IN HIS
Shadow

Also by Tiffany Snow

IN HIS
Shadow

A TANGLED IVY NOVEL

TIFFANY
SNOW

Montlake
Romance

Text copyright © 2014 Tiffany Snow
All rights reserved.

Published by Montlake Romance, Seattle

www.apub.com

Amazon, the Amazon logo, and Montlake Romance are trademarks of Amazon.com, Inc., or its affiliates.

ISBN-13: 9781477825860
ISBN-10: 147782586X

Cover design by Eileen Carey

Library of Congress Control Number: 2014940353

Printed in the United States of America

For Tammy and the summer we spent our days smoking
too many cigarettes and playing endless games of War.

CHAPTER ONE

"Hey, look. Your favorite customer is back, just in time before we close."

I glanced over at Marcia, my co-worker, who just grinned and tipped her head toward the door. Looking across the bank lobby, I stiffened, recognizing the man who'd just walked into the bank.

"Damn it," I muttered under my breath, my good mood plummeting. I took a deep breath. Another five minutes and my weekend would start; no need to let my last customer of the day ruin it.

He came every week, which would describe a lot of people, but he stood out, at least he did to me. Tall with light brown hair that might be blond if sunshine was allowed on it for a while, he was broad shouldered and lean hipped, and looked like he was in his mid-thirties. He always dressed casually, though I could tell his jeans were designer and his button-down shirts tailored. His name was Devon Clay, which I knew from the transactions he made, but we'd never exchanged pleasantries. It was always just business, which was fine with me.

Devon was one of those rare men whose every movement spoke

of someone who was capable of and accustomed to violence—a dangerous man. His eyes were cold, his expression always politely bland. While perhaps others didn't see it, I'd been conditioned from too young an age to be able to spot someone who was more than able to do me harm and not think twice about it. So from the first time I'd laid eyes on Devon a month ago, I'd instinctively and immediately disliked him—a dislike that only grew with each interaction I had with the man.

I'd mentioned my antipathy for Devon to Marcia, who hadn't understood. To her, he was just another customer, albeit a handsome customer who she said "oozed sex appeal." She'd also theorized he'd be "amazing" in bed, an assumption I silently agreed with but had no desire to explore despite his appeal.

For some reason, Devon always came to my line, even if I was the one teller with a wait. I had no idea why because, as I said, we didn't converse. He was the only customer with whom I didn't. Usually, I was a pretty nice person and I enjoyed interacting with people. Even on my crankiest day, I managed to dredge up a smile for my job as teller for one of the most exclusive and oldest banks in St. Louis. Except with Devon. There was something about him that got under my skin and made me want to run as far and as fast as I could in the opposite direction.

As I'd expected, Devon bypassed the two other tellers, one of whom was Marcia, to come to me. He handed me a few papers. I didn't greet him.

"Can I get these taken care of, please?" he asked, his cultured British accent smoothing the syllables like a warm blanket. His lips formed a thin sort of smile, which I didn't return.

"Of course," I replied, polite but not friendly, and avoided looking him in the eye. I reached for the papers, but he held them tight for a moment, just long enough for his finger to brush the top of my hand. It felt like an electric current ran through me.

My eyes flew to his in surprise. His steady gaze seemed to see right through me. For a moment, I couldn't move, then the papers were sliding into my hand.

I took a shaky step back, tearing my eyes from Devon's to start the transactions on my computer. It took several minutes and I was hyperaware of him studying me. It made me nervous how much that small touch had thrown me. Was he toying with me?

I had to cancel my work a couple of times and start over, which was irritating when I wanted to get him out of there as quickly as possible. Finally, I was finished.

I stepped over to the printer to retrieve his receipts and my toes screamed in protest from the two-hundred-dollar leather boots I'd been unable to pass by in the store. They looked amazing, but wearing them to a job where I stood for ninety percent of the time had been a mistake. I winced, grabbing the papers and glancing at the clock again. Two minutes. Thank God. I swore I was going to walk home barefoot rather than put up with these boots another second.

I handed him his receipts, careful this time not to touch him, or allow him to touch me.

"Everything all right, luv?" Devon asked.

His eyes were the lightest of blues with a web of fine lines at the corners, as though he'd spent too much time squinting into sunlight. Some might compare his eyes to an ocean or the sky. I likened them to ice.

I forced a stiff smile, thinking, *Don't call me that.* "I'm fine, thank you. Have a nice day." Now leave, I silently commanded.

The barest hint of amusement crossed Devon's face, as though he could hear inside my head, then it was gone. He leaned closer.

"It's been a pleasure, Ivy," he said softly, the words polite and harmless, but edged in something too close to seduction.

Devon had never before called me by name, though it was printed on the gold nameplate in front of my window. *Ivy Mason, Teller.* I watched him as he walked across the lobby and out the door.

"Girl, you are blind. That man is drool worthy and hot for you, my friend."

I turned at Marcia's teasing and grimaced. "I have no idea why he always comes to my line," I groused. "I'm not nice to him."

Marcia rolled her eyes. *"Gee, why does he come to my line?"* she mocked. "It's a total mystery. The fact that you could be a flippin' model wouldn't have a thing to do with it."

I sighed inwardly. Marcia meant well, but I wasn't a girl who valued my looks. They'd brought me too much trouble. I had hair that women paid thousands of dollars to try to achieve—pure white blonde that was thick, long, and straight. My eyes were a combination of brown and green so that they seemed gold, and I'd been blessed with high cheekbones and full lips. I'd been compared to a perfectly delicate porcelain Barbie doll. A comparison I hadn't appreciated.

Most women disliked me on sight, just on principle, so I went out of my way to be nice. Marcia was one of the few who'd befriended me immediately when I'd started working here six months ago.

"I think he's weird," I replied. "Something about him is just . . . off." I knew his type all too well. They presented a perfect face to the world, then were an utterly different person when no one was looking.

"He's rich and gorgeous," Marcia said wistfully. "I could overlook a lot of weird for those two things."

I burst out laughing, my good humor restored by Marcia's irreverence. She was completely unapologetic about her goal of finding a rich husband. Period. She'd moved to St. Louis a year ago from the middle-of-nowhere Iowa and had been "on the hunt," as she put it, ever since then. So far she'd dated a lot, but, as of yet, no proposals.

"He's got to be at least eight or nine years older than us," I argued.

"An older man who knows what he's doing," she retorted, waggling her eyebrows suggestively.

"You mean an older man who'll die first and leave you his money," I teased her.

She laughed. "I wouldn't complain. So, do you have big plans for the weekend?"

I shook my head. "Not really. Logan and I are meeting a friend of his for dinner. I don't really know what his plans are for the rest of the weekend. I'm counting on doing a whole lot of nothing."

Marcia shook her head. "I don't understand this relationship you have with Logan," she said. "You're living with him, but you're not together."

"I told you," I said. "We're just friends. I needed a place to stay that didn't cost a fortune when I moved here, and his roommate had just moved out. End of story." What I didn't say was that I felt safe with Logan. We'd met in the sixth grade and knew all there was to know about each other, including our secrets. "We just don't think of each other that way." I shrugged.

"No man can be friends with a woman he finds attractive," Marcia said, quoting her favorite movie of all time, *When Harry Met Sally*. "He always wants to sleep with her."

"Just because they said it in a movie doesn't make it true," I said, turning to sign off my computer. It was six o'clock. Quitting time.

"I'm just saying," Marcia replied, closing down her booth as well.

"What about you?" I said, changing the subject. "Have a hot date tonight?" It was rare that Marcia didn't have a date. Though she talked about my looks, she was really pretty, with honey-brown hair and blue eyes. She always complained about her weight, but she had curves I envied. I'd always been on the too-skinny side of thin.

"Yep," she said, pulling on her coat. "His name is John and he works at that big investment firm over on Broadway."

I grinned. "Sounds promising."

She winked at me. "I'll let you know Monday."

While my job was downtown, I lived in the Central West End near Forest Park. There's no way I would have been able to afford to live there on my own, but Logan worked for a big-name law firm and paid three-quarters of the rent. I'd argued about that when I'd first moved in, but he'd been adamant. I tried to make up for it by doing most of the cooking and cleaning.

I was just about to walk out the door when I heard my name being called. I turned around. Mr. Malloy, my boss, was hurrying toward me.

"Ivy, would you run this by Mr. Galler's on your way home?" he asked. "He wasn't able to make it in today."

Mr. Galler was one of the bank's oldest and richest clients, and by "oldest" I meant that figuratively and literally. He was a nice man, maybe somewhere in his nineties, and I'd taken things to his home before, even though it was out of my way. He lived in one of the multimillion-dollar mansions in Country Life Acres.

"Yeah, sure," I agreed, not that I had much choice, but I didn't mind. I liked old Mr. Galler, and we chatted when I went by on a bank errand.

After taking the packet, I headed outside, the bitter wind making my eyes water as I wrapped my black wool peacoat more tightly around me. My car was an old hand-me-down sedan from my grandma and made of the kind of heavy steel that meant I didn't have to worry about putting extra weight in the trunk when the weather got bad.

Rush hour was murder and it took nearly an hour to get from the bank to Mr. Galler's address. I called Logan to tell him I'd be late for dinner. He told me to meet him and his friend at the restaurant, since it wasn't far from where I was going anyway.

"You'll love Tom," Logan told me. "He's an artsy, creative type. Very hip. And his parents are loaded, which is great for him since he still hasn't made a dime from his work. Show a little leg and he might even buy your dinner."

I laughed. "You're implying I prostitute myself for a free meal?" I teased.

"Not your whole body. Just a leg. He'll be eating out of your palm, lovely Ivy."

"Logan!" I shook my head in exasperation. I wasn't interested in the kind of one-night stands that Logan dished out on a regular basis, but not paying for dinner sounded good to me. Eating out was something I loved to do, but it could get pricey and I had champagne taste on a beer budget, as my grandma said. The clothes I had on, black leggings under a cranberry dress that came to mid-thigh, would work for going out on a Friday night.

"You haven't had a date in forever," Logan went on, oblivious to my chastisement. "Your come-hither beauty is going to wither and fade away."

"Lucky for me I have a sparkling personality," I shot back, unable to help a smile even as I wanted to roll my eyes. "Just because your sex life is a revolving door doesn't mean mine should be."

"I just give the ladies what they want," Logan protested. "I can't help it if I'm irresistible."

"Right," I snorted. "Gotta go. I have to concentrate on this shitty traffic. See you soon." I hung up on Logan's protests.

He wasn't wrong, though. It had been a while since I'd dated anyone for longer than a few weeks, and even longer since I'd had sex. Not that I slept around like he did. On the contrary, I could count on one hand with three fingers left over how many times I'd had sex since high school, and both occasions had been mortifying and awful. Just remembering made me squirm in my seat. I just wasn't "into" sex. That much intimacy and vulnerability with someone made me uncomfortable and I'd avoided it ever since.

The guard manning the gated community let me through and finally I was knocking on Mr. Galler's door. He had a man who lived with him and did things like cook and run errands, and it should have been he who opened the door, but it was someone I didn't recognize.

"Hi," I said with a smile. "Mr. Malloy sent me to drop this off for Mr. Galler." I went to hand him the envelope, but the man stepped back to allow me inside.

"Mr. Galler is in the study," he said politely. "If you'll follow me."

Obediently I followed, a quick glance at my watch showing me I was going to be later than I'd thought, especially if Mr. Galler was feeling chatty.

The house was huge, beautiful, and luxurious, with expansive views of the trees and lawn. I caught a glimpse of a tennis court out back, then saw with dismay that it had begun to snow. I liked snow well enough so long as I didn't have to drive, but if I backed out of dinner, I'd never hear the end of it from Logan.

Mr. Galler was sitting in a leather armchair in front of a crackling fire. I missed having a fireplace. We'd had one back home and Grandpa had always made sure there was plenty of wood stocked up for winter.

"Hello, Ivy, my dear," he said when he saw me, his weathered face breaking into a smile.

"Hi, Mr. Galler," I said, and my smile was genuine. I liked old people. Maybe it was the years I'd spent living with my grandparents, but I felt they were underappreciated. "Where's Roger?" Roger was his usual assistant/cook/butler.

"He took ill quite suddenly," Mr. Galler said. "A company sent me William to fill in until Roger gets better. Please, have a seat."

I was grateful to sit down, the pinching of my toes making me long for my slippers. "Here you go," I said, handing him the packet once I'd sat on the sofa. "Mr. Malloy sent this for you."

He nodded, taking the packet and setting it aside. "Thank you," he said. "Would you like a drink? I can ring for tea."

"That's all right," I said apologetically. "I'm meeting friends for dinner, so I'm afraid I can't stay long. How have you been feeling?" Mr. Galler was usually in perfect health, but he'd complained of being ill lately.

"Better, I think," he said with a smile, though I wasn't sure I believed him. He looked a bit pale and drawn, but still I nodded.

"I'm glad. Did you finish that book yet?" Mr. Galler had told me he was writing his memoirs and often updated me on the progress.

"Nearly done," he said. "Some memories are more difficult to relive than others." His eyes became slightly unfocused, as though he were gazing inward. "Nineteen forty-five. A year I'd like to forget."

I did some quick math in my head. Mr. Galler would have been a teenager in nineteen forty-five, during World War II.

"Where were you then?" I asked. I loved listening to older people talk about their pasts. I found it fascinating.

Mr. Galler's gaze refocused on me. "Poland," he said. "My father was a physician."

"In the Army?"

He nodded. "He did research as well, some of which he entrusted to me."

"Did he die in the war?" I asked.

"Alas, he did," Mr. Galler replied. "My mother passed away when I was but an infant. My father did not survive the end of the war. I was an orphan sent abroad to charitable organizations that helped the parentless during those times."

I would have liked to ask him more questions and listen to his story, but I also knew Logan was waiting on me. "I really would love to read your memoir when you're through," I said. "Is there anything I can do for you? Anything you need before I go?"

Mr. Galler hesitated for a moment, his eyes shrewd as he examined me, then said, "Actually, yes. Would you get something for me?"

"Of course." I wondered what he could possibly need that William couldn't get for him.

"Go to my desk," he instructed, "and open the right drawer."

I did as he said and saw nothing but a thick stack of stationery and old-fashioned ink pens.

"In the very back, there's a small notch. Press it."

Reaching my hand in, I felt around, finally feeling what he described. When I pressed it, something sharp gouged my finger. Letting out a small gasp, I yanked my finger out and stuck it in my mouth. Ouch. A splinter, probably.

Looking back down, I saw another drawer open a sliver above the current one, which made me forget about my finger. Small and neatly hidden, I had to use my fingernails to pry it open. Inside lay a gold pendant. I picked it up, turning it curiously in my hand. It was heavy and ornate.

"Bring it here, my dear."

I closed the drawers and went back to Mr. Galler, handing it to him.

"This has been in my family for a long time," he said, examining it with hands that trembled slightly.

"It's very beautiful," I said. There was a crest imprinted on it with an elaborate design, but I hadn't gotten a close look.

Mr. Galler handed it to me. "I'd like you to have it," he said.

My mouth fell open. "I-I can't possibly—" I began, but he interrupted me.

"I insist. I have no children to leave it to and you've been a breath of fresh air these past few months." He smiled. "It would mean a great deal to me if you would accept it."

The gold was heavy in my hand as I stared into Mr. Galler's eyes. He seemed tired and sympathy struck me. It must be hard to be alone at the end of your life, no matter what luxury surrounded you.

"Okay," I said, my fingers closing around the pendant. "I'll treasure it. Thank you." Standing, I impulsively gave him a hug, which seemed to take him by surprise. His eyes were bright when I stepped back, and he cleared his throat before he spoke.

"Go," he said. "Have fun with your friends, dear Ivy. And thank you."

I understood I'd been dismissed so I headed for the door, but something made me glance back. Mr. Galler stared out the window, lost in thought, his shoulders bowed as though a great weight were on them.

I didn't see William on my way out. I climbed into my icy car and hurried to turn on the heat. By now, the snow was coming down thick and heavy. Since it was Friday night, I had a hard time finding a close parking spot, so by the time I got to the restaurant I was starving, my feet were killing me from walking three blocks in the snow and cold, and I was seriously cranky.

The warmth of the restaurant was a relief, the heavy aroma of Italian food comforting. Logan and Tom were already seated at a table in the back by the windows. From inside, the falling snow looked beautiful.

"It's about time," Logan said when he spotted me. I noticed three men at the table rather than just two, and they all rose when Logan did to greet me. I pressed a quick kiss to his cheek.

"Sorry," I apologized. "Traffic was awful." I turned to meet his friend.

"Ivy, this is Tom, the friend from college I told you about." I shook Tom's hand, plastering a smile to my face. "And this is Jared Ross, who just arrived in town, as luck would have it."

My *hello* died on my tongue as my gaze fell on Jared, because it wasn't Jared at all.

It was Devon.

"A pleasure," Jared, aka Devon, said. He lifted my lax hand and pressed his mouth to my knuckles. In shock, I just stood there. His lips were soft, his breath warm against my frigid hand. He lingered in that position, his gaze locked on mine, his thumb sliding across my skin.

I opened my mouth to say something, I didn't know what, but Devon suddenly pressed my fingers hard, a look of warning in his eyes. My mouth snapped closed, the twinge of discomfort from his grip making all the vague reasons I had for disliking him come into sharp focus, despite the shiver that ran through my veins at his touch. My eyes narrowed and I yanked my hand from his.

"Thanks," I murmured. Logan had pulled out my chair and now I sat between him and Devon with Tom across from me. Tom's eyes had lit up when he'd seen me and he was gazing avidly at me now.

"You didn't tell me Ivy was beautiful," Tom teased Logan, his eyes on me. I gave a stiff smile.

"Excuse me, but I thought you'd sworn off women?" Logan retorted good-naturedly.

"A temporary decision," Tom shot back with a grin.

Their ribbing was lost on me. All I could think about was Devon and what could possibly be going on. Though there was no mistaking the message he'd sent me. I wasn't to say a word.

"Fancy some wine?" Devon asked me. He didn't wait for my answer before filling my glass with the ruby-red liquid.

Logan and Tom carried the conversation, with an occasional comment from Devon. Our dinner came without me even remembering what I ordered. I drank my wine and barely touched the food on my plate, my stomach in knots over what was going on. What was Devon hiding? Should I tell Logan?

"I apologize, I've been monopolizing the conversation," Tom said. "Ivy, what brought you to St. Louis? Logan tells me you work at the Worcester Bank downtown."

"Um, well, I-I have one of those useless college degrees," I managed to stammer. "History, actually. And unless you want to teach, there's not a lot you can do with a degree like that. I happened to be talking to Logan a few months ago and he mentioned his roommate had moved out and that I should come here. So I did."

"No work for you back in Dodge City?" Tom teased.

My smile was stiff. "Not unless you want to sling hash in a truck stop or work at the local Wal-Mart." Nothing short of my own funeral would make me go back home.

Tom and Logan laughed. Devon did not. I didn't look at him, but could feel him watching me. He'd changed but was still dressed expensively, his wool suit a deep charcoal against a white shirt and striped silk tie. His hand was toying with his wineglass and I caught myself watching his fingers. He had strong, capable hands that looked rougher than I would have expected for a white-collar kind of guy. Hands that could snap one of my bones like a twig.

"Excuse me," I said, getting abruptly to my feet. I needed a moment to regroup, and a trip to the ladies' room would give me that time.

Devon politely stood as well, Logan and Tom hurrying to copy his movements as I left the table. Purse in hand, I hurried to the back of the restaurant and into the empty restroom.

I stood in front of the sinks, gripping the edge of the cold marble counter. Maybe I could just go home? But then I'd be leaving

Logan with a man I knew to be lying about his identity. And it didn't matter that I didn't know why he was doing it; people who lied about their name usually had reasons for doing so that were anything but benign. I'd have to stay and stick it out, if for no other reason than I wanted to look out for Logan.

Leaving the comfort and safety of the restroom, I turned the corner and nearly ran into someone in the tight corridor. Murmuring an apology, I glanced up, the words dying on my tongue. Devon stared back down at me and the look on his face was anything but friendly.

Barely had I processed this when his hands went to my waist and he turned me, pushing my back against the wall. I had no warning whatsoever before he kissed me.

CHAPTER TWO

Devon's lips were warm and soft, and I felt the roughness of his palms as his hands lifted to cradle my face, his fingers slipping into my hair. He wore a cologne with a scent unfamiliar to me—sandalwood and spice tinged with something else, his own skin maybe. His body was pressed fully against mine and was harder than I'd imagined it to be.

My surprise left me temporarily immobile, my jaw dropping in shock at his actions. Devon took the opportunity to deepen the kiss, his tongue sliding between my parted lips to brush against my own. I could taste wine on his tongue, hot and sweet.

Devon's hold on me was unyielding, keeping my head where he wanted it, and I couldn't have gotten away if I'd tried. It was overwhelming, my head spinning at the feel and taste of him. His jaw was roughened slightly with the day's growth of whiskers, their soft abrasion against my skin a masculine touch that turned my stomach into a nest of butterflies.

Just as suddenly as he'd begun the kiss, he ended it. I opened my eyes, but he wasn't looking at me. A man had just walked past us and out the back door. Devon was watching him.

"Have a lovely evening, Ivy," Devon said, his lips brushing my ear. His voice was a deep rasp that combined with the warmth of his breath to send a shiver down my spine.

I was utterly speechless, but it didn't matter, he was already gone, disappearing out the back door as well.

It took me several minutes to recover my composure and I went back into the ladies' room to repair my lip gloss with a hand that shook. What had just happened? I knew nothing about Devon, not even his real name, and he had just kissed me. It made no sense.

When I got back to the table, I wasn't surprised to find that Devon had made an excuse to leave.

"He said he had a meeting or something," Logan said with a wave of his hand, "which is fine with me. I hadn't planned on taking a client out to dinner tonight anyway. His arrival was unexpected."

I wanted to tell Logan about Devon's real name and quiz him on what he knew of him, but didn't want Tom to hear. I decided it could wait until later.

"I'm sorry, Logan," I said abruptly, "but I'm not feeling well. Do you mind if I head home?" Dinner was done, so technically I'd been there for most of it, but knowing Logan as I did, he was bound to drag Tom to a club or bar and be out late into the night. No way was I up for that.

And I really wasn't feeling well all of the sudden. My head ached and my mouth was cotton dry. I just wanted to get home, curl up with a blanket, and forget all about this dinner and Devon. Some people might have wanted to figure out the mystery. Not me. I'd learned a long time ago to avoid trouble, and Devon was trouble with a capital T.

"Sure, Ives," Logan said, slipping in his nickname for me. He frowned in concern. "Are you sick?"

"I'm sure I'll be fine," I said, grabbing my purse to pay for my share. "It's just been a long week."

"Dinner's on me," Tom interjected, and Logan winked at me.

I thanked him and when he stood for a friendly hug, I allowed it, though it lasted longer than it should have. I rolled my eyes at Logan over Tom's shoulder, but he just made a kissy face at me.

My car was covered in snow when I got back to it. I started the engine and got the defrost going full blast, but it still took me a while to clear it off. My motions were automatic as I scraped the windows. I was confused and out of sorts. Meeting Devon in that hallway had thrown me more than I wanted to admit, his identity a mystery that tantalized me even as better sense said I should leave well enough alone.

I was just about to get into my car when I heard a noise and paused. It was coming from the alley between the two buildings I'd parked in front of. I heard more noises, like someone grunting, and my pulse notched up. Was someone being mugged? In this weather?

I didn't know what I thought I'd be able to do to help and didn't really stop to think, I just hurried to the mouth of the alley, skidding to a halt when I saw what was making the noises.

Two men were fighting, both of them moving so fast it was hard to tell who was winning. The falling snow and the night obscured their forms. Suddenly, one broke loose and began running straight at me. A shot rang out. The front of the man's forehead exploded, sending red splatters of bone, flesh, and blood flying. His body crumpled not ten feet from me.

I stood, frozen in shock at the man on the ground. A pool of crimson stained the pristine snow.

My eyes jerked up as the man still standing moved. He had a gun in his hand and when he stepped into the dim glow of the streetlight, my heart lurched into my throat.

It was Devon.

He took another step my way and that's when I turned and ran.

I slipped and slid my way to my car—thank God I'd had it running—fell inside and shoved it into drive. I stomped on the gas and shot down the street, looking in my rearview mirror to see Devon standing in the spot I'd just vacated, staring after me. As I watched, he melted back into the shadows.

Panicked, I drove too fast, making myself slow down when the car skidded around a curve. I didn't know what to do. Should I call the police? Call 911? But Devon had seen me, knew that I saw him kill that man. I was a witness. Would he come after me now? Hurt me, too? And what would I tell the police? I didn't even know his real name.

In the end, I drove home, unable to make myself call the police. I'd talk to Logan. He'd know what to do.

Our apartment was on the third floor of an old warehouse that had been remodeled. The remodel hadn't included an elevator. Normally climbing the flights of stairs in the boots-from-hell would have me searching for more colorful expressions to describe how I felt about the lack of an elevator. But tonight all I could think about was Devon and the dead man. He'd kissed me . . . then murdered someone.

A chill skated down my spine at the memory. I had no idea why he'd done what he had—and I didn't want to know. I felt guilty for not calling the police, but overshadowing the guilt was fear. I didn't want to end up like the guy facedown in the snow. Did that make me a coward? Probably.

Logan and I each had our own bathroom, so I didn't have to worry that he'd complain about my leaving clothes on the floor. I took a long, hot shower, the warm water easing away some of the tension in my body. Every time I closed my eyes, I saw that man's head exploding, and Devon, standing with gun raised and pointed at me.

Shaking my head to dispel the images, I got out and wrapped myself in a towel. Grabbing my brush, I started combing through my tangled hair as I exited the bathroom and headed for the television in my bedroom.

I sat on my bed, watching TV, and brushed my hair until it was nearly dry. The long strands shone like spun gold in the glow of the lamp. It soothed me, brushing my hair. My grandma used to do it for me all the time. I missed her. If it wasn't so late, I'd call her, just to hear her voice. It would be something normal and ordinary after the events of tonight.

A sound from outside my door had me glancing at the clock. Strange. I hadn't expected Logan would be back so soon.

Another sound, the slight squeak of a shoe on the wooden floor, made the hairs on the back of my neck stand on end. Logan wouldn't be so quiet. He'd be thumping around the kitchen and would turn on the television in the living room.

My panicked eyes locked on the knob on my door. It was turning, ever so slowly.

Adrenaline iced my veins, making me feel like I'd just been dipped in a bath of cold water. I lunged for my bedside table and yanked open the drawer, pulling out the gun I kept there just as the door swung open.

"This is a bit unexpected," Devon said, his eyes on the gun pointed at him.

"You!" I exclaimed, horrified. "What are you doing here? How did you find me?" My grip didn't loosen on my gun, though my hands shook. I pointed it at Devon, who seemed unconcerned by the threat.

"You're not terribly difficult to find," Devon said evenly. His gaze raked me from my head to my bare toes. "Nice towel."

I swallowed, wishing I'd dressed. "What do you want?"

"It's a shame," he mused. "Who would have thought that the one person who knows my name would also be at dinner tonight? And see a rather . . . unfortunate incident outside."

I decided to play dumb. "I don't know what you're talking about. Now get out before I put a bullet in you."

Devon's lips twisted at this, as though he found the thought of me shooting him an amusing one. He took a step closer, bringing himself to within point-blank range.

"We have a problem," he said, ignoring my command. "By all rights, I should kill you."

His words made fear twist in my gut, the way he so casually talked about killing me. "I think you're confused as to who's going to kill who," I snapped. "I'm the one with the gun."

Faster than I could react, Devon knocked my arm aside, then snatched the gun from me.

I gasped in dismay and fear, suddenly weaponless, and scrabbled backward on the bed away from him.

Devon flipped the chamber open on the gun, emptied the bullets into his palm, then tossed the gun onto the bed. He pocketed the bullets.

"As I was saying," he continued as though nothing had happened, "we have a problem."

It struck me then. I was alone in my apartment with a man I'd already seen kill someone. He'd disarmed me as easily as if he'd been swatting a fly. I could die tonight, at the hands of a man to whom I'd barely spoken more than a few dozen words.

My mind was frantic as I tried to think what to do. "Please," I said, my mouth utterly dry. "I swear. I won't tell a soul. No one. Just don't . . . hurt me."

Devon frowned. He loomed over me, the planes of his face shadowed in the low light, his eyes hooded. The air crackled between us, his gaze studying me while I fought to draw breath. There was nowhere for me to go. I knew a little self-defense, but considering how quickly he'd taken my gun, I didn't think I'd be able to inflict much damage on him.

He took another step toward me and I let out a small cry, jerking back and stumbling from the bed to plaster my back against the wall. I was as far away from Devon as I could get, and there was a sharp tang of fear in my mouth.

Devon didn't move, his expression darkening into one that made a mockery of the pleasant façade I'd seen him assume at the bank and during dinner. His square jaw was set in bands of steel as he watched me.

"I'm not going to hurt you, Ivy," he said, his voice gentle and a stark contrast to the look on his face.

I didn't speak, my eyes wide and watching him for the slightest movement.

Devon held my gaze and carefully took a step back, then another. My panic eased ever so slightly. My chest was heaving and my palms were sweaty, but I found my terror receding as Devon made no effort to come at me.

"Better?" he asked.

I swallowed, pressing my lips together, and jerked a short, quick nod.

Glancing around the room curiously, he folded his tall frame into a chair in the corner, casually unbuttoning his jacket. Though it was snowing outside, he wore no coat. Lifting his hands to show me they were empty, he said, "Have a seat. I won't come any closer." The corner of his mouth lifted. "Unless you want me to, of course."

Relief flooded me, but I didn't trust him.

"Please," Devon added when I didn't move. He gestured to the bed.

Gingerly, I knelt on the bed, my shaking knees threatening to collapse in the wake of the adrenaline rush and fear.

His gaze calculating, Devon said, "I'm afraid I underestimated the intensity of your dislike of me."

"Dislike has nothing to do with it," I said, glad that my voice was steadier than my shaking limbs. "I saw you kill someone tonight. Then you come into my apartment—into my bedroom—uninvited, and tell me how you're going to kill me. How was I supposed to react?" I decided not to mention the kiss.

A small smile played at the edges of Devon's mouth. "My apologies. Was an invitation forthcoming?"

"Of course not!" I blurted. "I don't even know your real name."

"So you'd like me if you knew my name?"

I couldn't believe my ears. Was he . . . flirting with me?

"I watched you shoot a man in cold blood," I said bluntly. "I don't think 'like' is the word I'd use to describe how I feel about you."

Devon leaned forward, bracing his elbows on his knees, and said, "I've been coming to your window for weeks, Ivy. Didn't you wonder why?"

Ignoring that uncomfortable question, I responded with a question of my own. "So what's your real name? Devon or Jared?"

"Devon," he replied without hesitation. "Now answer my question."

"I thought you must be a glutton for punishment," I retorted.

His lips twisted again. I noticed his eyes crinkled slightly at the corners, softening the hard planes of his face. Marcia was right. He was . . . divine, and the memory of his kiss made me want to forget everything I saw in that alley. But nothing changed the fact that he'd said the word "kill" in reference to me, which kind of killed the attraction—no pun intended.

"Who was that man?" I asked. "Why did you kill him?"

Apparently we were playing a version of quid pro quo because he again answered right away. "You don't need to know who he was and I didn't kill him in cold blood. It was an act of self-defense. It was him or me. Though make no mistake, neither of us would win any points for virtue. He wasn't a good man and neither am I."

"He was running away," I argued. "It didn't look like you were in any danger."

"I didn't say he would've killed me tonight. Consider it an ounce of prevention."

Proactive murder. I wondered if a jury would buy that defense. "So why the two names?"

"My job occasionally requires a level of anonymity," he said. "My turn. You were afraid of me before tonight, before you saw me in that alley, before I came in here and sent you into a blind panic. Why?"

I hesitated. "Because I know men like you," I said quietly. "I know the type. You can hurt people, and I bet you don't mind doing it." More than a little bitterness edged my words.

It didn't surprise me in the least when no denials sprang from his lips. Instead, he said, "That's very . . . astute of you, Ivy."

"Stop saying my name."

"Why?"

"Because we're not friends."

"But perhaps I'd like us to be," he said. "Friends. It's a great deal better than the alternative."

The way he said "friends" made it clear he meant a whole lot more than that. And just in case I didn't catch his drift, his eyes took a leisurely trip down my body. I clutched my towel a little closer, cursing my long legs that left the terry cloth much too high on my thighs to be called modest.

"Are you threatening me?" I forced the words out.

Devon sat back in the chair. His hands went to his tie, leisurely undoing the knot and pulling the fabric from around his neck. The soft slide of the silk made my heart beat faster, and it wasn't from fear. I couldn't move as I watched his fingers deftly undo the top two buttons of his shirt, exposing the skin of his throat.

"I don't threaten," he said, making my gaze jerk back up to his. "I state the facts. You are now a liability, rather than a pleasant diversion. I'm willing to overlook the former, if you agree to the latter."

I couldn't believe my ears. Was he coercing me into having sex with him? "And if I don't?" I asked, not at all sure I wanted to hear the answer.

Devon stood and this time when he approached the bed, I made myself hold my ground no matter how badly my limbs trembled with fear. He towered over me, his blue gaze unblinking and searing right through me. I remembered the assured way he'd held his gun, completely unmoved at having killed someone, and swallowed hard.

He raised his hand and I couldn't help flinching, but he merely rested his fingers on my bare shoulder. The touch felt as though he'd applied electricity to my skin, shooting through my veins until every nerve ending was attuned to him.

The rough pads of his fingers were unexpectedly gentle as they traced the line of my shoulder to my neck, lower to brush my collarbone, then up the line of my throat. I could barely breathe, my eyes locked with Devon's. The fear I felt was tinged with something close to excitement, followed by desire. My heart raced and I knew by the subtle curve to his lips that Devon had seen the fluttering pulse underneath my skin.

"I think you will." The words were a soft murmur. "I'll be in touch, Ivy." Then he was gone as silently as he had come.

Next to me on the bed was his tie, and it seemed as though I was watching someone else's hands pick up the soft silk, bring it to my nose, and inhale the scent of sandalwood, spice, and Devon.

CHAPTER THREE

I didn't see Logan until late in the morning on Saturday. Hearing his keys jangling in the lock, I turned from where I was huddled under a blanket on the couch, sipping my coffee. The door opened and Logan walked in, spying me and sending a shit-eating grin my way.

"How was she?" I asked.

"Fantastic," he replied, breezing past me into the kitchen. When he reappeared, he had a mug of coffee as well and had discarded his coat. With a sigh, he plopped down next to me, grabbing some of my blanket.

"It's disgusting how a man can look just as good doing the walk of shame in the morning as he did the night before," I complained. Logan's dark hair was mussed, a day's growth of beard shadowed his jaw, yet with his blue eyes and wicked grin, he looked as though he could have stepped from the pages of a magazine.

"I have good genes," Logan said with a shrug. I rolled my eyes. "So I take it you didn't like Tom?" he asked.

I made a face. "I'm not into the artistic type," I said. "I'm guessing he found someone to ease the pain of my rejection?"

"I seem to remember him kissing some girl and then following her into a taxi, yeah," Logan replied.

"And your girl?" I asked. "Did she have a name? A number?"

"I'm sure she did," Logan said, taking another sip of the steaming coffee. He winked at me.

"You're unbelievable," I huffed, flipping the channel on the television. "I'm so glad we never got involved."

"I'd much rather have you as my best friend than a one-night stand," Logan said, unrepentant. It mollified me, but I still felt the need to at least make a token protest on behalf of all the women he laid and left.

"One of these days, you're going to find some girl you fall head over heels for and she's going to make you ditch your man-whore ways," I predicted.

"Maybe," Logan admitted. "But it wasn't last night."

I laughed at his cheeky grin and wink. It was impossible for me to stay mad at him. I loved Logan unconditionally. He was the brother I'd never had. Ever since I was twelve and he'd seen me crying in a dark corner of the school library, he'd been there for me.

"So who was that other guy?" I asked, bringing up the man I hadn't been able to stop thinking about since he'd disappeared from the apartment last night.

"Yeah, that was weird," Logan said. "He showed up at the firm yesterday afternoon, said he was looking for a friend of his, a client of mine. We can't just give out addresses, but he seemed legit so I said I sometimes saw the guy at this restaurant. Next thing I knew, he was there when I walked in with Tom. Invited himself to dinner so I just made the best of it." He eyed me. "Don't tell me you liked him? He didn't seem your type."

"Of course not!" I denied a little too quickly. "Just thought, like you did, that it was weird, especially when you hadn't mentioned him joining us when we were on the phone."

Our conversation was interrupted by the telephone, and Logan reached behind the couch to pick up the cordless off the table. He glanced at the caller ID.

"Hey, Grams," he answered.

I looked up at this, what we'd always called my grandma, even Logan. My grandma adored him and I rolled my eyes as Logan chatted with her for several minutes. Finally, he handed the phone to me.

"Hello, sweetheart!" she said. "How are you doing?"

"I'm doing great," I replied. "How're you and Grandpa?" It didn't matter if I was doing well or not, I always said I was great. My grandparents had raised me from the time I was thirteen and had dealt with enough pain and heartache for a lifetime. I'd vowed a long time ago to never cause them more.

Grams told me how Grandpa had sprained his wrist, and I got after her for not letting the hired hands do the work on the farm, though we both knew that Grandpa was too restless to just sit inside and let others do it. Finally, after a few more stories about one of the barn cats having kittens and a neighbor whose oldest son had just gotten remarried, she said, "So honey, I wanted to remind you, Jace is up for parole next week. Remember?"

I stiffened at the mention of my stepbrother. I hadn't seen him in ten years and I'd just as soon never see him again.

"Yeah, I remember," I said.

"I know you worry, Ivy, but even if he did get out, he doesn't know where you are," she said, trying to comfort me. "Me and your grandpa aren't going to tell him anything either."

"I don't want him anywhere near you guys," I said. "If he comes, you call the police."

"Your grandpa has a shotgun, honey, and he knows how to use it. We'll be fine."

Like that was supposed to make me feel better, my seventy-year-old grandpa toting a shotgun.

"How's Taffy doing?" I asked, changing the subject. I missed my little cocker spaniel, but Logan's apartment manager was quite clear that no pets were allowed.

"Oh, she's fine. She still wanders back into your bedroom though, like she's looking for you."

She talked some more about Taffy and when we ended our conversation, Grams promised to call and let me know as soon as she heard how Jace's parole hearing went. Logan was watching me when I hung up, the earlier mischievous look on his face replaced by one of concern.

"Was that about Jace?" he asked.

I nodded, setting aside my empty coffee mug. "Parole hearing this week," I said.

"He's had them before," Logan said, "and didn't get out. There's no reason to think this time will be any different."

"I know." But I also knew the twisting nausea in the pit of my stomach wouldn't go away until I'd heard from Grams. Logan must have sensed my unease, for he reached out and grasped my hand, slotting his fingers with mine.

"Did you ever tell them?" he asked, his voice quiet.

My gaze met his in surprise. Logan and I never talked about what had happened with Jace. Ever. "Of course not," I said. "With my mom and everything, they had enough to cope with. They didn't need to know that, too. And besides, it didn't matter. He was already going to prison."

"Yeah, but Ives," he said gently, "they love you."

"It would only hurt them," I insisted. "No one needs to know. Not now. It's in the past."

"Is it?" Logan asked a little sadly. "Or is that why you're not interested in anyone I introduce you to?"

"Don't go there," I admonished him. "I am not one of those women forever scarred by the traumatic events of my past." Logan looked skeptical and as though he were going to say something else, so I cut him off. "Enough! It's three weeks until Christmas and we haven't decorated at all. You're going to help me put up a tree."

Logan groaned. "I knew it was a mistake letting a girl move in here."

I grabbed a throw pillow and smacked him with it. "Too late. Time to decorate."

"Hey, that rhymes," he teased, grabbing my pillow away from me. "You're a poet and didn't even realize it."

I laughed, though he'd used the same bad joke on me many times. The thought of Devon and what had happened last night went through my head, but I decided not to tell Logan about it. It was so strange, so odd, and despite it having just happened hours ago, I had trouble believing it. Surely if I just didn't think about it, didn't dwell on it, Devon would disappear from my life. Telling Logan would make it real, and I'd have to try to explain something that was incomprehensible to me.

The guy last night is also a customer at the bank and he killed someone, then showed up here and threatened to do the same to me if I didn't sleep with him.

Yeah. Completely insane.

Throwing myself into decorating the apartment proved a worthwhile distraction, and by the time I crawled into bed that night, our living room was adorned with a six-foot tree festooned in bright, multicolored lights. I'd also added lights to any available flat surface and made Logan help string them along the ceiling. A skinny tree with white lights stood in the corner of my bedroom and I stared at it.

I never slept in the dark. The blackness was always broken by a night-light of some sort. The last time I'd slept without a light, I'd been twelve years old. For a year, I'd endured a hell that a night-light couldn't ease. Now I had something better—a gun at my side—should the stepbrother I both hated and feared find me.

The bravado I'd displayed in front of Logan was nowhere in sight now, and the thought of Jace made my stomach ache as I curled into a ball beneath the covers, overwhelming any residual fear of the man who called himself Devon.

∽

By the time Monday rolled around, I'd nearly convinced myself that Devon had been a figment of my imagination, our brief conversation the by-product of too much stress. Yet I found myself dressing more carefully than usual, in black heels with a platform sole, a black maxi skirt that hugged my legs, and a pale pink blouse made of thin chiffon. My hair I caught in a loose, low ponytail, draping it over my shoulder.

Logan glanced up from where he was standing at the kitchen counter, finishing his coffee while reading the paper, and whistled.

"You're in the wrong profession," he said. "Especially for how much you love clothes. You look amazing."

"Thanks," I said with a smile. "You're looking very lawyerly yourself this morning." I reached up and straightened his tie, one I'd bought for him. I didn't think I had a lot of vices, but shopping was definitely one of them. I adored fashion and spent way too much of my paycheck on shoes and clothes. Logan teased me about it relentlessly, but the warm male appreciation in his eyes gave me a much-needed boost of confidence.

"I'll drop you," he said, depositing his empty mug into the sink. "It snowed again last night."

I readily agreed. I didn't like driving in the snow, especially in my sedan, whereas Logan had an SUV. Because he was driving, I didn't even have to clean off my car.

The familiar warmth and quiet of the bank soothed me as I deposited my purse and coat in their usual spots before grabbing another cup of coffee. I spotted Marcia hurrying to clock in as I was headed to my teller booth.

"Good weekend?" I asked as I passed by.

She shot me a look. "I may walk funny today."

I burst out laughing. "I'll take that as a yes," I teased. "And I want to hear all about it."

Monday mornings were typically busy, so by the time I looked up at the large clock on the wall a while later, I saw half the morning had flown by.

"Ivy, could you come in my office please?" Mr. Malloy's voice over the phone intercom was tinny and I hit the button to reply.

"Yes, sir." I lowered the old-fashioned shade so people would know my line wasn't open, then headed toward the offices in the back. My heels echoed on the marble floors. I knew I didn't want to work as a teller forever, but I loved being at the bank, especially this one. Everything was old and ornate, and sometimes it seemed as though I'd stepped into the past and John Dillinger would come sweeping through the doors at any moment with a Tommy gun in hand.

I rapped my knuckles on the office door and opened it once I heard him call out. To my surprise, two other men were in Mr. Malloy's office as well. All three of them looked my way. Mr. Malloy looked upset, his thin, white hands twisting together.

"Come in, Ivy," he said. "These are Special Agents Lane and . . ." His voice faltered.

"Johnston," one of the men supplied, getting to his feet. He reached and shook my hand, as did Agent Lane. "We're with the FBI." He flashed some kind of elaborate ID at me. "You're Ivy Mason?"

Oh, no. Cops. And not just one of your friendly, local boys-in-blue, but big-bad-federal ones. Their presence didn't bode well.

"Yes, I am." I struggled not to let my panic show. They'd found out. Somehow they'd found out I'd seen that man murdered and hadn't told anyone. But how? And what would they do to me?

"You saw Mr. Orin Galler last Friday evening at his home?" Johnston asked.

"Um, yeah, I did." I was confused. What did Mr. Galler have to do with the guy in the alley?

"How long were you there?" the agent continued.

"I don't know," I said. "Maybe ten, fifteen minutes at the most." I glanced at Mr. Malloy. "What's this all about?" But it was Agent Lane who answered.

"Mr. Galler was found murdered in his home this morning," he said.

My jaw dropped open in shock. "What? Mr. Galler?" I couldn't believe it.

"The time of death was Friday evening," he said. "His body wasn't discovered until this morning by his cleaning lady."

"That . . . that's awful," I managed to say, my eyes watering. Mr. Galler had been a sweet old man. How horrible that someone had not only killed him, but that no one had been by to find him for days.

"From what we've been able to ascertain, you were one of the last people to see him alive."

That dried up my tears pretty darn quick. I'd seen enough TV shows to know by the way the agents were looking at me that sympathy was the last thing on their minds.

"Surely you don't think I had anything to do with it?" I asked in disbelief.

"There's no sign of forced entry into the home," Agent Lane said. "Whoever killed him was most likely someone he knew."

"He was a sweet old man! I'd never do anything to hurt him!" The panic was back now, but for an entirely different reason.

"What happened when you went there Friday night?"

I struggled to remember. "Nothing important," I said. "I sat with him for a few minutes and chatted. He hadn't been feeling well lately. I gave him the papers Mr. Malloy sent and left." Then

I remembered. "Wait! His usual butler wasn't there, Roger. Mr. Galler said he'd taken ill and that a company had sent a new guy, William, to fill in." *Yeah, go investigate that guy, not me.*

"Roger is dead, too," the agent replied. "After being tortured first. There's no sign of anyone else in the home and no record of any company sending a replacement."

My knees wobbled and Mr. Malloy grabbed my arm, urging me to sit in a chair. "That's impossible!" I insisted, sinking down onto the leather. "He was there, I saw him! Spoke to him!"

"Can you tell us what he looked like? Anything about him that you remember?" Agent Lane asked.

"Yes, absolutely." I told him what I could remember about William, not that there was a whole lot to go on. I'd only spoken to him for a few minutes, when he'd answered the door. Agent Lane wrote down everything in a little notebook. "But why is the FBI involved? Why aren't the police here instead?"

"Mr. Galler was a special case, an immigrant from World War II," Johnston explained. "His murder has raised some red flags. We're here to investigate whether it was foul play or something more. And that's all I'm at liberty to say."

I nodded. It sounded serious and I was glad when the agents stood to leave. Federal agents had a lot of power and they scared me. Lane reached into his pocket and handed me a card. "We'll be in touch, Ms. Mason," he said.

I took the card, staring up at the two men as they left the office. Agent Lane's shrewd gaze lingered a moment on me, but he didn't say anything before he closed the door behind them.

"Are you all right?"

I glanced at Mr. Malloy, glad to see he for one wasn't looking at me with suspicion in his eyes.

"I-I guess," I stammered. "I've never been questioned about a murder." At least not where they considered me a suspect. Though the agents may have just done that to scare me into telling them everything I knew, which totally hadn't been necessary. Their very presence had ensured I was scared enough to cooperate.

"Did anything unusual happen while you were there Friday?" he asked.

That was when I remembered the pendant Mr. Galler had given me, but for the life of me I couldn't see how that could have anything to do with anything, so I shook my head.

"No. It was just a quick visit, and I left."

Mr. Malloy and I sat in silence for a moment, then I stood up with a sigh, feeling suddenly tired. "I guess I'll get back to work." He nodded and I left his office, the agent's card burning a hole in my hand.

Marcia and I ate our lunches together in the break room, though it was hard for me to pay attention as she related the tale of the guy she'd gone out with Friday night, and, as it turned out, Saturday night, too.

"Ivy," she finally said with an exasperated huff. "You haven't been listening to a word I've said!"

"I'm sorry," I apologized, "it's just that, well, you know old Mr. Galler?" She nodded. "Well, someone killed him after I left his house Friday night."

Marcia's eyes practically bulged out of her head. "Oh my God!" she said. "What happened?"

I told her what little I knew and how the agents had been by to question me.

"You're lucky you weren't killed, too! What if you'd still been there?" She shuddered.

I hadn't thought of that. Yikes.

Lost in thought, I was barely aware of the afternoon passing by until my cell phone buzzed close to six o'clock. It was Logan texting me.

Have to work late. Sorry. Can you catch a cab?

I wasn't surprised. Logan often had to put in sixty hours or more a week at his job. I texted back.

No problem. See you at home.

It was nearly six thirty and already full dark when I left the bank. The wind was whipping through the streets of downtown, taking my breath away with its icy blast and making me regret wearing a skirt and thin blouse. I shivered, my teeth clacking together, and wrapped my arms more tightly around my middle.

Taxis weren't usually hard to come by, but tonight it seemed no one wanted to stop. After the third one roared past me, I bit out a curse and started walking just to keep the blood flowing. If nothing else, I could walk to Logan's office and just wait for him to finish working.

Another cab was barreling down the street and I stuck an arm up to wave it down. That's when I noticed the man.

About twenty feet away, he wasn't looking at the traffic. He was watching me.

It wasn't like men had never looked at me before, so just the fact that a man was watching me would have been innocuous, but there was something about the look in his eye and the focused expression on his face. It sent a chill down my spine.

My arm faltered and the cab zoomed by. I took two steps backward on the sidewalk, my gaze on the man, and he took three steps toward me. Echoes of the agents telling me how Mr. Galler had been killed, his butler tortured and killed, rang through my head.

Turning away, I started hustling down the sidewalk, cursing the fact that I'd worn heels today. Who wears heels when there's snow on the ground? An idiot like me, apparently.

A quick glance over my shoulder showed that he was following me, and gaining.

Abandoning all pretense that I didn't know he was chasing me, I started running. I passed by buildings that I didn't dare stop at to try to enter. This area of town was a business district and most doors would be locked. I'd lose the precious lead I had.

The bitterly cold air burned in my lungs, making my eyes sting as I ran. I thought frantically, trying to figure out what to do. Another glance behind made my heart stutter. He'd be on me any moment now. I couldn't outrun him.

The squeal of tires yanked my attention to the street, where a steel-gray sedan had just done a one-eighty and jerked to a halt. The passenger door flew open.

"Get in!" a voice called out.

I had a split second to make a decision. Keep running and be quickly caught by an unknown man? Or take what was behind door number two, though it may be worse?

I'll take door number two, Monty.

I didn't have time for second thoughts. Dashing into the street, I threw myself into the car. The driver stepped on the gas, the momentum slamming the door shut.

Panting for breath from fear and exertion, I turned to see who had so precipitously saved me.

"You!" I burst out.

I made a grab for the door handle, but Devon slammed his hand down on the master lock.

"You're going to jump out of a moving car?" he asked, his tone dry. "That'll leave a mark."

"Better hurt than dead," I retorted.

"Who was that?"

I gulped. "I have no idea."

Devon glanced at me, his gaze sharp as he took in my chest still heaving and the fear in my eyes. "Seems a bit odd," he said finally, looking back at the road. "A bank teller being chased by an unknown assailant."

"You could say my life's taken an odd turn the past few days," I shot back with a meaningful glare.

The ghost of a smile whispered across his lips and vanished. He glanced up in the rearview mirror, his mouth tightening slightly. I turned to look behind us.

"Is he gone?" I asked, searching the rapidly disappearing sidewalk for him.

"It appears so," Devon said. "A would-be mugger, perhaps? You should be more careful."

I shrugged, turning back around with a relieved sigh. "Yeah. I guess."

Now that I had a moment to breathe properly, I looked around. It was a nice car. A really nice car. The seats were heated leather and the interior made my car look like something out of the *Flintstones*. It was a sporty sedan and while I wasn't great with car logos, I thought it was probably a Porsche.

"Where are you taking me?" I asked, glancing at Devon. He was wearing another suit that perfectly encased his broad shoulders, and I could smell a hint of the intoxicating aroma I now associated with him.

This time when he looked at me, I saw a hint of mischief in his eyes.

"To dinner," he said lightly. At my surprised expression, his lips twisted in a near smile. "I'm starving."

Devon's gaze fell to my mouth and my pulse skittered. The impulse to lick my lips was nearly overwhelming. I dragged my eyes away from studying the man next to me and focused on the road.

He drove to a restaurant out of my price range and handed the keys to the valet. I glanced around as I got out of the car, looking for a cab, but Devon was already there, taking my elbow in a firm grip and steering me inside. We were led to a secluded table in a quiet corner. I unbuttoned my coat and Devon was there again, standing behind me, his hands on my shoulders as he lowered the heavy fabric down my arms.

His proximity made the air freeze in my lungs, the hard wall of his chest at my back, and I couldn't move. Lowering his head, Devon's lips brushed the skin of my neck, bared by the loose blouse and my side-swept ponytail. My hands clenched into fists at his touch, my body leaning ever so slightly into his, then he stepped away.

Devon's manners were impeccable and I had to keep reminding myself that this man had shot someone and threatened me. He ordered a bottle of wine and our dinners, though I couldn't fault his choices.

We sipped our wine, an excellent vintage, and took measure of each other, as though we were calculating an opponent's strengths and weaknesses. Unfortunately, it didn't seem Devon had any weaknesses. As for me, well, I just prayed I wasn't as transparent to him as I felt.

"Why are you doing this?" I asked once the waiter had brought our food. "Is wining and dining me supposed to make me agree to sleep with you and forget you shot someone?"

"You've already decided to sleep with me," Devon said, refilling our wineglasses. "That's a foregone conclusion."

The absolute certainty in his words, his demeanor, set my teeth on edge. There was confidence . . . and then there was Devon, who put a whole new level of meaning to the word *arrogant*.

"You seem very sure of yourself," I said stiffly. I took a bite of the lamb he'd ordered for me. No sense letting good food go to waste. I loved lamb. Like I said, champagne taste.

"Just stating a fact," he said. "Am I wrong?" His eyes studied me over the rim of his wineglass as he took a drink, his gaze like a palpable touch as it dropped to my neck, shoulders, and breasts.

I suddenly wished I hadn't worn the translucent shirt today, feminine as it was. If I was brutally honest with myself, in the back of my mind this morning I knew I'd wanted to wear something pretty . . . for him. But now that he was here and devouring me with his eyes, my instinct for self-preservation kicked in and it was only through sheer force of will that I didn't cross my arms over my chest.

"Why me?" I asked, avoiding his question. "I'm sure you could have your pick of women, a good-looking guy like yourself. Why accost me?"

"So you think I'm good-looking?" he teased.

I rolled my eyes. As if he didn't know how gorgeous he was.

"Why am I *accosting* you, then," he continued. "You mean besides the fact that you're beautiful, young, and detest me for reasons unknown?" His British accent made the question sound polite, friendly even, though the look in his eyes was anything but.

"I told you why I don't like you," I replied stiffly. "You were going to kill me, remember?"

"True. However, I proposed a much more . . . pleasurable . . . alternative," he said with a smile.

The smile was unexpected and warmer than I would have thought him capable. It softened the hard planes of his face and made his eyes appear less like chips of ice. It also had the effect of making butterflies dance in my stomach. The low noise of the restaurant grew distant as we stared at one another and his smile slowly faded.

I was drawn to Devon in a way I couldn't explain, with an intensity that I felt deep in my bones was dangerous and self-destructive. I'd been right to dislike him, my instinct pegging him correctly as someone who could hurt me. Not just physically—though he could obviously do that, too—but emotionally and forever.

If I was smart, if I had any sense of self-preservation at all, I'd get up and walk out. I don't know what kept me in my seat. It was akin to someone with their first taste of an illicit drug. Despite knowing all the dangers and warnings, they just couldn't help themselves from taking that first step, that first taste, that said there would be no going back.

I've never thought of myself as someone who was drawn to the unknown or as a girl who had a thirst for taking a walk on the wild side. I was Ivy Mason. Pretty, yes, but sensible. A girl who liked safety and comfort above all else. Someone who eschewed the fleeting thrill of the "bad boys" my girlfriends always *ooh*ed and *ahh*ed over and who never failed to break their hearts. I was smarter than that, wiser than that.

Or so I'd believed.

Dinner was over and it was time to go. I was so nervous, I was nearly light-headed, though maybe that was from the wine. I had no idea who Devon was, what he did for a living—though I was guessing he worked on the wrong side of the law—and yet here I was letting him touch my back and brush his fingers down my arms as he helped me into my coat.

Turning me to face him, his hands spanned my waist inside my coat. I was narrow and small, his hands so large his fingers nearly touched. I could feel the heat of his touch through the thin material of my blouse and it seemed to burn. A shudder went through me and I tipped my head back to look up at him. His eyes were intently studying me, their depths sparking with blue fire.

"Don't fight it, luv," Devon said, his voice a low thrum of sound. "You were mine from the moment I laid eyes on you." The possessiveness in his gaze made the breath catch in my chest.

It wasn't until we were outside in the brittle cold, Devon no longer enthralling me with his words and his touch, that sanity returned. What was I doing? This was insane. *I* was insane. Devon couldn't be trusted, no matter how inexplicably drawn I was to him.

Devon released his hold on me to take his keys from the valet, and I bolted. Another couple was exiting the restaurant, heading to a waiting cab, and I darted in front of them.

"Sorry!" I called over my shoulder, slamming the door behind me. "Go!" I told the driver, who stepped on the gas, unfazed by my rather abrupt entry into his car.

I turned in my seat to look out the back window. Devon was standing in the street by his car, gazing after the fleeing cab. I couldn't see the expression on his face, but the lines of his body were taut. Maybe he was angry, but I had the feeling my impulsive action had been more like waving a bloody flag to a hunter who lived for the chase.

Logan was already home when I arrived, and he was none too pleased.

"Where have you been?" he asked when I walked in the door. "I've been blowing up your phone, worrying about you."

"I'm sorry," I said, shucking my coat and setting my purse aside. "I . . . ran into a . . . friend. And we had dinner." The lie came easily, which was strange. I never lied to Logan. And yet, I didn't want to tell him about Devon.

"Oh," he said, the irritation fading from his expression. "Who?"

"You don't know him," I said, heading toward my room.

"It's a him?" I heard Logan call after me, but I could pretend I hadn't.

I brushed my teeth and got ready for bed on autopilot. Devon knew where I lived, had broken in here before, and maybe it was a testament to my irrational state of mind that a part of me hoped he'd show up again tonight.

In that, I wasn't disappointed.

Chapter Four

Devon came in the dead of night.

When I opened my eyes, I was disoriented for a moment, then I saw the outline of a man standing over me. His form was a deeper shadow than those around him and the instant I realized someone was in my room, I sat straight up and dragged in a ragged breath to scream.

A hand was instantly over my mouth, stifling me before I let out a whisper of sound. My heart was in my throat and I froze in terror, a cold sweat breaking out on my skin.

"You left before dessert," Devon said. "And without a thank-you, though I suppose thanks aren't necessary."

Oh, God. My eyes slid shut in overwhelming relief and I slumped back down on the bed. Devon's hand lifted from my mouth and I took a deep breath. I could smell the faint aroma of his cologne and it had a calming effect on me.

Opening my eyes, I focused on him. His face was cloaked in shadows, though light slatted through the open blinds from the street outside, sending bars of illumination across my bed, and my tree was still lit in the corner.

Turning away from me, Devon locked the bedroom door, then discarded the jacket he wore, draping it over the chair. My eyes had adjusted and I watched as he carefully set aside his gun before divesting himself of the holster, then he approached me again and I promptly lost all train of thought.

He sat on the edge of the bed, his hand moving to where my leg lay tangled on top of the sheets. My love for clothes extended to pajamas and tonight I wore my favorite despite the cold outside, a slip of a dove-gray gown that came to mid-thigh, held on by spaghetti straps, a panel of soft lace in the deep V neckline. His fingers brushed my calf, sliding up slowly to catch in the tender skin behind my knee. My heart was pounding so loudly, I was sure he could hear it, yet he said nothing.

"What are you doing here?" I asked, my voice barely above a whisper.

"You have to ask?"

I swallowed. So this was it. Was I going to allow this to happen, to possibly mark a third awful sexual experience to the other two? But this was different—Devon felt different. My body, my mind, both responded to him in a way I'd never felt before. The way he'd so blatantly stated his intentions, while perhaps not romantic, was freeing in a way. Sex with Devon wouldn't be about a relationship or love—it was only about two people finding pleasure in each other's bodies. No need to overthink or overcomplicate it.

Devon leaned over me and now I could see his face, fierce in the low light. His hand brushed the hair back from my face, his eyes looking so deeply into mine that I felt naked, stripped to my soul. The light trail of his fingers went from my knee up my thigh, catching the thin fabric and moving it upward with his touch until his palm cradled my hip. His thumb brushed the soft skin of my abdomen and the butterflies inside my stomach took flight.

"Who's the man you live with?" he asked.

It didn't occur to me to lie. "Logan. A friend."

"Just friends?"

I managed a nod, embarrassed at the rapid rise and fall of my chest as I breathed much too fast. The linen of his shirt was almost rough on my sensitized skin, the smell of him enveloping me. The cage of his body over me made me feel trapped, but in a way that left my body humming for more.

Devon caught the hem of my gown and tugged. I sat up, my heart in my throat, letting him raise the fabric and slip it over my head. The silk drifted to the floor, leaving me clad in just a pair of thin bikini panties.

I hadn't been this naked in front of a man in a long, long time. Instinctively, I crossed my arms over my chest. Fear warred with excitement inside me, but I was determined not to let the fear win. Not this time. Not with this man.

"Don't," Devon said, catching my wrists and pulling my arms inexorably downward. "You have nothing to hide. You're exquisite."

The flush of pleasure those words brought made my spine straighten. I'd always been self-conscious of how thin I was, my breasts barely able to fill a B cup, but the way Devon looked at me made me feel beautiful. Desirable.

Devon took my hand and lifted it, palm up, to his lips. Bending his head, he pressed his mouth to the inside of my wrist. Eyes wide, I watched him slide his lips down my arm to the sensitive skin inside my elbow, the touch of his tongue warm and wet.

"You're trembling," he murmured, his lips moving against my skin. He lifted his head, now much closer, our faces just inches apart. "Still quite afraid of me, sweet Ivy?"

Was I afraid of Devon? He'd killed a man. Broken into my apartment. Taken off my clothes and touched me. He was so much larger than me, his presence and physical size overwhelming.

Was I afraid of him? Yes. But God help me, that wasn't enough to stop me wanting him or wanting to bury the part of me that cringed from being sexually vulnerable to a man.

"Does it matter?" I asked.

A frown creased his brow at this and he didn't answer. His hand lifted to cup my jaw, the strength and size of his fingers making me realize just how easily he could break my bones if he so chose. But his touch was gentle, the pad of his thumb brushing my lips, then he was kissing me.

This kiss was different from the one we'd had before that had taken me so by surprise. His lips were soft, coaxing even, rather than demanding. Kissing had always been one of my favorite things, and Devon was very talented. He deepened our kiss and I found my hands creeping up to his shoulders, my body pressing closer to his.

I was breathless when his mouth moved from mine to trail down my jaw to my neck. Taking my hands in his, Devon moved them to the buttons of his shirt. Getting the hint, I started undoing them, eager to feel his skin against mine. His hands moved to cup my breasts, his thumbs sliding sensuously over the tips and sending a bolt of heat through me.

In a corner of my mind, I couldn't believe this was happening, that I was going to have sex with a man I barely knew. What I did know of him was that he was dangerous, a murderer, and someone whose job required him to lie. He knew even less about me, which was maybe why I found myself able to let go and just . . . feel. Devon wanted nothing from me except my body.

I tugged his unbuttoned shirt free of his slacks and he took his hands from me long enough to shed the garment, then he was laying me carefully back on the bed, his lips on mine, his body resting between my spread thighs.

The feel of him, his weight pressing me into the mattress, made my limbs stiffen. My heart sank even as I fought the feeling of being trapped. I didn't want to shut down, didn't want to feel afraid. But my body refused to obey my mind's commands, my breath coming too fast and my heart racing for an entirely different reason than arousal.

"What's the matter?" Devon asked, his voice soft. He raised himself on his arms so he could look down at me.

"Nothing," I quickly denied. I *would* do this. I'd vowed I would not be a prisoner to the past. Devon wanted me. I wanted him. It seemed so simple, but then again, when had sex ever been simple for me?

He gazed into my eyes for a long moment, searching, then abruptly sat up. Reaching for his discarded shirt, he began pulling it on.

My mouth dropped open, aghast. "What are you doing? You're leaving?"

"I'm afraid so," he replied, fastening a few buttons. "I've seen enough broken souls to know one when one is right in front of me."

Tears stung my eyes but I blinked them back. I pulled the sheet to me, covering my naked chest. "I don't know what you're talking about," I said. "I'm not . . . broken."

"Perhaps in another time, another life, I might be the man to heal you," Devon said, standing and reaching for his gun, holster, and jacket. "But I'm not. And as nonexistent as my ethics and moral code are, I'd like to think I'm not a man that would do more harm."

He stood over me again. His eyes were piercing and saw too much, even in the low light, and I couldn't hold his gaze. My eyes dropped to the bed, the familiar weight of my hair swinging forward to help shield me. I felt numb. I was being rejected by a man who'd been able to tell instantly that something was wrong with me. That I was . . . broken.

Devon's hand lifted my jaw, forcing my eyes to meet his.

"That old saying, 'It's not you, it's me,' is quite true," he said. "I'm a coldhearted bastard, sweet Ivy. And you . . . well, you are lovely." The last was said with a kind of sigh, his fingers caressing my cheek before tangling gently in my hair. He brought the long strands to his face, his eyes drifting closed as he inhaled deeply. "Yes, quite lovely," he murmured.

Devon bent, as though he couldn't help himself, kissing me with a fierceness I immediately responded to, hoping he wouldn't leave. I dropped the sheet to curl my arms around his neck, rising on my knees so I could push my fingers into the soft strands of his hair. His hands lowered to cup my rear through the thin fabric of my panties. He groaned and I could feel the hard press of his erection against my stomach.

"Don't go," I whispered. But he slowly took my arms from around his neck and stepped away. I watched as he disappeared from my room as silently as he'd entered.

Grabbing my nightgown from the floor, I dragged it over my head, then crawled back underneath the covers. I looked out the window to the cold night outside. This hadn't exactly been how I'd pictured things going when I'd opened my eyes earlier and realized Devon had returned.

I didn't cry. I just stared out the window until my eyes burned, imagining what it would be like if I were normal, and wondering if or when I'd ever figure out how to fix myself.

My life seemed to return to the usual routine after that. The next few days passed as most of my days did, without incident or any strangers chasing me down the street. I hadn't heard again from the federal agents regarding Mr. Galler's death, though his murder had made the papers.

Perhaps it was that very same monotony of my life that had once been comfortable, but which I now found to be tedious. Devon had brought a brief surge of the unexpected, of excitement, which logic demanded I shouldn't want, and yet I did. Thoughts of him were constantly in my mind. Who he was, what he did, why he'd killed that man. The feel of his body against mine, the touch of his lips, the hard planes of muscle stretched beneath warm skin.

"Hey, look who's here," Marcia said in an undertone to me. "Your stalker. And right before quitting time."

I glanced up and saw that Devon had walked through the door of the bank. He paused and our eyes met. I held my breath as he came toward me. He didn't pause or look around, just kept walking, his eyes on mine, until he had reached my window.

"You look beautiful today," he said, his gaze drifting over me. His voice was low, the comment meant for my ears alone. I was absurdly glad that I'd taken the time to curl my hair and leave it long, the black silk dress I wore cut a little low for December, but it looked fabulous against my fair skin.

"Thank you," I replied stiffly. "You look . . . nice, too." Nice wasn't exactly adequate to describe Devon. He had on another expensive suit that I could tell was hand-tailored, overlaid with a designer-brand black wool coat. His dark blond hair was cut to the perfect length, the strong square jaw had just a hint of shadow, and his eyes . . . his eyes were a clear blue that stripped away my clothes until I was back in my bedroom, Devon's hands and mouth on me.

With a jerk, I pulled myself back into the present. "Um, how can I help you?" I asked.

Devon smiled slightly, as though he knew exactly what I'd been thinking . . . remembering.

"Ah, yes," he murmured. "I should have some sort of excuse for coming here, other than I could smell your perfume on my skin the other night and I haven't been able to get the image of your body out of my mind."

My eyes flew to his, trepidation and pleasure curling in equal measure in my belly. "I get off in a few minutes," I offered, somewhat hesitant. I had to be insane. I hadn't liked Devon, should be glad he'd left my apartment. But I couldn't deny the palpable attraction between us, the pull he exerted on me. I'd say I was becoming obsessed, but that thought scared me, so I shied away from it.

"Shall I test that theory?" Devon asked.

It took me a moment to get his joke, and when I did, I could feel a blush stain my cheeks.

"How delightful you look when you're embarrassed," he said, his lips turning up in a flirting grin that made my toes curl.

"I thought you weren't interested," I replied with a raised eyebrow, remembering only too well my mortification when he'd said I was a "broken soul" and left me naked and alone.

"I could say the same for you," he replied. "Did you decide I wasn't so horrendous after all?"

"Maybe," I hedged. "Though I have to say I generally don't like it when a man walks out on me."

Devon leaned forward, resting his arms on the marble counter. "Maybe I was a bit hasty," he said.

I felt a surge of joy at that, but I needed the answer to a question. I leaned forward, too. "Are you a criminal?" I asked, my voice barely above a whisper.

"Does my answer affect yours?" he whispered back.

"It should."

"That doesn't exactly answer my question," he said, his lips still twisted in a half smile.

"And you're avoiding mine," I retorted.

Gunshots startled a shriek from me, and I jumped back. Three men with masks and guns had entered the bank and now surrounded the handful of customers in the lobby. Phil, our security guard, went to draw his gun but another shot rang out and he dropped to the floor. He didn't move. One of the armed men threw the locks on the door to keep people out. A woman screamed.

"Oh my God," I breathed in horror.

"Everybody get down on the ground!" one of the gunmen yelled, but no one moved. He fired two shots in the air, startling people out of their shocked immobility. Customers began dropping to the floor, facedown.

One of the men ran to the teller booths, pointing his gun at me and Marcia. "Out of the booth!" he yelled. Then he turned his gun on Devon, who I just realized hadn't lain on the floor like everyone else. "Get down!"

Devon was slow in complying, his body stiff with tension. The look on his face was hard and ice-cold, and it sent a shiver down my spine. Surely this couldn't be the same man I'd just been flirting with? This was the man I'd seen in the alley, the man who'd shot someone dead.

I followed Marcia to the door, and she had to punch in her code twice to unlock it, her hands were shaking so badly. The armed robber was waiting for us on the other side.

"You," he said, motioning to Marcia. "On the floor. You"—now he looked at me—"get the keys to the safe deposit boxes."

I gave a jerky nod, then headed for the back office. Another gunman was back there already, herding employees out into the lobby. I passed my boss, whose strained expression looked terrified.

It was when I was heading back to the lobby, keys in hand and gunman at my back, that I heard the sirens.

"Fuck," growled the man behind me. "Hey, we got company," he called to his partners once we'd reached the lobby.

"No shit," the man who appeared to be the leader replied. "Get her over here."

The man gave me a rough shove from behind and I stumbled, nearly falling. I gasped in surprise, my heart racing with fear and adrenaline. Regaining my footing, I hurried toward the leader, who stood in front of the door that led downstairs to the safe deposit boxes. I glanced at where Devon lay on the floor. He was watching the man behind me, his gaze narrow and calculating.

The safe deposit boxes were down a half flight of stairs and behind an iron cage. Two of the men followed me down while one remained behind in the lobby. I heard a phone begin to ring.

"That'll be the cops," the leader growled to his partner. He pulled off his mask. "I told you not to let them hit the panic button."

"I didn't see who did it," his partner said, pulling his mask off as well. "Could've been this bitch, for all I know." He turned his malevolent gaze on me.

They were both older than I'd thought, perhaps late twenties to early thirties, with lean builds that spoke of time spent working out. The leader had a scar down his cheek, a jagged white line that made his cruel face even more terrifying.

"Let's go," he said to me, taking my arm and pushing me toward the cage. "We need in box 928."

I knew as soon as he said the number that I was in trouble. "But, I-I can't get in that box," I stammered.

"What the fuck are you talking about?" the leader said. "You're holding keys. Now open the box."

"But that box is in our high-security range," I said. "All the nine hundreds are."

His hand shot out and grabbed me around the throat, shoving me against the wall so hard my head cracked against the hard surface. I cried out in fear and pain, then found I couldn't breathe.

"Bitch, you'd better not be lying," he snarled, his hand tightening around my throat.

He tossed me aside like a rag doll, and I fell hard against the bars of the cage and then to the floor, the keys flying from my hand. My vision was blurry and edged in black. I blinked rapidly to clear it. I was shaking like a leaf and gulping down air as I got unsteadily back to my feet. Both men were watching me, identical sneers on their faces.

"How do we get in the box?" the leader asked.

"Th-the high-security boxes have passcodes that change every hour," I explained. "The owner of the box has a fob that has the passcode, then the bank manager has a corresponding code where they unlock the box together."

"Show me."

I bent and picked up the keys just as a gunshot sounded from the lobby. Both the guys jerked toward the sound. The leader turned to his partner.

"Stay with her and get that cage open," he ordered. "We'll blow the box." He ran up the stairs.

"You heard what he said. Get the cage open."

I fumbled with the keys, finally shoving the right one into the lock and twisting it open. The man with me got on the mini walkie-talkie attached to his belt, pushing the button and talking into it.

"What's going on out there?" he asked. He released the button in a hiss of static, but there was only silence. After a moment, he repeated the question.

Suddenly, a body flew through the air from the stairwell, crashing to the floor at our feet. It was the leader and he looked extremely dead, his sightless eyes staring and his neck at an odd angle.

Both the robber and I were frozen in shock for a moment, then he lunged at me. I screamed and fell back, trying to get away, but he caught my sleeve. The fragile silk tore, then he had me. His arm wrapped around my neck and he yanked my body in front of his as a shield just as someone appeared at the foot of the stairs.

Devon.

He held a gun with both hands and had discarded his coat. I could see a thin trickle of blood trailing from his mouth, but his hands were rock steady.

"Trying to be a hero, buddy?" the man said to Devon. "You're just going to end up dead."

"Like your mates, you mean?" Devon replied. "Not bloody likely."

The guy pressed the barrel of his gun to my temple. "Take one more step and I'll—"

A shot rang out and suddenly, I was free. Warm blood spattered and the body of the man slowly slid down the cage bars to the floor. Looking down, I saw the entry hole for the bullet in the center of his forehead, the exit wound much larger in the back.

I couldn't breathe. I raised a shaking hand to my face, swiping my cheek. My hand came away bloody. His blood was on me.

"Ivy, are you all right?"

Devon's hand was on my arm. I looked at him and slowly blinked.

"There's blood on me," I said through lips gone numb.

Reaching into his suit, Devon produced his pocket square and began to gently clean my face. I stared at him, my mind slow to process what had happened. Assiduously, he wiped my cheek, forehead, and neck, slowly removing the blood. Finally, he finished and looked me in the eye.

"There," he said with a soft smile. "That's better?"

I couldn't speak, so I just nodded. Reaching down, Devon took my hand and led me past the dead bodies, up the stairs into the lobby.

Things were chaotic and a blur as the cops came in and the customers began giving their statements. Devon led me to one of the leather chairs in the waiting area and sat me down. I stared at my hands folded in my lap. They were still shaking.

Devon took off his jacket and slung it over my shoulders. An EMT took my blood pressure and shined a light in my eyes.

"She's in shock," he said to Devon, "but she'll be all right." He stood and moved on to someone else. The police were everywhere, questioning everyone, and Devon had to leave my side to talk with them. Before long, I heard someone say my name. Looking up, I saw Special Agent Lane.

"Miss Mason," he said, sitting down beside me. "It's rare for a coincidence like this. First you're at Galler's residence the night he was murdered. Today you're at an attempted robbery." He didn't say it in a mean or suspicious way. It was more like an observation, so I didn't bother trying to scrounge up a reply.

Someone brought me a cup of water before disappearing back into the crowd. I felt Lane's eyes on my shaking hand as I took a careful sip. I watched as two men carried a black body bag up the stairs to the lobby and out the door.

The last time I'd seen a body bag flashed through my mind. Tears stung my eyes and I had to set aside my water before I spilled it. I braced my elbows on my knees, covering my face with my hands as tears leaked from my eyes. I felt too close to coming apart.

"Miss Mason, are you—"

"Ivy!"

Logan's voice cut through the cacophony around me, interrupting whatever Lane had been about to say, and a moment later, he was there.

"Ivy, thank God you're okay," he said, crouching down in front of me. Gently grasping my arms, he pulled them away from my tear-streaked face. He took one look at me and knew.

"Come on," he said. "Let's go home." He helped me to my feet and wrapped an arm around my shoulders. I leaned into him, grateful he was there. Logan knew me. He understood.

Logan replaced Devon's suit jacket with his own, handing the garment to Lane, who automatically took it. "Thanks, buddy," he said, barely glancing at Lane before leading me away. I didn't bother correcting him on exactly who the jacket belonged to.

Logan drove me home, sitting me on my bed before removing my shoes and torn dress. He put me into the shower where I finished getting the blood off me, then he dressed me as carefully as one would a child, dragging a T-shirt over my head and helping me into a pair of soft, flannel pants.

When I was finally clean and comfortable, Logan sat with me on the couch, holding me in his arms and tucking a blanket around me. I settled against his chest with a sigh.

"Thank you," I said quietly. I didn't know what I'd do without Logan. He was my rock and always had been.

"Do you want to talk about it?" he asked.

Haltingly, I told him about the robbers. How they'd come in and shot Phil, then made everyone get down. Then how they'd singled me out to unlock the safe deposit boxes. When I got to the part about Devon, I hesitated.

"One of the customers must've been some kind of cop or something," I said, not quite lying. Devon wasn't a cop, but he was . . . something. "He somehow took out the guy in the lobby, then the other one went to find his partner and he got him, too. The last one he shot while I was there. The robber . . . he'd been using me as a shield . . . but the guy . . . he didn't even hesitate. He just . . . shot him. Right in the head."

"Holy shit," Logan breathed. I looked up at him and his eyes were wide. "He shot the guy *while* he was using you as a shield? Fucking moron! What if he'd missed by an inch? You could be dead right now." Logan's expression had shifted from shocked to pissed. His arms tightened around me and I felt him press his lips to the top of my head.

"I guess he was sure he wouldn't miss," I said, though inwardly I wondered if Devon had even cared if he hit me or not. The thought made me shiver. Logan felt it and squeezed me. "Then I saw the body bags and remembered when they pulled my mom out of the fire . . . and I just lost it."

"Well, I don't know about you," he said after a moment, "but all this excitement has made me hungry. What do you say to ordering a pizza? I'll even spring for the cheesy breadsticks you like. And after that, I'll pump you full of Xanax and put you to bed."

I smiled. "Sounds good to me."

Two hours later, belly pleasantly full, I was crawling into bed. I sighed when my head hit the pillow, and thanks to the Xanax, was asleep faster than I would have believed possible after the day I'd had.

⌒

It was a hot and sunny July Sunday afternoon. I could feel the warm breeze against my face as I rode my bike, cooling the sweat on my brow. It was late afternoon and Mom had said not to come home until dark, but the traveling carnival was packing to leave and there had been nothing left to do in town.

Not that I really wanted to go home. As a matter of fact, I dreaded it. But the longer I was gone, the longer Mom was home alone with him.

He'd been drunk last night and things had been bad. The sounds through the thin walls of the house had made me cower underneath the covers in my bed, despite the oppressive heat of the house. I'd been afraid he'd come into my room, too, but he hadn't for a change. Then I'd felt guilty for feeling relieved. I should help my mom, but I didn't know how.

This morning there had been bruises on Mom's face and her hands shook as she made breakfast, but her smile was as steady as ever for her only child. Then she'd calmly handed me some money and told me to go have fun in town for the afternoon.

"Don't come home until dark, sweetie," Mom had said. Then she'd kissed my cheek and hugged me long and hard.

The carnival had been fun. I'd bought a corndog and snow cone, and wandered around watching people play the games. At five, they'd started packing up to move on to the next town, so I'd gotten back on my bike and started the trek home.

I thought about going to see Logan, but remembered that he was out fishing with his dad today. His home was a refuge to which I often retreated. Logan was always ready with a joke and a smile. Maybe I could sneak over there tonight and we could lie on our backs in the field and watch the stars. We did that a lot. Staring up at the expansive Kansas sky had a way of making a person feel small, irrelevant, but in a good way.

Parking the bike in the yard, I hopped off and headed to the back door. When I was a few steps away, I stopped and sniffed. Something smelled. A sour odor that grew stronger with each step I took toward the house. Alarmed, I hurried to the door.

Placing my hand on the doorknob, I turned it, and then there was nothing at all.

CHAPTER FIVE

I woke with a start, drenched in sweat, and sat straight up in bed. My chest heaved as I struggled to breathe, as though I'd really been trapped in the fire of my nightmare.

I hadn't dreamt about that day in a long while, though I knew what had brought it on. It had been seeing the body bags. They'd carried my mom's body from our burned-out house, while telling me how lucky it was that I hadn't been home.

No one seemed to know how my mom and stepdad had missed the smell of gas, but one spark had set the house ablaze, killing them both. I'd been blown clear with such force that it had knocked me out. When I'd woken, it was to see that flames had engulfed the place I'd called home, but in reality had been far from it.

Logan was the only one I told about how my mom had sent me away, how I was sure she'd done it on purpose, to save herself the only way she knew how.

And to save me.

Some days the guilt was enough to paralyze me.

Normally, I'd go crawl into bed with Logan when nightmares from my past visited me in the dead of night, but he'd already dealt with one crisis of mine today and he had to be up early for work in the morning.

Knowing I wouldn't be able to sleep, I climbed out of bed and headed to the bathroom. A long, steaming shower would relax me, and maybe temporarily wash away the terrors of the past.

I piled my hair on top of my head and stepped under the hot spray, just this side of scalding. A sigh escaped me. I tried to clear my mind. I didn't want to think about the past or remember the look on my mom's face as she watched me from the porch as I pedaled away that fateful morning.

The next day, I'd gone to live with my grandparents.

I was crying without even realizing it, the water mixing with the tears sliding down my cheeks. So many memories and remembered horrors streamed through my mind, and overwhelming it all was a nearly crippling grief for my mother and guilt that she'd done what she had for me.

Hands on my shoulders made me gasp in fear. I spun around, terrified, only to be stunned into immobility. Devon was there with me, naked in the shower. Relief washed over me so fast, I thought I might pass out.

"Didn't mean to give you a fright, luv." His brows were creased as he studied me, his hands lifting to cradle my face, then he was kissing me. The long, hard length of his body pressed against mine and thoughts of the past fled.

I lifted my hands, resting them on his arms as his mouth moved to trail down my neck. The suits Devon wore hadn't done justice to his body. His biceps were massive under my fingers, his shoulders wide and layered with muscle. Now that I could see him in the light, he took my breath away.

"Don't think," he murmured against the skin of my shoulder. "Just feel."

I don't know why it was easier to do this time, maybe because after what I'd been through today, his touch felt more like comfort than a threat, and I did as he said. His hand moved to slide between my thighs and my eyes drifted shut. His fingers slipped between my folds, his touch gentle but sure. I clutched at his shoulders as he stroked me, my eyes flying open when a thick finger pushed inside me.

Devon was watching me, the icy blue of his eyes penetrating my soul the way he was penetrating my body. His arm had moved to curve around my waist, supporting my weight as my suddenly weak knees threatened to collapse.

My heart raced, the steam from the water feeling almost cool against my overheated skin. I could feel the hard press of his erection against my hip, an answering flush of heat between my legs coating his fingers. Each thrust of his finger stroked my clit until I was panting with desire. My eyes slid shut as he brought me closer and closer to the edge.

"Open your eyes," he said roughly. "Look at me."

I obeyed, though it took effort, my nails digging into his skin. His eyes were darker now, the pupils wide.

"I won't hurt you," he said, careful to enunciate each word.

I tried to concentrate on what he was saying, but all I could feel was what he was doing to me. His hand moved faster, the pressure building inside me until I was moaning.

I felt helpless to do anything but let him touch me, and I knew by the look in his eyes that there was nothing I could have said or done to stop him.

"Come for me, sweet Ivy," he rasped.

Devon's finger pressed hard and my whole body seemed to explode into a pulsing wave of pleasure. His mouth covered mine and I greedily opened my lips to kiss him. His tongue stroked mine, his hand still touching me in a way that made my legs tremble.

Lifting me, Devon shifted my legs around his waist and I clung to him. He turned off the water and carried me to my bed, still kissing me. His cock was hard as a rock and I whimpered, his size and length making me want him inside me, a feeling that was unknown to me before this moment. I didn't give a thought to our wet skin dampening my sheets, my every sense locked on to him.

I felt his arm reach for the table next to my bed and he shifted slightly. Then he was settling between my legs and pushed inside me in one hard thrust. I gasped at the slight pain, jerking my mouth from his. Devon must have sensed my discomfort because, although he was settled deep inside me, he didn't move.

"You're beautiful," he murmured, pressing light kisses to my cheek and brow. "Just relax. Trust me."

The words penetrated the panic that had begun to creep over me and I opened my eyes. He lifted his head to look at me, a hand brushing the hair back from my face.

"Better?" he asked softly.

I nodded, unable to speak. It was . . . overwhelming. The feel of him inside me—I'd expected to be afraid, panic-stricken, desperate to get away. But instead, I felt marked. Possessed. And it felt good. It felt . . . right.

Devon began to move, slowly pulling out of me, then pushing back in. I felt every inch of him. He watched my face closely, as though trying to detect any hint of fear or discomfort. I reached to twine my arms around his neck, my fingers sliding into his hair, and tugged him down to kiss me.

That must have sent the right signal because he groaned into my mouth, the sound making pleasure curl low in my belly. I locked my legs around him and his hands moved to my hips, his fingers digging in as he thrust harder. I held on, closing my eyes and losing myself in him.

It was Devon, taking me hard and fast, the strength of his body surrounding mine. He was big, his cock filling and stretching me, the head brushing against my womb with each thrust. But I didn't mind the twinge of discomfort. The slight pain set fire to my senses, as though this was what my body was meant for—for Devon to possess.

The repeated slide of his cock against my clit pushed me over the edge again. Cries and gasps fell from my lips as my body intimately gripped the hard length of him, as if to hold him to me. But he didn't stop. If anything, he moved harder and faster, pounding into me until he ground hard against my overly sensitive flesh, his cock emptying its load deep inside. He was quiet when he came, though his whole body shuddered in my arms and his breathing was labored. The feel of him pulsing inside me made me moan in response, tipping my hips upward as though to take him deeper than he already was.

His body was slick with water and sweat underneath my hands, the muscles bunched tightly as he held me to him. My heels dragged the backs of his thighs as I relaxed. Devon was breathing hard, his face buried in the crook between my neck and shoulder. His lips moved, caressing my shoulder before gently sucking on the tender skin under my jaw.

I was sorry to feel him move away from me, which he did too soon. The intimacy of the moment, Devon sliding out of me and turning away, struck me. I'd never liked being that intimate with anyone before. Not to where it was a good thing, something that made me feel warm inside.

Devon reached down and slid a condom off his penis, tying it off before tossing it into the small trash basket. Standing, he headed to the bathroom, closing the door behind him. I heard the water running.

I sat halfway up, resting my weight on one elbow. Suddenly self-conscious, I reached down and tugged the sheet and blanket up over me, covering my nakedness. What would happen now? Would he leave? Would I ever see him again? The anxiety pressing on me, the sudden sharp *need* of him that I felt, took me by surprise.

The bathroom door opened and Devon stepped out. He was an impressive sight in his clothes—without them, he was just as formidable. A scattering of hair covered his broad chest, narrowing to a thin line below his navel. My eyes followed it down . . .

"Why are you covering yourself, darling?" he said, sitting on the bed. He made short work of pulling the covers off me. "Your body deserves to be admired."

The endearment warmed me and I didn't know what to say. No one had ever said something like that to me before, complimented me on something so personal. Devon was so comfortable in his skin, as though not wearing clothes was as easy as being fully dressed.

He reached for my leg, raising it and resting it across his lap, spreading me wide open. I gasped sharply, heat flooding my cheeks. Devon just chuckled.

"A bit late for modesty," he said. That's when I saw the washcloth he held. He pressed it between my legs, gently cleaning me. "I thought you might be sore. This should help."

The cloth was very hot and it did feel good against the parts of my body he'd just put to more use than they'd seen in ages. I was in awe of what had just happened. I'd actually had sex. And not just the crappy, embarrassing kind of sex I'd had before, but the mind-blowing, earth-moving kind with the most amazing specimen of a man I'd ever seen.

"So do you want to tell me?" he asked, his voice casual, intent on his task.

"Tell you what?"

"Tell me who abused you."

I stared at him, the blood draining from my face. He knew. Of course he did. He'd known the other night when he'd decided to leave. Which reminded me—

"I thought I was too broken for you?" I asked, more than a hint of bitterness in my voice. "That's what you said the other night, right before you walked out. Why did you come back?"

Devon set aside the washcloth. When he turned back, he moved to lie beside me. I scrambled to put some space between us, but his arm hooked around my waist, drawing me back to him. He quickly had me pinned flat on my back, his leg between my thighs and his torso lying half on top of mine.

"I decided I didn't give a damn," he said, studying my face. His gaze followed the path of his fingers as he traced my brow, down the line of my nose to my lips, brushing across my cheek to my jaw. "I wanted you, and I thought you wanted me to." He paused. "Was I wrong?"

The selfishness of his words was in stark contrast to the tender way he was touching me, the firm but gentle hold his body had on mine. I swallowed.

"No. But what if I'd been afraid?" I asked.

His eyes met mine. "But you weren't, were you," he said. It wasn't a question.

"No," I finally said, the word barely more than a whisper. "And I don't know why."

"It's because I saved your life today," Devon said, "and now you trust me. In here." He leaned down, pressing his lips to the valley between my breasts. "Though perhaps not up here." His finger tapped lightly at my temple.

"I barely know you," I said.

He smiled thinly. "You know me as well as anyone does."

"But I—"

"Shh," he hushed me, pressing his fingertips to my lips. "Go to sleep. I need rest, and so do you."

"You're staying?" I asked, unable to keep the surprise from my voice.

"You'd rather I go?" he asked, his brows rising.

"N-no, of course not," I stammered. "I just thought you . . . would. That's all."

"I like the feel of a woman next to me," Devon said matter-of-factly, settling himself beside me.

Reaching down, he tugged the covers up over us, then turned us on our sides. My back was pressed against his chest, my bottom cradled by his hips. His arm rested in the curve of my waist and his hand settled over my breast, his thumb brushing idly over the nipple.

It seemed I didn't really have a choice in the matter, not that I was protesting. Devon was so large, I felt small next to him. Protected. It was natural for him to take control, easy for me to let him. He was almost absently caressing my body, as one would a pet.

Just before I drifted to sleep it struck me that he'd said he liked the feel of "a woman." Did that mean any woman would do? And did I care if that answer was yes?

I was awakened in the early hours of the morning to Devon draped over me, his mouth covering a nipple. If I'd been more awake, I would've turned away. I had always been self-conscious about my on-the-smallish-side breasts. But Devon didn't seem to mind, turning me so he could wedge his hips between my spread thighs.

"Once more, luv, before I go," he murmured, his lips moving against my skin.

I wasn't sure if it was a question or a statement, but I nodded my acquiescence, my breath caught on a gasp as he slid inside me.

The dawn light was enough for me to see his face clearly as he looked at me. His hand skated down my thigh to hook behind my knee, drawing my leg up higher. The new angle was better and I bit my lip at the feel of his cock thrusting inside me, tingles of pleasure radiating outward from where we were joined. My eyes fluttered closed.

"Look at me," Devon commanded. I pried my eyes back open. His gaze was intense, his hips moving faster. "I want to watch you," he said.

I held on to him, memorizing the feel of him against me, inside me. His eyes stared deeply into mine as he moved, and it was as though he could see my soul. His skin was warm beneath my fingers, his brow growing damp. I was awestruck by how this time, with this man, I'd finally found what had eluded me all these years. It didn't seem like he was taking something from me. It felt like I was giving myself and he was giving it back.

He waited for me, not allowing himself to come until I was digging my nails into his shoulders, my body quaking beneath his. Only then did I feel him shudder in my arms, his mouth landing hard on mine.

Afterwards, he seemed reluctant to release me, but he eventually did. He turned and I heard the slight crinkle of the trash can liner as he threw away what I assumed was another used condom. Then he leaned over to brace himself on his arms above me.

"Women are lovely," he said, almost to himself, "and you even more so than most, sweet Ivy." He kissed me again, his tongue dipping inside my mouth to stroke mine. But before I could wrap my arms around him, he was gone.

I watched him dress, though it seemed he forgot me the moment he left the bed. He didn't glance my way as he buttoned his shirt and added his holster and gun. His tie he folded and tucked into a pocket. A man's watch—his watch—was sitting on the table and he wrapped it around his wrist, then grabbed his jacket.

Glancing at me, he winked, then was out the door, closing it silently behind him. Though I listened, I heard nothing of him exiting the apartment.

Flopping over on my back, I stared at the ceiling, wondering what in the hell had just happened to me. I'd had sex—incredible sex, twice—with a practical stranger. And not just any stranger—someone who I thought was a criminal and yet who had stopped a robbery yesterday. Granted, he'd shot a bullet into a man's skull not two inches from my own, but it had saved me from an unknown fate at his hands.

I didn't know how to feel. I was happy. My fears had been overcome in the heat of the moment and I hadn't gone cold and panicky. Devon would probably never know, or care to know, what he'd done for me. I hadn't been permanently broken. He'd proven that.

Which brought me to the other half of what I was feeling, which was rather alone. I thought I probably shouldn't feel that way. After all, it wasn't like Devon hadn't taken great care to make sure I enjoyed it, too. But it felt as though when he walked out, he'd taken a bit of my soul with him. I wondered if that was how the women felt when Logan left, and if they did, why they kept doing it.

Regardless of my confused emotions, my body knew quite well what it was feeling, which was elated . . . and sore. I moved a little and winced. Yes, I'd be remembering Devon today. As if I could forget him.

After another shower, I did my hair and makeup, then dressed in a pair of wide-leg trousers and a thin white blouse, adding a wide black leather belt. Glancing in the mirror, I thought it made my waist look even smaller, which I liked. After slipping on a pair of black Mary Jane heels, I headed to the kitchen. Usually I was the last one out the door, but today I'd beat Logan to the coffee pot. I was on my second cup and half watching a morning news show on the television when Logan made an appearance.

"Good morning!" I said cheerily.

He looked at me askance while he poured himself a cup of coffee.

"You're up early," he said, frowning slightly, "and are way too happy for this hour. I take it you didn't have any bad dreams?"

I shrugged. I'd nearly forgotten the dream that had woken me. Devon and what had followed had driven it from my mind. "It's okay," I said.

"You could've come in with me," Logan replied. "I wouldn't have minded."

I smiled. "You're too good to me," I said. "Besides, I knew you needed your sleep. You've been putting in twelve-hour days lately." And there was the small detail that I'd been comforted by multiple orgasms.

He sighed. "The life of an associate. At least I have a few years under my belt. I feel sorry for all the first-years now. Well, I would if I hadn't done it myself, not so long ago." He grinned.

"Any chance of making junior partner soon?" I asked.

"I sure as hell hope so," Logan said. "I'd hate to think I've been killing myself for nothing." His eyes narrowed as he studied me. "You okay today? To go in, I mean? You look a little worn out."

I felt heat flood my cheeks and quickly looked away. I thought about telling Logan about Devon, but it was just so weird. A man was sneaking into our apartment late at night and last night he'd had sex with me. Logan would go ballistic if he knew. The breaking-in part would piss him off, but he'd be more upset that I'd slept with a man I hardly knew.

Logan had been protective of me since we were kids, and I knew he wanted me to be happy, to find a guy and be in a good, healthy relationship. He knew I had issues, so despite his teasing over how little I dated, he'd launch right into overprotective-brother mode if he found out about Devon. So I kept my mouth shut.

"I'm fine," I said, going to the sink to rinse out my mug. "I don't even know if we're open today or not, but thought I'd go in anyway. It's better than moping here at home."

"Why don't I take you?" he offered.

"Won't you have to work late tonight?"

He shrugged. "I'll come get you and we'll grab some dinner. I can go back into the office afterwards."

"I don't want you to have to do that," I protested.

"I insist." Logan held my coat for me to slip into. "There's nothing I'd like better than to have dinner with the most beautiful woman in the city." He smiled.

I didn't answer, just gave him a tight hug and felt his lips brush the top of my head. I felt better, normal even, with him around.

It turned out the bank was open today, and aside from the police tape still cordoning off the safe deposit box area, you wouldn't have been able to tell a robbery had nearly occurred yesterday. Regardless that we were open for business, it was still slow and I found myself doing busywork when Marcia sidled up next to me from her station.

"Can you believe your hunky hero?" she asked in an undertone. "Talk about keeping cool under pressure."

"So what happened yesterday?" I asked. "There were two of them, one out here, and then suddenly they were dead."

"Well," she said, easing closer and looking like she was about to explode if she didn't tell me all the juicy details, "your guy—"

"He's not my guy," I interrupted.

Marcia rolled her eyes. "Whatever. Well, he was here with all of us, on the floor. Then he started acting funny, like something was wrong or he was going to be sick. So the bad guy came over to him, but before he could even say or do anything, your guy just jumped him! So fast, no one even had time to react. The next thing I know, the bad guy's on the floor and not moving and your guy had his gun."

I stared at her, eyes wide. "So he killed him? With his bare hands?"

She nodded. "It was all action-movie-Jason-Bourne shit. Then he fired a shot straight up into the ceiling and went and stood by the stairwell, waiting. When one of the guys with you came out, he did it again."

And this had been the same man who had slept next to me in my bed last night. I swallowed. Hard.

"Wow," I said. "He, uh, sounds like someone you wouldn't want to mess with, right?"

"And it was weird, too," she continued excitedly, "because when the cops talked to him, I thought they'd be all up in his business about taking matters in his own hands and endangering us and blah blah blah, but they weren't. They talked to him and then they just let him go on his way. Just like that." She snapped her fingers.

Okay, now that *was* weird. The red tape of an investigation in progress took forever to get through. I knew that from personal experience.

"He sure was hovering over you, though," Marcia said, adding a wink for good measure. "I think he likes you."

I should have known Marcia, even with all the chaos going on, would be keeping tabs on what Devon was doing. Though I didn't tell her exactly how *much* Devon liked me.

"Did you find out anything more about the robbers or overhear the cops say anything?" I asked, deciding to ignore her comments about Devon and me.

Marcia sobered. "Yeah. I guess the box they were trying to get into was Mr. Galler's."

"No way!" I said in surprise. "That puts a whole different spin on him being killed. I wonder what they were after."

A customer stepped up then and Marcia went back to her window. Business picked up a little after lunch, but I still had too much time with my thoughts.

I hadn't heard back from the FBI after that one time, so I hoped they'd realized how absurd it was to think I had anything to do with killing him. Personally, though it was a cliché, I still thought the butler did it. The guy they couldn't find but whom I had met that night.

It hurt in an uncomfortable spot in the center of my chest to think too much about poor Mr. Galler and what he'd endured just shortly after I'd left that night, so I shoved the thought from my mind.

My cell phone rang then, and while usually it was frowned upon if we answered it, I saw it was my grandma and grabbed it anyway.

"Oh, Ivy, thank goodness you're all right," Grams said. "I saw it on the news about the bank yesterday."

"Yeah, it was a little scary," I admitted, "but I'm okay."

It took several more reassurances from me before Grams would believe I was really okay, but she finally let it go.

"Sweetie, I've got some bad news," she said. "It's about Jace. His hearing . . . well, they let him out, Ivy. We just got word a little bit ago."

A shiver of ice went through me and my palms began to sweat. Logically, I'd known this was possible, but logic wasn't controlling me now.

"Sweetie, I'm so sorry," Grams said when I was silent. "Try not to worry. You're staying with Logan, your name isn't on the lease or any of the utilities, there's nothing he can trace to find you."

I finally found my voice. "It's not just me," I said. "It's you and Grandpa, too. I don't want him coming there."

"Don't worry about us," Grams said. "We'll be fine. I hated having to tell you at all, but I knew you'd be upset if I didn't. They don't let just anyone out on parole, sweetie. He may have changed. Prison may have changed him from what he used to be."

"Not likely," I retorted. Jace was cunning. I could see him in my head now, telling the parole board about how "sorry" he was and how he'd been "rehabilitated." I was one of the very few who was able to see through Jace's lies.

I had to go and, after promising to talk to her later, I ended the call just as a customer stepped up to me. Smiling automatically, my mind was far away as I processed the transaction, my fingers flying by rote over the keyboard before handing over the receipt.

Jace was out.

The twelve-year-old girl still within me wanted to curl inside a closet and hide, just like she used to do. But the adult in me knew I couldn't. Grams was right. The apartment, utilities, everything was in Logan's name. My regular mail went to Grams. There was nothing that could lead Jace to me.

And yet my hands still shook as I went through the motions of shutting down my station for the night.

I waved goodbye to Marcia and shrugged into my coat as I headed out the door. Logan had texted that he was on his way so he should be pulling up any minute.

But another car, a familiar one, was already waiting at the curb. I paused uncertainly, staring at the tinted windows. The driver's side door opened and Devon stepped out, his gaze on me.

A thrill shot through me as our eyes locked, stealing my breath. He wore another designer suit tailored to fit the broad expanse of his shoulders and girth of his biceps. Marcia's recounting of Devon's deeds flitted through my mind and my gaze dropped to his hands. His large, capable hands that had killed two men yesterday, then had held me and touched me . . .

He stalked toward me, his stride long and purposeful. Instinctively, I took a step back, but wasn't quick enough to escape him. In the span of two heartbeats, he was in front of me, his body too near mine.

"We-we're closed," I stammered.

The hint of a smile curled his lip. "Brilliant, because I'm not here for the bank," he said, his soft accent making the words sound like a promise.

"Oh." It was all I could come up with. Too busy examining every detail of his face, breathing in his scent that I could just catch on the chilled breeze, my mind couldn't spare the brain cells to compose a proper reply.

"Come with me," he said, taking my elbow and steering me toward his car.

It was only after I'd obediently taken several steps that I remembered.

"Wait . . . I can't," I said, putting on the brakes. "I-I have plans."

"Break them," he said, opening the door for me.

I looked at him, appalled. "I-I . . . can't," I sputtered. "I won't. Listen, you can't just show up here—"

Curving a hand around the back of my neck, he pulled me to him and kissed me, cutting off my words. It wasn't a sweet, tender kiss. It was dark and deep, thrusting me back into memories of last night. His mouth was hard against mine, his tongue hot. The hold he had on me was firm but didn't hurt, though my neck felt fragile in his grip.

When Devon lifted his head, it took me a moment to open my eyes. The anger that had been building over his arrogant high-handedness had disappeared, replaced by a languid desire that crept through my bones. I found that I was clutching the lapels of his jacket like a lifeline, my fisted hands crumpling the expensive fabric.

I lifted my eyes to find Devon watching me, his icy blue gaze so intense, I couldn't look away. Neither of us spoke.

"Ivy?"

The familiar voice calling my name shattered the spell and I pulled myself out of Devon's grip, taking a couple of unsteady steps back. Our eyes were still locked together, but he made no move to come after me.

"Ivy!"

Turning, I spied Logan. He'd rather haphazardly parked his car across the street and was dodging traffic as he hurried toward me.

Seeing Logan knocked some sense back into me, and my back-bone. I glanced back at Devon.

"I have plans."

With that, I turned and walked away, though part of me wanted to run. I was scared of Devon and yet, he drew me with a force so compelling, it was in and of itself frightening. My head was shouting all kinds of warnings and danger signals about him, which I would be wise to heed, no matter what had transpired in my bed last night.

I met up with Logan halfway down the sidewalk.

"Who's that?" he asked, looking over my head at Devon. His brow was creased in a frown.

"No one," I said, grabbing his arm and tugging him back in the other direction toward his car. "Come on, let's go."

Logan looked down at me in disbelief. "He was kissing you! That doesn't sound like a 'no one' to me. Unless you're suddenly in the habit of making out with strangers in public?"

"I'll talk to you about it in the car," I said, shaking my head. "Now please, let's just go, okay?" I tugged again on his arm, but he wasn't moving.

Logan glanced back toward Devon, his jaw clenching. I didn't turn around to see if Devon was staring back, though from the way Logan was glaring, I could very well guess that was exactly what he was doing.

"Fine," he said curtly, finally letting me pull him away.

A few minutes later we were in Logan's car and speeding away from the bank . . . and Devon.

CHAPTER SIX

"You want to tell me what's going on?"

I turned to look at Logan from where I'd been watching Devon out the back window. Logan looked tired and pissed. His tie was loosened and the top button of his shirt undone, but his eyes were sharp.

"I know that guy," Logan continued when I didn't answer. "That's the guy that came to my firm, the guy who invited himself to dinner that night. Did he follow you?"

Logan was doing exactly what I'd predicted, heading straight for the overprotective-big-brother zone.

"It's not like that," I said, trying to think of what to tell Logan that wouldn't piss him off more.

"So then what's the deal? You're seeing him or something? I mean, that's fine, you know, whatever, but you could've told me."

"It's not like that," I said. *We're not doing something as normal as dating. I'm just using him for sex and vice versa. Geez.* Logan would think I was taking a page out of *his* book.

"Then what's it like?" he shot back. "Because I know you, and there's no way in hell you'd be letting some guy you barely know kiss you."

It was true. Logan had seen me date guys in high school and college, and I'd never been a girl who liked being touched and kissed before I felt secure and comfortable with the guy. Usually, I'd broken it off before it ever got to that point.

Devon had blown past all that, all my insecurities and hang-ups that kept men at arm's length. I didn't know if it was because he hadn't given a damn, as he put it, or if it was just the fact that it was . . . him. I could tell none of this to Logan, of course, so I decided to tell a sanitized version of the truth.

"He was a customer at the bank," I said, "and that night, at dinner, we kind of connected," which was a nice way of saying he'd kissed me breathless in the hallway. "I've seen him a couple of times since, had dinner," all of which was perfectly true. I shrugged. "So he kissed me. It's not a big deal."

Logan glanced back at me from the road. "Why wouldn't you tell me?" He was looking at me like I'd betrayed him, the hurt in his voice making me wince.

"I don't know and I'm really sorry," I said. "I-I guess I wasn't sure what to make of it at first, so I didn't want to say anything. Please don't worry." Again, all true, though I didn't think I'd be getting any awards for veracity anytime soon.

Logan looked back at the road, the set of his jaw grim and his hands tight on the steering wheel. He was silent for a moment.

"Ivy, I've been watching out for you since I was fourteen and too much of a kid to do anything to help you except be there when you showed up at my window in the middle of the night." He paused and it seemed both of us were recalling those nights that now seemed so long ago. "I know you're a grown woman and it's your life," he looked back at me, "but please don't ask me to stop looking out for you. I don't even know if I could."

My heart twisted at the worry in his eyes and I reached for his hand, prying it from its death grip on the steering wheel.

"I know," I said quietly, folding his hand in both of mine. "I love you, too."

Logan's face softened and I knew he was over it. I gave a little sigh of relief. I hated it when we argued, not that it happened very often.

"So tell me about this Romeo," Logan said with a sigh. "What was his name again?"

My stomach lurched and I was glad he didn't recall the fake name Devon had given him at dinner. "It's Devon," I said. "His name is Devon."

"Ah," Logan said. "Devon. Well, to hell with Devon for tonight. I've had a shitty week and there's no way I'm going back into the office on a Friday night, no matter my lofty intentions this morning." He grinned at me. "I'm in the mood for drinking and dancing, Ives. You in?"

I grinned back, pushing thoughts of Devon aside. "You read my mind."

Logan was one of those dream guys who could actually dance and loved it. He'd taught me and now one of our favorite things was to go to the same club we always went to, have a few drinks, and spend hours on the dance floor.

The club was a country bar called Whiskey Tango. They didn't allow smoking, which was kind of nice for us nonsmokers. We ordered burgers, fries, and beers before Logan shed his jacket and tie and pulled me out onto the floor. A lot of guys liked to two-step, even to the fast numbers, but Logan liked the fifties' style swing dancing. We'd danced together for so long, it was like we were telepathic, our moves smooth and sure.

We took a break to eat, but soon I'd pulled my hair up into a ponytail and undone a couple more buttons on my blouse as I fanned myself. Logan had rolled back the cuffs of his shirt and his skin was hot through the fabric, a thin sheen of sweat on his forehead, but that didn't stop him. He spun me around the floor until I was breathless and grinning.

"Gotta take a break," I panted at the end of a song.

"Wuss," he ribbed me good-naturedly.

"There's a blonde in the corner eyeing you," I suggested, raising an eyebrow. Logan glanced over, winked at me, and headed her way.

I sank gratefully onto my stool at our table, taking a sip of my Crown and Coke. I wasn't a big drinker so it didn't take much to make me tipsy. I watched as Logan took the blonde onto the dance floor, and it was obvious that she was a novice dancer. Considering how pretty she was, though, I didn't think Logan minded.

"Hey, beautiful. Can I buy you a drink?"

Looking around, I saw a man slide onto the stool next to me. He was tall and dark-haired, an easy smile on his face. Lifting a hand, he signaled for a cocktail waitress.

"Um, I'm actually with someone," I hedged. I was awful at turning people down. It was the people pleaser in me, I thought, that hated to disappoint someone, even strangers. But neither did I want to encourage an unknown guy.

"Does he know that?" the guy said with a grin, jerking his head toward the dance floor where Logan and the blonde were laughing together.

I gave a weak smile.

The harried waitress came by and the guy ordered another round. When she left, he held out his hand. "I'm Steve. And you are . . . ?"

Manners made me give him my hand and answer. "Ivy."

"Nice to meet you, Ivy," he said, folding my hand in his much larger one. He was still smiling and seemed nice enough. He wasn't drop-dead gorgeous, like Devon, but he was good-looking and his wide, friendly smile made him more attractive. I relaxed ever so slightly.

"Would it be just too cliché if I were to ask if you come here often?" Steve asked.

I laughed at that. "Maybe," I said. "But yes, I do. My friend and I like to dance."

"You from around here, Ivy?"

I shook my head. "No. You?" I was always vague when people asked where I was from and didn't give any more information than necessary. Call it an ingrained sense of caution, but I didn't think strangers had a right to know my life story just because they bought me a drink.

"Born and raised," Steve said, handing the waitress some money when she returned with our drinks.

We chatted for a little while and he told me he sold insurance for a living, which you wouldn't think was very interesting, but he had some funny stories that had me laughing.

Steve was a nice, normal guy. He wasn't dark and mysterious, and he probably didn't shoot people or kill them with his bare hands.

I sipped the drink Steve had bought me while we talked. It was in an old-fashioned rather than tall, the way I usually ordered, and it seemed the liquor went straight to my head. My vision grew blurry and I tried to focus on what Steve was saying, but couldn't.

"I'm going to the ladies' room," I said, sliding off my stool. To my shock and embarrassment, my knees almost immediately folded.

"Easy there," Steve said, catching me as he jumped to his feet.

"I'm sorry," I mumbled, trying to blink my vision clear. I tried to hold on to Steve, but I had trouble making my muscles obey my commands. "I think I need some water."

"You'll be fine," Steve said. "Let me give you a lift home."

"N-no, I need L-Logan," I forced out, my lips slurring the words. I was starting to become alarmed now, in a hazy, fuzzy way. Alcohol had never affected me like this before.

"I'll take care of you," Steve said, half carrying me toward the door. "Don't you worry." Something in his eyes was different now, calculating instead of friendly, and I got scared.

"Let m-me go," I said, trying unsuccessfully to pull away, but it was like swimming through molasses. I turned my head, trying to find Logan through the crowded dance floor.

But we were already out the door. The air was frigid against my skin, my coat still in the club. By now, I couldn't move, my body weight entirely supported by Steve. To any passerby, it'd look like a guy helping his girlfriend after she'd had too much to drink. My head lolled against his shoulder, my arms hanging uselessly at my sides. The hold he had around my waist was painfully tight and I knew I'd have bruises tomorrow—if I survived tonight.

A car pulled up, skidding to a stop at the curb in front of us. Steve jerked open the back door and shoved me none-too-gently inside. He climbed in after me, slamming the door behind him.

"Go!"

The driver took off down the street. Steve grabbed me and hauled me upright from where I'd slumped against the passenger door. My eyes were heavy and I had trouble keeping them open. I felt strange. I was afraid and panicked, but it was as though those emotions were covered by thick blankets, their sharp edges muted against my lethargy.

"Tell me about Galler," Steve said.

I stared at him, the words slow to penetrate my mind.

"Galler told you something," he said. "What did he tell you that night you were there?"

"She looks like she's about to pass out," the driver said. "How much did you give her?"

"I paid the waitress to do it," Steve shot back.

"Well, she ain't gonna be any use to us if she can't talk."

"You think I don't know that?" Steve focused on me again and my eyes slipped closed.

Pain exploded in my cheek. Steve had slapped me. Hard. He did it again and I tasted blood.

"Wake up, you stupid bitch!" he snarled. "Tell me what Galler said!"

I was confused and I hurt, and I couldn't think what he wanted me to tell him. I could barely see him now, black clouding my vision as I fought to stay conscious.

I heard the sound of breaking glass and Steve turned to the driver, but the driver slumped over in his seat. There was a small hole in the windshield in front of him.

The car careened out of control and Steve threw himself toward the steering wheel, but he was too late. We crashed, the sound of screeching metal and shattered glass loud in my ears. Steve flew forward, his body striking and then breaking through the windshield. My limp body ricocheted against the backseat, my head slammed into something hard, and then everything went dark.

Oh, God, what a hangover. My head ached and my stomach felt like I was going to throw up any minute. How in the world could I have let myself drink so much? And why had Logan not stopped me? He knew I couldn't hold my liquor.

Something ice-cold pressed against my cheek, making my eyes fly open as I instinctively jerked back.

"Easy now," Devon said, laying a hand on my shoulder. "I gave you something to counteract the drug, but you need some more time."

And it all came rushing back to me. Steve. The drink. The car crash. Oh God . . .

"Where am I?" I asked, looking around. Devon was right. I felt incredibly weak, though the fog that earlier had clouded my brain and weighed down my limbs had lifted. "How did I get here? Where's Logan?" I struggled to sit up.

"Stay put," Devon said, pushing me gently but firmly back onto the couch. "If you attempt to stand up, you'll fall." He replaced the cold pack against my cheek, holding it there. That's when I felt that my face hurt. Oh yeah, that asshole had hit me.

I was in an unfamiliar apartment and I guessed it to be Devon's. He sat beside me on the couch I was lying on. He'd discarded his tie and jacket, and I wasn't a bit surprised to see the shirt he wore was still immaculately white and unwrinkled.

His expression was carefully blank as he watched me, but when he pulled away the ice pack to check my face, his jaw tightened and his eyes grew cold.

I grimaced. "How bad is it?" I didn't like to think I was vain, but I wasn't an idiot either. I'd be lucky if Steve hadn't left a mark.

"It'll heal," he replied, his voice curt. "Tell me what the bloody hell happened?"

My eyebrows went up. "*Me* tell *you* what happened," I said. "Shouldn't you be telling me? How did you find me? Did you kill that man?" I remembered how the driver had been shot right before we'd crashed.

For a moment, I didn't think he'd answer me, but then he said, "I wasn't looking for *you*. I was looking for *them*. Imagine my surprise when I opened the back door and you came tumbling out."

"So it was just a happy coincidence that you came along when you did?" I asked, not believing a word of it.

"What else did they do to you?" Devon asked, ignoring me. He nodded toward my blouse. "Your clothes are ripped."

I glanced down. Sure enough, though I'd undone a couple of buttons, the fabric was now torn and gaping.

"Nothing like that," I said, searching my memory. "He said he'd had the waitress put something in my drink, then he was mad because it made me sleepy. That's when he hit me." Devon's lips pressed into a thin line. "He kept asking me about Mr. Galler."

"Mr. Galler," Devon repeated.

"He was a customer at the bank," I explained. "He was killed last week."

"And why would you know anything about Mr. Galler?"

"I have no idea," I said with a tired sigh. "He liked me, I guess. I was the one always sent to his house. But that's all. It's not as if I was related to him or something." Pushing aside Devon's hand, I sat up, holding my shirt together with one hand. I noticed a hypodermic needle on the table next to the couch and wondered what Devon had given me, not that I was complaining. Bruises aside, I felt better than I had before.

The whole Mr. Galler thing was strange. "You know," I said, "the men who tried to rob the bank, they wanted into his safe deposit box."

"They must be looking for something," Devon said, "and think you have it."

I shrugged, pushing my hair back from my face with my free hand. "All I have from Mr. Galler is a pendant that he gave me the night he died."

Devon said nothing and, after a moment, I glanced up at him. He was looking at me as though I were an idiot.

"What?" I asked.

"Mr. Galler gave you something—*the night he was killed*—and it didn't occur to you that it might be exactly what they're looking for?" Besides looking at me like I was an idiot, he also looked angry.

"But it's nothing!" I said, stung. "It's just a pendant. See?" My necklace had twisted, the heavy pendant I'd attached to the chain this morning now hung down my back. I tugged it around, showing it to Devon.

Rather than just looking at it, Devon reached up and undid the clasp for the chain and dumped the pendant into his palm.

"So this is what everyone's after," he murmured.

I was confused. "Who? Do you know who those guys were? Why were you following them?"

Devon spoke while still scrutinizing the pendant. "I'm trying to locate a man. A very dangerous man. The men who took you had just been to Galler's home. The man I'm looking for is searching for this."

"Wait," I said. "You knew they came from Mr. Galler's home? How? Did you know him?"

Now he looked at me.

"No," he said shortly. "But I suspected what they did. That you knew something, had access to something." He fisted his hand around the pendant. "This should help."

Devon's words took a moment to sink in and I gaped at him, dismay and shock rippling through me. At last, I found my voice. "You mean all of this," I waved my hand to indicate him and me, "was a setup? To get that?" I pointed to the pendant in his hand.

"Much easier than attempting to rob the bank," he said, matter-of-fact.

I was horrified. I'd been so, so stupid. I'd thought Devon and I'd had a connection, that there was something between us, something I'd never felt with anyone before. I'd let him touch me, kiss me, have sex with me—

Abruptly, I felt like I would be sick. Embarrassed mortification crawled over my skin.

Devon must've realized this revelation wasn't going over well with me because he said, "Not that it wasn't pleasurable." Then his lips tipped up in a half smile.

I swung my hand without thinking, rage spiking hard. But Devon's reflexes were lightning fast and he grabbed my wrist before my palm could make contact with his cheek. His eyes were narrowed shards of ice, the smile wiped from his face as our gazes locked.

"Let me go, you sonofabitch," I said through gritted teeth. His hold on me was just this side of painful. I tried, and failed, to pull my arm away.

But he didn't let go. Instead, he slowly pushed my arm down and away from his face, overwhelming my strength with his. Then he leaned over me until we were mere inches apart.

"Don't try that again," he said, and the menace in his voice and danger in his eyes made my insides quake.

As soon as he let me go, I was up and rushing for the door, my vision blurred with the tears swimming in my eyes. I refused to cry in front of him. I just wanted to go home and lick my wounds in private. How could I have been so gullible?

Clutching my shirt closed with one hand, I laid the other on the doorknob and pulled open the door a scant two inches, only to have it slammed shut by Devon's palm.

He stood behind me, so close I could feel the heat of his body as he leaned his weight on his hand to keep the door closed.

The warmth of his breath fanned my cheek. I could barely breathe, my heart pounding from fear and anger.

"You walk out that door," Devon said in my ear, "and you won't last a day."

"You can't possibly think I'd stay here?" My voice was barely more than a pained whisper, but I was hurting too much to care what I sounded like.

"They know who you are and they've already attacked you twice," Devon said. "If I hadn't been there tonight, they'd have succeeded."

I was caught, caught between what seemed to be two equally dangerous sides. Devon had lied to me and used me. The taste of that was bitter in my throat. But he'd saved me, kept me from bodily harm, though I wasn't so sure about the psychological and emotional damage he'd wrought.

Devon's hands moved to settle on my shoulders, which he may have meant to be comforting, but I felt too narrow, my bones too fragile beneath his palms. His strength and size controlled me and the force of his will overpowered mine.

I felt him brush my ponytail aside, then the soft touch of his lips to my skin at the place where my neck met my shoulder.

"Does this feel like a setup to you?"

I was stiff under his touch as he gripped my upper arms, slowly drawing the ruined fabric of my blouse down and exposing more of my skin to his mouth. He pulled my hand from its death grip on the door handle. Devon's touch was an addiction I couldn't tear myself away from. A knot of bitter anger still burned in my belly, but I could no more stop my body's reaction to him than I could have resisted the drug I'd been given tonight.

Cooler air touched my stomach and I realized Devon had removed my blouse completely, the fabric falling from my wrists to land in a soft brush of silk on the floor.

His hands were unhurried, giving me plenty of opportunity to try to stop him, but I did nothing when he unclasped my bra, letting it slide down my arms to the floor as well. Devon's palms cupped my breasts and I drew in a lungful of air with a gasp. His mouth sucked lightly at my neck and my head lolled back to rest against his shoulder.

The buzzing of my cell phone in my pants pocket tore my attention away from what Devon was doing to me. It had to be Logan, no doubt worried about me and where I'd disappeared to.

Devon didn't pause in kissing or caressing me as I fished the phone out and answered.

"Hello?" The greeting was breathier than my normal voice.

"Ivy! Where the hell are you?" Logan's voice penetrated the haze of desire Devon had wrapped around me and I pried my eyes open.

"Sorry," I said, searching for a white lie about what had happened with Steve. "I decided to get some air, then ran into Devon."

"You left your coat, and your purse is still in my car," Logan said. "Jesus, Ivy, you're not usually this inconsiderate. I mean, I don't care if you want to ditch me for a dude, but you could have at least mentioned it." His irritation made me feel guilty, even though I knew it wasn't my fault.

Devon suddenly turned me to face him, bracing my back against the chilled wooden door, then his lips were closing over my nipple. The wet heat of his tongue sent a sharp flash of arousal through me. My eyes slammed shut and my free hand clasped him to me, my fingers buried in his hair.

"Sorry . . . Logan," was all I could manage.

"What's the matter?" Logan asked suspiciously. "Are you all right?"

I couldn't reply, my thoughts incoherent as Devon's mouth skated upward to cover mine. Our tongues slid together and I could feel the hard press of his erection against my abdomen. Logan's voice echoed in my ear, but I didn't listen to what he was saying.

Suddenly, the phone was lifted from my hand.

"She's busy at the moment," Devon spoke into it. "She'll have to ring you back." He pressed the button to end the call, then tossed the phone carelessly behind him. It thudded to the carpet.

The brief moment brought clarity. I wedged my arms between us and pushed against Devon's chest while trying to cover my exposed body.

"Stop," I said, angling my head away from where his mouth was drifting over my collarbone. "I don't want this."

Devon stilled, his proximity unchanged from my attempt to push him away. I waited to see what he'd do, barely breathing. I knew that if he pressed the issue, disregarded my wishes and continued kissing and touching me, I'd fold like a cheap tent. Even now as I struggled to keep a clear head, my body was wet and aching for him.

He lifted his head, his ice-blue eyes staring down into mine.

"Are you quite sure about that?" he asked.

Devon's hands spanned my waist, the pads of his fingers rough against my skin. A shiver ran through me and the whisper of a smile drifted across his face. I felt a blush crawling up my neck, but my words were firm.

"I'm sure. You used me, lied to me." I shook my head. "I don't want to have sex with someone who treats me that way."

"I also saved your life—twice," Devon said.

I raised an eyebrow. "So you require sex as a thank-you?" I was hoping to hit a nerve, because Devon was too arrogant to ever have sex with a woman who viewed it as an obligation.

Devon's face was unreadable. "I don't *require* anything," he said, stepping away from me and confirming my suspicion. I let out the breath I'd been holding.

Bending down, I grabbed my shirt, clutching it to my chest as though it were a shield. Devon had disappeared from the room and I eyed the door. Was he right? Would someone come after me again if I went home? Or was he lying to me again? Should I leave now while I had the chance?

But before I could make up my mind, Devon was back.

"Here," he said, handing me what had to be one of his shirts. "Put this on."

I turned my back and dropped my ruined blouse before shrugging into the much-too-large shirt. I buttoned it up and had to turn back the cuffs several times. The fabric was a thick, soft cotton and carried a whiff of Devon's scent. When I turned, Devon was watching me, and the look in his eyes made me fleetingly regret calling a halt to his seduction.

"Are you hungry?" he asked, walking over to the kitchen. "Something in your stomach will help get the drugs out of your system."

"Okay," I replied, noncommittal. Picking up my discarded blouse and bra, I folded them and set them aside, then took the opportunity of Devon not standing over me to look around the apartment.

It was nice, like it-was-obvious-he-had-money kind of nice. The furniture was top-of-the-line and everything went together too well for me to think anyone other than a professional had decorated the place. There was a wide expanse of windows that showed the city skyline, so I could tell we were close to downtown, but in a more expensive neighborhood than my own.

Something felt strange about the apartment and it took me a moment to pinpoint what it was. There was nothing personal in it at all. No photos, no books, no knickknack memorabilia sitting on shelves. It was like an apartment from a magazine, devoid of sentimentality or intimacy.

My ponytail was falling out, so I reached up and pulled the band until my hair fell to my shoulders and down my back. I ran my fingers through it, trying to comb through the tangles. That felt better.

I didn't see a television, which I thought was strange, then I noticed a closed cabinet in the corner. Ah. It was probably there.

I could hear Devon rummaging around in the kitchen as I headed for the white cupboards. The apartment had a lot of space and a hallway led back to where I assumed the bedroom was.

My thoughts skittered away from that. Didn't want to think about it. Though if I was going to stay here, where would I sleep?

Best not dwell on that right now either.

"Come sit down."

Devon had approached without me hearing him and now his hand was on my waist, moving me toward the couch. There was a tray of food sitting on the coffee table that held a couple of different types of cheese, some crackers, grapes, and strawberries.

"Strawberries in the winter?" I asked as I sat on the couch. Those weren't cheap.

He shrugged. "I like strawberries." Snagging one, he sat back, watching me as he bit down into the soft red fruit.

My gaze was rapt on his mouth, now slightly pinker because of the juice clinging to his lips. His tongue swiped and the juice was gone, leaving behind a wet sheen. Tearing my eyes away, I picked up a cracker and some cheese.

"Will you tell me who you are?" I asked, nibbling on the cracker. "Who you are really?"

"I've already told you," Devon replied.

"But who do you work for? How can you kill so many people without the police catching you?" I couldn't look at him as I asked, maybe because now that I was saying it aloud to him, it made it more real. If he realized I knew all he'd done, would he hurt me, too?

"My job is a bit . . . above the law." He reached out, snagging another strawberry.

I swallowed the bit of cheese in my mouth, wondering if I wanted an answer to my next question. "And what is that job exactly?"

"I'm a spy, of course."

CHAPTER SEVEN

I stared at Devon, then slowly blinked.

"You're a what?" I asked.

"A spy," he repeated, "though perhaps not how you're used to thinking of one." He ate another strawberry.

"I generally don't think of spies at all," I said honestly. "I kind of thought they were extinct after the Cold War."

"Extinct?" He raised an eyebrow. "Surely I'm not that old. Besides, spies never go away, nor does the need for them."

I let this ruminate for a moment. "So," I said, "you're a . . . British spy? Spying on America?" Nice. I'd hooked up with someone who could probably get me arrested for treason or some such thing.

"Don't be ridiculous," he dismissed. "We don't spy on allies."

The way he said it made my response a little dry. "Of course you don't."

His lips twitched at my tone. "I told you I'm looking for someone," he said. "My search led me here."

"And Mr. Galler is . . . was . . . involved?"

"It would seem so."

I waited, but Devon didn't elaborate. "That's all you're going to tell me?"

"That's all you need to know."

"Why didn't you just tell me that from the beginning?" I asked. "Why the lies and . . . and the pretending to like me . . . and taking me to dinner and . . . and stuff?" Blurting all of that out made me look away in embarrassment, but I wanted to know. I'd fallen for it, hook, line, and sinker. After years of being so cautious, it burned to know how easily Devon had seduced me.

His hand cupped my chin, making me turn to face him. I lifted my eyes reluctantly to his.

"I didn't tell you because I thought you might be working with them," he said. "And I do like you. If I hadn't . . . well, there are other ways to make someone talk."

Yeah, I didn't really want to know the details.

"What convinced you I wasn't?" I asked instead.

Devon's hand slid to my cheek and I resisted the urge to tip my head farther into his hand.

"The night you were afraid," he said. "You couldn't have faked that, nor would there have been a reason to, if you'd been working for them."

That night flashed through my mind, how quickly he'd known what I'd been trying to hide.

He was so close, and the words he said soothed my mangled pride. But I didn't trust him. He could lie so easily, and considering his life probably depended on how well he did so, it would be foolish to believe him now. Should I even believe that he was a spy? Maybe he was playing a game with me, seeing if I'd believe such an outlandish story.

I eased back, putting some space between us. "So you're just going to keep me here?"

"For now," Devon said, the calculating look coming back into his eyes. He stood. "Come. You need to rest."

Taking my hand, he pulled me to my feet and led me down the hall to the bedroom. He flipped on the switch and a lamp illuminated the room. Although spacious, the huge bed dominated the space and my eyes were drawn inexorably to it.

"You can sleep in here," he said. "I'll take the sofa." The way he said it, almost with a wry smile, had me glancing at him.

"You don't have to give up your bed for me," I protested. "I mean, it's not like you're a gentleman." I didn't know why I added the dig, maybe I wanted to push him and see how far he'd go.

But his lips only twisted further. "I can pretend as well as the next man," he said.

Devon moved closer until we were nearly touching. I stood my ground, though I wanted desperately to take a step back.

"What are you doing?" I asked, immediately hating the throaty sound in my voice.

Devon didn't answer me. His gaze dropped to my mouth and my pulse leapt. Leaning down, his lips brushed mine in a feather-light touch. His lips were soft and warm, teasing gently and coaxing a response from me as his tongue swiped my bottom lip.

It was electric and I moaned softly, opening my mouth so he could deepen the kiss. He tasted of strawberries, his tongue sliding along mine as his hand palmed the back of my head. Devon kissed me as though he had all the time in the world, until I was breathless and clutching his shoulders, my body pressed against his.

"Your body was made for me," he murmured, his lips sliding along my jaw to leave my skin burning. "That's why you're not afraid. It knows me. It wants me between your legs, buried inside you."

The words curled in my ear like the sweet, silky promise of a viper. I stiffened, but before I could push him away again, Devon pulled back.

"Good night, sweet Ivy." Then he was gone, the door closing softly behind him.

How the hell was I supposed to sleep after that?

And yet, sleep I did. When I woke, I realized I'd slept longer than usual and it was already late in the morning. I showered in the master bath but didn't have any clean clothes. Devon's shirt came down to mid-thigh, so I put that back on. My black pants went on right over my bare skin—looked like I was going commando for the time being.

When I emerged from the bedroom, I smelled food. Following the scent to the kitchen, I was momentarily taken aback at the sight of Devon with his back to me as he cooked something on the stove. His upper body was bare. Though he wore pants, his shirt had been discarded and the sunshine lighting up the apartment threw his skin into stark relief.

Three bullet-wound scars decorated his back. A long scar that must have been from a knife arched across his shoulder blade before disappearing around his torso. The thick muscles rippled underneath his skin as he moved, the pants riding low on his lean hips.

I sucked in a breath as I avidly drank him in. Usually scars would be a detriment, but Devon's only added to his appeal— badges of honor earned through his pain and blood. I questioned again what he'd told me about being a spy. He definitely did something dangerous, but maybe he just hadn't wanted to tell me it was illegal so had made up the spy thing.

Did it matter to me? No. Not really. Should it matter? Without a doubt.

"Sleep well?" he asked, still cooking something on the stove.

I frowned, wondering how he'd known I was there when I was sure I hadn't made a sound.

"Um, yeah, I guess," I replied, sliding onto one of the barstools at the granite counter.

Devon reached for two plates and slid some food onto each, then turned and set one in front of me. He'd made omelets.

"You can cook," I said, stating the obvious, but it surprised me. It seemed like such a mundane activity for a man like him.

"Everyone has to eat," he said, taking a good-sized bite of his omelet.

My mind churned as we ate in silence. Devon wasn't the chatty type, but my thoughts were going a thousand miles a minute and I couldn't help expressing the most worrisome of them.

"It doesn't seem to bother you, killing people," I blurted. "You don't even hesitate. I've only known you a couple of weeks and I've seen you kill . . ." A pause while I counted. "Six men."

He glanced at me, then took another bite before responding. "I wouldn't be very good at my job if I hesitated or if killing people was bothersome to me."

"Are you good at your job?"

Devon's eyes were steady and cold. "Very."

Suddenly I wasn't hungry anymore. I pushed my plate away. "I think I'd better go," I said.

"I told you, it's not safe," Devon replied.

I gave him a look. "Somehow I don't think I'd be safer here with you."

Devon wiped his mouth with a napkin and picked up the plates, setting them into the sink. "I wasn't attempting to frighten you," he said, walking toward me. I swiveled the seat so I could track him, which might have been a mistake because he didn't stop until he stood right in front of me. He wedged his body between my knees, forcing my legs apart to accommodate him.

"I'm not frightened," I managed to say, "but I don't know what to believe. This could all be a lie for all I know. Maybe *you're* the bad guy." My eyes were drawn to his chest, the width of his shoulders. I knew I should feel afraid, and perhaps I was, a little. But the fear only made me want him more, which was a red flag waving on the path of self-destruction if I ever saw one.

"Quite right. I suppose it would depend on who you asked," Devon quipped, a smile playing at the corners of his mouth.

He smelled like soap and spice, the nipples on his chest begging me to lean forward just a little and lick them. He'd shaved, the tinge of musk from his aftershave teasing my nostrils as my fingers itched to test the smoothness of his jaw.

"So why do you care what happens to me?" I asked.

"Because I like having sex with you," he said, his bluntness making my jaw gape. "Last night was a bit rough, so I let you have your space." His hands moved to the buttons of the shirt I wore. "However, knowing you're not wearing anything underneath those clothes has me rethinking my efforts at chivalry." The buttons slipped easily through the holes, and before I'd even had time to react, Devon had it undone to my waist.

Devon had saved me—pursued me—only because he'd thought I'd known something about Galler . . . and because he wanted to fuck me.

Talk about a blow to a girl's ego.

He felt absolutely nothing for me, even after we'd slept together. In fact, Devon gave the adage about men thinking only with their dicks a whole new level of meaning. Perhaps some women might have found it flattering. I did not.

"Yeah, listen," I said, pulling my shirt closed just as Devon was about to slip his hand inside, "I thought I could do the sex-without-strings thing, but it's not really me, so I'll just be going." I swiveled on the stool again and hopped down. I buttoned my shirt on the way to the door to put on my shoes, then grabbed my cell from where Devon had set it on a table and slipped it into my pocket.

"Even after what I've told you, you're just going to leave?" Devon asked, following me.

"I own a gun, so I'll be sure to have it on me," I replied, keeping my gaze averted. I didn't want to get sucked into the almost-magnetic pull he had on me. "Besides, you don't care, remember? You have the pendant. You've had me." Now I fixed him with a fake smile. "I doubt I'll cross your mind."

"I don't believe in things like *love* and *forever*, and I don't apologize for it," Devon said with a shrug, pushing his hands into his pockets.

"I barely know you," I retorted. "I'm not asking for either of those things."

"Then what do you want?"

"In exchange for what?" I asked. "Sleeping with you?"

Devon didn't speak, but he didn't have to. The cold fire in his eyes as his gaze raked me from head to toe said enough. My skin prickled as though he'd touched me, and I clenched my fists, angry at my body's response to nothing but a look from him.

"Sorry," I sneered, "but I'm not a prostitute. Find someone else to scratch your itch." Then I was out the door.

A cab ride and a quick call to Logan to bring down my purse to pay the driver and I was back home.

"You've got to be freezing," Logan said, holding the cab door for me while I climbed out. "I can't believe you didn't even take your coat last night."

"I know," I said, wrapping my arms around my torso and shivering. I glanced up at Logan as the cab drove away. "Thanks for bringing down some money for me."

"It's not a—" Logan's voice cut off and his eyes went wide. The blood drained from his face as he stared at me.

"What the fuck did he do to you?" Logan's hands gripped my upper arms as he hauled me closer, his gaze inspecting my bruised face. "I swear to God, I'm going to kill him!"

Alarmed, I hurried to explain. "Logan, it's not what you think!"

Logan didn't reply, his face livid now with anger.

"Let's go inside," I pleaded with him.

Relenting, Logan pulled me into the building. To his credit, he didn't say anything more until we were in the apartment and I was ensconced on the couch. Wrapping a blanket around me, he said, "I'm waiting for this explanation."

I winced at the leashed fury in his voice. Time to tell all. Logan had been with me too long, had seen too much in my life, for me to wait any longer. So I spilled the whole tale. From when I'd first begun seeing Devon in the bank, to the night I'd watched him kill someone and right on up to my abduction last night and the car crash.

At some point, Logan sat down next to me, the anger on his face turning to surprise, shock, then back to anger. When I finished, Logan was quiet for a moment as I nervously waited to hear what he'd say.

"This guy has broken into my apartment, assaulted you in your bedroom, *killed* several people, and I'm just hearing about it *now*?" Logan's voice rose until he was nearly shouting at me. His fury was palpable and I flinched away from him. Seeing that, he closed his eyes and took a deep breath, as though trying to regain his calm.

"I'm sorry, Logan," I said. "I didn't know how to tell you. It was just so strange. And he didn't assault me." I swallowed. "I was . . . willing." My cheeks burned. We discussed Logan's sex life all the time. Mine, not so much, and there were good reasons for that.

"I don't understand it," Logan said, his brow furrowed in confusion. "You don't like this guy, tell me he scares you, yet you slept with him and you say he didn't force you. Why would you do that?"

Logan was my best friend, but it felt weird discussing this. "I don't know," I said. "It just . . . happened. I don't really want to talk about it."

He stared at me and I had to look away. "You know what I think?" he asked, as if I wasn't going to hear it anyway. "I think this guy has some kind of sick hold on you, and you can't even see it."

"What are you talking about?"

"The only man you've allowed to touch you in years is me," Logan retorted. "And now you're screwing some guy you barely know after he threatens you? It's too much like your past and you know it."

I felt the blood drain from my face. "Did you just say that to me?" I whispered.

Logan shoved a hand through his hair. "Christ, Ivy. I'm sorry. Can you blame me for being upset? This guy sneaks around, scares you, and I'm not supposed to be concerned when you tell me you slept with him?"

I threw off the blanket and leapt to my feet. "This conversation is over," I snapped. "I wish I hadn't told you at all." I hurried back to my bedroom.

"That makes two of us," Logan called angrily after me. I slammed my bedroom door shut.

I was shaking, I was so angry, and I was crying. I'd known Logan wasn't going to react very well, but I hadn't expected this level of anger. I got that he was concerned, but he was treating me like I was a brainless idiot who didn't know what I was doing.

Well, if the shoe fits . . .

Shoving that traitorous thought away, I stripped off my pants and borrowed shirt, pulling on a pair of yoga pants and a thick, cotton sweater. It had been beyond the pale for Logan to bring up my past, especially in this context. I was appalled and dismayed that he thought that about Devon and me. Not that there was a "Devon and me."

I flopped down onto my bed, sniffing away the tears. I stared listlessly out the window until I drifted off to sleep.

⁘

I woke when it was already dark, and for a moment I didn't remember the fight. When I did, my mood plummeted. How was I going to face Logan, knowing he was thinking there was something wrong with me for sleeping with Devon?

Who were we kidding? There *was* something wrong with me.

I brushed my teeth and hair, then went in search of Logan to apologize and talk things out. But the apartment was quiet and empty, save for me. I found a note on the counter.

Had to go in to work. Sorry we argued. Talk tonight. —Love, L

That made me feel a little better. At least I wasn't the only one upset that we'd fought, though I didn't know how we'd talk through it. What was done was done. It wasn't like I was going to see Devon again. He'd made it quite clear that I was useful for only one thing. Well, two things if you counted the pendant, which still pissed me off when I thought about it. I'd rather Devon had just told me what he was after instead of lying.

My stomach growled so I peered into the fridge, wondering if I should go to the grocery store. Just then, a knock sounded at the door.

I looked through the peephole first, then jerked back with a gasp.

Devon was there.

My palms immediately began to sweat and my heart rate kicked into overdrive. Taking a deep breath, I opened the door.

"Forget how to break in?" I asked coolly, glad my voice didn't betray my nerves.

Devon's lips twisted. "I was being courteous," he replied, taking a step closer.

I didn't back up, my body still blocking the doorway, and had to tip my head back to look him in the eye. He was wearing a tuxedo, of all things, that looked like it had been lovingly hand-woven to fit his body. The bowtie was actually tied, rather than the pretied ones I'd always seen at weddings and such.

"You're awfully dressed up to be stopping by for a visit," I said snottily. "Or were you hoping for a booty call?"

Devon's grin spread wider. "I came with a purpose, though I'm not opposed to a . . . booty call." He said the words as though they were foreign to him, and maybe they were. He acted and spoke as though he came from a higher class of society than me, a farm girl from Kansas.

"Forget it," I said, then tried to shut the door, which came to an abrupt halt when Devon wedged his foot in the opening.

"I brought a peace offering," he said.

"Not interested."

"And . . . an apology."

I paused. "I'm listening."

"I've been a bit . . . dodgy with you when perhaps being more forthright would have been the wiser choice," he said.

"That doesn't sound like an apology."

Devon's eyes twinkled with humor at my dry response. "You have my most sincere apologies," he said. Though the words were serious, his eyes held more than a trace of humor.

I thought about it, how upset I'd been earlier. He was right, though, he had saved my life. Twice. And the sex had been good . . . very good.

"Apology accepted," I said finally.

"Excellent," he said, brandishing a hanger with a long, opaque plastic covering over it. "Now for the peace offering." He held it out to me, but I didn't take it.

"What is it?" My eyes narrowed suspiciously.

"A dress."

"What *kind* of dress?"

"The kind you've only dreamed about wearing," he said with a knowing glint in his eye.

That perked up my interest and I eyed him. "Why do you have a dress for me?"

"I was hoping you'd accompany me tonight," he replied. "Dinner and dancing at a very fancy party."

"Is this a date?" I asked.

"It is if I buy you dinner."

The excitement I felt at seeing him again couldn't be denied, and the dress he held—still hidden from view by the protective plastic—was like catnip to me. Clothes—my Achilles' heel.

Wordlessly, I stepped back and allowed him inside. He gallantly handed over the dress, his lips still tipped up in a knowing smile.

"I'll just be a few minutes," I said, taking it from him. I left Devon standing in the living room and hurried back to my bedroom.

I unwrapped the dress carefully, hardly able to contain my excitement, and I gasped when it was fully revealed.

It was a two-piece dress in an avant-garde Indian style, the fabric a thick silk tapestry in black with shades of bronze and silver. The top fit tightly across my chest and had short sleeves that reached almost to my elbows. A draping ruffle of fabric wrapped around me from underneath my breasts and stopped a few inches above my navel to bare my midriff. The bottom was a pair of snug shorts in the same material as the top, overlaid with several layers of sheer, black organza that hung to the floor. The three-inch wide band at my waist hit right at my hips and was encrusted with tiny crystals that sparkled when I moved. You could catch a glimpse of the shorts I wore through the skirt, depending on the shift and thickness of the organza layers as I walked.

"Wow," I breathed in awe, eyeing the dress in the mirror. I scurried into the bathroom to put on my makeup. Heavy foundation concealed the bruise on my cheek and I was glad it wasn't swollen any longer. I applied heavy eyeliner and smoky shadow along with a dusting of glittery powder. Pulling my hair back into a low bun, I added long, dangling earrings. A pair of sky-high heels with a strap that wrapped around my ankle completed the outfit.

I had no idea how Devon had gotten this dress and probably didn't want to know. It was a tiny size and for once I was glad of my smallish chest. If I'd been better endowed, there's no way I could have fit into it.

Grabbing a black clutch to use as my purse, I stood straighter, my shoulders back, as I emerged from the bedroom. A dress like this deserved to be worn with pride and I was determined to do it justice. And I must have succeeded in some measure because Devon had poured himself a drink and was taking a sip, but he froze when he saw me, his hand halfway to his mouth.

I let a moment pass, then raising an eyebrow, I said, "So . . . I like the dress."

Devon's gaze swept me from head to foot and back, then he tossed back the contents of the glass he held. I watched his throat move as he swallowed.

"Me, too," he said, his voice rougher than usual.

Hiding a satisfied smile, I rummaged in a kitchen drawer for a pen, then flipped Logan's note over to write on the other side.

"What did you argue about?" Devon said, his lips at my ear. He'd come up behind me silently and his hands settled on my waist. The touch of his skin against mine was as though an electric current had gone through me. I bit my lip against the sigh that wanted to escape.

"Um . . . about y-you, I guess," I stammered. Focusing my attention back on the paper, I scrawled *Went out for a while. Love—me.* I didn't want to say who I'd gone out with or when I'd be back. If I was honest with myself, I didn't know if I'd turn down that booty call, despite the hurtful words Logan had said to me. "He thought you had hit me."

"Did you tell him I'm not the type of man to hit a woman?"

The warmth of his breath fanned across my skin and I shivered. His words didn't even register for a moment, too consumed was I with the feel of him and the scent of his cologne.

"Why would I tell him that?" I asked. "I don't know if it's true."

Devon went still, then turned me to face him.

"Let's get one thing perfectly clear," he said, and gone was the note of seduction in his voice. This was pure command. "I have not, and will not, hurt you. You may not trust me, but you can be assured that I will not deliberately harm you." His clear blue gaze searched mine. "Is that understood?"

He actually seemed a bit disgruntled and insulted that I'd insinuated he'd hit a woman. But he was right, I didn't trust him. Yet he asked me to believe he wouldn't hurt me. Did I believe him?

Well . . . yes. Yes, I did.

I nodded. "Understood." My voice was small, but steady.

"Then we're off."

Devon held my coat for me and I slipped my arms into the sleeves, then locked the door behind us as we left.

His car waited downstairs at the curb, the steel-gray Porsche a decadence I enjoyed as I slid into the front seat. It was scary how accommodating I could be for a man who brought me a designer dress and drove a luxury sports car, even if he killed people and worked as a spy.

Nice ethics, there, Ivy, I thought, rubbing the soft fabric of my skirt between my finger and thumb. Despite my self-chastisement, a familiar pleasure curled in my belly at the pretty dress. Sheesh. What a girly girl cliché I was.

Devon drove us to the Four Seasons Hotel downtown, handing his keys to the valet who scurried to open my door. The valet's jaw dropped a bit when I emerged from the car. I winked at him and his ears flushed bright red.

Appearing at my side, Devon offered me his arm, which I took as we entered the hotel and he led me to the elevators.

We emerged onto a floor high in the building. I glanced around, confused.

"I thought we were going to dinner and a party?" I asked.

"We are," Devon replied, heading down the hallway. He stopped in front of a door. "Just dropping off your coat first." Pulling a key card from the pocket inside his jacket, he unlocked the door. I followed him into the room.

It was one of the big suites that had a separate bedroom, and an amazing view of downtown and the Arch, all lit up and shining. Devon took my coat from me while I tried to figure out why he had a room here. I thought about asking, but then was a little afraid of his answer, so I kept silent.

"You're beautiful," he said, his hand trailing down my arm to my hand. His thumb brushed my knuckles as his gaze met mine. "No matter what happens tonight, do exactly as I say. Understand?"

A flicker of trepidation crawled under my skin at his words and the dead-serious way in which he'd said them. "That sounds ominous," I said with a tremulous smile, trying to keep it light.

"Caution and warnings are better than pain and regret."

Letting go of my hand, Devon turned away, reaching into his jacket to pull out a gun from a holster underneath his arm. My eyes widened in alarm and I couldn't tear my gaze away as he ejected and checked the magazine before slamming it home and replacing the weapon in its holster.

Now my trepidation had grown into full-fledged fear. What had I gotten myself into? But before I could think of how to extricate myself from this night, Devon was pulling me back into the hallway and leading me down the corridor.

CHAPTER EIGHT

"Take this," Devon said, handing me a plastic key card.

I went to put it into my clutch, but he stopped me.

"Put it somewhere you won't lose it."

Okay, well in this dress, that left few options. I hadn't worn a bra because I hadn't wanted the outline of the straps through the fabric to spoil the effect of the dress, so that was out. That left . . . I slipped the card underneath the band of my skirt. The shorts were tight enough to hold the card without letting it slip.

"I've never wanted to be an inanimate object quite so much," Devon quipped, slanting a glance at me.

"If that's your oblique British way of saying you want to get in my pants, then you should know it's going to take more than an expensive dress." Though this particular dress went a helluva long way. I kept that part to myself.

Devon's lips tipped up at my sass. "What was the room number?" he asked.

"What?"

"The room. Do you remember the number?"

I thought for a second. "Nineteen seventeen?"

Satisfaction gleamed in his eyes. "Very good." The way he said it made me feel as though I'd passed some kind of test. "Remember it." Reaching down, he grasped my hand, drawing it through to rest on his bent arm.

We took the elevator to a lower level that had hardwood floors rather than the usual carpet that muffled the hallways where guests stayed. My heels clacked as we walked to the far end where two wooden double doors stretched high.

I could feel the stiffness of Devon's arm underneath my fingers, but he appeared outwardly calm and coolly serene. His face was a blank mask of indifference and I tried to emulate him as we walked inside.

There were more people than I expected, all of them dressed to the hilt. The hum of conversation drifted through the ballroom, complete with chandeliers hanging from the ceiling high above our heads. Music played through unseen speakers and I could hear the clink of dinnerware and glasses among the chatter.

A man approached us, obviously the host or maître d'. "Good evening," he said. "And you are?" He held what I assumed was a guest list and began scanning it before Devon even gave his name.

"Devon Clay."

I was surprised Devon gave his real name. Weren't spies supposed to have an alias or something? Or maybe he was still lying to me about his name. I didn't really want to think about that option.

"I'm sorry, sir," the maître d' said, "but your name is not on the list."

Well, this was awkward.

But Devon just gave him a thin smile and said, "I'm an old school chum of the groom's. We went to university together."

Hold up! What had he just said? I snapped my head around to look at Devon. He ignored me, so I started scanning the room.

Sure enough, I spotted a woman in a billowing white gown at a table near the front.

Oh. My. God. Devon had brought me to a *wedding* reception. And while the gown I wore was gorgeous, it was so not appropriate wedding-guest attire. I cringed and shrank back a bit behind Devon.

"Of course, sir," the maître d' said, obviously unwilling to make a scene. And really, who'd crash a wedding reception in a tuxedo? "Right this way."

"Where's the sexy strut from earlier?" Devon asked quietly as we followed the maître d'.

"This dress isn't appropriate for this," I whispered back.

"You look like a luxury package of sex and decadence," Devon hissed. "Own it."

Sex and decadence.

The words turned over inside my head. Was that really how he saw me? How I appeared? I liked that. I liked that a lot.

I'd watched many a fashion show on television and the Internet, the models beautiful women with haughty expressions who walked down a runway as if they owned it.

I could do that.

I straightened my spine and pulled my shoulders back. Lifting my chin a notch, I added a sway in my hips as I walked, knowing that the crystals on my skirt would catch the light. Devon was a gorgeous man, the tuxedo adding elegance to his tall frame, and together we made a striking couple. Heads turned as we walked by.

"Here we are," the maître d' said, stopping at a table only three away from where the wedded couple sat. Reaching down, he plucked two name cards from the table and gestured for us to take the empty chairs. Guess there'd been a no-show.

Devon held the chair for me, scooting it forward as I sat, then took the seat on my left. There were three other couples at the table, all eyeing us with open curiosity, but Devon didn't introduce us, merely acknowledging them with a curt nod of his head. I noticed two of the women looking at me with distaste, their gazes taking in my dress and bare stomach, but I was used to other women disliking me because of my looks, so it didn't bother me. I turned my attention to Devon, dismissing them without uttering a word.

"You said dinner and a party," I said softly so only Devon could hear me.

"We're at the party, and here comes dinner now," Devon said just as a waiter stepped up and placed two small plates in front of us. It looked like a first-course *amuse-bouche* type of thing, with just one bite of food.

"You didn't say I would be your plus one at a wedding reception," I pressed.

"I thought women adored weddings," he replied lightly.

I rolled my eyes. It was obvious he was unrepentant about bringing me to a wedding, and now that we were here, I worried even more about the warning he'd given me and the gun he carried. I'd assumed he had the gun in case there was trouble. I really hoped *he* wouldn't be the trouble.

Another waiter came by and poured the wine that was paired with the course. That, I took a drink of immediately. I might need it to get through the evening.

Four more courses followed and, after a while, I started to relax. The food was excellent and I savored it. Devon even played the doting date, feeding me bites here and there and whispering in my ear. His arm rested along the back of my chair, his fingers brushing the bare skin of my neck in an unconsciously seductive sort of way. I didn't know what or who the performance was for, and I was enjoying it too much to care.

After dessert, the bride and groom took to the dance floor. I watched them, trying not to feel envious of the obvious affection between them. The bride was beautiful, with dark hair that was fashioned in an elaborate updo. Her dress was strapless, the white a nice contrast to her olive skin.

The groom seemed completely enamored of her, his smile blinding as they danced. He was older than I expected given the youth of the bride, perhaps early forties. But the look of adoration on his face was sweet to see, though it made my chest hurt. That was the kind of love marriage should be about, not what my mom had endured. Watching the couple, it seemed love—true love—did exist for some people. I wondered if I'd ever be one of them.

Others started joining the couple on the dance floor and Devon suddenly took my hand.

"Let's dance," he said, pulling me from my chair. Taking the wineglass from me, he set it on the table.

Okay then.

It was a slow, romantic tune and Devon took me in his arms. I'd had just enough wine to make me sloppily sentimental and forget all the things I'd said to him this morning. His hands were warm on the skin of my back and I smiled up at him, looping my arms around his neck.

"It doesn't take much to make you happy," Devon wryly observed. "A pretty dress, a nice dinner, dancing."

"I'm a simple girl," I said with a shrug.

Devon eyed me, a smile playing about his lips. "Now why don't I believe that?"

"Would I lie to you?"

He leaned down and put his lips at my ear. "I think you'd try."

A shiver ran through me and I could tell he felt it because he pulled me closer until our bodies were pressed together.

Our eyes locked and my smile faded, his icy blue gaze held me captive. In a flash of stark insight, I wondered what limits this man was capable of pushing me to, and what I wouldn't do for him.

Maybe Logan was right after all. Maybe I was all messed up inside, and my attraction to Devon was tainted and wrong.

Devon looked away, glancing over my shoulder. "Do you think you might dance with the groom?"

Taken aback, I said, "Um, yeah, I guess."

"Perfect. Off you go." He spun me around and out of his arms, then murmured in my ear, "Tell him Devon sends his regards."

I swallowed, sure I was missing something important in what was going on, but then I spotted the groom. He was dancing with a bridesmaid and I felt weird cutting in, but I walked over and tapped him on the shoulder anyway.

"May I?" I asked.

The groom smiled and his brow creased, as though he was trying to remember who I was, but he nodded a thanks to the bridesmaid and reached for my hand.

"Your bride is lovely," I said as we turned in time to the music.

"Thank you," he replied. "She most certainly is." He had a British accent as well.

I smiled and he studied me, a slight frown on his face.

"Please forgive me," he said, "but have we met? I'm afraid I can't quite place you."

"I'm a plus one," I explained. "I'm here with Devon, who sends his regards."

The effect of those words was immediate. He stopped in his tracks and the blood drained from his face.

"How? How did he find me?" he murmured, almost to himself.

I didn't know the answer to his question and the look on his face alarmed me. I took a step away, but he grabbed my arm in a painfully tight grip and jerked me closer.

"Where is he?" he hissed. "Where's Devon?"

I flinched in pain. "I-I don't know," I stammered. "He's here. I was just with him."

He looked around the room, searching and obviously frantic. Dragging me with him, he approached another tuxedo-clad man.

"Have you seen Anna?" he asked.

The man shook his head. "No. I thought she was dancing." He turned and scanned the dance floor.

The groom didn't wait, but went to another three people, dragging me along and asking if they'd seen Anna. No one had. Finally, the sixth person he approached said, "I thought I saw her go outside." Then he was pulling me with him as we went out onto the terrace.

It was cold, but huge heating lamps had been set up along with three outdoor fire pits that burned brightly. The Arch gleamed and the lights of downtown twinkled. Small groups of people clustered around the fires, but there was only a scattering of people out there.

I spotted Anna at the same time the groom did, standing near the clear, waist-high barrier that surrounded the terrace next to a heat lamp. Devon was with her and they were talking.

Barely did I have time to process this before the groom dragged me toward them. I could hardly keep up and I knew I'd have bruises tomorrow from where he gripped my arm.

When we came to a halt, I was out of breath and frightened. Anna glanced over, a smile on her face.

"Clive," she said, "your friend Devon was just telling me how you and he met! You've never mentioned you'd been to Singapore."

Clive looked stunned and relieved at the same time. His gaze swiveled to Devon, who merely smiled in a way that had me thinking the "friend" appellation probably wasn't the best to describe his relationship with Clive.

"Hello," Anna said to me when Clive didn't speak. "I'm Anna." She held out her hand.

"Ivy," I replied, giving her hand a light squeeze. I forced a smile, though I was more attune to the tension radiating between Clive and Devon.

"That's a lovely dress," Anna said.

My cheeks grew warm. "Thank you," I replied. "I wore it without realizing I'd be attending a wedding reception."

"Oh?" Anna glanced curiously at Devon.

"Anna, sweetheart, would you mind going inside? I'm afraid the coordinator is in need of your guidance regarding how you'd like the cake served." Clive finally released me and took Anna's hand. "I'll speak with Devon for a moment and be right behind you." His smile was thin but warm, and Anna accepted the dismissal with good grace.

"Of course," she said. "Nice meeting you, Devon. And you, too, Ivy."

I watched longingly as Anna walked back inside, wondering if I'd be allowed to follow her. But when I took a tentative step back, Clive grabbed me again.

"What do you want, Devon?" he snarled. "Sending in a decoy so I wouldn't see you kill my wife?" He gave me a hard shove and I gasped as I stumbled hard against Devon. I would have fallen, but his arm snagged me around the waist, hauling my body against his side.

"Why would I do that? She's not the one who betrayed me." Devon's voice was cold and smooth—and utterly terrifying.

I saw Clive visibly gulp.

"I had no choice," he said. "You don't know these people. They would've killed me. They would've killed Anna." He paused. "They promised if I did what they said, they'd leave us both alone."

"Yes, but you didn't extract any such promise from me." The menace-laced words hung in the air like a prophecy.

I began to shiver. The cold air and Devon's threat combined to rob me of any warmth or comfort. Was Devon going to kill Clive? Right here and now? I knew he had the ability, just as I also knew there wasn't a thing I could do to stop him.

To my surprise, Devon's arm tightened around me, bringing me closer to the heat of his body. My shivering eased slightly.

"You double-crossed me and left me for dead," Devon accused. "Did you really think you could get away with it? That I'd *let* you get away with it?"

My feelings toward Clive changed instantly on hearing the information that he'd left Devon. The bastard. Who betrays their friends and leaves them to die? I scowled at him, suddenly not so sure I'd be sorry if Devon exacted his revenge.

"Please," Clive said, and the note of hopelessness in his voice almost made me pity him. "I didn't know what to do, didn't see a way out. I did the only thing I could do."

"Everything has a price," Devon said. "Are you really so stupid as to forfeit your life for a woman?" His contempt for Clive's choice was clear and I tried not to be offended.

Clive gave a shrug, the look on his face one of resignation. "I love her, Devon."

His confession was stark in its simplicity, as was his calm acceptance of his fate. A man who'd die for love. Clive had earned back a little of my respect, but I doubted I could say the same for Devon, who'd already made it clear what he thought of love.

"An ephemeral emotion predicated on hormones and fervent declarations of affection. For this, you'd die. I don't know whether to laugh at you, pity you, or just kill you and put you out of your misery."

The scathing words made me wince and I thought I saw a nearly imperceptible flinch cross Clive's face, too.

"I can help you find them," Clive said. "They're here."

"I already know they're here."

"But you don't know what they're planning. I can find out. I'm sure the Shadow would want to know."

I frowned at this. The Shadow? You could practically hear the capital letters on that. Who was Clive talking about?

"You'll say anything to save your life," Devon replied.

"Maybe. But can you take that chance? If Vega were to find out—"

"You know not to say the name," Devon cut him off, and for the first time I heard outright anger in his voice.

Clive glanced at me, surprise etched on his features. "She's not an agent?" Devon didn't reply and Clive's lips thinned. "You're such a bastard, Devon. I could easily have killed her. Is your revenge so dear to you that you'd send an innocent to slaughter?" Now it was Clive's turn to be disgusted. "Meet me tomorrow on the Landing. There's a pub called Shay's. Eight o'clock." With a last somewhat pitying glance at me, Clive turned and left.

I was left reeling in shock. Clive could have killed me? And Devon had not only known this, but practically shoved me at him anyway?

I guess Devon's promise that *he* wouldn't hurt me was literal and didn't extend to others I might be thrown in the path of.

Pushing against him, I tried to get away, but his hold only tightened.

"Let me go, you bastard!" I seethed, struggling as hard as I could. "You didn't care if he'd hurt me or not!"

"Enough, Ivy!" Devon barked. His hands on my upper arms drew me upright and held me immobile. "I knew he wouldn't kill you."

"How lucky for me that you knew," I sneered, "because he sounded pretty certain that it was an option." I renewed my struggles, which I knew were futile, but damned if I was just going to give up.

"I wouldn't have deliberately put you into danger," Devon said.

"Why should I believe you?" I asked in exasperation. I was furious and hurt at the same time. I pushed against his chest, which was like trying to push a brick wall.

"Because I said I wouldn't hurt you and I bloody well meant it!"

His raised voice made me go still and I stared up at him, trying to read his eyes.

"I've known Clive for a long time. He wasn't going to kill you or hurt you in any way. Not while I had his bride."

I swallowed, my anger leeching away. "He was terrified," I said. "Is that what you came to do? Kill her?"

"I was making a point," Devon replied. His grip on me had loosened, but now I didn't try to get away.

I shivered, cold again now that I was separated from the warmth and security of his body. Without a word, Devon released me and slid his jacket down his arms, then swung it around my shoulders. The fabric still held his body heat along with his scent. He pulled the lapels closed and tugged me toward him.

His gaze drifted from my eyes down to my lips. It seemed in slow motion as he bent and kissed me, his mouth settling gently over mine.

I couldn't touch him—my arms were locked inside the jacket as he held it closed—and I couldn't move away. I could only stand there and allow him to kiss me senseless, until I didn't feel the cold any longer, only heat and desire.

His tongue slid against mine, our breath mingling in the chilly air, and I pressed as close to him as I could. When he lifted his head, I stretched upward, keeping the contact as long as possible. A soft whimper escaped me when his mouth left mine. Devon's lips curved, satisfaction gleaming in his eyes. I should have been offended by how easily he'd ensnared me, but I wanted him too badly to spare any thought for righteous indignation.

"I've had enough of the party," he said. "Haven't you?"

I nodded. Going back into the wedding reception seemed like a bad idea. Sliding his arm around my waist, Devon kept me close as we headed for a side exit from the terrace. I handed him his jacket once we were inside and he put it back on, hiding the gun underneath his arm. A few minutes later, we were exiting the elevator on our floor.

Our room was at the far end and I noticed two men in the hallway, one pushing an empty luggage cart. They glanced at us as we walked by, but didn't smile.

Devon suddenly took my hand. I turned to him with a smile, which rapidly faded.

His expression was that cold, blank mask again.

"What's wr—"

Devon squeezed my hand, hard, and slanted a glance my way. I got the message and shut up.

He pulled me to a stop in front of a door that wasn't ours. Taking out the plastic key card, he fumbled with the lock.

"Damn," he said, more loudly than usual and with a slight slur to his words. "Can't get the door open, luv."

Putting his hands on my waist, he dragged me in front of him, pinning me between his body and the door at my back. Then he was kissing me. But it was different and I realized something was very wrong, and that I was supposed to play along.

I reached up and rested one hand lightly on his shoulder, not wanting to hamper him in any way should he need to move quickly. I heard the muffled squeak of wheels on the luggage cart as it rolled slowly toward us.

The only warning was the slight sound of cloth rustling.

Devon pushed me to the side just as wood splintered over my head and I heard the stifled report of a gunshot. He launched himself at one of the two men, pushing him through the door marked *Stairway* that I just realized was opposite from where we'd stopped in the hallway.

The door crashed open under Devon's assault and he didn't stop his momentum, throwing the man with the gun over the rail and into the open cavern below. I could hear the thuds his body made as it hit parts of the stairwell on the way to the bottom.

The second man was already on Devon. He didn't have a gun. Instead, he held a wickedly long knife. Devon spun around, grabbing the man's arm as it lifted to strike.

The door swung shut on them, blocking my view, and I had an instant's indecision of what to do. But in the next moment, my panic and fear for Devon outweighed my fear for myself and I rushed to the stairwell door and flung it open.

Devon and the man were grappling and had fallen down to the next flight. Devon pulled his gun, but the man knocked it aside and it went flying down the stairs in a clatter of metal against concrete.

They moved so fast, it was hard to follow. I'd never seen a fight like this before, a fight to the death, and it terrified me. The guy was big, as big as Devon, the collision of their bodies sending them ricocheting off the guardrail and falling down more steps. The man was on top of Devon and the knife flashed. Blood coated it before Devon slammed the man's arm against the edge of a stair.

I followed, catching sight of the gun on the next landing down past where they fought. If I could just reach the gun, maybe I could help Devon.

I ran down the stairs, then had to press myself into a corner as Devon slammed the guy into the wall, his arm pressed hard against the man's throat. I threw myself past them, terror clawing at my chest. Then something hit me in the back and I went sprawling hard onto the landing below.

The men grunted as they fought, sliding past me, then the man got loose of Devon and scrabbled for the gun. Devon threw himself on top of him, putting him in a choke hold. The man reached for the gun but it was too far. He thrust his body back at Devon, flinging them both onto their backs.

In a flash, he straddled Devon's torso, his hands around Devon's throat. I watched in horror as he began to choke Devon.

Oh my God. Devon was going to die if I didn't do something. I couldn't get to the gun, it was past where they were fighting and I was too afraid to try to reach it.

Frantic, I looked around and spotted a fire extinguisher hooked to the wall behind the man trying to kill Devon. Without thinking or planning, I rushed to it and grabbed the canister. Spinning around, I closed my eyes and swung as hard as I could.

The metal connected with a solid *thunk* against the man's head and he went sprawling. I dropped the canister, its clanging ringing in my ears, and flattened myself against the wall. My panicked breathing was hard and shallow.

Devon was up immediately, and flung himself at his gun. He flipped over onto his back just as the man stood, swaying slightly on his feet. He caught sight of Devon and went to rush him again, but the sound of a bullet's report echoed in the stairwell.

The man froze, a red stain blossoming on his chest, then he fell backward against the stairs. His body slid down a step or two, crumpling, and didn't move.

Blood was rushing in my ears, my heart pounding so hard it felt as though it were going to leap from my chest. My throat burned with my ragged breaths as my gaze stayed locked on the dead man.

I'd seen Devon kill before, but this had been different. It had been up close and personal, and I'd had a hand in the man's death. Yes, I'd been helping to save Devon, but it didn't make it any easier to swallow the knowledge that I'd just helped kill someone.

Devon got laboriously to his feet, his chest heaving. His face was coated in sweat and blood dripped from his mouth. He'd lost his jacket at some point in the fight and I could see that a sleeve of his shirt was torn, the white fabric bloodied, and remembered the crimson knife blade. He went to the man first and checked for a pulse.

"Get upstairs to the room and don't come out," Devon ordered. "I have to take care of the bodies."

I didn't move. I couldn't. I felt as though my limbs had been dipped in ice. I just stared at the dead man.

Devon glanced at me. "Now!" he said, the sharp command jerking my attention to him. "Move!"

I gave him a shaky nod, turned, and somehow managed to climb the stairs to our floor. I was moving on autopilot as I stopped in front of our door and fished out my key card. My hands were shaking so badly it took what felt like forever before I could hold the card steady enough to slide it into the slot.

The door swung shut behind me and I stood there, unsure what to do next. Devon hadn't told me what to do.

In some corner of my mind, I realized I was close to losing it, but I couldn't clear my head enough to get a grip. The fight kept replaying inside my head, the sound the fire extinguisher had made as it hit him, the look on the man's face when he had the split-second knowledge that he'd been fatally shot.

The skyline looked serene outside my window and I drifted toward it, sliding open the glass doors to step onto the terrace. I stared at the lights twinkling, the cool silver of the Arch reaching for the sky. I could breathe better out here and I sucked in a lungful of air.

I didn't know how long I stood there, but after a while I heard the door to the room open and close. Distantly, I hoped it was Devon, but I couldn't bring myself to care if it wasn't.

Slow footsteps approached, and large warm hands settled on my hips.

"What are you doing out here in the cold?" Devon asked, his voice soft.

"It was p-peaceful," I stammered through chattering teeth, only now realizing my entire body was racked with tremors.

"You're freezing," he murmured, wrapping his arms around me. He drew me back against his chest. He was warm and solid and safe, and the sharp edges of fear still cutting me finally eased.

"Come inside," he said, and I nodded, allowing him to draw me back into the hotel room.

CHAPTER NINE

Devon flipped back the heavy down comforter on the bed and sat, pulling me down next to him. He arranged the comforter over us and leaned back against the headboard, enfolding me entirely in his arms. My cheek was pressed against his chest and his chin rested on the top of my head.

Chills shook me from my head to my toes, but Devon's hold didn't loosen, and the heat from his body gradually began to seep into my icy skin.

We lay there for a long time. Once I stopped shaking from the cold, my body relaxed, molding itself to Devon. His hand was gently caressing my head now, his fingers finding and carefully removing the pins that held my hair in place. When they were gone, he lifted the long strands and unwound them. I sighed at the sensation.

"Better?" he asked.

"Yes." And I wasn't just talking about my hair.

Silence descended for several long minutes, then I spoke again.

"I helped kill a man tonight."

"He would have killed me. And you."

Yes, that was true. Still . . .

"I've never done something like that before."

A pause. "Some people deserve to die."

I considered that. "Yes," I said slowly. "You're right. There was a time when I wanted to kill someone. Or maybe myself." The words just slipped out, surprising me, and Devon, too. His hand stilled for a moment in my hair before resuming its caress, his fingers sliding through my hair.

"Tell me."

In our cozy cocoon, the scent of Devon surrounded me. Not so much his cologne now, but the smell of only him—his skin, his sweat, his blood. I felt safe and protected. So I talked.

"He used to come in my room late at night, hours after I'd gone to sleep. We'd never gotten along, so the first time, I couldn't understand why he was there. Then he made me do . . . things." My voice cracked, but I kept going. "In one breath he'd tell me he loved me, then the next he'd swear to kill me if I ever told. I had a kitten I'd gotten from the farm next to ours. He cut off its head and left it underneath my pillow. I wanted to kill him then. It was only later, months later, that I thought about killing myself. But I wasn't brave enough to do it."

Devon had stopped stroking my hair now, but I didn't mind. I was saying things I hadn't spoken of in years and years.

"One night, it hurt—real bad, more so than usual—and I couldn't hide it from my mom the next day. She figured it out, even though I didn't tell her. She called the cops, but they couldn't do anything. He found out, though. When I got home from school, he was waiting for me. He had Mom's chef knife. I made it to my room and barricaded the door. He practically knocked that door down, screaming and yelling that he was going to kill me. I sat with my back to the door, holding it as much as I could, and I prayed the whole time." I fell silent, lost in the memories of that awful day.

"What happened?" Devon asked.

I pulled myself back to the present with a sigh. "He left, got drunk, and wrecked his car, killing a man. He was sent to jail for manslaughter."

"And this was . . . your father?"

"Stepbrother. My dad died when I was little. He was in the Army."

"How old were you when . . . this started happening?"

"Twelve."

Devon didn't ask more questions, which was good because I didn't want to talk anymore.

"I want to shower," I abruptly decided. I felt dirty, bloodied, even though there wasn't a mark on me.

I expected Devon to just let me go, but instead he got out of bed, took my hand, and led me into the bathroom. He started the water and I automatically began undressing. My earrings I tossed to the counter before pulling my top off over my head. I carefully folded the expensive fabric before hooking my thumbs into the band of my skirt and sliding it and the shorts down my legs. I'd worn a tiny black G-string, which I discarded as well.

When I turned around to get in the shower, Devon was staring at me. His eyes burned and naked need was written on his face, but he didn't approach.

"I'll leave you to it then," he said, his voice slightly hoarse. He stepped toward the door.

"Wait," I said, laying a hand on his arm. He glanced at me.

I didn't say anything else. My eyes caught on the blood on his shirt and I could see more underneath the torn fabric. He was hurt and bleeding, and yet he'd been comforting me all this time.

Reaching for the buttons of his shirt, I quickly undid them, sliding the shirt down his arms, then lifting the hem of his white T-shirt up and over his head. There was a nasty cut on his arm and a huge red and purple bruise on his abdomen. It must have been a heavy hit to have bruised so deeply and so quickly, yet Devon didn't utter a word of protest or so much as cringe in pain. It was almost as though he'd separated himself from it and felt nothing, and I wondered if that was something he'd had to learn in a job fraught with danger.

I dropped my hands to his belt and hesitated. The blunt truth was that I'd never undressed a man before, and to start with a man like Devon . . . well, it was a little daunting.

He must have sensed my uncertainty because his much larger hands suddenly covered my own.

"I'll do it. You get in the warm."

I nodded, crossing to the shower and stepping underneath the steaming spray. It crossed my mind that I liked hearing him talk to me. What little emotion Devon did show, he most often did with his voice rather than express anything on his face. Just now, his voice had been a gentle command wrapped in the curves of his accent, like a tender caress meant to protect and care for. I liked it.

Water and soap ran from my scalp down my face and over my shoulders as I bathed. The bubbles tickled as they sluiced down my body, and I hoped I could so easily wash away the blood on my conscience.

Devon stepped in behind me, closing the shower door and enclosing us in a steam-filled cocoon. I turned toward him, blinking away the water from my eyes. He was so much larger than me; the width and depth of his shoulders and torso took my breath away.

He seemed content to let me wet a cloth and gently clean the blood from his face and arm. Scrapes marred his ribs and the backs of his knuckles. I was as gentle as I could be, not that I thought I would have been able to tell if I'd been hurting him.

Lifting his hand, I pressed my lips to his raw knuckles. I didn't know why and I didn't think. I just did it. Devon seemed so strong, invincible. Yet here was evidence, proof that he was just a man, and bled like any other man.

Devon moved his hand to cradle my cheek. I closed my eyes, tipping my head into his hand. His thumb brushed my cheekbone.

We stood there in silence and I reveled in the quiet peace he'd brought to my mind. Devon was strength and safety, the events of tonight making it clear to me in a way words couldn't that he would never hurt me, not like I'd been hurt before.

I expected him to kiss me, touch me, but he did nothing except continue caressing my face. I opened my eyes and looked up at him. His forehead was creased in a frown as he studied me.

"What's the matter?" I asked.

But he just shook his head. Reaching behind me, he turned off the water, then wrapped me in a towel. I grabbed another for my dripping hair and followed him into the bedroom. A towel was wrapped around his hips and I felt a bit disappointed. Perhaps he just wasn't in the mood. He had just fought off two would-be killers, after all. I'd be tired, too.

I dried my hair the best I could, then finger-combed it. My hair was so straight there were few tangles. I sat on the bed and watched as Devon opened the closet. To my surprise, he had clothes hanging in there. Reaching inside, he grabbed a shirt and slipped it off the hanger.

"Here," he said, handing it to me. I stared questioningly at it.

"You're giving me your shirt?" I asked in confusion.

"We'll sleep here tonight. Thought you'd like something to wear."

That made my eyebrows climb up my forehead. Devon had been perfectly fine with us sleeping naked together the other night. In fact, he seemed to prefer it. It took me a few moments to figure it out and when I did, I heaved a sigh.

"I shouldn't have told you," I said.

Devon didn't even glance at me as he busied himself doing something on his cell phone.

"That's why, isn't it," I persisted.

"I don't know what you're talking about."

His muttered reply only made me angry.

"I don't want your pity, Devon," I said. "I shared something with you. That doesn't make me . . ." I searched for the right word. ". . . less . . . or fragile or any other adjective you have inside your head."

"It's been a long night," he said, still not looking at me. "We both could use some rest."

Tears stung my eyes and I furiously blinked them back. I'd finally found a man who treated me like a desirable woman, and whom I desired in return. We'd had amazing sex and I craved the intimacy again. But the moment he found out I'd been abused, he'd labeled me off-limits.

"So you don't want me anymore?" I asked, my voice louder than I'd intended. I was getting more and more upset, which just made me angrier.

Devon ignored me.

"Answer me, damn it! Since when do you care about my past? You told me you didn't give a damn. What happened to that?"

"Well, I do give a damn!"

Devon's shout startled me into silence. He'd spun around, his furious eyes glaring at me. His mouth was set in a hard line and his hands clenched into fists. When he spoke again, his voice was much quieter and more controlled, but no less furious.

"I do, and I don't like it."

Devon felt something for me. Cared about me. I was so shocked at his admission, I just gaped at him.

After a tense moment of charged silence between us, he turned away. He dropped his towel from around his waist, pulled a pair of pants from the closet, and began to dress.

My mind raced as I tried to figure out how to get past this new barrier he'd put up between us. He was a man, which meant he had one universal weakness, though it would perhaps take more effort than usual to exploit it.

"Before you, no man was able to reach me," I said bluntly. "It was as if I'd been frozen in ice, and I didn't know if it was only fear that froze me, or if I was just broken beyond repair."

Devon made no indication he'd heard me or that he was even listening, but I kept going.

"Then you came along, and showed me I'd just needed the right man. That I'd needed *you*."

I unwrapped the towel from around my torso and tossed it. The terry cloth landed in a puddle near Devon's feet. His head dipped down to gaze at it and his hands that had been busy fastening his belt stilled.

"Over the years, I had to take care of myself. I couldn't let a man close, but my body wanted to feel. So I learned what to do."

I sat back against the pile of pillows at the headboard. My nerves were stretched thin at what I was going to do, the wild idea that had struck me. There was a chance Devon would be disgusted, but I was betting that would be the last reaction he'd have.

Pulling my knees to my chest and planting my feet flat on the mattress, I spread my thighs apart. Devon still had his back to me.

"Watch me, Devon."

The mere idea of Devon watching made me wet and my hand drifted from my knee down my inner thigh. I didn't know if he'd do it, if he'd turn around, and I held my breath. At last, he turned, almost reluctantly, as though he couldn't quite help himself.

The blue of his eyes transfixed me and I focused on his steady gaze as my fingers brushed the flesh between my legs. I slipped a finger between my folds, the wetness there coating my skin. Rubbing my throbbing clit, I fought the urge to close my eyes. Devon's gaze seemed to burn as I watched him watch me.

"I think of you now," I managed to say. I pushed a finger inside and bit my lip at the sensation. Moving my finger in and out, I imagined it was Devon's hand and my eyes fluttered shut.

A strong grip on each of my ankles had my eyes flying open. Devon pulled me to the edge of the bed until my legs dangled off, and before I'd even recovered from my surprise enough to wonder what he was doing, he'd dropped to his knees on the floor and his head was between my legs.

The breadth of his shoulders pushed my thighs apart, exposing me even more than before. His hand opened me wide and then his mouth was on me, his tongue lapping at my clit.

I cried out at the pleasure of it, the intimacy thrilling me. He pushed a thick finger inside me and I groaned. My hands clutched at his head as my body responded to what he was doing to me. My pussy was engorged and pulsing with heat. There wasn't a thought in my head as every sense was focused on the touch of his mouth and hands.

Moans and gasps fell from my lips and his tongue moved faster, flicking at me until my legs trembled. My fingers dug into his hair as I lifted my hips, needing what was almost within reach. Devon groaned, adding a second finger to the one thrusting inside me.

My eyes squeezed shut and it felt as though I fell apart from the inside out as my orgasm exploded in waves. Wordless cries erupted from my throat and I could feel my body spasming around Devon's fingers still deep inside me.

Heaving as though I'd just run a marathon, I pried my eyes open. Devon had stopped when his touch became too much and was now nuzzling the skin at the juncture of my thigh to my hip. He pressed his lips against my abdomen as I threaded my fingers through his hair.

I craved his skin against mine, wanted the hard length of him inside me. I pulled at his shoulders until he lifted his head. His lips were wet and red and I licked my own in response.

Devon crawled up the bed, straddling me, until he hovered over me on his hands and knees. I whimpered, my gaze fixed on his mouth, and he kissed me. His kiss was deep and I could taste myself on his tongue.

My hands went to his belt and the shyness I'd felt earlier had evaporated. It was a matter of a few tugs to unlatch the belt and draw down his zipper. He had nothing on underneath the slacks and his cock was heavy and thick in my hand. Devon groaned against my lips.

The head of his cock was as soft as silk and my thumb brushed the sensitive skin. Devon's kisses turned hungry and urgent. Sliding an arm underneath me, he moved us farther back on the bed, away from the edge. I barely noticed. I wanted him inside me.

"Please," I whispered. "Make love to me."

For a fraction of a second, Devon went still, then he hooked a hand underneath each of my knees. Drawing them up toward my chest, he spread my legs and sank inside me in one hard thrust. I whimpered at the friction against my overly sensitized flesh. It felt too much, the hard stroke of his cock as he moved, and yet I wanted more.

"Watch me now," he rasped. "Watch me take you."

I gazed down at where our bodies joined, mesmerized at the sight of his glistening flesh sliding into mine. It felt as though he was staking his claim on me. I watched until a second, more powerful orgasm took me and my eyes squeezed shut again.

Devon's hips pistoned hard into me, a wordless shout torn from his throat as he came. He hadn't used a condom this time, which didn't bother me at all. I was on birth control and somehow his not using the condom gave the act more meaning between us than it had before.

He lay on top of me and my legs cramped slightly as I circled them around his back. The warmth of his breath teased my neck as

I held him close. The rapid beat of his heart overpowered mine as his chest pressed against me.

Pulling away, he rolled me with him, arranging us so he could pull the duvet to cover our bodies. There was a bit of a chill in the air and I let out a deep sigh. My body was sated and my mind was in a warm, fuzzy place with rainbows and cupids.

Devon lay facing me. I smiled a little at him, my chest full of feelings I didn't yet want to put a name to.

He didn't return my smile, but he did reach out and brush a stray lock of hair back from my face.

Despite my sated exhaustion, questions nagged at me about tonight. "Who were those men tonight?" I couldn't help but ask. Though I was loath to bring back up the topic of the dead men, I wanted to know what was going on. What if I hadn't been there tonight? Would Devon have managed to break free of that man's choke hold?

"They work for a man," he said. "A man who knows I'm looking for him."

I frowned. "I thought the man you were looking for was Clive?"

"I let him think that, yes," Devon said. "I was betting he'd give up information to save his own hide. And I was right."

My hand rested in the empty space between us on the mattress. Devon seemed lost in his own thoughts as he threaded his fingers through mine, his thumb absently stroking my skin.

"Are you going to meet him tomorrow?"

"Of course."

I swallowed. "But what if he double-crosses you again?"

Devon's gaze focused on mine. "Then I'll kill him."

A cold chill went through me and I shivered. Wrapping an arm over my waist, Devon pulled me closer to him, tucking me into the warmth of his body.

"So why are you looking for this man?" I asked.

"He stole something very important," he replied, "a seventy-year-old secret."

"What could he possibly do with a secret that old?" I asked.

"Kill millions."

I pulled back so I could look at Devon, my jaw gaping. Our eyes met. "You're serious," I said.

"I never joke about things like that."

"And Mr. Galler?"

"Had known the secret for a very long time," Devon finished.

"What is it?" I asked, unsure if I wanted to know such a thing or not.

"The details are still sketchy, which is why I need Clive's help in order to stop them."

"I'll worry about you," I hesitantly confessed.

Devon didn't say anything. He just pulled me back toward him again until my cheek rested against his chest. His silence hurt. I felt like I'd been stripped bare tonight, revealing things about my past that no one besides Logan knew. Devon's and my relationship, if you could even call it that, was a sexual one of convenience for him. Even with his earlier admission of caring a little for me, he'd also said he didn't like it, which I took to mean he didn't *want* to care about me.

Which was too bad, considering I was falling in love with him.

"Wake up, brat."

I shuddered at the sound of his voice in my ear. I should have known that pretending to be asleep wouldn't make him go away.

The covers were jerked out of my fisted grip, the cool night air in my room chilling me. A rush of cold sweat skated across my skin. I knew what was coming, and in that moment, I would have done anything to avoid it.

Jace yanked the sweatpants I wore down and off my legs, taking my underwear with them, and I knew better than to fight him. If I fought, he made sure it hurt. I despised myself for fearing the pain too much to fight him.

Pushing me, he made me turn over, and I heard the crinkle of paper as he unwrapped a condom. I hadn't even known what that was the first time he'd done it. I'd learned quickly enough.

I buried my face in the bedcovers and tried not to make a sound. It hurt. It always did.

His guttural moan made me want to vomit and I choked back the bile.

"You like it, don't you, brat," he hissed.

Jace liked to talk and I tried my best to tune him out. I thought about school, about homework, about Logan, about how I could take a knife and slash my wrists and I'd never have to go through this again.

In spite of myself, I let out a whimper of pain.

Instantly, he slammed his palm into the side of my head.

"Not a sound, brat."

My head throbbed from where he'd hit me, but I bit my lip until I tasted blood and didn't make a sound.

I pretended I was somewhere else, a warm summer field, staring up at the clouds racing by overhead, Logan by my side. We'd make pictures of the clouds, laughing at some of the ideas we came up with. Rabbits skipping rope, elves lying side by side, bears reaching for a kite . . .

"Turn over," he ordered, his harsh command dragging me back from where I'd retreated inside my head.

He was done and I knew what came next—what always came next. I hated it possibly more, but I also knew that he'd leave afterwards, so I did as he ordered, staring up at the dark ceiling rather than at him as he stood by my bed.

Jace leaned down, pressing his lips to mine. I didn't move or even breathe. Finally, he lifted his head.

"You know I only do this because I love you," he whispered. His hand brushed my hair and cheek. "You're so pretty, and I love you so fucking much." His fist tightened in my hair, making my eyes water, but I didn't make a sound. "What the fuck am I supposed to do, brat? You make me do this. It's your fault I'm this way."

The moment my door closed, I was up and in the bathroom. I couldn't shower, not so soon or he'd hear and come back to punish me. But I'd snuck antiseptic wipes from the kitchen into my bathroom and I used those to wipe between my legs.

My hands were steady and my mind blank. I couldn't think about it. It just . . . was. Maybe Jace was right. It was my fault he did this to me. But I couldn't understand why, if he said he loved me, why he'd hurt me? Would he ever stop? Or would this be my life from now on?

At that thought, I started to shake. I had to get out of there. Logan. I needed Logan.

I dressed again and shoved my feet into my tennis shoes; my only thought was Logan. I had to get to Logan.

LoganLoganLogan . . .

༄

"Shhh."

I woke to confusion, the few seconds of not knowing where I was before memory returned.

Devon was holding me, holding me much more tightly than when we'd fallen asleep. And he was shushing me.

"What's the matter?" I asked, easing away slightly. Why had he woken me?

He looked down at me, his expression stark. "You were . . . having a nightmare," he said finally.

That's when I realized my cheeks were wet. A flash of a dream, like smoke, flitted through my mind. I'd been dreaming about Jace. I shuddered.

"Sorry about that," I said. "I don't usually have the nightmares anymore." And I didn't. Worrying about Jace must have brought my past to the forefront of my subconscious.

Devon gently swiped my cheeks, erasing the tracks of my tears. He pressed his lips to mine once. Twice.

"Go back to sleep. I've got you."

The warmth in his voice made me relax and I obediently closed my eyes. This time when I slept, there were no nightmares waiting for me.

With room service for breakfast came clothes for me to wear. I didn't question how Devon had gotten the hotel to acquire them; I just put them on. The pair of black slacks and crimson cashmere sweater fit perfectly and didn't look too odd with my black heels.

Devon was knotting his tie when I finished pinning my hair back up. I carefully packed the dress I'd worn last night into a plastic laundry bag to take with me.

"Did you eat something?" Devon asked.

I nodded. He'd ordered some of everything, it seemed. "I had the yogurt."

A slight frown creased his forehead. "You didn't try the pastry?" He snagged a Danish from the tray and took a bite. Approaching me, he wrapped an arm around my waist. "Try it," he said, holding the Danish to my lips. "You'll adore it."

I opened my mouth and he fed me a bite, the flaky dough melting on my tongue. I liked being in Devon's arms too much to protest as he patiently fed me the entire pastry. He smelled good, his jaw smooth from his shave, and he wore a suit as comfortably as most men wore jeans.

It was sunny and cold outside and I hugged my coat closer as Devon held the door to his car for me. Soon we were speeding down the road in the direction of my apartment.

I wasn't sure what to say. Would I see Devon again? Did he want to see me again? Had I said too much last night, gotten more personal than he ever wanted? I couldn't help but think that was true, that no matter the connection between us, Devon wasn't looking for any kind of relationship that would tie him down.

When we arrived, he walked me upstairs to my door and we didn't speak. His hand was warm and solid at the small of my back. Once we were outside my door, I turned to him.

"Thank you for a—" I was going to say "nice evening," but in light of the men attacking us, that seemed rather inappropriate. "Just . . . thank you," I said instead.

Devon's lips twitched and I thought he must have known what I was thinking.

"You're welcome," he said. Slipping inside my coat, his hands circled my waist as he tugged me closer. I tipped my head back to look at him and my heart skipped a beat.

"Will I . . . see you again?" I asked.

Instead of replying, Devon kissed me. I became lost immediately, tuning out my surroundings as I wound my arms around his neck. His tongue slipped between my lips and I moaned, my body responding to his touch.

We were pressed tightly together, our bodies straining toward each other even through the layers of clothes, when the door to my apartment was suddenly thrown open.

Devon turned immediately, his arm keeping me shielded behind him, and I saw him reach automatically for his weapon.

"No, don't!" I said, gripping his arm. It was Logan at the door, staring at us as if in shock. But he recovered quickly, his furious gaze landing on Devon.

"You sonofabitch," he ground out, and his fist came flying through the air.

CHAPTER
TEN

Devon moved so fast, I could barely track what he did. Before I could say or do anything else, he had slammed Logan face-first against the wall. Devon had Logan's arm in a tight grip and bent up behind his back, and I could tell by the grimace on Logan's face that it wasn't pleasant.

"Devon! Stop!" Oh my God, he was going to break Logan's arm.

"Let me go, damn it," Logan ground out.

Devon took a moment, but he released him. Logan turned around, still glaring at Devon before his gaze settled on me.

"What the hell, Logan? You were just going to punch him? Seriously?" I was upset and flustered, not sure how to react to him being like this. He'd never been this way before with any other guys I'd dated, though granted he'd never caught me making out with them either.

"Where have you been? I've been worried sick!" he retorted, ignoring my questions.

"I left a note, for crying out loud," I snapped. "I'm not a child, Logan."

He scrubbed a hand across his face and heaved a sigh. "Never mind," he said. "Thank God you're okay." Crossing to me, he pulled me into his arms. He hugged me so tight, I couldn't help but hug him back, despite his attack on Devon.

"Why wouldn't I be okay?" I asked, pulling back to look up at him. "What's going on?"

"Just a minute," he said to me. He glanced at Devon and his expression turned guarded. "Devon, I'm guessing?" Logan's tone was stiff and anything but friendly.

Devon didn't immediately reply and I noticed his gaze was fixed on Logan's arms still wrapped around me. When he lifted his eyes, they were icy cold, the blue chilling even from a distance.

"Correct," he said, his easy reply belying the hard set of his expression. "And you must be Logan."

"I am."

"Pleased to meet you." Devon held out his hand. Logan seemed reluctant at first, but a lifetime of midwestern manners couldn't be ignored. A moment later, he clasped Devon's hand in his own for a perfunctory shake.

"Wish I could say the same," Logan replied, and my eyes went wide.

"Logan!" I couldn't believe he'd be so rude, but he ignored me.

"I'd appreciate it if you wouldn't break into our apartment again," Logan said, his tone one of barely leashed anger. He released me, but still had an arm locked around my waist, keeping me pressed to his side. "Especially if you're just looking for a quick lay."

I sucked in a sharp breath and opened my mouth to say something, I had no clue what, but Logan shot me a swift look. I knew that look. We'd been best friends for over ten years. There was little I *didn't* know about Logan. And that look meant *I'm pissed so shut up now.* So I did.

Devon showed no outright reaction to Logan's words, instead he took a step forward and said, "Perhaps you and I ought to have a little chat."

"That's a good idea," Logan said. Taking my arm, he moved me to the open doorway of the apartment. "Give us a minute, Ives."

The first thing I wanted to do was to tell them both that no, I most certainly was not going to "give them a minute" to discuss me like a misbehaving child. But logic and common sense kicked in and I realized it might not be a bad thing for Logan and Devon to talk alone. They'd certainly gotten off on the wrong foot. Maybe this would help, though if Devon wasn't coming back, it was a bit pointless. Still, I allowed Logan to steer me inside. Before he closed the door, I glanced back at the two of them.

Logan was younger and not as broad as Devon, though they were evenly matched for height. While Devon wore a suit and tie, Logan was more casual in jeans and a gray button-down shirt he wore tucked in. The cuffs were turned back, exposing the wide leather bracelet I'd bought for him ages ago that he hardly ever took off.

With one last glance, I shut the door, leaving the two of them alone in the hallway.

Not that I was going to let it go at that, of course. I pressed my ear to the crack in the door and listened.

"You're protective of Ivy," Devon stated. He didn't sound friendly or unfriendly, just matter-of-fact.

"You would be, too, if you knew the hell she's gone through." Logan's reply was even more rude now that I wasn't around. "I know men like you. You're not fit to breathe the same air she does." His contempt was obvious.

"Men like me," Devon repeated. "Somehow I doubt you know many men like me."

"You broke into my apartment and seduced my best friend," Logan said. "That tells me all I need to know."

The floor creaked in the hall and when Devon spoke again, his words were quieter but clearer. He'd stepped closer to Logan.

"She likes me, mate. I don't see that changing anytime soon, and there isn't a damn thing you can do about it."

There was silence for a moment. "Listen to me," Logan said, "Ivy is . . . damaged. She's fragile. You can't just play with her, screw her, and leave. She deserves better than that."

"Maybe that's why you're still just her mate," Devon shot back. "Because you see her as damaged. I don't look at her that way."

"Listen, I don't know what kind of hold you have over her," Logan replied, "but I see what it's doing. You're putting her back into a mind-set that she worked hard to escape. A way of thinking that made her believe she was only good for one thing. And I'm not going to let you do that to her."

I stood at the door, stunned at what I was hearing. Was that how Logan thought of me? Damaged? Fragile? And was he right? Was my being with Devon putting me back into the prison of feeling worthless and degraded? I couldn't think that, couldn't believe that.

Not wanting to hear any more, I backed silently away, retreating to the couch where I sat, lost in thought. It wasn't long before Logan reentered the apartment. He spotted me and headed my way, taking a seat beside me. He sat hunched over, his elbows braced on his knees and his hands clasped loosely together.

Neither of us spoke and the silence grew heavy. "Is that what you think of me?" I asked finally. "That I'm . . . damaged?" I didn't look at him, just stared straight ahead, not seeing anything.

"Ives," he began, "we've been together a long time. I love you more than anyone on the goddamn planet. But what you've been through . . . I just don't think you've ever really put it behind you. It's still there, just under the surface."

Anger suddenly burned away the hurt, or at least obscured it for a while, and I jumped to my feet. "Who the hell are you to play psychiatrist and tell me what I've put behind me or how damaged I am?" I demanded. "You don't know the first thing about it!"

Logan got to his feet, too, and grabbed my arm. "Don't pull this shit with me," he ground out. "I was the one you came running to, remember? I was the one who helped you into the bathtub when you were bleeding and hurting so bad you could hardly walk. I was the one who held you when you were too scared to go to sleep. And all that time, there was *nothing* I could do to make it stop. So don't tell me that I don't know anything about it! I was fucking *there*, Ivy!"

His yells echoed through the apartment while I stared at him in shock, the blood leaving my face in a rush.

Logan was right. He'd seen me through the worst of it and now it seemed I was punishing him for watching out for me. My vision began to blur. "I'm so sorry, Logan," I choked out.

He muttered a curse and pulled me into his arms. I buried my face against his chest. I felt guilty for treating him badly. Logan was my rock and I didn't want to take him for granted. Then I remembered.

"Wait, why were you worried about me?" I asked, sniffing away my tears.

Logan was stroking my hair and he paused at my question. Pulling back slightly, he looked down at me. His eyes were sad when he said, "Because Jace skipped on his parole, Ives. No one knows where he is."

My knees buckled and if Logan hadn't been holding me, I was sure I would have collapsed. He maneuvered me onto the couch.

"Take it easy," he said soothingly.

"How?" I asked, hearing the fear in my voice that I couldn't hide. "How can that be?"

"Grams called last night," Logan explained. "She didn't want to scare you, but she wanted to warn me."

I felt cold all over. He would come for me. Jace had told me he'd never let me get away and he was going to find me and when he did—

"Ives, listen to me," Logan said. "He won't find you. I promise. Nothing and no one is going to hurt you, okay?" His hand cradled my cheek, gently lifting my chin until he could look in my eyes. "Not this time. I swear it."

He was so sincere and so intent, I almost believed him. But in the end, Jace had a way of getting what he wanted, and if he wanted me, nothing would stop him. Not even Logan.

"So why did you go all crazy on Devon?" I asked, wanting to change the subject. I wouldn't—couldn't—think about Jace right now. "That's not like you."

"I don't trust him."

Logan's flat reply made me frown. "I appreciate your concern, I really do," I said as gently but as firmly as I could. "But it's my life and if it's a mistake to be involved with him, then it's my mistake to make."

He didn't reply and I hoped that was the end of the argument. Anxious to turn the conversation to something a bit lighter, I asked, "So was the blonde entertaining Friday night?"

Logan glanced at me, confusion in his eyes. "Who?"

"The blonde who was eyeing you. The one you danced with," I reminded him.

"Oh. Her. Yeah, she was fine," he said dismissively.

"Are you going to see her again?" I asked, though I thought I probably already knew the answer to that.

Logan snorted at me and I sighed. Maybe someday he'd find a woman who would capture his interest. It obviously hadn't been the blonde.

Reaching up, I pressed a kiss to his cheek, then stood and headed for my bedroom. A Sunday afternoon nap sounded just the thing, especially after the night I'd had. I didn't want to think about the men Devon had killed, or Jace, or what Logan had said about my past. So I slept.

Come that evening, I started getting antsy. I remembered what Clive had said about meeting Devon at eight o'clock. At seven, I was fidgety. By seven fifteen, I was pacing. And by seven thirty, I'd decided to go.

I dressed in dark jeans, a black turtleneck, and black knee-high boots. I pulled my hair back into a long, straight ponytail, all the while trying to convince myself that it wasn't a big deal if I went. I'd just pop into the pub for a drink, like any other customer, and if I happened to see Devon there with Clive . . . well, then I could make sure he was all right. If Clive tried to double-cross him again, I'd—

Well, I didn't know what I'd do.

With that thought in mind, I retrieved my gun from the drawer in my nightstand. It was a semiautomatic 9mm Glock that I'd chosen for its size. It fit comfortably inside a purse. I had a concealed carry permit so I had no qualms about taking it with me. If Devon ran into trouble, I'd at least be packing heat.

Logan had papers spread over the kitchen table as he sat, bent over a thick sheaf while a legal pad and pen sat near his right hand. He glanced up when I walked in.

"Going out?" he asked.

I grabbed my coat from the hook by the door. "Meeting a couple girlfriends for dinner." I kept my gaze averted as I lied, guilt making my stomach squirm uncomfortably.

"Anyone I know?"

I shook my head. "Just a friend from work and her roommate. I shouldn't be very late." I grabbed my keys off the counter and hooked my purse strap on my shoulder.

"Be careful," Logan called after me. I blew him a kiss as I pulled the door shut.

I made it to Shay's in record time, parking around the corner. Sunday nights weren't busy on the Landing, so I saw few people as I made my way inside.

It was dimly lit, which worked in my favor. Several people were sitting at the long bar, so I took an empty stool. The chairs at the dining tables were dark green leather and the floor was hardwood, giving the place a warm atmosphere.

The bartender was a young guy wearing black pants and a black T-shirt with a small imprint of the bar's logo. He smiled when he saw me, his teeth very white against his dark complexion. Paired with his dark hair, I thought he might have a touch of Italian in him.

"What can I get you?" he asked.

"Crown and Coke, please," I said. "Tall." A moment later, he set the glass down in front of me.

I sipped the drink as I tried nonchalantly to search the place for any sign of Devon or Clive. My nerves were stretched taut, not only because of the danger I felt Devon to be in, but how he'd react to my presence if he saw me. I didn't imagine it would be good, and yet I couldn't make myself leave.

A movement in a shadowy corner caught my eye and I realized it was them. Devon had his back to the wall and Clive sat across from him. They were deep in conversation.

I watched for several long minutes. Clive slid something across the table to Devon, who palmed it. Clive got up, glancing casually around, and left. Devon swallowed the last of his drink, then followed where Clive had disappeared through the exit.

Tossing some money on the bar, I grabbed my purse and hurried after them. Maybe I could see where they went. Were they done meeting? Or had that been a precursor to a longer discussion somewhere else?

As I exited the bar, I glanced to my left and right. To my right, the narrow cobblestone street led down to the river; to my left, it rose up the steep hill. The street was nearly deserted and a thick fog was rolling in from the river. I could hear the faint lapping of the water as the current rushed by.

A familiar figure in an overcoat caught my eye off to my right just as he turned the corner. Devon.

Without thinking much as to why I was doing this—probably not the best idea—I hurried to follow him. The streetlamps left pools of light at regular intervals, but the fog, combined with the snow still covering the uneven cobblestones, made walking fast a dicey proposition. Still, I made it to the corner without mishap.

There was an alley between the buildings, which were old and had been built fairly close together. Uneasy now, I crept into the alley, searching for any sign of Devon or Clive. My hand slid into my purse and I pulled out my gun. I'd rather have the weapon in my hand and not need it than be scrabbling inside my purse searching for it and be too late.

The alley emptied into another street and I approached the corner carefully. The fog muffled sounds so it was not only hard to hear, it was difficult to tell where noises were coming from. The back doors to a couple of restaurants emptied into the alley and there were several dumpsters loaded with trash and debris, which I carefully skirted.

My pulse was racing and my heart was in my throat. I was regretting coming out tonight after all, but my worry for Devon kept me putting one foot in front of the other. For some reason, I just had a really bad feeling about what was up around that corner.

I hesitated when I reached the end of the alley. Pressing against the wall, I took a deep breath. The blood was rushing in my ears so badly I could hardly hear anything over it. Despite the cold, my palms were sweaty as I gripped my gun.

A sudden clatter made me nearly jump out of my skin. I spun around, my gun at the ready, only to see a skinny cat behind me. He blinked at me, then primly stepped over the mess he'd just made tipping over a box of trash. Daintily sniffing an overturned jar, he batted it with his paw.

I let out the breath I'd been holding. I was shaking like a leaf, either from fear or adrenaline, probably both.

"Damn cat," I muttered, wiping a hand across the cold sweat that had formed on my brow. "Scared me half to—"

A hand landed hard on my shoulder, spinning me around just as another knocked the gun from my grip. It landed on the cobblestones with a clatter. A scream clawed its way up my throat, but then I was pressed with my back to the wall and a man's palm covering my mouth, silencing me.

"Following me, Ivy?"

Oh, God. It was Devon. Relief flooded through me, so overwhelming in the immediate aftermath of being terrified that I thought I might pass out.

He was pressed close to me, his body blocking the meager light in the alley. I expected him to remove his hand, but he didn't, not right away. I breathed in the scent of his skin, his hand warm despite the weather. My eyes were locked on his, their depths unfathomable in the darkness. Finally, he slid his hand from my mouth and I took a deep breath.

"How did you know it was me?" I asked.

Devon leaned down until his lips were near my ear. His proximity, the hard length of his body against mine, sent my thoughts careening off into a much more carnal direction.

"I was downwind," he said, his warm breath fanning lightly across my ear. "I caught the scent of your perfume." He nuzzled the spot underneath my jaw. The touch of his tongue against my skin made me gasp and my eyes slid shut. His hands moved to the inside of my coat to rest possessively on my hips. "And why are you following me this evening?"

It was hard to think with him doing that, and it took a moment for me to stammer a reply. "B-because I w-was afraid something might happen to you." My voice was too breathless and my arms reached up to clutch at his shoulders.

Devon lifted his head and I released a tiny sigh of disappointment. I'd become addicted to him so quickly, craving the feel of his skin against mine the way a pet craved its master's touch.

"I didn't ask you to care," he said, the words so cold I couldn't suppress a shiver. When I didn't speak, he continued. "It would be better if you didn't. Our involvement is a fleeting one."

I swallowed hard at that. Devon certainly wasn't one to give a girl the warm fuzzies, that was for sure.

"Fine," I said stiffly, my anger just under the surface. "Forget I gave a damn." Pushing out of his grip, I got two steps before he had me back against the wall, his body pressed against mine to hold me in place.

"What did you think you were going to do?" he asked, his face so close to mine I could see into the depths of his eyes.

"I-I don't know," I said. "I brought my gun." I shrugged. "You know. Just in case." Yeah, because I'd just pull it out and shoot someone. Right. What had I been thinking?

Devon's lips twitched. "So you were going to have a go at rescuing me," he said.

Okay, now it did seem ridiculous. I remembered seeing him fight with those men in the stairwell, remembered the bank robbers he'd killed.

"I helped last night," I said defensively.

"Do you want to help again?"

I gave a hesitant nod, my lips pressed tightly together. I had no idea how I could help him, but the need to be around him outweighed the need for self-preservation, in spite of and perhaps especially because he'd outright said he wouldn't be with me for long.

Reaching down, Devon scooped up my gun and handed it back to me.

"Then you may need this," he said.

Taking the weapon, I slipped it back inside my purse.

"Come with me," Devon said, reaching to take my hand. He led me out of the alley and down another street to where his car was parked. I thought about mentioning my car, but decided I didn't really care. I'd come back for it later.

The confines of the car felt safe to me, especially with Devon only inches away. I watched his hands move on the gearshift and steering wheel, flashes of memory of those hands on me going through my mind. Devon had discarded his suit for a change, tonight wearing slacks and a dark sweater that was either black or navy. The sleeves were pushed up, exposing the heavy bones of his wrists and muscles in his forearms.

I marveled at how just a few weeks ago, Devon frightened me. A man of his size and demeanor always had and probably always would, but now I felt sheltered by him rather than threatened. Deep inside, a part of me knew Logan was right, that I was treading a dangerous path, yet I couldn't stay away from him.

I didn't speak until we were out of the city. "Where are we going?" I asked, dragging my eyes from his hands to his profile, shadowed in the darkness.

"To the scene of the crime," he said cryptically. Glancing at me, he clarified. "Galler's residence."

"Why? What did Clive tell you?" My curiosity was rampant now that the immediate danger had passed.

"Clive gave me information," Devon said cryptically. "We'll see if it works out. He's still not to be trusted."

"He told you why he did what he did," I reminded him. "He said they were going to kill Anna."

Devon's gaze slanted my way for a moment, then returned to the road. "It doesn't matter," he said.

I frowned, confused. "Doesn't matter that she would've died? He obviously loves her. Of course he did what he had to do to protect her."

Devon's lips tipped up in a humorless smile. "Love. A worthless, debilitating sentiment expressed by a fool."

I was sure I hadn't heard him right. "You think love is worthless?" True, he'd been less than enthusiastic about the emotion when speaking to Clive. At the time, I'd thought that had been due to his anger at Clive's betrayal more than a deep-seated antipathy.

"Don't you?"

"Of course not!" Yes, I sounded like a cliché, but his dismissal of an emotion that was too close to what I was feeling for him stung.

"Emotions are subject to change, they make one irrational instead of logical, and are impossible to predict. Fear, anger, frustration. Lust, jealousy, hate. And yes, even love, are to be avoided."

He recited the words as though he'd memorized them and taken them wholly to heart. While depressing, I didn't want him to stop talking. This was the first he'd really told me about himself and I wanted to know more.

"You're referring to your job," I said. "Emotions are dangerous to you because of what you do for a living."

"Obviously." Very British, the way he said that, with condescension in his tone.

"So you're impervious to emotion then?" I asked.

Devon's eyes were fixed on the road. "I never said that."

"But you just said—"

"I said they're to be avoided, not that I was immune. No one is immune. But they can be controlled, so they don't control you."

"Like the Force, right?" I joked, deadpan. He glanced questioningly at me. "You know, 'Anger, fear, aggression. The Dark Side are they,'" I quoted Yoda.

Devon gave a sudden bark of laughter. "I suppose that would be one way of looking at it," he acknowledged. His smile was still intact and I took a minute to enjoy it.

"But then why do you do what you do?" I asked.

"What do you mean?"

"I'd think it would take a great deal of commitment—of emotion—to do a job like yours," I said. "Be it from patriotic fervor, or anger, or love of country. So why?"

That seemed to take Devon utterly aback and it took him a while to answer me.

"I didn't have a lot of alternatives," he said at last.

"Why not?" I couldn't imagine he wouldn't have been smart enough to have a different career.

"I was orphaned at a young age and sent to live within the system. When I was of age, I joined the Royal Marines, then moved into the SBS"—he glanced at me—"Special Boat Service. I was . . . recruited from there."

That was a lot of history he'd just glossed over. I had the feeling getting personal information out of Devon was going to be like playing a game of Twenty Questions. I decided to start at the beginning.

"How did your parents die?"

"Why do you want to know?" His voice was hard.

"Excuse me?"

"I said, why do you want to know?" he asked again. "I've repeatedly told you our arrangement is a temporary one. You've been put in danger because of your association with me. Why do you want to know my personal history?"

"Because . . . I'm curious," I said with a shrug. "I like you. I want to learn more about you. Is that wrong?"

"Not wrong," he admitted. "Just perhaps . . . misguided."

I just loved being told I was stupid, even if it was cloaked in a polite euphemism. I held my tongue, though, and waited him out.

"They were killed by an IRA attack in London," he said with a sigh. "I was ten."

A pang of sympathy struck me. Despite my grandparents, being an orphan was something I could relate to.

"My father died when I was three," I said. "He was in the Army and died in combat. My mother was never the same. She thought I needed a father, and she needed someone to help pay the bills, so she remarried when I was six." I swallowed and looked out my window, not wanting to say the next part, but if I expected Devon to share his past, then I had to do the same. "She killed my stepfather and herself when I was thirteen."

Silence reigned in the car.

"Considering what you've told me of your stepbrother, I would guess she did that to save you," Devon said.

Surprised at his insight, I glanced at him. "It was a gas leak," I said. "Officially an accident. But I know the truth. Yes, that's exactly what she did. My stepdad drank, and when he was drunk, he was mean. He hit her. Me, too, sometimes. Then he stopped hitting me, and he started—" But my throat closed off and I couldn't speak anymore.

Devon turned to look at me, and our eyes met. I saw that he already knew what I couldn't say. There was no pity in his gaze, which

I couldn't have withstood, just an understanding that sometimes life could be real shitty.

I cleared my throat. "So how long have you done this job? Been a . . . spy?" It still felt weird saying that.

"Sometimes it seems like a very long time indeed," he said. His vague answer didn't surprise me.

"Ever thought of doing something else?" I didn't dare hope what his answer would be.

Looking over at me, he said firmly, "Not for a moment."

Well. It wasn't like he was leading me on, I supposed. Brutal honesty, though I could do without the "brutal" part.

"I heard Logan say I was 'damaged,'" I said. "You don't see me that way?" I'd really liked hearing him say that and wanted to hear it again, this time to my face.

"We're all products of our past," Devon said. "What we choose to do with it is our decision, no one else's. You can choose to be damaged, fragile. Or you can choose to be more than the broken elements of your psyche. Fire tempers steel. Pain tempers character.

"I think you are stronger than your friend Logan gives you credit."

We pulled to a stop then, and I noticed we were parked adjacent to Mr. Galler's property, which was probably wise. Everyone knew he'd been murdered. Parking in front of the house would be a dead giveaway that we weren't supposed to be there.

The snow crunched underneath our feet as we walked, much of it had melted but some patches still remained. I slipped at one point and Devon caught my arm before I fell. From there on, he held my hand, which I didn't mind at all.

"Did Galler tell you anything else that day?" he asked as we approached the dark and silent house.

"No," I said. "He was writing his memoirs and mentioned his

father was a doctor, that he died in the war. That was all. I wasn't there for very long. He gave me the pendant and I left."

We walked over the large patio in the back and past the swimming pool covered with a large, black tarp. I hadn't brought my coat and was freezing. I stood with my arms wrapped around myself while Devon fiddled with the lock on the back door. Quicker than I would have thought possible, he had the door open and we were inside.

The house was still and as silent as a mausoleum. No one lived there anymore, and I could feel it. Strange how it's like that. I wasn't a believer in the sixth-sense kind of thing, but couldn't deny the shiver that went down my spine as I gazed around. Scattered moonlight filtered through half-closed window blinds and I could feel the underlying hum of electricity through the house.

Devon took the lead and I let him, the darkened house giving me the creeps. When we reached the study, he flipped on the light.

"Did you see where he kept the pendant he gave you?" he asked.

I nodded. "In his drawer," I said, walking to the ornate desk in front of the windows. I showed Devon the drawer and the secret compartment. To my surprise, he yanked the entire thing out of the desk.

"What's this?" he murmured, inspecting something in the back, next to the notch I'd pressed to open the drawer. I leaned in for a closer look.

The point of a needle lay hidden far up inside the recesses of the drawer.

"That must have been what pricked me," I said, thinking out loud.

Devon glanced sharply at me. "When?"

"The night I was here," I explained. "Mr. Galler didn't get the pendant out, I did. He just told me where it was and how to open the drawer. When I reached in, something poked me. I thought it was a splinter."

Devon didn't say anything, turning his attention back to the drawer. Brute force was enough to crack open the hidden compartment farther, enough for both of us to see that the needle was attached to a spring. Taking a pen, Devon pressed lightly on the button and I watched in amazement as the spring instantly jabbed the needle forward.

"Wow," I breathed. "That was really fast." A disturbing thought occurred to me. "Devon? Why would he have that in there?"

Devon's gaze met mine again. "I don't know."

Well.

I swallowed, wondering what I was supposed to do now, how I could find out. Devon replaced the drawer while I drifted aimlessly around the room, searching for I didn't know what.

I ventured out of the room and down the hallway. There was enough ambient light to see. I turned into an open doorway, wondering if I could find Mr. Galler's unfinished manuscript. It might have something written there that would help Devon. I fumbled for a light switch, the room too dark to see anything.

"Ivy, wait—"

But Devon's words were cut off by my scream as someone reached out of the blackness and grabbed me. I blindly fought him, trying to get away and retreat the way I'd come. He grabbed a fistful of my hair and yanked me around. I cried out in pain, but when I felt the cold press of steel against my neck, I froze.

The lights clicked on and I blinked in the sudden glare. My heart was pounding with fear and panic, which only notched higher when I saw Devon standing in the doorway. His gun was in his hand, but his eyes were on the knife at my throat.

I swallowed, feeling the knife slide against my skin at the slight movement.

Two other men were in the room, along with the man hold-ing me. All of them looked menacingly lethal, as did the guns they held, all pointed at Devon.

"Drop the weapon, mate," the man holding me said, "or I'll slice her from ear to ear." He yanked my hair again and my eyes watered at the pain. I pressed my lips tightly together so I wouldn't make a sound.

Devon's eyes flicked to the two men, then back to me, and I knew with a sinking sensation in my stomach that, if not for the threat to me, Devon could have gotten out of this. I could see it in his eyes.

And right as Devon tossed his gun to the floor was when I understood why he was so averse to feeling anything for anyone.

CHAPTER
ELEVEN

I watched in horror as one of the men approached Devon, who stood his ground. If he was afraid, he didn't show it. His face didn't even register mild concern. I was terrified they were going to kill him.

I squirmed when one of the men stepped behind Devon, unable to stop myself from wanting to help him. The guy holding my hair pressed the tip of his knife to my carotid artery and I sucked in a breath as he yanked me back.

"Don't move," he hissed.

Devon's head jerked toward us, his body tightening and his hands fisting, but before he could act, the man behind him cold-cocked him with the butt of his gun. I watched as Devon's eyes rolled back in his head and his body collapsed to the floor.

I was unfortunately very much conscious as they dragged me across the hall. They left Devon on the floor, but I saw someone else coming down the hallway with rope dangling from his hands. The last I saw of him, he was entering the room before the door was slammed shut.

The man with me had sheathed the knife, but still held my hair. My scalp was burning, my body bent sideways as I tried to keep up with him and ease the pressure as much as possible. He finally let go, only to backhand me. I went flying, careening right into a table at knee height. I fell on it, knocking it over and dumping everything onto the hardwood floor. The tinkling sound of breaking glass filled my ears as I lay facedown on the floor, struggling to catch my breath.

My head ached, both from the punishment my scalp had taken and the blistering hit to the side of my face. I groped for my purse, but realized too late that I'd left it in the study.

"I imagine they'll have your boyfriend awake in no time," the man sneered. "Let's give him a little motivation, shall we?"

That was all the warning I had before his boot slammed into my side. I choked on a scream, pain lancing through me as I curled into a ball.

"I barely heard that, love," he said. "Try a bit louder."

Another kick, this time in my back and I couldn't stop the scream that clawed its way up my throat.

"There. That's better."

He kicked me again. And again. I screamed, the pain excruciating. As small as I tried to get, he still found a way to hurt me.

I was suddenly hauled up by a hard grip on the back of my neck. I scrambled to my knees. My body hurt everywhere and tears leaked from my eyes.

The door opened, giving me a moment's respite from whatever my torturer had planned. That was when I heard the yell. A man's yell of pain.

Devon.

"Is he talking yet?" my captor asked.

"No, but he reacts when she screams, so keep it up."

They were using me against Devon. Using my pain to force him to cooperate. I heard another guttural yell from behind the closed study door.

I could be quiet. God knows, I'd had enough practice. Jace had taught me well.

The next blow elicited nothing but a grunt from me, as did the next and the one after that.

I was lying on my side again, my breath heaving and my entire body broken out into a cold sweat. Pain radiated from everywhere now and I tasted blood inside my mouth.

"She's clamming up," the second guy said. "Try something else."

"Take her shirt off."

I had no energy to move away from the hands grasping at me. "No, stop," I mumbled through stiff and swollen lips. But my turtleneck was pulled over my head and tossed aside.

He grabbed my arm and hauled me to my knees, my back to the other guy. His hand held the back of my neck in a tight grip, the fingers bruising my flesh. I heard the rasp of a lighter, then nothing. I trembled all over as I waited. The familiar sense of impending pain made my mind go blank in search of a way to disconnect, the same way I had so long ago.

"Hold her," the guy said.

I braced myself, but nothing could have prepared me for the feel of the white-hot steel of the knife, heated by the flame, as it pressed against my back. A scream of pure agony tore from my throat.

Relief came when he finally lifted the blade. I choked on a sob, tears streaming from my eyes. My throat was raw from screaming.

"Please, I'll do whatever you want," I begged. "Please." But I had no idea what they wanted from me. They hadn't asked me a single question. All they wanted from me was my pain.

"Enough, gentlemen," a new voice said.

I heard another yell from Devon and it made me want to die. He was being hurt, I'm sure worse than me, tortured just steps away. And I could do nothing. My very presence had put him in this situation. It was a very real possibility that neither of us would survive the night.

The hand holding me up disappeared and I folded limply to the floor. Staring up, I saw a man I hadn't seen before. He was dressed expensively and was smoking a cigarette.

"Please," I managed to croak. "Please don't hurt him anymore." Just talking made pain ricochet through me and I swallowed on a dry throat.

"Devon Clay, you mean," he replied before taking a long drag.

I gave a fractional nod and forced my lips to move again. "I'll do whatever you want. Just please, don't kill him."

Another muffled yell from across the hall that I felt down to my bones.

"Will you?" the man asked, eyeing me. "Will you really?"

Pain wrenched a moan from my lips and I tried halfheartedly to get away from the hands lifting me. A stab in my side forced a hoarse scream from me.

"Shhh, it's all right. I've got you."

It took an act of will to pry open my eyelids, and when I did, I saw Devon above me. He was carrying me.

"Devon," I croaked, hardly daring to believe my eyes. His face was bruised and bloodied. I lifted a shaking hand to touch him, wanting to make sure he was real.

"Don't try to talk," he said, laying me down on something soft. I didn't care enough to try to figure out where I was.

That's when I heard the sirens. They were loud and coming closer. I focused on Devon, though, his eyes so blue even in his battered face. He was looking me over and his jaw was clenched tight, a nerve pulsing in his cheek.

"Ah, my sweet Ivy," he murmured, his hand gently brushing my hair. "What have they done to you?"

I sighed at his touch, my tired eyes drifting shut. I wanted to stay conscious, to be with him, but the pain in my body was dragging me back under.

"You're okay," I mumbled, my thoughts a twisted jumble of relief, fear, and pulses of agony.

The sirens were really loud now and so close. I heard a door crash open just as Devon pressed his lips to my forehead, then I knew nothing.

⌒

Fog seemed to cloud my mind as I tried to open my eyes, but they wouldn't open. As hard as I tried, everything stayed cloaked in unrelenting darkness. My body felt simultaneously heavy and empty, and I recognized the effects of powerful pain medication.

I relaxed, the absence of pain made me realize I was probably in the hospital. Listening closely, the noises around me confirmed it—the soft whirring of machines, the muted voices from outside the room, the soft yet scratchy linens covering my legs, and the pillow underneath my head.

Someone was with me, holding my hand, but I couldn't squeeze or do anything to let them know I was aware of their presence.

I heard the sound of a door opening, the whoosh of air, the scuff of a shoe. The hand holding mine tightened its grip.

"What the hell are you doing in here?"

It was Logan who was next to me and it was he who spoke. His hand dropped from mine and I heard a chair scrape the floor as he stood. He sounded very upset, very angry. "Haven't you done enough?"

"I want to check on Ivy. You don't have an exclusive right to care about her."

My heart leapt in my chest to hear Devon's voice. I hadn't been hallucinating. He really was okay.

"This is how you care about her?" Logan spat. "Look at her! She's in the fucking hospital, you piece of shit!"

I didn't like to hear him getting so angry with Devon. It hadn't been his fault. He had a dangerous job. I'd been the one to follow him, to tell him I wanted to help.

"Stop yelling," Devon ordered. "You're upsetting her."

"She's asleep," Logan said defensively.

"Look at her heart rate."

They were both silent for a moment. The modulated beeping I'd heard earlier had indeed sped up.

I felt a hand lightly brush my cheek and forehead before sliding into my hair. Devon. The beeping slowed again.

"Don't you think I know what I've done?" Devon asked quietly. "I never meant this to happen. Never wanted her to get hurt."

"That doesn't really matter, does it," Logan retorted. "You've done nothing but fuck her over since you met her." The acid in his tone hadn't changed; he just kept his voice down.

"I'm not going to abandon her, just because her guard dog says so," Devon snapped.

"Oh yes, you are," Logan hissed. "If you care anything about her at all, you'll walk out that door and never see her again."

There was silence and I wanted so badly to tell Logan no, to stop, but the drugs were dragging me down again even as I tried to stay conscious. I had to hear what Devon said. He cared about me, I knew that, but was it only skin-deep? A sense of responsibility easily sloughed from his shoulders as he moved on? Or did it go deeper?

But I didn't get to hear what he said as the arms of the drugs pulled me back into darkness and silence.

∽

When I woke again, the drugs weren't nearly as heavy-duty and I could move. I opened my eyes to see I was in a small hospital room. It was dark outside, and, as before, I wasn't alone. But it wasn't Logan or Devon in the room with me.

"Who are you?" I asked the woman who stood in the shadows near my bed. My voice was scratchy and hoarse from disuse.

"Good. You're awake," she replied. It was obvious she wasn't a doctor or nurse, or if she was, I would hate to be her patient.

Tall and forbidding, her face was all sharp planes and angles. Her lips were flat and her eyes lacked any warmth or humor. It was hard to determine her age, but I guessed late fifties or early sixties. An expression of mild irritation seemed permanently etched on her face.

"You're Ivy Mason," she continued, taking a step closer to the bed.

"Who are you?" I repeated.

"You could say I'm Clay's boss."

Clay. She called Devon by his last name. Devon was a spy and this was his boss? I suddenly wondered if I was safe in her presence. Would she want to eliminate me for what I knew about Devon? My hand groped for the call button.

"I'm not here to harm you, if that's what you're worried about," she said dryly. "Besides, my guard at the door wouldn't let anyone through anyway."

Okay then.

"What do you want?" Somehow I knew this wasn't a friendly getting-to-know-you chat and I was instinctively wary and distrustful of her.

"I want you to tell me exactly what happened the other night. Specifically, what you told them."

"I didn't tell them anything," I said. "They didn't ask me anything."

"Given your injuries, I find that hard to believe."

I'd been awake for all of thirty seconds and this lady was already starting to piss me off.

"Believe what you want," I retorted. "They wanted me to scream. That's all."

This made her pause and her dark eyes narrowed as she studied me.

"Is that so?" she murmured, almost to herself.

I squirmed under her penetrating gaze. *God, what I wouldn't give for a drink of water.*

"You should leave," I said, resting back against the pillow and closing my eyes. "I know nothing else to tell you."

"My dear, you've told me more than you even realize." Her dry condescension made my eyes open again, but she was already walking out the door. It swung shut behind her and I let out a deep breath.

I lay awake until morning, wondering about the woman and what had become of Devon.

"You're conscious! Finally!" Logan said as he walked into the room around seven in the morning.

I smiled, glad to see him. I vaguely recalled he and Devon arguing that one night, but it was like a half-remembered dream.

The aroma of the coffee he carried made me long for a cup, the smell only intensifying as he sat in the chair by my bed.

"When can I go home?" I asked him.

"Since you're awake, I'm guessing today or tomorrow," Logan replied. His tone was light but his eyes were serious.

"What day is it?"

"Wednesday," he said. "Been here since Sunday night. The night you got mugged." He looked away from me, taking a sip of his coffee.

So that's what Devon had told everyone. I hadn't thought that far.

One look at Logan's face and I knew what he was thinking, the worry and panic I'd no doubt put him through.

"I'm sorry, Logan," I said.

His gaze flicked back to mine. "Don't apologize, Ives. This wasn't your fault." And he didn't have to say any more for me to know whose fault he thought it was. Speaking of which—

"Where's Devon?" I asked, because I couldn't go any longer without knowing.

"He left," Logan said. "Early Monday morning, I think."

I stared at Logan. "When is he coming back?"

"Ives . . . he's not."

Shock rippled through me, followed by the tearing agony of despair. My throat thickened and my eyes burned. It couldn't be true. He couldn't have left me for good. Not really. Devon cared about me. We had something—something more than just sex.

I turned my head away from Logan, swallowing down the tears that threatened. Maybe I'd been wrong. It wasn't as if he hadn't told me flat out that our relationship, such as it was, would be anything long-term. Though after what had happened the other night, what we'd gone through together, I'd thought—

I cut that thought off. I didn't want to think about it anymore, and I shoved it to the back of my mind. I was being ridiculous. I'd only known Devon a couple of weeks. The heartache I felt was too acute for such a short period.

Then why did my chest feel like someone had a vise around my heart, slowly squeezing until it hurt to breathe?

Logan left for work shortly after that, brushing his lips to my cheek and promising to call me later. A nurse came in to check my vitals and, at my request, she helped me into the shower. Everything ached and the hot water helped to ease my cramped and abused muscles. Two cracked ribs made every movement slow and painful. A good look in the mirror made me wish I hadn't.

Bruises decorated my torso and back, deep purple and black against my skin. My face still had a faint bruise from where the guy had hit me the first time. If I turned just right, I could see the scar from the knife on my lower back. Livid and about four inches long, seeing it made me shudder at the memory of what it had felt like. Yet, I was grateful that all they'd done was hit me. I'd rather that than rape, though neither was preferable.

True to his word, Logan called me late in the afternoon. He asked if he could bring me dinner, but I refused. I wasn't hungry and told him to go home.

"You've been here every day," I said. "They're letting me out tomorrow anyway. I'm fine. Take it easy tonight."

He protested but I insisted, and in the end he didn't come. I was glad of it. I didn't want to have to try to put on a happy face. I lay in bed and stared out the window, picking at the watery Jell-O on the hospital dinner tray.

They put me on a lighter pain medicine to help me sleep and I welcomed the oblivion. It meant I didn't have to think about Devon. I hadn't cried again. I just buried my heartache deep inside, in the same place I put everything that made me hurt.

But I couldn't stop my subconscious from dreaming about him.

I felt his touch, the warm brush of his fingers on my arm, my shoulder, my cheek. His smell surrounded me and I heard the low murmur of his voice. Unable to make out what he said, I just listened to the timbre and cadence of his words. His hand clasped mine, our fingers slotting together, and the emotions I'd tried to ignore surged to the surface. Then he was pulling away. I reached for him, but he was gone, leaving me cold and alone.

I gasped, coming awake with a start. Tears pricked my eyes and streamed down the side of my face into my hair. I stared up at the ceiling, inhaling deeply as I struggled to control my emotions.

Then I caught a scent in the air.

Without even thinking, I jumped out of bed, my muscles screaming in protest. A moment later I was at the door and flinging it open. I looked expectantly down the hallway, first to my right, then my left.

He was gone.

⌀

Logan wanted me to take Friday off work, but I refused. I felt like I needed to get back to my life, back to being normal, because "normal" was the last adjective I'd use to describe how I felt.

I'd never been so at sea before or felt so lost, and I never would have thought that losing someone would make me feel that way.

Being in a relationship—caring for someone, being sexually involved with them—had always been a vague, distant sort of thing to me. Yes, it would happen to me . . . at some point. The fact that it had happened, and so suddenly, made its loss that much more acute and I didn't know how to handle it.

"You okay?" Marcia asked as she poured herself a cup of coffee. We were in the break room grabbing a refill, and she was watching me stir my coffee while I absently stared off into space.

"Hmm? Oh, yeah, I'm fine," I replied, giving her a wan smile.

"Uh-oh," she said, eyeing me. "I know that look. I've *had* that look. It's a guy, isn't it. Tell me." She leaned back against the counter expectantly, taking a cautious sip of the hot coffee.

I shook my head. "You wouldn't believe it if I told you."

"Try me," she insisted.

I heaved a sigh. Maybe it would be good to talk to someone. Lord knew I couldn't talk to Logan about it. We'd been carefully polite since I'd gotten back home, neither of us bringing up Devon or what had happened.

"Remember that guy?" I asked. "From the robbery?"

"The one who was all about protecting you that day? The guy you can't stand?"

I nodded. "Well, he and I kind of got . . . involved."

"O. M. G.," she said, her eyes wide. "I'm so jealous right now. Not only gorgeous, but a badass, too." She grinned and winked at me. "You go, girl."

"Yeah, well, I thought we kind of had something, you know?" I continued. Talking about it did help, and now that I had started, I wanted to tell her everything. Well, almost everything. "But then he just . . . ended it. And now, I just feel so alone and I-I really miss him." I cleared my throat past the lump that had formed and blinked back the tears that threatened.

"Did he say why he ended it?" Marcia asked.

"No. Not really." I didn't want to voice the fear inside my head—that he'd tired of me.

"Have you tried calling him? Texting him?"

I shook my head, too embarrassed to admit I didn't even have his number.

"I'm not usually a big fan of chasing a guy if he's not that into me," she said, "but in this case, maybe you should go see him. At least get him to give you some kind of explanation or a decent goodbye-have-a-nice-life."

"I don't want to look desperate," I hedged.

"He owes you that much," she insisted. "Besides, you only live once, right?"

She had a point there. Several, actually.

"I'll think about it," I said as we headed back toward our booths.

"Let me know how it goes," Marcia said.

And I thought about it. All day. I couldn't *not* think about it, just like I couldn't stop thinking about him. I wondered if the woman who'd come to see me had told Devon about that visit. Maybe she'd told him to not be involved with me anymore, not mix business with pleasure, etc., etc. In which case it was very likely he'd obey her, considering how dedicated he was to his job.

I was caught in a wave of indecision. Was Marcia right? Should I go by his apartment? I'd been there, I remembered where it was. Or should I just leave things alone? I really didn't want to look like the needy female, no matter how much I felt like one.

It was the week before Christmas, and true to Midwest form, when I left work more snow was falling to replace the last batch that had melted. Logan was spending the weekend with a buddy in Colorado. His friend had a place in Breckenridge and Logan loved to ski. They'd left early that morning.

I wasn't that upset he was gone. I thought maybe Logan and I needed a break from each other. Things had been pretty tense recently; his disapproval over decisions I'd made about my life—about Devon—had driven a wedge between us. Some time apart would probably do us good.

Eating didn't appeal to me, but I forced down some canned soup. Since the hospital, I'd lost my appetite. I figured it was the broken-heart cliché.

I lasted until almost midnight.

"Screw it," I muttered to myself, climbing off the couch where

I'd planted my rear end all evening to zone out in front of the television.

The gnawing ache inside me wouldn't go away. Maybe if I just saw him again, heard him tell me it was over, I could move on.

It's funny how things that have no rationale in the cold light of day suddenly make perfect sense in the middle of the night.

Changing out of my sweats, I pulled on a pair of dark leggings with an oversized, crocheted sweater. I wore an ivory tank underneath because, although the sweater was really pretty, the large knit made it see-through. The snow made boots necessary, and I didn't bother with my hair, leaving it to fall straight down my back.

Logan had retrieved my car for me and I was glad of it as I scraped the snow off. I tried to stay calm on the ride to Devon's apartment, but I was too keyed up at the prospect of seeing him again. Would he be glad to see me, and would I even be able to tell if he was? Or was I making a colossal mistake?

By the time I pulled up to the building, I had convinced myself I was insane and needed to turn around and go right back home. Instead, I found myself parking and locking the door before stepping out onto the pavement.

Flakes of snow hit my cheeks and I pulled my coat tighter around me, wishing I'd stopped long enough to think to wear gloves and a scarf. Too late now.

Entering the building, I took the elevator to the top floor. It was an expensive residence and there were only two apartments per floor. When I stood in front of Devon's door, I took a deep breath, then knocked.

Nothing.

I knocked again, harder. Still nothing. I tried again.

The door behind me suddenly opened. I turned, spotting a man standing in the apartment across the way. He was probably in his mid-thirties. It seemed Devon had a neighbor. His eyes flicked over me and he smiled.

"Hi there," he said. "I heard you knocking. Guess you didn't know he's gone?"

I stared in surprise. "Um, no, uh-I guess not," I stammered.

"Yeah, he left earlier," the guy continued, leaning against the doorjamb and crossing his arms over his chest. "Said he was leaving the country. Didn't say how long he'd be gone."

Leaving the country.

Well, he *was* British. It had probably been a fluke that Devon had been here in the first place.

I forced a smile. "Thanks for telling me," I said.

"You want to come in?" he asked. "Have a drink before you go? I'm Beau, by the way."

His smile was friendly, but all I could think about was that Devon was gone—forever out of my reach—even for a goodbye.

That had a lot of implications that I didn't want to think about right now.

"Um, sorry, but I'd better go. Thanks anyway." I didn't bother waiting for the elevator and took the stairs instead.

I was crying again by the time I hit the sidewalk and angrily brushed at my wet cheeks as I walked. Well, I guessed that was that. You couldn't get much more permanent than leaving the damn country.

I wondered if the guys who'd taken us captive had gotten anything out of Devon, if my screams had made him reveal things he shouldn't have. Maybe that's why his boss had shown up.

Thinking of what had happened made me remember something, or really, someone.

Clive.

Had he betrayed Devon yet again? Was that how they had known to lie in wait at Mr. Galler's mansion?

The thought was infuriating, a cold rage filling me that I hadn't felt since the last time I'd seen my stepbrother.

I knew what I'd do. I'd find Clive and make him pay. Somehow. I'd make him hurt for what he'd done and regret throwing away the second chance Devon had given him.

But even with that resolve made, I was still dejected on the drive back to my place.

My place.

It wasn't really, though, and I thought maybe it was time I rectified that and got my own apartment. I couldn't afford something as nice as Logan's, but at least it'd be my own.

I parked my car in the same spot in the lot it'd been in before. The snow was falling in a thick sheet now, and usually that would put me in a good mood, thinking of a white Christmas and all that. But tonight it only increased my sense of loneliness and isolation as I trudged my way to the back door of the apartment building.

I was concentrating on finding the right key for the door when I felt more than heard someone behind me.

Whipping around in fright, I saw a man in a long black coat, the collar turned up to ward off the cold. The snow was too thick to see him properly and my first thought was of Jace. Had he somehow found me?

Groping in my purse for my gun, I jerked it out and pointed it at him. "Stay back! I have a gun and I *will* shoot you!"

He took a step toward me, just enough so the light shining through the glass door at my back fell on him.

Devon.

CHAPTER TWELVE

O h God," I whispered, stunned at seeing him. "You're here. I-I
thought you'd gone . . ."

Devon didn't say anything; he just stepped closer, right up
to me. I tipped my head back to look him in the eye and barely
noticed as he took the gun from my hand and slipped it into the
pocket of his coat.

The corners of his mouth tipped up. "Did you think I'd go
without saying goodbye?"

His hands came up to cradle my face and time slowed as he
bent down and pressed his lips to mine.

The heat of his mouth was a stark contrast to my chilled skin.
I opened my lips and his tongue slipped inside to stroke mine. A
whimper escaped and I twined my arms around his neck, to clutch
at him, not caring where we were or that he hadn't contacted me
all week. I just wanted him. It seemed he felt the same way because
his kisses grew deeper and more urgent, his body pressing mine
against the glass.

Skating his mouth along my cheek, he whispered in my ear, "Give me your keys," and I was ever so happy to obey. There was no way I could do something as complicated as unlock the door to get us inside. At the moment all I could think about was how much I needed to feel his skin against mine.

Somehow he got us into the building. I didn't pay too much attention, clinging to him like a vine. Even when he tore his lips away to focus on unlocking the door, I just fastened my mouth to the skin of his neck and sucked.

Devon got us into the stairwell, my legs hooked around his waist and his hands underneath my butt supporting my weight. He climbed a flight of stairs while I traced the shell of his ear with my tongue.

"I want you," I whispered in his ear.

The words had barely left my mouth before Devon had my back pressed against the wall of the landing and was kissing me again. I didn't care that we were in a stairwell. I needed him, needed him to make me feel whole again.

I squirmed out of his hold and he let my legs drop back to the floor. Once I was standing, I reached for his belt and started tugging.

"Ivy, wait—"

"No," I interrupted. "Now."

Thank God he had on slacks and not jeans; the button was much easier to undo. I hurriedly toed off my boots and Devon's hands were at my hips, pushing down the leggings I wore. It was the matter of a moment to fling them and my underwear aside, then he lifted me again. My ribs gave a sharp protest at the movement, but I pressed my lips together and didn't make a sound.

He pushed inside me in one strong thrust and I gasped at the sensation, a mixture of pleasure and pain. His mouth came down hard on mine, our breath mingling as our tongues dueled and slid hotly together.

The pain became inextricably linked with the erotic pulse of desire and need in my body. Each thrust of his hips sent a stab through me, but I welcomed it. The slick friction of his cock increased the urgency pulsing in my blood.

I tore my mouth from his. "Harder," I begged, needing more.

Devon groaned, burying his face in my neck, his teeth nipping at my skin. He did as I asked, moving harder and faster. The pleasure and pain notched upward until all I could feel was what he was doing to me. Pain was good, burning through my soul. I deserved to feel the pain with the pleasure—they were two sides of the same coin.

I bit the inside of my lip to keep quiet. I had to keep quiet.

Devon's fingers bit into my flesh as he ground hard against me, the pressure making exquisite sensation explode through me, centering between my legs and radiating outward all the way to my neck and toes. It was hard to breathe, my ribs stabbing me like a knife with every expansion of my lungs. The pulsing orgasm of Devon's cock deep inside me was my reward for enduring. My ecstasy was edged with beautiful pain, until I couldn't tell which was which.

"Why are you crying?"

My eyes flew open at Devon's shocked question, momentary panic seizing me. Was he angry? Had I done something wrong?

He was gazing at me, bewildered dismay etched on his face, and I choked in a gasp of air. I'd been holding my breath so I wouldn't make a sound, but tears were streaming down my face. Without the pleasure to take the edge off, the pressure of his body pressed against mine, and my body pressed into the concrete wall at my back, made the pain in my ribs unbearable. A whimper I couldn't keep inside escaped and I tasted blood from where I'd bitten clean through the skin of my lip.

Then everything went dark.

When I came to, I was lying flat on my back on my bed. I went to sit up, gasping at the ache the slight movement produced. I decided lying down was fine for now and relaxed back into my pillow. I was naked under the blanket tucked up underneath my arms.

"You're awake," Devon said, walking into the room. He was carrying a glass of water and had discarded his coat, jacket, and tie. "Excellent. Time for your pain medication."

I shook my head. "No. I don't like how they make me feel."

Devon sat next to me, setting the glass on the bedside table next to a pill bottle. "I found your discharge papers in the kitchen," he said. "Cracked ribs. I know how much those hurt. Why didn't you tell me I was hurting you?"

My face grew hot and I glanced away, unable to look him in the eye. "It wasn't bad."

"Bad enough to make you pass out," he retorted. "I saw the bruises, Ivy. Don't try to hide from me."

"It's fine," I insisted. "You know I liked it." My face grew even warmer. "You felt it."

"Yes, darling," he said with a sigh, his voice gentling. Reaching for me, he brushed his fingers through my hair, caressing my cheek in a soft touch. "I felt you come, but that doesn't tell me why you would let me hurt you. I don't want that."

I shrugged. I couldn't explain it to myself, much less put into words the impossible emotions and twisted thoughts going through my head in those moments in the stairwell. I didn't want to think about or examine them, afraid of what it would say about me.

Logan was right, I thought. Devon's hold on me was utter and absolute. I'd do anything for him, even if it meant my own pain and destruction.

Devon drew the covers down, exposing my body to his gaze. I didn't try to stop him. He owned me now, body and soul, whether he knew it or not—whether he wanted to or not. Despite my embarrassment and mortification at the bruises marring my skin, it didn't occur to me to try to stop him. I was his, to do with as he pleased. Maybe it was love I felt, maybe obsession, perhaps gratitude, or fear that I'd lose him. Whatever it was, it was more powerful than my instinct for self-preservation and I didn't question the why or how—I just accepted it.

Devon's gaze traveled slowly from my face down my black-and-blue torso to my legs, then back up. Reaching out, he gently turned me over onto my stomach. I knew my back looked just as bad, perhaps more so because of the knife imprint branded on my skin.

His fingers lightly brushed the mark and I stiffened, even that gentle touch causing a pang of discomfort from the still-healing wound.

"They marked you," he murmured. "I hadn't realized . . ."

But I didn't mind the permanent scar. It was a battle wound I'd earned protecting Devon, and it reminded me that I had value and worth.

Devon leaned over me, his lips settling just above the brand and pressing a gentle kiss there. His tongue swiped the abused skin and the slight twinge made me sigh, my eyes slipping shut.

He kissed me everywhere, his mouth drifting up to my shoulder, then sliding down to my waist. It felt as though he was kissing my bruises and he was exceedingly gentle. His hands brushed my hair aside, then skated lightly down to my rear. His tongue traced patterns in my skin, dipping into the cleft between my cheeks.

By the time he reached the backs of my thighs, my breath was coming in pants and my hands were fisted in the bedsheets. I wanted to see him, touch him, and tried to turn over, but he stopped me.

"Lie still," he commanded roughly, his warm breath sliding over my sensitized skin.

I obeyed, not moving as he licked and sucked his way to the backs of my knees. My core was pulsing, dripping with need, and I desperately wanted to slide my hand between my legs to ease the ache. But Devon had told me to lie still.

He kissed the inside of my knees as his hands moved to my hips. Carefully, as though I were made of spun glass, he turned me onto my back.

Braced over me, his arms and legs caging me, our gazes met. His eyes burned a cold, icy blue as he stared at me. I couldn't look away from him and couldn't reach for him as I wanted to. I was naked to my soul and I wondered if he could read in my eyes how much I felt for him.

Dipping his head, Devon brushed his lips across my collarbone and my eyes slid shut. He treated my chest the same way he'd treated my back, kissing and licking every mark and bruise. His tongue traced my ribs and delved into my navel. I bit my lip again, the pain on the same spot making tears burn behind my eyelids.

"Don't," Devon whispered against my lips. His kissed my lower lip. "I want to hear you, sweet Ivy."

His words were permission and I gasped when his tongue brushed a nipple, then his mouth closed over the tip and he sucked. I moaned in response, my back arching helplessly toward him. He moved to my other breast, giving it the same treatment, and I couldn't control the loud hiss of my breath.

I whimpered at the loss of his mouth on me, my eyes fluttering open to watch him. He unbuttoned and discarded his shirt, and I saw bruises marked his torso as well. Grasping my wrist, he tugged.

"Come this way," he urged, pulling me toward him as he lay back on the bed. Not understanding what he wanted me to do, I rose to my knees and hesitated.

"Straddle me, sweetheart," he said, tugging again.

I looked in confusion at the pants he still wore, though by the way his slacks tented, he was enjoying this as much as I was.

Devon laughed lightly. "Not there. Here."

He grasped my waist and pulled me over him until one knee was braced on either side of his head. I was shocked at the position and what he wanted me to do. It was too aggressive. Too demanding. Not me at all.

"I-I can't do this," I stammered, my face burning. I tried to squirm away, but Devon's hands settled on my hips, holding me in place.

"Don't tease me," he said, his voice a playful rasp. "You'd give me a glimpse of the paradise between your legs and not let me taste you?" His mouth fastened to my inner thigh and I gasped at the sensation.

"You're beautiful," he said, his lips moving against my skin. "Your pussy is red and plump, begging for me to lick you."

Oh, God, had he just said that? Before I could process my utter embarrassment at his vivid description, he was pressing on my hips, urging me down until his mouth was on me.

His tongue was a slick heat against my body, the position he'd put me in spreading me wide open. His hands held me in place while he devoured me. There was no other word for it. Yes, he'd done this at the hotel, but now it seemed different somehow. As though, like the way he'd kissed all my bruises, he wanted to show me the opposite of the pain I'd endured.

I couldn't keep my eyes open, the pleasure spiking through my body was too much. He teased me, his tongue lapping softly at my clit, then harder and faster, bringing me to the edge and holding me there as his touch gentled. I stopped thinking about how awkward I felt in this position. I stopped thinking at all. Moans and pleas fell from my lips, a gasp when his tongue dipped inside me. I thought I'd die if he didn't let me come, his mouth and tongue tormenting me in the most intimate of ways. I was mindlessly begging for release when his lips fastened around my engorged clit, sucking hard as his tongue slid against the sensitive flesh.

The orgasm was immediate, my body convulsing hard as a ragged scream left my throat. It seemed to go on forever, Devon prolonging the ecstasy until I couldn't take any more.

My body was boneless and trembling with aftershocks as Devon gently lay me down on the bed. I pried open my eyes to see him lying next to me, his head propped on one elbow as he watched me.

I swallowed and cleared my throat, but my voice was still rough when I spoke. "That was . . ." But I had no words. I'd never felt anything so intensely before, and I was still reeling. The ache in the center of my chest only intensified, telling me I felt way more for this man than was wise.

Even while my body still hummed with the glow of a mind-blowing orgasm, I wanted Devon, wanted him inside me. I reached for his belt, but he caught my hand.

"There's no need," he said, threading our fingers together.

I frowned. He was a man, and from what I could see of his erection through his slacks, he definitely had a "need."

"But I want you," I said, frowning in confusion.

"Do you?" he asked. "Or do you just think you should?"

It took me a moment to get it, and I had to marvel at his shrewdness. "Therapy through sex, Devon?" I asked, raising an eyebrow. Making a joke of it made it less uncomfortable that he'd been almost too perceptive of the underlying issues I had with sex.

"Do I look like a therapist?" he deadpanned.

I smiled. "Then finish what you started," I taunted him. "I want you." This time when I reached for his belt, he didn't stop me.

When he was as naked as I was, I stopped and took a minute to admire him. Scars, new and old, decorated his torso, the muscles underneath his warm skin rippling when he moved. His stomach was flat, the indentation between muscles begging for my touch. Narrow hips led to strong thighs and my eyes were drawn to his cock nestled between them. It was thick and hard, jutting out from his body in a way that made me weak in the knees with desire. His length would have been intimidating if I hadn't already known how well we fit.

I didn't think at all, I just settled over him as though I'd done this dozens of times before. I was wet from my own juices plus Devon's mouth, so it was easy to slide his cock inside me. The twinge of my body as it expanded to accommodate him was familiar in a way that was comforting to me.

Bracing my hands on his chest, I lifted, letting him slide almost all the way out before lowering and taking him inside again. We both groaned. The wet friction against my clit made me suck in a breath, and gave me incentive to repeat my actions.

It felt freeing, to be the one to set the pace. I concentrated on achieving that peak of pleasure again, moving faster on Devon. His hands were on my hips, holding on or guiding me, I couldn't tell and didn't care.

"That's right," he encouraged through gritted teeth. "Get yourself off. Faster, luv."

My thighs were trembling with the effort, our bodies slick with sweat, when Devon took over. His fingers pressed into my hips to hold me still, his body thrusting hard up into mine. So fast, the pounding against my clit was too much and I cried out as I came. A split second into my orgasm, Devon let out a shout, pulling me down hard on him as he thrust upward. The pulsing of his cock inside me matched the ripples of pleasure centered where we were joined and lights exploded behind my closed eyes.

My body was a limp rag doll as I crumpled to lie against his heaving chest, our bodies still connected. Sweat dotted my brow, but I didn't care. I could no longer feel any pain from my body, the endorphins from two incredible orgasms driving the discomfort away.

I would have been happy to just roll over and go to sleep, but Devon had other ideas. I mewled in disappointment when he slid out of me and rolled me onto my back, then disappeared into the bathroom. A moment later, I heard the tub filling.

The wet stickiness between my thighs made me smile. I was marked by him. Despite the tenuousness of our relationship, we were bound by blood and sex. An irrational part of me didn't want to wash away the evidence of him on me, inside me. But I didn't protest when he returned, lifted me in his arms, and carried me to the steaming bathwater.

⌒◡⌒

"Where's Logan?" Devon asked.

It was morning, and dusky sunlight filtered through heavy cloud cover to lighten the bedroom. I'd slept the sleep of the dead, curled in Devon's arms.

"Mmmm," I said, stretching out the kinks in my body. I arched my back and Devon took the opportunity to skate a hand up my side to cup my breast. "He's out of town with a friend, skiing." If I could have, I would have purred at his touch.

"How did you meet him?"

It took a moment for my sleepy brain to focus on the question. "We've been friends for a long time," I said. "Since we were children." I left out the part where Logan used to be my refuge after a visit from Jace.

"A man and woman living together, just as friends. You don't see it very often," Devon mused.

I shrugged. "It works for us." Devon's fingers were working their magic again, brushing my nipples in a teasing seduction that made it hard to concentrate on the conversation.

"Does it?" he asked.

But I wasn't paying much attention. "If you don't stop that, we're never going to get out of this bed," I complained.

Devon suddenly flipped me onto my back, pinning my arms above my head as he crouched over me.

"And you have a problem with that?" he asked.

The lust in his eyes made my heart skip a beat and my mouth go dry even as a warm rush of heat flooded the flesh between my thighs.

"Not really," I breathed, my gaze dropping to his mouth.

Which was why it was another half hour or more before I did finally climb out of bed.

It was Saturday, and thanks to Devon, I was feeling pretty darn good. Not only physically, but it made me happier than I wanted to think about, having him here with me.

I dressed in a pair of jeans and a black, oversized, thin cotton shirt with long sleeves. Not bothering with a bra, I brushed my hair until it shone a pure white gold and hung perfectly straight down my back. Devon had dressed as well and was in the kitchen when I emerged from the bedroom.

"What do you eat?" he asked, surveying the contents of the refrigerator. "There's nothing in your icebox."

"We eat out a lot," I said. "Or Logan cooks. When he's out of town, I order takeout." Cooking wasn't my thing. Granted, I liked to eat—who didn't?—but cooking bored me. Combined with my penchant for spending too much money on clothes plus my distaste of generally all things domestic . . . well, let's just say that someday I'd make a terrible wife.

"You don't cook?" he asked.

I wrinkled my nose and gave a small shake of my head. "But I can rock a pair of skinny jeans and four-inch heels like nobody's business," I said, poking him lightly in the chest.

"I'll bet you can," he said, his lips tipping upward in the hint of a smile.

"Want to go out?" I asked. "Or we can order pizza or something." Even as I said it, though, Devon didn't strike me as a pizza kind of guy, so I wasn't surprised when he was shaking his head before the words were even out of my mouth.

"Put your heels on," he said. "I'll buy you dinner."

No need to tell me twice. I dug out a favorite pair of nude platforms that were perfectly conservative, until you saw the wickedly tall and sharp stiletto heel. Before long, I was walking those heels into another very nice, and very expensive, restaurant. The maître d' took our coats and I felt the warmth of Devon's hand on the small of my back as we followed him to a table.

Devon sat across from me, his back to the wall, and once the waiter had come by to get our drink order, he settled back in his chair. His gaze rested on me, a smile playing about his mouth.

I looked at him as I opened the menu, my brow creasing in a frown as I smiled tentatively back. "What?" I asked. "Why are you looking at me like that?"

"Like what?" he asked innocently.

I rolled my eyes. "Like that."

Resting his elbows on the table, he leaned forward as though he were going to tell me a secret. "I like to watch you," he said.

Okay, that was an odd thing to say. "What do you mean?"

"The way you carry yourself. The way you walk," he said. "It's what first drew my eye. You're beautiful, and you know it. You carry yourself with confidence and have a charisma about you. It's . . . mesmerizing. Intoxicating." He reached for my hand with both of his, lifting my arm to press his lips to my palm, then my wrist. "Addicting." The brush of his lips and breath made my pulse speed up.

It felt as though the air had been frozen in my lungs and I couldn't think what to say. I'd always been pretty, but it was something I'd just dealt with and taken for granted. It was the way I'd been born, like being left-handed or tone-deaf.

Devon released me and I could breathe again, my skin tingled from where he'd touched me. I struggled to get my bearings, though the gleam in his eyes said he knew exactly what he could do to me.

"So are you really leaving town?" I asked once the waiter had brought and uncorked a bottle of wine. Devon had again ordered for me.

He nodded. "The man I'm looking for, the one who trapped us, has what he's after or is very close to it. I intend to stop him."

My gaze dropped and I took a sip of the red wine. He was leaving. And just like that, my good mood was gone.

"Do you . . . need any company?" Maybe he'd take me with him?

"I nearly got you killed," Devon said, "and I still don't know why they let us go. Taking you with me would be a mistake."

"Do you think you'll be back?" I asked, taking a different tack and carefully making my voice as nonchalant as possible. I studied my fingers playing with the stem of my wineglass to avoid looking him in the eye.

"Ivy."

I didn't look up.

"Ivy," he repeated. The tone of his voice was such that I had to obey and reluctantly lifted my gaze to meet his. "I'm afraid not," he said gently.

I felt that blow down to my bones, like a sucker punch out of nowhere. I gave a jerky nod.

"Of course not," I mumbled. "Why would you?" I took a large gulp of wine.

"You don't like me, remember?" he said, a teasing note in his voice that told me he was trying to make things a little easier on me.

Pride came to my defense. I had not, nor would I ever, cry and moon over a man who didn't want me.

"It's fine," I said a little too brightly. "Let's just have dinner, shall we?"

Our food arrived, but I barely tasted anything and only picked at it. Somehow I didn't feel much like making small talk.

"So your boss is a lady," I said after a while. "Vega is her name?" That last part was a guess. She hadn't introduced herself to me at the hospital, but that was the name Clive had said.

Devon's gaze met mine as he took a bite of beef from the tines of his fork. He chewed while I waited, then he took a sip of wine before answering.

"Why would you say that?" he asked.

"Because she came to see me."

My blunt response must have taken him off guard because his eyebrows lifted ever so slightly. A major reaction, coming from him.

Setting aside his napkin, he nodded at the waiter, who removed the empty plate. Resting his elbows on the table, his hands steepled beneath his chin, he asked, "And when was this?"

"While I was in the hospital," I answered. "She seemed very concerned that I'd said something I shouldn't, or that perhaps you had."

"How long was she there?"

"Not long." I frowned, just then realizing something. "Was she not supposed to know about me?"

Devon shrugged. "It doesn't really matter."

Those words reverberated inside my head. *It doesn't really matter.* In other words, I didn't really matter, because I wouldn't be in the picture for long.

What the hell was I doing? Putting life and limb in jeopardy, alienating my best friend, all for a man who was good in bed? I must've lost my mind. Sweet Jesus, I was nothing but a vagina on legs to him, whereas he had become my whole world. Would I fall apart without him?

I was up and out of my chair in an instant, grabbed my coat in the next, and was out the door. The cold hit me like a slap in the face and I shrugged on my coat while I hurried down the sidewalk.

"So stupid," I muttered to myself, jerking the heavy wool closer to my body. There were a few people on the sidewalk, some going the same direction I was and some the opposite way. I avoided them all.

"Ivy, wait!"

I heard Devon's voice, but just walked faster, hoping to lose myself among the people, but there just weren't enough to hide me.

In a way, I was surprised he'd come after me. If I meant so little to him, what did it matter who owned the vagina he put his dick in?

"Ivy!"

His voice was closer and I still ignored him, my heels *click-clacking* on the sidewalk that someone had thoughtfully cleared of snow.

Devon's hand gripped my upper arm, yanking me to a halt before spinning me around to face him.

"Don't just walk away from me," he said, his tone dangerously even. "We're not through, you and I."

"Oh yes we are," I retorted, trying unsuccessfully to pull my arm away. "You don't give a shit about me. Find some other girl to fuck, Devon."

Grabbing my other arm, he jerked me close, our bodies colliding. I tipped my head backward to look at him, anger giving me courage against the ice in his eyes. Gritting my teeth, I struggled in his hold, but it was useless. In seconds, he had me pinned against a wall.

"But I don't want to fuck another girl," he said, his lips by my ear. "I want to fuck you."

The words slithered into my ear and I shivered at the warmth of his breath. My body was already betraying me, my breasts full and nipples hardened into sensitive peaks, waiting for his touch. The flesh between my legs began to throb.

"You're as addicted as I am," Devon whispered, his hands moving from my arms to slip inside my unbuttoned coat. "You crave my touch the way I can't stop thinking about the way you taste, how soft your skin is against mine, and how it feels when I'm inside you."

The words eased my battered pride and I didn't stop him when he undid the button of my jeans and lowered the zipper.

"The chase, the fight—it makes you damn near irresistible to me. And you want this—you want me—too much to care about your bruised ego," Devon said, slipping his hand inside my jeans and underneath the silk panties I wore. "I'd wager you want me so much that you'd stand here on the street with me and let me finger you, wouldn't you, darling."

Words were beyond me now. His hand had insinuated itself between my thighs, his middle finger sliding between my folds to stroke me. I was wet and ready for him.

"There's a girl," he sighed. "Spread your legs, sweet Ivy."

I couldn't have disobeyed even if I'd wanted to, and when I opened farther to him, my reward was his finger slipping inside me. I clutched at the lapels of his coat, its voluminous folds shrouding our embrace.

"You'll do what I say because this," he slowly pumped his finger, sliding over my clit in smooth strokes, "is very, very good, isn't it, Ivy."

It wasn't a question and I didn't try to answer. I closed my eyes and concentrated on his touch and the sound of his low voice whispering in my ear. His touch was sure, knowing. We could have had an audience of a hundred people and I wouldn't have cared.

His hand moved faster, making my breath come in pants.

"Oh God," I breathed. "Devon . . ."

He kissed his name from my mouth and I eagerly opened my lips, letting him deepen the kiss into a warm, slow slide of his tongue against mine.

His finger curved, pressing inside me, and I came apart. Devon swallowed my cries, moaning slightly as my body convulsed around his finger, still buried inside me. I turned away, gasping for air, and his mouth again settled by my ear.

"What you do to me," he murmured. "I should leave you far, far behind, sweet Ivy."

My knees were weak and I didn't try to move away as he took his hand from my body and fastened my jeans. I leaned into him, his hands sliding underneath my shirt to cup my breasts, his palms a rough friction against my nipples.

Opening heavy-lidded eyes, I could just see beyond him to the darkened sidewalk and street. What few people had been around had mostly cleared, and my gaze settled on a shadow across the street. I watched as the figure stood very still, and I realized he was watching us.

Devon had slipped his hands from my shirt and was now fastening my coat, but I was still staring at the man across the street. Something about him looked familiar . . .

"Devon—" I began as a car drove by. The flash of headlights briefly illuminated the man's face . . . and I screamed.

Faster than I would have believed possible, Devon had spun around, pushed me behind him, and drawn his gun.

But the man was gone.

I couldn't breathe. Air inflated my lungs, but I couldn't breathe. I couldn't possibly have— No. It was impossible.

"Ivy! Ivy, what's wrong?"

I couldn't feel my hands or feet, and I just couldn't breathe. Devon's arm was a steel band around me supporting me, his face anxious as he studied me.

"Talk to me," he said evenly. "Breathe, Ivy. You're all right. Just tell me what you saw."

My lips were numb as I forced them to move.

"Jace."

CHAPTER THIRTEEN

I didn't remember the trip back to the apartment. I barely remembered Devon helping me inside or sitting on the couch. I stared into space, my hands ice-cold, and tried to come to grips with Jace having found me. Devon disappeared into my bedroom, but I didn't ask what he was doing. Instead, I grabbed my phone and hit speed dial, letting out a relieved breath when Grams picked up.

"Hi," I said, suddenly realizing I had no good excuse for calling this late on a Saturday night. "I was just, um, thinking about you. How are you?"

"Oh, we're fine, sweetie," Grams said. "Your grandpa spent this afternoon chopping some firewood with the neighbor." She went on, as I knew she would, telling me about all they'd done that day and how Grandpa had run to the store to get some more birdseed. "My birds just expect to be fed now when there's snow on the ground," she said, "even with the barn cats hanging around."

"Um, have you heard from or seen . . . Jace around?" I asked.

"Not a peep," she replied. "The police have some posters up at the QuikTrip and Kroger, but he hasn't come by here."

My eyes slid shut. Thank God. I couldn't handle Jace doing something to my grandparents. Though they were in their seventies, I wouldn't put anything past him.

"Now you're coming home for Christmas, aren't you?" Grams continued.

Oh no. Christmas. If Jace had followed me here, somehow, would he follow me home? No way was I leading trouble back to Grams and Grandpa.

"Um, actually, I've had something come up," I said, improvising on the spot. "A friend asked me to travel with them for a few days, so I think I'm going to go."

"Oh? Where are you going?"

I said the first thing that came to mind. "Florida."

"That'll be nice and warm down there," Grams said. "We'll miss you, but I think it'll be good for you to get away, take a vacation. Is Logan going with you?"

"No, he's not."

"Well, just be careful," she admonished. "Two girls alone isn't very safe. Don't go out at night."

I smiled ruefully, wishing I didn't have to lie to her. I'd be barricaded inside my apartment come Christmas. Even now, I was terrified to step foot outside my door.

"I will," I promised. After another round of warnings and I-love-yous, I ended the call.

I stared at my phone. The urge to call Logan was strong. But it wouldn't be fair to him. He was on vacation two states away. What could he do about Jace?

"What are you thinking?"

I looked up to see Devon staring down at me.

"Of how much I want to call Logan," I answered honestly.

"Why?"

I shrugged. "He's always been there for me, been the one I turned to when I had no one else."

"Because of Jace?"

I nodded.

Devon sat next to me on the couch. "I'll protect you," he said.

I grimaced. "You're leaving, remember?"

"I'll only be gone for a day. You'll stay at my place while I'm gone."

I glanced at him in surprise. "What?"

"I can't leave you here, not with your stepbrother mucking about."

That's when I saw the suitcase behind him. "Did you . . . pack for me?"

"Yes. It's time to go."

A moment of clarity hit me then, the kind where you see a fraction of time as a turning point—a fork in the road. I could stay here, alone, and await whatever Jace was planning. Or I could go with Devon, a man who made me feel more alive than I ever had before, though he was dangerous and being with him took a toll on my physical and emotional well-being.

It was perhaps a little mortifying how quickly I chose.

"Okay," I agreed.

Devon held out his hand and I took it.

⤳

We were outside Devon's apartment door and he was unlocking it when the door across the hallway popped open.

"Hi, again!" Beau said cheerfully. "Looks like you found him."

"Um, yeah," I said, heat rising in my cheeks. Devon glanced at me, raising his brows in silent question.

"Good evening, Beau," Devon said cordially. "I take it you've met Ivy?"

"Not formally," Beau said, thrusting out a hand, which I shook.

"Beau is a salesman of sorts," Devon said, his lips twisting slightly. "What's the business this month, Beau?"

"Time-shares, my man," Beau said with a grin. "I have a great place in the Bahamas that's got your name written all over it."

Devon laughed outright. "I'll bet you do." He ushered me into the apartment as Beau tried again.

"I can get you a great deal!" he called out.

"Good night, Beau," Devon said, closing the door behind him. He leaned his back against it and looked at me.

"He's . . . ah . . . interesting," I offered.

"Beau is a used car salesman who sells everything except used cars," Devon replied dryly. "Don't ever buy anything from him. He will completely screw you over."

I laughed. "Sounds like you speak from experience," I teased.

He grimaced. "I prefer not to talk about it. And considering my reaction to our . . . transaction, I'm surprised he'd try to sell me anything again."

I was, too.

"So you came looking for me last night?" he asked.

"You didn't come to the hospital," I said, deciding not to tell him I'd known he was there. "I-I wanted to see you. I hoped you'd want to see me, too."

I couldn't read the expression on his face as I laid bare my desire to be with him. I didn't tell him how he'd been consuming my thoughts for days or how I felt lost without him.

Picking up my suitcase, Devon took it to the bedroom. Not sure what else to do, I followed.

"How long have you lived here?" I asked, breaking the nearly awkward silence. I glanced around again at the impersonal room. Comfortable and well appointed, yes, but that was all.

"A few months," he replied, glancing at his watch. "You'll be all right here alone?"

"Of course," I said, patting my purse. "I'm packing heat, remember?"

"How could I forget?" he quipped, approaching me. Carefully removing my purse strap from my shoulder, he set it aside. "You'll be safe here. I'll be back Monday night. Keys are on the kitchen counter."

"It might not have been Jace I saw," I admitted. "Maybe it was just someone who looked like him." I hoped that was true. It gave me a chill to think Jace might've tracked me so quickly.

"Maybe," Devon said, his hands resting on my hips. "When does Logan return?"

The way he said Logan's name gave me pause. There was a slight hint of disdain or maybe contempt, but so nearly indiscernible, I decided I must have imagined it.

"Tomorrow night. He has to work on Monday. I can go back home then." I was amazed as it was that Devon wanted me to stay in his apartment. That seemed a line not normally crossed for him, and it was hard not to be pleased at this development, even if the cause for it was Jace.

"You'll stay here until I return," Devon said, his tone final.

My eyes widened. "Why? Once Logan's home—"

"I really don't want to hear his name anymore," Devon interrupted with a sigh.

"But—"

His mouth landed on mine, cutting off my protest.

I forgot everything I was going to say and melted into him, my body molding to his. His hands moved to my rear, pulling me closer, and I could feel the hard length of his erection at the juncture of my thighs. His kiss was deep and slow, the soft brush of his tongue against mine making my toes curl.

"I have to go," he murmured against my lips.

I made a mewling sound of protest as he unwound my arms from around his neck.

"Will it be dangerous?" I asked, gazing up at him. I was worried, even though I knew he didn't want to hear it.

His smile was crooked. "No more so than usual."

Not exactly comforting.

Devon pressed his lips to my forehead, then he was gone.

Somewhat at a loss, I glanced around the bedroom. My suitcase was sitting by the bed, dutifully waiting for me to unpack it, and yet I decided to explore.

The closet was a huge walk-in and Devon's clothes were carefully arranged and grouped by type and color. It was incredibly precise and I remembered him telling me that he'd served in the military. I guessed old habits die hard.

I poked around more than was decent for a guest, but found nothing interesting. I thought maybe I'd run across the pendant Mr. Galler had given me, but it was nowhere to be found.

It was strange, being in Devon's apartment without him. Yet, it made me feel closer to him. I fell asleep in his bed with the scent of him clinging to the pillow underneath my cheek.

◠◡

My cell phone woke me Sunday morning and I blindly groped for it on the bedside table.

"Mmm 'lo?" I mumbled into the phone.

"Miss Mason?" The voice on the other end was businesslike and I pried open my eyes.

"Yes?"

"This is Special Agent Lane," the man said. "We met at your work regarding the death of Mr. Galler?"

Okay, now I was wide-awake. I sat up, clutching the phone to my ear.

"I remember."

"I'd like you to come meet with me, answer a few more questions."

My palms were sweating now. "Um, okay."

"Can you come this morning?"

"Sure. I-I'll come as soon as I can," I stammered.

"Thank you." He gave me an address, which I scrambled to jot down, then he ended the call.

I sat in panicked befuddlement, staring at the wall as I tried to figure out what he could possibly want from me. I desperately wanted to talk to Devon, but I had no way of reaching him.

It didn't take long for me to get up and dress. Devon had been thorough in packing for me and I pulled on a pair of skinny jeans and a long-sleeved shirt that I threw a black jacket over. My coat went on over that and I added my tall black boots. I may not have known what awaited me, but it never hurt to look fabulous.

There was a note on the kitchen counter next to a set of keys.

Try not to scratch the car.
−D

I grinned, practically hearing the dry phrase uttered inside my head. Nice. He'd left me his car keys, and apparently had very little faith in my driving ability.

I'd never driven a Porsche in my life and it made me nervous to drive one now, but I realized I could get used to driving a luxury sports car pretty darn quick. I really should have been born into royalty.

The sun was blinding off the snow and I was glad of my oversized sunglasses as I found the address. I pulled up to a guard booth in front of a four-story building surrounded by a black iron fence. I told the serious-looking man in uniform my name and who I was there to see. He took my ID, scrutinizing it carefully and checking a clipboard before allowing me through. I parked the car and went inside.

I passed two guys coming out, one of them holding the door for me, and both paused in their conversation, turning to stare as I walked by.

"I'm looking for Agent Lane," I told the woman behind the reception window.

A few minutes later, the agent was striding toward me. I jumped to my feet from where I'd been waiting in an orange vinyl chair. I combed my fingers nervously through my hair, brushing it back from my face. I saw Agent Lane's dark gaze follow the movement, his Adam's apple bobbing up and down as he swallowed. He was taller than me, his hair a deep chestnut that fell in waves over his forehead.

"Miss Mason, thank you for coming," he said. I noticed he was much more polite this time than when I'd first met him at the bank. "Please, come with me."

I followed him through a door and between a maze of desks. Though it was a Sunday, there were plenty of people working and some glanced up as we walked by. Finally, we reached what I supposed was his desk. He motioned me to the chair next to it while he took the one behind it.

Lane was an attractive guy, his jaw lightly shadowed with stubble that gave him an appealingly unkempt look. His shirt was wrinkled in a way that said he was a bachelor who couldn't be bothered with an iron, and a cheap tie was knotted loosely around his neck.

His shoulder holster held his gun, which gleamed from the care and attention he reserved for it alone.

Taking off my sunglasses, I slid them into my purse. "So why did you want to see me?" I asked, crossing one leg over the other.

"I hear you were mugged last weekend," Lane replied instead.

I shrugged, glancing away from his penetrating gaze. "It's the city. It happens."

"You didn't report it," he persisted, making me wonder how he'd known. The hospital maybe?

"I just want to forget it," I said.

"The man who was with you when you were . . . mugged," he said. The way he said "mugged" made me think he didn't believe a word of our story. "You know he didn't give a name to the hospital. Paid his bill in cash and walked out. Did you know him?"

"He's a . . . friend," I said, not sure what else to call him and wary of why the agent was asking about Devon.

Lane looked at me for a moment longer, then reached for a manila file folder on his desk. Opening it, he turned it around to face me. "Is this your friend?"

It was Devon, but the shot was a candid one and looked like it had been taken at a distance, the quality grainy.

Hesitantly, I nodded. "Why do you want to know?"

"We found your fingerprints, and an unknown set, at Mr. Galler's residence," Lane said. "The unknown prints didn't match your friend's, but running his through our system brought up some . . . interesting information."

I swallowed but remained silent.

"Miss Mason," Lane said with a sigh, "I think you've gotten mixed up with some bad people, in particular, this man." He tapped the photo of Devon for emphasis. "How did you meet him?"

Thinking quickly, I said, "He was there when the bank was robbed. He helped apprehend the robbers."

"He didn't apprehend them, Miss Mason," Lane said flatly. "He killed them."

The reminder chilled me and I lashed out. "If you think he's so dangerous, why didn't you arrest him then?" I snapped.

"We weren't allowed to," he said.

I frowned. "What do you mean you 'weren't allowed to?'"

Lane sat back in his chair, crossing his arms over his broad chest. "Your friend must have friends of his own in high places. One phone call was all it took and word came down he was to be released with no further questioning." He leaned forward again. "But I think he's in this up to his neck, Miss Mason, and I think you know that."

There was no way for me to answer that without incriminating either Devon or myself, so I stayed silent.

"Law enforcement is a small world," Lane said. "No matter what agency we work for, we're all on the same side. So I did some digging, and your friend has turned up in a few other places." Taking a stack from the file, he began flipping through the papers.

"Sri Lanka, five years ago, seven men dead." He placed a piece of paper in front of me, then photos. I blanched at the sight of several bodies. "Amsterdam, three years ago, thirteen dead." Another sheet. More pictures. "Beirut, right after Amsterdam, nearly an entire village was wiped out." More sheets and this time the pictures were of burned-out homes in the desert. "Stockholm, two years ago, ten dead, two of them women." A photo of a beautiful woman, her eyes vacant beneath a bullet hole in the center of her forehead.

The words fell on my ears, but I barely comprehended. My stomach churned with nausea. I'd known, in a visceral, dreamlike way, that Devon hadn't been lying when he'd told me what he did for a living, but to have it handed to me, in cold black and white, all the murder and mayhem that he wreaked around the globe . . . it was too much to take in.

"Interpol sent me these earlier," Lane said, flipping through the file to another picture of Devon, this time at airport security. "Looks like he left the country late last night, headed for London."

I waited, sure there'd be a question.

"Any idea when he'll be back to the States? *If* he'll be back?"

I shook my head, my lips pressed tightly closed. Lane stared at me.

"The mugging was pretty brutal," he said, suddenly changing the subject. "I hear you were bruised up pretty bad, even a couple cracked ribs." Reaching forward, his fingers tipped my chin up, turning my cheek toward the light streaming in from the window. "Hard to cover completely with makeup."

I jerked away from his touch. "Excuse me," I snapped, "but what's your point?"

Lane's eyes narrowed. "My point is that your friend leaves a trail of dead bodies in his wake without so much as a flicker of remorse. Now I don't know who he is or who he works for, but I believe your involvement with him is not only a severe threat to your life, but also may not be . . . consensual." He rested his elbows on the desk and leaned forward.

"Miss Mason, I want to help you," he said, his voice gentling. "I think you *need* my help. You're a beautiful, innocent young woman who somehow became involved with a man who may get you killed . . . if he doesn't kill you himself."

I stared at him, eyes wide, and hesitated, indecision and fear now creeping into my mind. Lane was a good guy, trying to do the right thing and help someone who he saw as a damsel in distress. Was that me? Would I be the body Lane identified in a few days or weeks, his words a prophecy of what was to come if I stayed involved with Devon?

"Please," he said, laying a hand atop mine. His palm was warm and calloused. A hardworking man's hand. Lane sensed the conflict within me. "Let me help you."

I remembered all the people Devon had killed, the men who'd held me captive and made me scream. I shuddered to think of that happening again, but what choice did I have? And Lane didn't even know the half of what I couldn't tell.

"I'm scared," I whispered, the words falling out of my mouth. It was almost a relief to say it, to admit my fear. "But I can't get out. I just . . . I can't. You don't understand." Tears stung my eyes and I grabbed my purse, jumping to my feet.

"Wait! Miss Mason!" Lane called, but I was already rushing through the maze of desks and out the door. I didn't stop until I was back in the Porsche.

I started the car but didn't leave. I just sat, hands on the wheel as I tried to think what to do. Tears trickled down my cheeks but I barely noticed.

Not only was I in this too deep to get out, I felt too much for Devon to have the willpower to leave. It was a demoralizing realization. Would I really gamble my life for a man I was obsessed with, maybe in love with, whose only tie to me was his desire to have sex with me?

A knocking on the window startled me. I looked up to see Agent Lane standing there. Cautiously, I rolled down the window.

"Take this," he said, his gaze pained as he took in my tear-stained face. "In case you change your mind. My cell is on the back." He held a white business card between two fingers. I took it.

"Thank you," I managed to say, before rolling up the window and backing out the car.

Glancing in my rearview mirror, I saw Lane standing there watching me until I was out of sight.

❧

Logan called me late that night.

"Hey, Ives, how're you feeling?" he asked.

"Good. I'm feeling good," I said. "How was your trip?"

"Fantastic!" he enthused. "Met a couple of snow bunnies that kept us warm, didn't break anything, so all in all, a successful trip."

I smiled, shaking my head at him. That was typical Logan.

"I should be home within an hour or so," he said, "but don't wait up."

Shit. "Um, yeah, I'm not at home," I said. "I'm, um, staying with a friend for a few days." I winced at the white lie.

Except I never could get a lie past Logan, and his silence was telling.

"Why would you do that?" he asked. Gone was the lightness in his voice.

"I, um, well, I think I might've seen . . . Jace."

"What? Are you kidding me? Are you all right?" His frantic questions came one after the other.

"I'm fine," I hurried to reassure him. "It might not have been him at all, but I thought it might be wise to stay somewhere else for a few days."

"Well, I'm back now so you can come home tomorrow," he said. "No one's going to hurt you while I'm around."

His sweet protectiveness made my chest hurt, which made it even harder to say what I had to say. "Actually, I think I'm going to stay here for a few days longer."

A long pause. "You're with Devon, aren't you."

I didn't answer. I didn't need to. It hadn't been a question.

Logan let loose a string of curses and I flinched.

"Logan, please—" I began.

"He put you in the hospital, Ivy," he said, cutting me off. "And don't give me that story about being mugged—I know that's bullshit."

"Logan," I tried again, "it's just for a few days—"

"Until what?" he broke in. "Until I get another call that you're in the hospital again? Or the morgue?" He let loose a heavy sigh.

"God, Ives, please just listen to me. I'm begging you. Come home. Forget about that guy. He's such bad news for you. Please, Ives."

Logan was the second person that day to tell me I was in over my head with Devon. The second man who thought he knew what was best for me, who would take my choice away without even attempting to understand what I was feeling and without knowing the circumstances that tied me to Devon. And my temper snapped.

"Last I checked, Logan, I wasn't still twelve years old. And while I appreciate your concern, I think it's really crappy of you to have so little faith in my ability to make decisions for myself. I already know you think I'm 'damaged.' Must you add insult to injury?"

"Ives, I didn't mean—"

"Save it. I know all too well what you meant. I'll talk to you later, Logan." I ended the call.

I was angry and upset, combined with worried and afraid, which made it really hard to get to sleep.

☙

Work the next morning seemed surreal. After all that had happened in the past couple of weeks, the normal pace and tasks of my job were strange to settle back into. Marcia wanted to know about the mugging, and I got away with not saying a whole lot by telling her I didn't really remember. My boss, Mr. Malloy, was kind and solicitous—I think he realized that between Mr. Galler's death, the attempted robbery, then a mugging, I'd had a rough time of it lately. It was midafternoon when he approached me.

"The estate attorney for Mr. Galler requested the contents of his safe deposit box," he said. "Would you mind boxing up the contents? They're sending a security guard to pick it up here shortly."

"Yeah, sure," I said, taking the dual set of keys he handed me.

I headed down to the safe deposit box area and unlocked the

cage. The keys he'd given me were the set I'd had the day of the robbery along with an additional set—customer override keys. They were only to be used in situations like this, and I was glad I hadn't known where they were kept. If they'd kept using me as a punching bag that day, I was sure I'd have given in to their demands.

My curiosity about what was in the box was raging as I scanned the numbers, finally settling on box 928. The two keys went in and the box slid out of its chamber.

I'd brought a cardboard bank box with me to place the items into and I'd set it on the table in the privacy room adjacent to the cage. Moving aside the heavy curtain that separated the room from any prying eyes—electronic or human—I rested the safe deposit box next to it. I raised the lid with anticipation.

To my disappointment, only a stack of papers and an envelope of photographs were in the box. I glanced through the photographs as I transferred them. They were old photos, mainly black and white, of various people who seemed to have no bearing on one another. No one face was recurring the way you'd see in a box of family photos.

"The security guard is here," Mr. Malloy called out, poking his head down the stairwell.

"Nearly finished," I called back.

I was hurrying to put the papers into the box when a small, leather-bound notebook slipped from the stack and landed at my feet. Finishing the transfer of the papers, I leaned down to pick it up, and froze.

The emblem on the cover was the exact match for what had been on the pendant Mr. Galler had given me.

I hesitated, my pulse skyrocketing. Grabbing the notebook, I quickly stuffed it down the back of my slacks. The jacket I wore covered it up and I stood, replacing the safe deposit box, and adding the lid to the bank box before carrying it upstairs.

"Here you go," I said with a fake smile, handing it to the serious-looking security guard waiting in the lobby. Mr. Malloy was there and had me sign a form that he signed as well. My palms were sweating and the pen was slippery in my grip. I was terrified they'd both realize what I'd done.

I gave Mr. Malloy the keys and then hurried back to my booth. I slid the notebook into my purse and tried not to think about how many laws I was breaking. I justified it by telling myself that Mr. Galler had gotten me into this mess and he was dead. I had to do what I could to make sure I didn't end up the same.

The rest of the day passed as a blur, my only thought was on getting home and taking a look inside the notebook. Though the definition of my "home" was nebulous since I was staying at Devon's and I hadn't talked to Logan since our argument.

I clocked out and waved goodbye to Marcia, then went out the back way to where I'd parked the Porsche. My phone chirped and I dug it out of my purse. Logan had texted me.

I can't stand not talking to you. Give me a chance to grovel over dinner?

I smiled a little, my irritation at him melting away. I texted back, walking slowly across the parking lot.

No need for groveling. We had a fight. It happens.

It only took a few seconds for his reply to come through.

You know it's just b/c I love you.

My heart ached. I was glad Logan had texted. Though an unapologetic player, he was a softie on the inside.

I know. Love you too. Dinner tomorrow?

It's a date.

I was texting back a reply when someone stepped in front of me. Stumbling back, I jerked my head up to say *Excuse me* but the words died on my tongue.

"Miss me, brat?"

CHAPTER
FOURTEEN

My phone clattered to the ground as I dug inside my purse for my gun, but then Jace had me by the throat.

"I've been thinking about you for ten long years," he hissed. "I reckon that tight little pussy of yours is just begging for old Jace."

Prison had changed him, his hair now cut so short you could see his scalp through it and a long jagged scar marked his cheek. But his eyes . . . his eyes were exactly the same. Cold and without a shred of humanity in them.

"Let me go," I gritted out, trying fruitlessly to pry his hand from my neck.

"You and me are going to get reacquainted," he said, his grip tightening.

I couldn't breathe and spots started to crowd my vision, my fingers scrabbling uselessly at his arm.

"I've had a long time to think about how I'm going to make you pay," Jace continued, his face so close to mine I could feel the fetid heat of his breath. "I'm going to make you bleed, brat. You'll be sorry you ever turned your back on me."

Dragging me by the throat, he pushed me up against an SUV in the lot.

"Feel that?" he hissed, pressing his hips against me. "My dick's aching for your sweet cunt, just like we used to, brat."

My arms hung limply at my sides, Jace's hand around my neck the only thing keeping me on my feet. Everything started to go black.

"Freeze! FBI! Let the girl go!"

I vaguely saw Jace turn around, then suddenly I was free. A shot rang out and I heard the sound of breaking glass as I collapsed to the asphalt, sucking in clean, wonderful air. I didn't have the strength to move, even though I could tell I'd landed in a puddle of slush, the icy cold water seeping through my clothes.

"Ivy! Are you all right? Ivy!"

A man skidded to a halt next to me, dropping down to his knees. I pried open my eyes, shocked to see it was Agent Lane.

He helped me onto my back, one arm supporting my shoulders while his hand pushed back the hair from my face. "Talk to me," he said anxiously. "Are you okay?"

I swallowed, an action I immediately regretted as a flash of pain went through me. "I'm fine," I said, my voice hoarse. I coughed, which burned my abused throat.

"Who was that guy?" Lane asked. "Did you know him?"

I nodded, struggling to sit up. Tears leaked from the corners of my eyes and my hands shook as I tried to gather my purse and phone. Dropping it had shattered the glass screen.

"He's my stepbrother," I said. "He's out on parole. Where'd he go?"

"I fired a warning shot, but he ran off and I stopped to help you. What's his name? I can get an APB put out on him."

"Jace Croughton," I answered.

"Take it easy," Lane said, helping me struggle to my feet. My knees felt as though they were made of rubber, wanting to immediately fold and dump me back on the ground.

Shoving my phone into my purse, I dug out Devon's keys. "Thank you," I said to Lane. "I don't know what I would have done if you hadn't been here."

He smiled a little. "Yeah, let's focus on that and not how I was following you, 'kay?"

My smile was wan. I didn't care why he'd been there, just that he'd stopped Jace.

"You sure you're okay to drive?" he asked as I got into Devon's Porsche.

"I'll be fine," I said, anxious now to get to Devon's. A clawing need to feel safe was churning in my gut. "Thanks again."

Lane stood in the space of the open car door, peering down concernedly at me. After a moment, he crouched down to my level.

"Be careful, Ivy," he said, reaching out to brush my cheek. "I have this feeling, like this may be one of the last times I see you alive."

On that ominous note, he stepped back, closing the car door. I managed to get the keys into the ignition, then tore out of the lot in the direction of Devon's apartment.

Jace was back. And not only that, he'd found me. So quickly and so easily, it was laughable how I'd thought I'd be able to hide from him.

The things he'd said replayed in my mind, terror taking hold of me until all I could think about was finding a place to hide.

I let myself into Devon's apartment almost mechanically. I dropped everything I was carrying to the floor before getting on my knees and dumping out my purse. Grabbing my gun, I hurried into the bedroom, frantically looking for a place to hide. If I hid well enough, maybe Jace wouldn't find me.

My eyes fell on the closet and, in three steps, I was in front of it. The space was dark, full of clothes, and had little nooks and crannies in the back. Dropping to my knees, I pulled the door shut behind me and crawled into the farthest corner. It was pitch-black, but that was okay. Maybe Jace wouldn't look in here. Maybe I'd be safe.

Don't make a sound. Don't even breathe too loud. Just sit and watch the door.

My old mantra repeated inside my head as I sat, knees drawn to my chest and gun cradled in both hands. If he came, I'd be ready for him.

I sat there for hours, time ceasing to have meaning after a while. My eyes grew heavy and my head bobbed from exhaustion, but I jerked upright each time, determined to stay awake.

I had no idea what time it was when I heard the sounds of someone in the apartment.

Gripping the gun tight in my suddenly sweaty palms, I focused intently on the door, just barely able to see the faint edges of the cracks. I thought about praying and my lips moved silently, even as I knew praying had never helped me before. I'd prayed and prayed that some miracle would stop Jace from coming into my room. That miracle had never come.

I made myself as small as possible in the corner, the footsteps coming closer now as he walked into the room. I heard him pause. My pulse was racing and I was light-headed with fear and panic. I would *not* let him do to me what he'd done before.

The door to the closet suddenly flew open and the light came on, blinding me after hours in the dark. I screamed, terror spiking in my mind, and pulled the trigger.

The gunshot was loud in the confined space, making my ears ring, but with it brought a semblance of sanity. I wasn't in my adolescent bedroom closet hiding from Jace—I was in Devon's closet, and he'd said he was coming home tonight, which meant I'd just shot—

"Oh my God!" I cried out, dropping the gun. Now I could see a man lying on the floor outside the closet. I scrambled forward on my hands and knees, terrified that I'd killed Devon. "Devon! Oh my God." I was crying, near hysterics by the time I got to him. I reached out a shaking hand—

His hand shot out and wrapped tightly around my wrist. I gasped in surprise and relief as he sat up, apparently unharmed.

"Oh thank God," I said on a sob. "You're okay. Thank God you're okay."

Devon was staring at me, a frown creasing his brow. "Yes, a good thing for quick reflexes or else I certainly would not be 'okay.' Do you want to tell me why you're hiding in my wardrobe with a gun?"

I was crying too hard to explain, so I said the only word I could. "Jace."

The change in Devon was immediate. Gone was the irritated confusion, replaced by stark worry.

"Jace? What did he do? What happened?" he asked. His hands cupped my face, making me look at him, but I was still crying. Relief that he was here and unhurt overwhelmed me.

Realizing that I couldn't speak yet, Devon drew me onto his lap and held me. I rested my head against his chest, the cotton of his shirt soft against my cheek. His hand held the back of my head, slowly petting my hair as he murmured soothingly to me.

"Shh, it's all right now. I've got you."

Gradually, my sobs eased and I realized how out of my mind my fear of Jace had made me. I could have shot Devon, killed him.

"I'm so sorry," I managed to whisper.

"Shh, no harm done," Devon said gently. "Can you tell me what happened?"

Haltingly, I told him about Jace's attack, the things he'd said, and how Agent Lane had intervened. When I was through, he made me sit up slightly so he could inspect my neck. I imagined there was a handprint from where Jace had nearly strangled me.

Devon's gaze met mine. "You've never told anyone, have you," he said. "Never talked through what happened when you were a child."

I gave a hesitant shake of my head. "He told me he'd kill me if I ever told," I whispered. Logan had known without me telling him the excruciating details. I'd maintained my silence all these years.

"Tell me."

I stared wide-eyed at Devon, sure I'd misheard him. "You don't want—" I began.

"I do," he interrupted. "And you need to say it. You need to say the words, let the light shine on it so you can see it for what it was. Your silence has gained you nothing. Tell me. When did it start?"

His eyes were so blue, so intently focused on me, and I could feel the strength of his arms around me, his body against mine. And maybe it was because there was no pity in his gaze, only the frank knowledge that he'd seen horrible things as bad as mine, maybe worse, and nothing I could say would surprise him.

So I began to talk.

I told him everything. From the very first night Jace had come into my bedroom and how it began with him just touching me, to how eventually he'd grown bold enough to come in several times a week. How he'd turn me over and pull my pajamas down. The way it had hurt but if I made a sound, he'd hit me with his fist. That he never stopped calling me "brat."

It took a long time and I had to stop several times when the words became too hard to say, but Devon was patient, waiting silently for me to continue. His hold on me didn't lessen. He didn't push me away in disgust.

I finished with the last time, the day he'd gotten so mad he'd threatened to kill me with a knife from the kitchen. I told Devon how I'd barricaded my door and sat with my back to it, praying I could hold him off. I'd been so scared that day.

Finally, I ran out of words. The room seemed too quiet when I stopped talking.

I was afraid to look at Devon, realizing I'd glanced away at some point while I'd been speaking. I'd been lost inside the horror of my own memories. What would I see in his eyes now?

Devon's finger brushed my chin, gently turning my face toward his. "Look at me," he said.

Reluctantly, I lifted my gaze to his.

"None of that was your fault, Ivy," he said.

I shrugged. I'd heard that phrase often enough before to grow tired of it. "Yeah, I know."

"No, listen to me. Really listen. Nothing you said or did made him do that to you. It wasn't your fault."

Devon's words were so earnest, so passionate, it made me pause. Is that what I thought? Deep down, did I blame myself for the monstrous things Jace had done to me? That didn't seem right. I knew it wasn't my fault, but suddenly I wondered if I really *knew*— in the heart of me—that I wasn't to blame.

"You were the victim, Ivy," Devon said. "Don't blame yourself. Put the blame where it belongs. On him."

At the third time he repeated that, I could feel my face crumpling into tears. "But why?" I managed to say. "Why would he do that to me? What had I ever done to him?" They were questions I only now realized had been buried inside, that I'd never allowed myself to dwell on but had been there all the same.

Devon pulled me close to him again, cradling me tightly against his chest. "Shh, sweet Ivy. The why is simply because he's an evil man. And I know this because I've seen a lot of evil in the world. Evil that preys on the innocent, the defenseless. It wasn't anything you said or did. You were just . . . convenient."

The truth of his words hit me in a way I couldn't explain. It was painful to realize that he was right—the awful acts that marked my past, that still marked me—were nothing more than a product of a sick, twisted person with a victim close at hand. And that victim had been me. There was nothing I could have done to prevent it, just as there was nothing I did to cause it.

"He said he loved me."

Devon tipped my chin up until our eyes met. "That wasn't love, Ivy. What he did wasn't out of love. Don't ever believe someone who hurts you also loves you. The two don't go hand in hand."

"What do you know of love?" I asked sadly. "It's a useless, foolish emotion, remember?"

His gaze was steady on mine, his fingers tenderly brushing my cheek. "I may know little of love, but I know what it is *not*."

I mourned the innocence I'd lost all those years ago, and how I'd punished myself for what had happened in the years since, thinking it had been my fault. Subconscious though it had been, I could see now how I'd kept myself in a pristine shell, not allowing anyone to get close. Only Logan had made it past my defenses, and now, Devon.

Devon's hold on me didn't let up, his presence steady and solid while the ground shifted underneath me, putting my entire life into a different paradigm and perspective.

My tears eventually dried and I quieted. My body was folded onto Devon's lap and I realized we'd been sitting on the floor for a long time. That couldn't have been comfortable for him, though he gave no sign of tiring.

I shifted to move off Devon's lap. I was exhausted, emotionally and physically spent. He got to his feet and took my hand to help me up. His palm was warm against mine.

"How long were you in there?" he asked.

I shrugged. "I don't know. Since about six thirty, I guess. What time is it now?"

Devon glanced at his watch. "Almost two in the morning. You must be starving."

As if to illustrate his point, my stomach let loose a long growl. Devon laughed softly.

"Come on," he said, tugging on my hand. "I know an all-night diner. It's not far."

But the thought of leaving my sanctuary had me digging in my heels. Devon turned as I remained rooted to the spot, an unspoken question on his face.

"I-I'm scared," I confessed. "He's out there. Waiting for me."

Devon stepped close to me and I tipped my head back. His hand cupped my jaw.

His voice was solemn when he spoke. "I swear to you, I won't let him hurt you," he said. "Never again. Do you believe me?"

I stared into his eyes. The look in them was fierce and I wanted to believe him, wanted to believe I didn't have to be afraid of Jace, but Devon must have seen the doubt in my eyes.

"It's all right," he said, his lips lifting in a soft smile. "You don't have to believe for it to be true." Lifting my hand, he pressed a kiss to my knuckles. "Now let's get something to eat. I'm famished."

I saw that my stuff was strewn on the floor where I'd left it, but Devon just stepped over everything, grabbed his overcoat from where it lay over a chair, and drew me with him out the door.

When we were in the elevator, Devon folded the coat over my shoulders, carefully lifting my hair from beneath the heavy fabric. He wore his usual impeccable suit and tie. Even after sitting on the floor with me, it was still remarkably unwrinkled.

"Why do you always wear a suit?" I asked.

His lips twisted a little at my question. "Rounds out the edges," he said.

"Rounds out the edges?"

"People are less likely to look twice at a man in a suit. We're ubiquitous. Nonthreatening."

The idea of anyone looking at Devon and seeing someone "non-threatening" was laughable. I rolled my eyes.

Devon laughed, tugging me closer. It felt good to be near him and I slid my arms around his waist. "What was that for?" he asked.

"People would have to be pretty stupid to not see you as dangerous," I said. "It's the first thing I noticed about you."

"Not everyone is as observant as you are," he replied, tucking a stray lock of hair behind my ear.

The elevator let us out and soon we were in Devon's Porsche and pulling up to an honest-to-goodness diner. I didn't think there were any in the city and was surprised that Devon would know of it, much less actually eat there. But sure enough, he parked out front and was quickly opening my door for me.

A tired-looking waitress showed us to a red vinyl booth in the nearly empty diner and I slid in, shrugging the coat aside. Devon sat across from me, bracing his elbows on the white lacquer top scored with cuts and scrapes that looked like they'd been there since before I was born. Music played over the speakers, the strains of Johnny Cash walking the line.

I glanced over the laminated menu the waitress had left, but all I could think about was Devon, sitting across from me. I looked up to find him watching me.

"Do you already know what you're going to order?" I asked.

"I always have the same thing," he replied.

"You come here a lot?"

"Often enough."

Another vague answer. I sighed, returning my attention to the menu.

"What?" Devon asked.

I shook my head, chagrined. "I bare my soul to you, and you won't even tell me how often you come to an all-night diner." It was grossly unfair. He was able to maintain his emotional distance from me, whereas I had no more secrets to hide behind.

The waitress returned just then and Devon ordered coffee and a Denver omelet. I asked for the same. She went away, coming back quickly with our mugs of coffee. I doctored mine with cream and sugar while Devon drank his black.

"My time is off when I return from overseas," Devon said in the silence. "I ran across this place a few months ago since I rarely feel like cooking at midnight after a ten-hour flight."

"How often are you . . . overseas?" I asked, wondering if he'd divulge more to me.

"Lately, not very much," he said. "But I don't expect I'll be in the States for much longer."

I nodded impassively, though inside a part of me winced at the thought of him leaving.

"This federal agent, he had me come to the station yesterday," I said, though wondering if it was a good idea to open this particular can of worms. "He had a whole file on you."

"He did?" Devon didn't seem surprised or concerned at this information.

"Yeah, he showed me papers, and photos, of these places he'd said you'd been. Where people had died, lots of people. He said you were responsible." I looked up at him.

"I may have been."

His unequivocal response should have thrown me, but maybe it was a signal that I was growing accustomed to his . . . lifestyle . . . that it didn't.

"Will I end up dead, too?" Agent Lane's warnings echoed in my ears.

Devon stared at me, neither of us speaking. I waited, barely breathing, for his answer.

"No," he said at last. "Not you."

"Not me?" I echoed.

The waitress interrupted, setting our plates in front of us and refilling our coffee mugs. I waited until she was out of earshot before speaking again.

"That sounds like you've made that promise before," I said. "What happened?"

Devon was eating and I wasn't sure he'd answer me. I picked at my food and waited.

"This is a dangerous world," he said, "and my path in it more treacherous than most. I don't make promises I can't keep. Not anymore."

"How can you possibly promise me that I won't end up like the woman I saw in the photos?" I asked.

"I'm not forcing you to stay," he countered.

He had a point there. It wasn't like I was beating a path to the door.

"But if you do," he continued, "I'll do everything in my power to keep you safe."

"Aren't I just baggage you don't need?"

"Absolutely," he replied with ego-deflating rapidity.

Stung, I sat back in my seat. The chill from outside crept through the window next to the booth and I took another sip of my tepid coffee.

Devon wiped his mouth, silently eyeing me. I kept my gaze on the beige coffee in my mug.

"You haven't asked me why," he said at last.

I glanced up.

"You haven't asked me why I'd do this. Put myself and my mission at risk for a bank teller from Kansas."

I swallowed. "Because you like to fuck me." The vulgar words tasted bitter on my tongue, but it was what it was and I didn't want to sugarcoat it.

A humorless smile curved his lips. "I did say that, didn't I," he murmured, and maybe I heard a tinge of regret in his voice.

I didn't think I had to answer that.

"That is correct," he said. "But I could find that anywhere." He shrugged, as though to underscore how easily he could get laid.

"Why then?" I asked, wanting to hear the answer and yet afraid of it at the same time.

"I feel . . ."

My breath stopped for a moment.

". . . responsible for you."

My breath let out in a rush as I tried to conceal my disappointment. Why had I hoped for more? Because I knew, really knew, that I was already in too deep with him.

"Responsible for me," I repeated, shoving the thought aside. "I don't want to be anyone's . . . responsibility."

"Too late for that," he dismissed. Picking up my fork, he speared a bite of my barely touched omelet and lifted it to my mouth. "Eat something."

I shook my head, my appetite gone. "I'm not hungry."

"Eat, Ivy, please," he persisted, then added, "for me."

Our eyes locked and that's when I knew that *he* knew my last secret, that I was falling for him.

I opened my mouth and he fed me the bite. I didn't resist as he patiently fed me until over half the omelet was gone. We didn't speak, the silence between us needing no words to fill it. We both knew the power he had over me, understood that it was real and absolute. It should have frightened me, how much trust I was placing in Devon's hands, but it didn't. Though I didn't want to think about the devastation I'd feel when he left.

Finally, when I'd had enough, I gave a minute shake of my head and he placed the fork on my plate.

"Let's go, darling," he said, pulling some bills out of his wallet and leaving them on the table.

I drifted to sleep in the car while Devon drove us back, the brush of his hand against my cheek rousing me when he'd stopped the car. As though understanding how exhausted I was, he didn't try to talk as we walked to his apartment.

Once we were inside, he peeled the clothes from my body while I stood, unresisting and unembarrassed.

He lay me down in the bed and I watched in the soft glow of the bedside lamp as he undressed as well. His body was golden hued in the light, the muscles of his abdomen drawing my eye as the scars on his skin were muted. He was beautiful and when he climbed into bed and took me in his arms, I went willingly.

❦

I called in to work the next morning. I never took sick days so I thought maybe I had one or two coming, despite, or perhaps due to, my recent hospital stay. The sad fact was that I didn't want to give up the remaining time I had with Devon. Other than what he'd said last night, he hadn't mentioned when he'd be leaving again and I hadn't asked for a timetable. I was sipping my coffee when he emerged from the shower, wearing a pair of slacks.

I'd picked up the stuff I'd left strewn on his floor and set it on the bar. As Devon poured a cup of coffee, he glanced at the stack.

"What's this?" he asked, holding up the notebook I'd taken from Mr. Galler's safe deposit box.

"That was Mr. Galler's," I said, explaining how I'd seen the insignia on the front and stolen the notebook. "I thought maybe it would have something important in it." With Jace showing up right after work, I'd completely forgotten about it.

Flipping through the pages, Devon frowned. "I wonder . . ." he murmured, then disappeared back into the bedroom, emerging a few moments later holding the pendant Mr. Galler had given me. I wondered where he'd kept it and how I'd missed finding it when I'd searched.

Grabbing the notebook, he came to sit next to me on the sofa. I scooted closer and peered over his shoulder as he began to read.

"Wait, it's not written in English," I said, disappointed.

Devon snorted. "Of course not. Galler was German and so was his father."

"Do you know German?"

"Yes."

Okay then. All I knew was English and a few Spanish words I'd learned from Dora.

I waited impatiently while Devon read, watching him turn the pages at a pretty brisk pace. When I couldn't stand the curiosity anymore, I said, "Well? What does it say?"

Devon frowned as he replied. "It's a journal," he said. "Dr. Galler was a doctor during World War II. He joined the Nazi Party early on and was close to the upper echelons of Hitler's inside circle."

My eyes widened. "Wow."

Devon flipped a few more pages. "It seems Dr. Galler became intrigued with the idea of human subjects."

"What do you mean?"

He glanced up at me. "The Nazis were notorious for using human subjects for all kinds of heinous experimentation during the war, the concentration camps provided an unlimited supply of . . . patients."

My stomach turned at this information. It had been a while since high school history.

"Was Dr. Galler one of those doctors?" I asked, hoping the nice old man I'd known hadn't been related to a monster.

Devon nodded. "It would seem so," he said, thumbing through some more pages. I was suddenly glad I couldn't read German.

I was quiet while Devon read, though when he neared the end of the book, he paused again.

"What's wrong?" I asked.

"He's going on about this particular experiment with a virus," Devon said. "A virus that is airborne and kills within hours once the victim is infected."

A chill ran across my skin. That sounded like something out of a movie.

"But they didn't have anything like that back then," I said. "If they had, they would have used it."

Still reading, Devon said, "They had viability problems. It didn't last long outside of the lab and it wouldn't transmit person to person. Only direct exposure worked. To compound those issues, they couldn't create a vaccine to immunize themselves. Without the vaccine, they couldn't risk using the virus."

I sat for a moment, confused. "This is all interesting, but what does this have to do with me or the pendant or those people who are after it?"

"I would guess they think that either Dr. Galler or his son—the man you knew—eventually worked out the problems or came up with the vaccine, and they want to use this virus."

Staring at him, I said, "No, surely not! That's . . . that would be ridiculous! Who would do such a thing?"

"Lots of people," was his grim reply. "A bioweapon like this . . . there are those who'd pay millions for such a thing. Billions."

Taking the pendant in his hand, Devon pressed a tiny latch on the side and the rectangle clicked, opening up like a locket. Intrigued, I leaned closer.

"What's inside?" I asked.

"It's a key code," he replied. "The last few pages of the journal are written in code. This is probably the key." He showed me the letters etched inside the gold locket. "We'd have to take it to a code breaker to see what it really says."

"Would they be able to break it if it's that old?" I asked.

Devon nodded. "With it being World War II, I'm guessing the last bit was encrypted using the Enigma machine. That code was broken. So we just need to find someone who can translate the code for us."

"What does the virus do to you?" I asked.

"From the patients Dr. Galler infected," Devon said, the word *patients* marked with heavy irony, "it's a mutation of the Ebola virus, and somehow he managed to speed up its effect. The victims' organs would liquefy within hours of exposure rather than days."

I shuddered at that particular mental image. "They knew about Ebola back then?"

"Obviously Dr. Galler knew about it," he replied.

We sat in silence for a moment while I tried to digest all this information. So the people Devon was after maybe had this virus and wanted the vaccine before . . . what? Unleashing it on an unsuspecting populace? Selling it to the highest bidder? It seemed incomprehensible to me and as far removed from my life as a boring bank teller as . . . well, as Devon's life as a spy.

"These people," I began, "are they the kind of threat you deal with all the time?"

Devon was still scouring the pages. "Yes," he answered simply. "There's always someone wanting to rule the world."

It was a strange thought, but I wasn't surprised. I supposed history had shown what lengths some will go to for the power to control and rule others.

"So what will you do now?" I asked.

"Now I need to find Clive and see who turned them on to Galler and his research. Why, after all these years, did they come looking for this?"

"Clive will know that?" I asked.

"He should," Devon replied. "He's worked undercover for them for the past twelve months."

"Them?"

"Nanotech," he explained. "The bad guys." He stood. "After I talk to Clive, I'm going to their headquarters. You're coming along."

Stunned, I just stared at him, sure I'd misheard. "What?" I asked.

"I said, you're coming along," he repeated.

"But I-I can't just leave," I sputtered. "I have a job."

"It's Christmas week. You'll take vacation, or call in sick, or quit. I don't really care. But you're coming with me."

"Why? Won't it be dangerous?" Not that it would probably keep me away if he said yes. I just wanted to be clear on what I was getting into.

"You'll be safe and sound at a posh hotel, I promise," he replied. I noticed he didn't answer the why part of my question.

Well. If a posh hotel was involved, how bad could it be? And did it really matter? I'd be with Devon. That was all I cared about.

"Okay, I'll come," I said. "Now, where are we going?" I'd never heard of a place called Nanotech. Was it in the Midwest?

"Ever been to Paris?"

CHAPTER FIFTEEN

B efore we went anywhere, I needed to pack. It was late afternoon by the time Devon drove me to my apartment. He sat in the living room waiting while I tried to figure out what in the world to pack for a spontaneous trip to Paris. At Christmas.

I could have done a pirouette in delight at the thought of spending a few days in Paris, despite the fact that it was really more of a . . . business trip for Devon. He was taking me with him. I decided to focus on that and *not* on what kind of danger awaited me by being at his side.

I was nearly done, just trying to decide whether or not to take the designer dress Devon had given me, when I heard the rattle of keys in the front door. Glancing at the clock in dismay, I realized it was way too early for Logan to be coming home. I'd hoped to be gone and just leave a note before he arrived. Looked like that wasn't going to happen.

Dropping the dress, I ran into the living room just as Logan opened the door. I definitely did not want to see him and Devon go at each other again.

Logan's gaze fell on me and his face lit up in a smile.

"Ives!" he exclaimed in delight. "There's my girl!"

I was really glad he hadn't seen Devon yet, and I rushed to give him a hug.

"You're home early," I said, squeezing him around the neck. He dropped his briefcase and wrapped his arms around my waist. "Taking off early today?"

Logan buried his face against my hair and inhaled deeply. "Mmm," he said on a heavy sigh. "No one's there this week anyway. Hard to find the motivation to work. I thought I'd leave early, take you to a nice pre-Christmas dinner like we planned yesterday. I'm glad to find you home and not still at his place." The disgruntlement in that last part had me wincing.

"Um, yeah, about that—" I began.

"Afraid we won't have time for dinner, mate," Devon interrupted.

Logan's head jerked up and I turned to see Devon had stood. He'd leaned a shoulder against one wall, his arms crossed as he surveyed us. The look in his eyes had me rethinking my current position in Logan's arms.

"But thanks for the invitation," he added.

Logan had gone stiff as soon as Devon had spoken, and though I squirmed a bit trying to unobtrusively detach myself from him, his arms only tightened around me.

"What the hell are you doing here?" Logan bit out. "I told you in the hospital, haven't you done enough?"

"Logan—" I tried again, but Devon cut me off.

"Tell me," he said, "for how many months and years did you stand by and watch while your best friend was assaulted night after night in her own bed?"

I sucked in my breath at the accusation in Devon's voice, the blood leaving my face in a rush.

Logan must have been as shocked as I was because when he spoke, his voice was a choked hiss of sound. "What did you just say?"

"I said," Devon pushed himself off the wall and dropped his arms to his sides, as though readying himself for a fight, "why would you let Ivy go through such hell when you, and only you, could have helped her?"

"I was fourteen years old," Logan ground out. "I didn't know what to do." His fingers were biting into my flesh, his hold on me was so tight.

"Didn't know what to do? Or didn't *want* to do anything?" Devon retorted. "How often would she come over, Logan? Twice a week? Three times?"

Logan swallowed so hard I could hear it.

"I was there for her—" he began.

"Did it not occur to you to tell your parents, a teacher, a cop, *someone* what was going on?" Devon cut in and the venom in his voice sent a chill through me. "Or did you like playing the knight in shining armor just a little too much?"

Logan thrust me away and sprang at Devon, who was ready for him. His first swing missed, but his second connected with Devon's jaw. The crunch of bone against bone was loud in the room. Devon retaliated, his blow snapping Logan's head back.

"Stop it! Stop it, both of you!" I yelled, afraid at how far they'd go in trying to hurt each other.

They ignored me, now in close quarters and grappling. It was quickly apparent that Devon was much more skilled at hand-to-hand combat than Logan. They knocked over a chair and shoved the kitchen table before Logan was facedown on the floor with Devon's knee in his back, his arm twisted up behind him.

"You bloody arsehole," Devon hissed, only slightly out of breath. "She trusted you, and all you did was stand by and watch it happen."

"Fuck you," Logan snarled.

I hurried forward, latching on to Devon's upper arm. "Please," I said. "It's not his fault! Come on, please don't do this." I hated to see them fighting and was at a loss as to the why of it. They barely knew each other yet hated one another.

Devon didn't respond for a moment, the hard set of his jaw making me worry that he would end up breaking Logan's arm no matter what I said. But at last he released him. Standing, he took my elbow and pulled me toward him as Logan scrambled to his feet, his chest heaving.

"You don't think I regret every single fucking day that I didn't do something?" Logan yelled at Devon. "I was young and stupid and scared. One day I see a girl who looks like an angel sitting in the corner of the library. She's crying and won't tell me why. I tried to help her, be her friend, make her smile. Then one night she shows up outside my bedroom window, couldn't talk, couldn't tell me why she was there, just with a look in her eyes that made my soul bleed."

He stopped, taking a deep, shuddering breath as he shoved his fingers through his hair. When he looked up, his eyes were haunted with pain.

"I'd give anything to be able to undo the past, but I can't. All I *can* do is protect her now, from men like you."

"You don't know a damn thing about me," Devon growled.

"I know enough," Logan retorted.

"Stop it!" I broke in before they started on this path again. "Enough with the fighting already! I'm sorry to be the one to break it to you, but neither of you is in charge of my life." I turned to Logan. "Logan, you're my best friend and I love you dearly, but I have to be free to make my own decisions, even if you don't agree with them."

Facing Devon, I said, "And I didn't tell you those things so you'd blame Logan. You just told me only hours ago that it wasn't my fault. Neither is it Logan's."

Devon didn't reply, our eyes locked in a battle of wills. But I wasn't backing down. He'd been wrong to say those things to Logan. After a moment, he gave me a curt nod and I knew I'd won. But I didn't want to push it, with either of them, so I said, "Devon, would you please grab my suitcase from my bedroom?" He left to do as I asked and I turned back to Logan.

"I'm sorry, for all of that," I said, rushing to apologize for Devon. "He's just upset, I think."

"Ives, don't—"

"Please don't say it," I warned, interrupting him. "I know how you feel about him, but it is what it is."

Logan's jaw was locked tight, his lips pressed firmly closed.

"I'm going away with him for a few days," I continued, reaching out to straighten Logan's tie, which had gone askew during their fight. "But I'll text you and I'll be back soon."

Standing on my toes, I rested my hands on his shoulders, leaning forward to press a kiss to the bruise that was beginning to darken his jaw where Devon had hit him.

"Merry Christmas, Logan," I said. "I want a rain check on that dinner, okay?" I smiled, hoping he'd smile back. It took a moment, but he did, his lips curving ever so slightly.

"Like I could say no to you," he said softly. His smile faded and his brows drew together in a frown. "Just please, Ives, please be careful. I don't know what I'd do if—"

"Ready?" Devon interrupted.

Logan's eyes flicked behind me and his jaw locked again, a pulse throbbing in his cheek.

Anxious to keep the peace, I stepped away from Logan and turned around. Devon was holding out my coat and helped me into it. A moment later, we were heading out the door.

"I'll talk to you soon," I assured Logan, who stood in the doorway, watching us. The look on his face made my chest hurt and I smiled again, but this time he didn't smile back.

Devon took my hand, tugging me down the stairs, and I lost sight of Logan.

❦

We stopped at a nondescript house in an upper-middle-class neighborhood on the way back to Devon's apartment. He turned off the car's headlights as we drove down the street to the last house on the corner.

"Why are we here?" I asked.

"Clive lives here," he explained, getting out of the car.

The house was dark as we approached, no lights glowing from the inside. We went to the front door and Devon lifted his hand to knock, but froze.

"What is it?" I asked.

Devon didn't answer me, he just reached inside his jacket for his gun. Looking down, I saw the door was slightly ajar. My breath caught in my throat as Devon pulled me behind him, then eased open the door.

Inside it was as still and quiet as Galler's home had been, and my nerves felt an inch from snapping. Every doorway loomed as a possible danger. Were they waiting here for us? This time would I be able to survive?

But not even my overwhelming terror could prevent me from following Devon. He held his weapon with both hands and at eye level now, ready to meet any threat that would come our way. I cowered behind as I followed him, too afraid to stay alone by the door.

We crept along the hallway and I saw the faintest light glowing from underneath a door. Devon must have seen it, too, because he paused outside the door. Positioning me behind him and well away from the opening, he turned the knob and pushed.

My breath was a thready catch in my throat, adrenaline pouring through me in a cold wash of ice. But nothing happened.

Devon stepped inside the room, gun at the ready. Whatever he saw made him pause. He lowered the gun.

"What are you doing, Clive?" he asked.

Cautiously, I poked my head in and saw Clive sitting in a chair. He looked bedraggled, like he hadn't shaved for a couple of days, and his eyes were red and swollen. A gun sat on the table at his elbow, next to a decanter of amber fluid. He held an empty glass in his lax grip.

Clive didn't answer Devon. In fact, he didn't seem to hear him at all. He just stared off into space.

"Clive," Devon repeated, louder this time. He took a step toward him, his movements steady but cautious. "Clive."

At this, the third mention of his name, Clive finally reacted, but not in the way I expected.

"They took her," he said, his voice flat. "They took Anna. They said they knew I was helping you, and that if I ever wanted to see her alive again, I had to kill you." He didn't even look at Devon as he spoke, his gaze still focused away from us, unseeing.

"Who took her?" Devon asked.

Clive laughed, a bitter, hard sound that sent chills crawling over my skin.

"Who do you think?" he retorted. "He knows you're on to him and he's not just going to let you or anyone Vega sends waltz into his labs and sabotage their work. He's worked too hard, stepped on too many people, to get so close and lose."

"Are you going to kill me, Clive?" Devon asked the question almost idly, as though he were asking if they'd be drinking white wine or red with dinner.

"You know I can't," Clive replied, resigned. He added more of the liquor in the bottle to his glass and swallowed it in one gulp. "Anna and I are both as good as dead. If she's even still alive." His eyes shone bright, but no tears fell.

I was horrified by all of this. That beautiful, sweet bride had been taken by the same people who'd tortured me and Devon? How long would they torture her before they killed her?

I must have made a noise because both men suddenly looked at me. Swallowing hard, I stepped into the room.

"C-can't you go get her?" I stammered. "You know, rescue her?"

"You're still with the girl," Clive observed, frowning slightly. "Doesn't she know she'll end up dead? Just like Anna." Leaning his elbows on his knees, he covered his face with his hands.

Way to be a pessimist there, Clive. I looked questioningly at Devon. "Can't you find her? Save her? They could be hurting her, like they did me, or worse . . ." I didn't want to think about it, my imagination painting too clear a picture of what Anna might be enduring.

Devon was gazing shrewdly at me, and I couldn't read his expression. He might have thought I was being sentimental and naive, that I had no idea what I was asking. And he'd be right. But if I were Anna, I'd want someone to ask—someone to take a chance and help me, if any help were possible.

"Do you know where they have her?" Devon asked, still looking at me but his question directed to Clive.

Clive sniffed and swiped at his eyes before lowering his hands. "Yeah," he said roughly. "I guess so."

"Can you still get us in?"

Clive glanced up, his mouth falling open slightly. "Uh . . . yeah. But—"

"But what?" Devon cut him off. "Your wife's being kept prisoner and tortured while you sit here getting pissed and feeling sorry for yourself? Get off your arse, Clive. Anna's waiting for you."

It took a moment, but it seemed to finally sink in that Devon was going to help get Anna back. Clive jumped to his feet. "I'll get my stuff," he said, hurrying from the room.

I walked to Devon as he holstered his gun.

"Will you be able to rescue her?" I asked.

His smile was thin. "Perhaps. The odds are slim, but I've beaten the odds before."

"I don't want you to get hurt," I said, my teeth biting my lower lip.

Devon reached up, brushing his thumb across my cheek. "I don't have a choice," he said softly. "With those gold eyes looking at me as if I'm the hero rather than the villain—what's a man to do?"

I didn't know what to say, so I stretched up on my toes and kissed him.

"Thank you," I said, tentatively laying my hand along his jaw. I could feel the slight abrasion of his five o'clock shadow against my palm.

"Don't thank me yet," he said wryly. "We still have to find her and get out alive. And you're going to help."

"What? Why me?" I asked, and yes, it was a bit rhetorical. I hadn't asked for my life to be turned upside down and be in constant danger. I hadn't liked Devon from the start, had known he was bad news, and yet . . . here I was.

"Are you regretting letting me in your bed, sweet Ivy?" Devon's hand lifted to my hair, his fingers trailing through the long, silken strands. He was so close that I had to tip my head back to look at him. The whiskers that shadowed his jaw gave him a menacing edge that was more easily disguised when he was clean shaven.

It was more exciting and intoxicating than I wanted to admit, being this close to a man as dangerous and lethal as Devon. I never would have thought it of myself, but feeling like the gazelle sidling up to a lion made the blood pulse in my veins and gave me the heady sensation of being high. Logan had been right and so was Devon. I was hooked, addicted. Even knowing the danger I'd be in at his behest didn't stop me from wanting him.

"Regret is a wasteful emotion," I replied at last.

"Exactly."

⌒⌒

We were sitting in Devon's car, engine off, staring at what looked like a dance club across the street. I could feel the music thumping, even from this distance, and whenever the door opened, swirling neon colors shone through the opening.

Devon, Clive, and I had been sitting there for several minutes, just watching. We'd changed, both the men now in jeans and dark shirts, Devon sporting a tight black T-shirt that had made my eyes linger. But it was my outfit that had me squirming slightly.

It was something Clive had given me and I assumed it belonged to Anna. A black lace dress, though it barely deserved the name. Anna had been shorter than me and the hem barely brushed the tops of my thighs. The fabric was skintight, wrapping my torso and one arm, leaving the other shoulder, arm, and way too much of my chest bare. I'd had to use a little double-sided tape to make sure I wouldn't fall out of the top.

I'd made the mistake of bending over to slip on the towering stilettos I was also borrowing while dressing in Anna's spacious walk-in closet. A moment later, Devon's hands were cupping my exposed ass, his fingers tracing the line of the black thong I wore. I jerked upright with a squeak and the hem moved up farther as Devon's hands slid to my hips.

"Promise me you'll strike that exact same pose later," he rasped in my ear, the brush of his lips sending a shiver through me.

The memory brought a smile to my lips as I sat in the backseat, waiting for Clive and Devon to finish whatever it was they were doing. Reconnaissance, I supposed?

"Let's go," Devon said. He couldn't take his gun inside, but I'd seen him strap a knife to his ankle.

He opened the car door for me and I modestly kept my knees together as I swung my legs out. No need to flash a crotch shot.

"Damn," I heard him murmur, and I smiled to myself.

"You can get up close and personal later," I promised in an undertone.

"I'm looking forward to it."

Devon and Clive flanked me and I threaded my arms through theirs as we crossed the street to the club entrance. My sky-high heels made me as tall as Clive, though Devon still had a couple of inches on me.

I walked with a strut, realizing without being told that I was the eye candy who was going to get us into the club. Tossing my hair back over my shoulder, I was glad I'd used Anna's makeup to add thick liner to my eyes and a deep red gloss that made my lips shine.

There were two bouncers at the door when we arrived and they both cast a practiced eye over me, their eyes lingering on my legs. Devon had given me two hundred-dollar bills and I untangled my arms so I could reach inside my cleavage.

"Hey there," I said, my lips curving in a smile as I picked the bouncer that I thought was the one in charge. I left Clive and Devon behind as I stepped up close to him. "I'm looking for a party. Help a girl out?" I held the money up between two fingers and waited.

After a breathless moment, the bouncer grinned and took the money. "Shit, girl. You walk in and the party'll just be gettin' started."

"You bet your ass," I said with a wink. Devon and Clive stepped up to join me then as the bouncer moved aside. I blew the second bouncer a kiss as we breezed by into the club.

"Perfect," Devon breathed in my ear.

A flash of pride went through me. I'd helped out, which would hopefully end with us rescuing Anna.

The music and heat inside the club were overwhelming. Lights I'd seen from outside swirled through the dark room, illuminating a mass of people moving to the beat. I stopped, unsure where Devon wanted me to go, but then he took my hand, following Clive as he skirted the crowd.

We followed, though my eyes were drawn to the people there. An early- to mid-twenties crowd, they were all dressed similarly to me, though maybe with more Goth and urban flair. The girls were showing lots of skin while the guys sported tats and body piercings. A round bar with three busy bartenders took up one corner and the line was six deep.

This was where some biotech company was keeping Anna prisoner?

Clive stopped near a darkened corner and I saw him and Devon speaking in each other's ears, but couldn't hear what they were saying over the techno dance mix beating at my eardrums. I caught a strong whiff of marijuana, then Devon was pulling me forward and down a nondescript hallway that looked like it would lead to the restrooms.

A locked door with a keypad was halfway down the dim corridor and Clive punched in some numbers. The door clicked open.

"Stay here," Devon said, releasing my hand.

I made a grab for him, latching on to a fistful of his T-shirt. "Wait! Don't leave me behind."

"It's too dangerous," Devon said, prying my fingers loose. "Wait ten minutes. If I don't return, leave." He handed me another hundred. "This should take care of a cab to get you home."

I was starting to panic now. What would happen to him? Would I even know if they captured or killed him?

He pressed his lips briefly to mine, his thumb sliding along my jaw, then he and Clive were through the door. It slammed shut behind them and locked.

Unnerved, I stared at the door for a moment, wondering what to do. Finally, I backed away, turned to head down the hallway, and ran straight into someone.

"Looking for something?"

I jerked my head up from the massive wall of chest I'd run into. The man was huge, taller than Devon, and was built of solid muscle. His eyes were small and cold, his thin lips twisted in a malevolent grimace.

"I-I, um, no, not really," I stammered.

"That's too bad because you found it."

He grabbed my arm in a viciously tight grip that made me wince. After punching a code into the panel, the door swung open again and he dragged me through.

My palms were sweaty as I tried to keep up with him, but my heels made it difficult. Useful for getting us in to the club, they were a total pain in the ass if I actually had to move quickly, like now.

"Let me go now and I won't press charges," I bluffed.

The man just snorted at me, yanking me down the stairs. "Women are good for two things," he said. "Fucking and leverage. Guess which one you are."

We went down two flights of stairs and I could barely hear the music at all, only the thump of the bass as we reached the bottom of the stairwell. A man was standing in front of another door, but all he did was open it.

The room we entered was old and would have seemed out of date, if not for the glass cage in the corner. He gave me a shove and I stumbled forward, glad he'd finally let go of my arm.

Devon and Clive stood shoulder-to-shoulder mere feet away, both of them looking at me. I automatically took a step toward Devon, freezing when he gave a minute shake of his head. It was impossible to read the look on Devon's face, but I thought I saw disappointment in his eyes.

Sorry, I mouthed.

My eyes were drawn to the cage and my mouth dropped open in horror. A woman was inside the room walled in glass, sitting on the concrete floor with her knees drawn to her chest. I thought it was probably Anna, but couldn't tell for sure. Her head rested on her knees, her face turned away.

"So good of you to join us, my dear."

I jerked toward the sound of the voice, only now seeing another man there. He was sitting behind a white desk in the corner but then stood, buttoning his suit jacket as he rose. Something about him seemed familiar and it took me a moment to realize where I'd seen him before.

Mr. Galler's home.

He'd been the one to come in while I was being tortured. Once I made the connection, I gasped. His gaze flicked to mine.

"Devon. Did you learn nothing the last time about bringing your plaything with you?"

"Heinrich," Devon replied. "I'm surprised to see you here. Don't you usually send your minions to do your dirty work? Or has the corporate life grown boring for you?"

"Running a business is more cutthroat than you would imagine," Heinrich replied. "Besides, I have people to handle things I might find . . . distasteful."

At his words, the man who'd let us into the room stepped inside, along with three more men, all of whom held automatic weapons pointed right at us.

"I think you've met Hugo?" He motioned to the huge guy who'd dragged me down here.

Hugo, huh? Yeah, I could see that. I swallowed, suddenly wishing I'd heeded the warnings of Agent Lane and Logan. My knees were practically knocking together, I was so scared. They'd used me before to get to Devon. Would they do it again? My bravado from earlier was gone, lost in the terror of the unknown. The only comfort I had was the fact that Devon was here. I prayed he had some kind of plan, though what it could possibly be I had no idea.

"We've come for Anna," Devon said. "It's a bit beneath you, isn't it? Using the man's wife like this?"

"I'm afraid it's a dog-eat-dog world out there," Heinrich sighed with mock sympathy. "If Clive would have done as he was told, his wife would be safe at home, writing thank-you cards for her wedding gifts."

Devon took a few steps toward Heinrich, placing himself between him and me. The men with guns watched him carefully. Clive was ignoring everyone, drifting toward the cage that held his wife. She had yet to notice anyone else in the room and I wondered if the cage was soundproof or if it was one-way glass—we could see her but she couldn't see us.

"I know what you're after," Devon said, "and it doesn't exist. The vaccine to the virus Galler developed was never found, not by him, and not by his son."

"I'm afraid you and I have to agree to disagree," Heinrich replied. "I have proof that he did."

I realized that's what Devon wanted to know, what he'd mentioned earlier. The reason behind why they'd suddenly come after Galler, and consequently, me.

"And what's that?" Devon asked.

"Why, he did what any good German capitalist would do. He tried to sell it."

My stomach sank. Mr. Galler had been such a nice man. To hear that he'd tried to sell a virus and its vaccine to the highest bidder was heartbreaking. I'd never considered myself a bad judge of character, but I kind of thought I was batting zero.

"And you tried to buy it?"

"Mr. Galler ended up having second thoughts. I suppose a guilty conscience at his age made him consider things best left to priests and philosophers. I . . . took issue with him reneging on the sale."

"You had him killed," Devon said.

"Which I would *not* have done had I known he'd hidden the vaccine," Heinrich replied, sounding put out.

A hysterical laugh bubbled in my throat and I swallowed it down. He'd tortured and killed Roger, Mr. Galler's butler, to try to find that vaccine. Yet you would have thought he was discussing how neighborhood kids had trampled his lawn.

"If the vaccine exists," Devon said, "and I'm not convinced it does, it still won't solve your delivery or viability problems. You'll have a vaccine for a virus useless outside a lab."

"Technology's come a long way in the past seventy years, Mr. Clay. Aerosol delivery via air ducts . . . imagine a filled-to-capacity passenger plane. My, what a mess that would be." Heinrich laughed, sending a chill down my spine.

"That's not going to happen," Devon said. "You know we won't let you sell it to be weaponized."

"Vega can do whatever she wants," Heinrich dismissed with a wave of his hand, "but the Shadow's power over this ends here. We're not enemies, Mr. Clay, but if the Shadow attempts to thwart us, we won't hesitate to obliterate you, Vega, and every agent under her command."

"I'll be sure to pass on the message," Devon sneered.

"Oh, I'm sure you will," Heinrich said, gesturing to Hugo. "Especially once I demonstrate what we can do."

Hugo holstered his gun and started toward me. Devon immediately put himself between us. In an instant, the three other men were on him, two holding his arms securely behind his back while the third pointed his rifle at the center of Devon's chest.

"Heinrich, haven't you hurt enough innocent people? Leave the girl alone."

But Devon's words fell on deaf ears as Hugo stepped in front of me. I was rooted to the spot, fear icing my veins. Taking my arm in a crushing grip, Hugo began to drag me toward the glass cage.

"I'm hardly to blame," Heinrich replied. "You are the one who insists on toting your weakness with you for all to see, and use. I'm just taking the opportunity you so graciously provided. Be glad you have someone disposable with you. Trust me, you don't want us to demonstrate on you."

At that, I began to fight, realization hitting me too late. But Hugo was impossible to get away from and my heels slid on the floor as I tried to halt our progress to the cage. We reached it and Hugo punched a code into the keypad. The door buzzed and the lock clicked. Moving swiftly, Hugo swung open the door and flung me inside, the door closing soundly behind me.

I fell hard to the floor, wincing as my hands and knees struck the cold concrete. It took my breath away and I had to take a moment to recover. I rolled to my back and sat up, realizing that the cage wasn't soundproof as I'd assumed. I could still hear them talking and see them. Puzzled as to why Anna hadn't shown any response to our presence, I glanced at her. From this position I could see her face turned toward me.

I screamed and screamed, scrabbling backward away from her until I hit the wall and could go no farther.

Anna's eyes were bloodred, the irises and pupils indistinguishable from the rest of her eye awash in a sea of red. Blood streamed from her nose and mouth, wet against the dark brown of dried blood coating her chin and neck. Patches of livid, raw skin marked her once flawless complexion, and now that I was closer, I saw it on her arms as well. Her fingernails were jagged and bleeding, dried blood caked beneath her nails, as though she'd tried to scratch and claw herself.

She opened her mouth to reveal a bloody tongue and toothless gums. I stared at her in horror, unable to believe my eyes. A sound gargled in her throat, as though she were trying to speak but was drowning in her own mucus and bile.

I turned away, my stomach heaving as I retched. The cage smelled foul, the stench of bodily fluids and blood combining to make tears stream from my eyes. I threw up until there was nothing but dry heaves. When I finally turned back, Anna had lifted her head toward where Clive knelt outside the cage. His arms and hands were pressed flat against the glass as he stared at Anna.

"You see the power I wield, Mr. Clay?" Heinrich asked, his voice sounding tinny through the glass cage. "Do not cross us and do not interfere. Vega would be wise to listen to me, as would you."

"You're not going anywhere," Devon snarled. "This ends here and now."

Heinrich laughed outright. "I admire your persistence, I really do," he said. "But I'm leaving. You have two choices. You can follow me, try to stop me, kill me, whatever Neanderthal plan you can come up with against my men—which will likely fail—or you can stay and attempt to save your plaything." He glanced at his watch. "In sixty seconds, the timer will release a dose of the virus into the cage. Though it doesn't survive long, it'll be long enough, as you can see from Anna's condition."

I couldn't understand, couldn't believe what he was saying. I had sixty seconds before being infected with a virus for which there was no cure, the effects of which were literally staring me in the face. My stomach rolled and I thought I was going to throw up again. I swallowed it back down.

"It's your choice, Mr. Clay," Heinrich said, waving a careless hand toward the cage. "And I do hope we won't meet again." Giving another nod to the men, they released Devon.

"Let her go, Heinrich," Devon said. "We can make a deal."

But Heinrich ignored him, disappearing through the door and trailed by his men.

"Heinrich!" Devon yelled, but the only answer was the clanging of the steel door as it swung closed.

CHAPTER SIXTEEN

I watched, wondering which choice Devon would make. I'd assumed he'd come help me, but given the extreme unlikelihood that he'd be able to get me out in that short of a time, maybe he'd just go after Heinrich. After all, that seemed like a no-brainer: one life—my life—weighed against the millions Heinrich had the capability of destroying. Which was really tragic—for me.

Devon stood in the room, immobile, facing the door that had swung closed behind the men. I didn't breathe, afraid that the last thing I'd see would be Devon walking out the door and leaving me to die.

"Devon?" I asked, tentative. How did one beg for help from a man who professed to feel nothing for anyone?

Devon spun around and ran toward the door to the cage. I let out a pent-up breath. "Clive, come help me," he called out, but Clive didn't move from where he was frozen at the glass, staring at Anna. "Clive!"

This time Devon got a response and Clive jerked around. Scrambling to his feet, he rushed to help Devon. I couldn't see what they were doing but could hear the beeping of the lock as Clive pressed buttons on the keypad. I listened desperately for the clicking of the lock, but nothing happened.

"I don't have the code for this," Clive said.

"Try anything," Devon demanded.

"I am! Nothing's working!"

A clock was ticking inside my head as ten seconds went by, then twenty.

"Stand back, Ivy," Devon said.

Obediently, I took several steps from the door. I jumped when I heard the loud report of a gun. I didn't know where Devon had gotten it and didn't care. Shooting the glass out of the cage seemed like a fine alternative to me, but the expected shattering didn't come.

"Damn it," Devon fumed. "It's bulletproof."

The clock in my head said I only had about thirty seconds left.

I watched helplessly as he turned and ran for the wall. An ax was mounted in the concrete and Devon grabbed it. He ran back for the door and I watched him swing the blade. It clanged loudly against the hand lever, but held firm.

Twenty seconds.

He swung again, and again, but nothing gave. I suddenly realized . . . this was it.

"Devon," I said, heading for the glass wall next to the door. "Devon!" My shout made him stop and he finally looked at me. His chest heaved from exertion and the panicked look in his eyes made mine fill with tears. "It's no use," I said quietly.

He stared at me. "I'll get you out," he said, the words sounding like a plea for forgiveness.

"It's all right," I said, shaking my head. It wasn't, not really, I mean, I hadn't wanted to die today, but I'd come along willingly.

I placed my hand flat against the glass. Tears spilled down my cheeks but I didn't look away from Devon. I wished in that moment that I had the means to kill myself. I didn't want his last image of me to be what Clive had of Anna.

Ten seconds.

Devon dropped the ax to the ground and stood opposite me. Raising his hand, he pressed his palm against mine, mirroring me.

"I'm sorry," he said, his voice a choked rasp. "I'm so very sorry."

"Don't leave me until . . . after," I whispered, unable to say the words *I'm dead*.

He shook his head, his eyes unnaturally bright, and the blue of his eyes no longer reminded me of ice, but of the sea, warm and gentle as it lapped the shore.

Zero.

A sudden hiss made me start and I glanced upward to see a billowing cloud of white descending from the vent slats in the ceiling. Fear struck like a bolt of lightning and my knees gave out, making me crumple to the floor.

"Ivy!"

Devon's shout tore through me, the stricken expression on his face almost immediately obscured by the cloud as it filled the cage. I couldn't see anything and the cloud was thick, pressing against my lungs and eyes until I choked—deep, hacking coughs that went on and on and on.

The hissing finally stopped and I was flat on my stomach, my cheek pressed against the cold concrete. The coughing fit was over, leaving me wrung out. The smooth floor was icy against my bare legs and I didn't move. My eyes were streaming when I forced them open, realizing the fog was starting to clear. I almost lifted my hand to brush away the wetness, then fear that it was blood made me stop.

"Ivy! Ivy! Speak to me!"

Devon's voice was frantic, but I didn't want to turn toward him. I didn't want him to see me like this. I wanted him to remember me the way he'd last seen me. Beautiful. Heinrich hadn't said how long the virus took to break down the internal organs, but I was hoping it wouldn't take too long or be as painful as that sounded.

"Ivy, please," Devon begged.

That almost broke me. I managed to sit up, then echoed Anna's position. I pulled my knees to my chest and laid my head on my arms, letting my falling hair obscure my face. I still faced away from him toward the back wall. I didn't feel any pain, not yet, and I wondered when it would start. Anna hadn't made a sound and I wondered if she even could anymore.

"I found the decontamination program," I heard Clive call to Devon.

"Then activate it, for chrissakes!"

The sound of a fan whirring filled the cage, making the last of the fog lift away. A light mist fell from above, coating my hair, clothes, and skin. It didn't matter now. It was too late.

A loud buzz followed by the click of the lock, and the door flew open. An instant later, Devon had fallen to his knees beside me.

"Look at me," he insisted, grabbing my upper arms, but I kept my head down, suddenly overcome by lethargy. I didn't even have the energy to speak.

His hand was beneath my chin, forcing my face up, and I managed to moan in protest. I didn't want him to see me. He pushed my hair back and I forced my eyes open, afraid of the horror I'd see on his face once he got a good look at me. But he showed not a flicker of reaction.

"You're going to be all right," Devon said. "I'm going to get you out of here."

A tortured groan made Devon jerk his head around and I realized Clive had followed him into the cage. He held Anna in his arms, his hand lovingly wiping the blood from her face.

"My Anna," he said in a broken whisper. "This is my fault. They did this because of me. Please forgive me."

But Anna was dead. Even I could tell that. Clive clutched her to him and sobbed into her hair, begging her lifeless body to forgive him. My eyes streamed more, the ache inside my chest like a vise around my lungs as I watched.

"Come on," Devon called to Clive. "Help me get Ivy out of here." But Clive didn't move, didn't even hear Devon's words. He just rocked back and forth, crying inconsolably as he murmured to her.

Devon stared for a moment, as though assessing what to do with Clive, then he was lifting me in his arms and carrying me out of the cage. He didn't call again for Clive.

My body hung limp like a rag doll, my head lolling weakly against his shoulder. My eyes slipped shut and I lost some time.

When I opened them again, Devon was arranging me in the front seat of his car. He reclined the passenger seat and yanked the seat belt over my torso.

"Stay with me, darling," he murmured, his hand brushing my cheek. Then he shut the door and rounded the car to slide into the driver's seat.

The engine roared as we tore down the street. If I'd been more aware, Devon's driving would have scared me. I'd never driven so fast. His weaving between cars on the road made me dizzy. I closed my eyes.

And I lost some more time.

When I became aware again, Devon was carrying me down a hallway. He stopped, kicking a door until it opened.

"Help me," he demanded.

"Holy shit," I heard Beau say. "What happened to her?"

"Just get my door open. Here's the keys."

The jangle of metal was loud to me and I stared upward. Devon glanced down.

"We're almost there," he said, lifting me higher and pressing his cheek to my head as I lay against his shoulder. "Just a bit more."

"There's nothing you can do," I murmured, forcing my lips to move. It felt like my tongue was made of lead.

"Shh, don't try to talk," he said.

"Got it," Beau said, then Devon was carrying me into the apartment and back to the bedroom. He placed me carefully on the bed as though afraid of breaking me.

"Thank you," he said to Beau, who'd followed us.

"What can I do to help?" Beau asked.

"Stay with her for a moment," Devon replied, pulling his cell phone out of his pocket. He walked out of the room and I heard him talking but couldn't make out the words.

Beau looked down at me, his face creased in concern. He shifted uneasily from one foot to the other.

"How do I look?" I asked, unable to bear not knowing any longer.

"You look like hell," was his frank reply.

I closed my eyes again, feeling my sticky eyelashes mat together. I still felt no pain and I said a prayer of thanks for small blessings.

When I opened my eyes, Beau was gone and Devon sat next to me on the bed. He held my hand and I felt a hard pinch in my arm. Turning, I saw a stranger there and a needle in my arm.

I made a noise and tried to pull my arm away, but Devon held it firm.

"Let him," he told me. "It will help."

It didn't matter if I believed him or not, there was nothing I could do. When the guy finished with the injection, he took four vials of my blood. I watched the red fluid fill the small tubes and wondered. Why was Devon doing this? Did they think they'd be able to stop Heinrich by learning more about the virus? I supposed I couldn't really argue with that, even if I had the energy to do so.

And time passed.

Consciousness came slowly and, with it, pain. My entire body ached as though I'd done a three-hour workout, but even with that, I recognized that I could move again.

I turned my head, realizing that I'd been moved. Devon now sat behind me on the bed, my body cradled between his legs as I lay back against his chest. A thin blanket covered me and a quick glance down showed me the dress had been removed and I was naked.

At my movement, Devon woke.

"Ivy?" he asked, his arms lifting to wrap around me. "Can you hear me?"

"Of course I can hear you," I said, my voice so harsh and dry, it made me cough.

"Here," he said, grabbing a glass of water from the table by the bed. He held it to my lips and I took a cautious sip. It felt wonderful on my parched tongue and throat. When I was through, Devon set it back on the table and I sighed, lying back against him again.

"What happened?" I asked. My memory was fuzzy, the last clear thing was watching Clive embracing Anna's dead body.

"You've been very ill," Devon said. "How do you feel?"

"Okay," I said, silently taking inventory of my body. "A little sore and achy."

Devon carefully shifted me to the side and crawled out from behind me. I glanced at him and gasped. He had several days' growth of beard.

"Oh my God," I said. "How long have I been unconscious?"

"Today is Friday," he clarified. His eyes were bloodshot and red-rimmed with dark shadows beneath them.

I'd been out for nearly three days. It suddenly occurred to me, was I on my deathbed?

"Am I . . . am I going to die?" I stammered. How much longer did I have? But Devon was already shaking his head.

"No, sweet Ivy," he said. "You're going to be just fine." His smile was weak but triumphant as his hand settled on my forehead, lightly brushing back my hair.

"But . . . how?" I was confused. The virus should have killed me.

Devon turned away and walked into the bathroom, talking as he went. "It must need multiple exposures to kill," he said. I heard the water running, then he returned a few moments later with a steaming washcloth. "You're not dying. Not today." He sat next to me and gently pressed the warm cloth to my cheek, tenderly cleansing my eyes. When he finished, the cloth was stained pink.

"Have you been taking care of me?" I asked.

"Not exactly Florence Nightingale," he replied with a wry smile, "but I did my best."

My heart turned over in my chest. Devon may have said many times that he didn't love and didn't care, but his actions spoke much louder than his words.

He brought me something to eat, some soup that he'd heated up in the microwave, then helped me to the bathroom. Brushing my teeth felt awesome and the hot spray from the shower even more so. I stood under the cascade of water and let it wash over me. There's little that feels better than washing your hair after being sick and unable to for several days.

When I finally emerged from the bathroom wrapped in a bath sheet, I felt much better. The heat had helped with the residual ache in my limbs. A close inspection in the mirror showed me that my eyes were a bit bloodshot, but otherwise just fine.

It looked like Devon had showered and shaved, too. He'd changed the sheets and now lay on his stomach on the bed, shirtless with wet hair. I sat down and opened my mouth to say something when the sound of a soft snore met my ears. Leaning over, I realized he was sound asleep. I smiled and drew a blanket up over him. He didn't stir. Closing the door behind me, I left him to get some rest. As for me, I decided I was tired of lying in bed.

My luggage was in the living room—Devon must have brought it in at some point while I was sick—and I dug through it for clothes. Yoga pants and a soft fleece shirt felt like heaven.

A buzzing noise distracted me and I followed the sound to Devon's cell phone on the counter. Someone had texted him. I glanced at the screen and saw the beginnings of the message.

Tests confirmed. You were right.

Hmm. Devon was right about what? What tests?

My fingers itched to pick up the phone and be nosey, but I refrained. Sitting on the couch, I flipped on the television and found a rerun of *Friends* to watch. I must have dozed off because I woke to the sound of a door flying open and hitting the wall with a crash.

"Ivy!" Devon's anxious call was loud in the apartment.

"I'm here," I said, climbing off the couch and hurrying back to the bedroom. He met me in the doorway, his expression relieved as he pulled me into his arms.

"I fell asleep," he said, his chin resting on the top of my head.

"I know. I didn't want to disturb you."

The skin of his chest was warm beneath my cheek and his body felt strong and solid against mine. I reveled in the moment. Devon cared about me, whether he said the words or not, and it was the silver-and-gold lining to the cloud that hovered over me.

"How are you feeling?" he asked, his hand brushing through my damp hair.

"Good," I replied, tipping my head back to look up at him. "I'm good. Thanks to you."

Devon's face was serious as he gazed at me, his hand moving from my hair to my cheek. "I thought I'd lost you," he murmured, "and I've lost too many."

I wanted to pursue that statement, ask him exactly who he'd lost and how, but he bent down and kissed me.

It was a warm, tender kiss, gentle and reverent, the soft brush of his tongue against mine a question rather than a demand. I opened my mouth beneath his and he pulled me closer, his hand sliding to the back of my neck underneath my hair as he deepened the kiss. Languid and sweet, it seemed Devon was trying to say with his body what he couldn't say out loud.

He pulled me back to the bed. "You should rest," he said, easing me down until I was lying flat.

"But I'm not tired," I protested, though I didn't fight him. It felt nice, him fussing over me.

"Perhaps not, but it will make me feel better."

He lay beside me and I turned on my side to face him. The sun was shining brightly in the room, making his hair gleam like burnished gold with elusive copper highlights.

I reached for him and he caught my hand in his, slotting our fingers together. His gaze was tinged with something I couldn't name as he stared at me.

"What?" I asked, suddenly self-conscious. "What's wrong?"

Devon hesitated before answering. "I'm just memorizing how you look right now with the sun behind you, how you're staring at me as if I were a hero."

"You are," I said with a relieved smile. "My hero."

But Devon didn't smile back. If anything, my words seemed to bother him, his brow creasing in a frown as he studied me.

"Will you tell me about what you said earlier?" I asked. "About those you've lost?"

Devon's eyes flicked away from mine and down to our joined hands. "You don't want to hear about that," he said lightly. "It's a sad, tragic tale."

"You know my sad, tragic tale," I countered.

His gaze met mine and the grief I saw in his eyes made my heart lurch.

"My life," he began, then hesitated before continuing. "It's not exactly conducive to forming attachments. It's dangerous, for me and those whom I care for. I learned that lesson long ago."

I waited, hoping he'd go on. Eventually, he did.

"There was a woman," he said, his eyes dropping back down to our joined hands. "Her name was Kira. She was . . . beautiful and clever, loving and kind, far kinder than I deserved. But she wasn't an agent, just an ancillary victim to events beyond her control. Beyond my control. She did love me, I think. She said she did. It was . . . a revelation. No one had said such a thing to me before, at least, no one that I remembered."

Tears stung my eyes but I blinked them back. He was still talking, the words seeming to come with difficulty to him, and I wondered if he'd spoken about this to anyone before.

"I was on a mission when I found out they'd discovered her, and what she meant to me. By the time I was able to reach her, she was dead. They'd . . . tortured her, cruelly, and left her to die. There was nothing I could do, except avenge her."

Despite my resolve, tears streamed from my eyes, falling into the pillow beneath my cheek. Devon's grip on my hand was painfully tight, but I didn't protest.

"I'm so sorry," I whispered.

Devon glanced up at me, seeming to come back from the memories he'd been reliving inside his mind. He quickly swiped the tear tracks from my face.

"Shh," he said. "Don't cry. I want you to know, to understand."

"To understand what?"

His face was grim. "To understand why we can't be together."

Tears fell again and this time, Devon didn't tell me not to cry. Instead, he gathered me in his arms and held me.

"Do you think you'll feel up to traveling tomorrow?" he asked me later as we sat cuddled on the couch.

I'd had a craving for pizza and he'd caved, ordering from my favorite place and adding extra cheese. I was finishing my slice as I rested against his chest, his legs on either side of me.

"Probably," I said. "Why?"

"I promised you Christmas in Paris, remember?"

I inhaled sharply, then twisted so I could see him. "Really? You'd still take me?" It might be the only chance I'd ever have to visit someplace like that, but I thought he'd changed his mind after all that had happened.

"Absolutely," he said with a wink.

"But what about, you know, Heinrich and the virus and all that?"

His smile faded. "I passed on the intel I gathered to my boss. They've left the country and another agent is tracking them down. He'll sort it."

I was surprised. Devon didn't seem like the type to not finish something.

"So you're just . . . giving up?" I asked.

Devon's face darkened. "Not giving up," he said. "Choosing to keep you alive."

"By going to where Nanotech is headquartered?"

"There's more in Paris than Nanotech," he countered.

I considered this. "I thought we couldn't be together?"

"We can't, not in the long term," he said, tracing a lock of my hair between his fingers. "But it's Christmas, and I'd like to keep you just a little while longer." His smile was a bit forced and more than a little sad. I suddenly realized what he *wasn't* saying.

Devon had no one else.

No one wanted to be alone on Christmas, not even secret spy agent Devon Clay.

I squirmed around, turning until I straddled him, the T-shirt I wore riding up on my hips to expose the tiny panties I wore, now pressed against the crotch of his jeans.

"I don't know if I have the right clothes for Christmas in Paris," I teased, feeding him a bite of my slice of pizza.

"I hear they have shops in Paris," he countered. His hands slipped under my shirt to rest on my waist.

"I won't have shoes to go with dresses from Paris," I said thoughtfully, taking one last bite before setting aside the crust. I swallowed, then licked my fingers, catching Devon staring at my mouth.

"Are you angling for a shopping spree?" he asked.

"*Spree* sounds a bit much," I said with mock thoughtfulness. "But you can't go to Paris and not buy clothes and shoes, right?"

"Oh, absolutely," he agreed, pushing the hem of my shirt up. I crossed my arms and tugged it over my head, letting it fall to the floor.

Devon's mouth settled over my breast, a groan from deep in his throat making me smile. His tongue flicked my nipple, then sucked while his hand covered my other breast, brushing the tip with his thumb.

"Then I'll need a place . . . to wear it," I said, my voice breathless as I tried to concentrate.

"I'll take you dancing," he murmured against my skin, his mouth moving to my other nipple. His teeth lightly grazed my flesh, then his tongue laved the tender skin.

"That sounds . . . lovely," I breathed on a sigh as his lips captured mine.

CHAPTER SEVENTEEN

My nose was nearly pressed against the glass as I took in the dazzling array of lights laid out beneath me. We were on a huge private jet. I'd gawked like a hick from Kansas when we'd gotten on it—oh wait, I *was* a hick from Kansas.

I'd slept during some of the long flight, leaning against Devon, who sat next to me. Now we were landing in Paris, a place I never in a million years thought I'd get to visit.

Devon took care of our luggage when we landed, ushering me to a car that was waiting for us.

"Wow," I breathed, watching out the window as we drove through the city. If I craned my neck I could see the Eiffel Tower, all lit up. The streets were lit up as well, rows of Christmas lights wrapped the trees lining the road we were on. It wasn't until I saw the Arc de Triomphe, remembered from my ninth-grade French class, that I realized we were on the Champs-Élysées.

Tears stung my eyes and I sniffed. It was hard to believe I was actually there.

A snowy white handkerchief appeared and I glanced up. Devon pressed it into my hand, a smile playing about his mouth.

"Sorry," I apologized, embarrassed at my reaction. I dabbed at my eyes. "You must think I'm a real country bumpkin."

"Don't be sorry," he said quietly. "And no, I don't. Your tears mean you're still capable of wonder. I'd forgotten what that's like. It's a pleasure to see Paris through your eyes." He leaned closer to me. "One thing I've learned is to enjoy the moments you're given. Moments are fleeting—ones worthy of remembering, even more so." He lifted his hand to trace the line of my jaw, his fingers threading through my hair.

Our gazes met and held. The icy blue of his eyes no longer sent a shiver through me. Instead, it was comforting. Devon allowed so little emotion to show, yet his touch, his words, the way he looked at me—it all added up to more than he would ever say. What that meant, if it would make any difference in how it all ended, I didn't know.

We pulled up to a hotel and a valet opened the door. Devon got out, then extended his hand to help me. I stood, openmouthed on the sidewalk and gazing all around as the valet removed our luggage from the trunk.

He slotted his fingers through mine and led me into what could only be a five-star luxury hotel—the brand was one that I'd read about but had never thought I'd ever be able to afford to stay in.

The lobby was sumptuous with marble floors, plush rugs, and with various sculptures and floral arrangements dotting any available flat surface. Huge gilded mirrors hung on the walls next to paintings, and employees in spotless uniforms worked behind the desk.

Devon motioned for me to sit in one of the velvet-covered chairs while he went to the desk. I people-watched while I waited, then wished I hadn't. Watching the men and women coming and going made me acutely self-conscious of the jeans I wore. The women wore expensive, tailored clothes or gowns, and I imagined they were going to an elaborate seven-course French dinner, or perhaps to the opera house.

I was more than a little envious of their clothes. I was sure that I was watching more designer gowns than I could rattle off walking through the doors of this hotel, draped lovingly over the women's figures.

One couple in particular caught my eye. A striking pair, the man was tall with inky black hair and deep, intense blue eyes. He carried an aura of danger about him that instantly reminded me of Devon. The woman at his side was a stark contrast. A petite little thing, her hair was an unusual color of strawberry-blonde and hung in gorgeous waves down her back. He caught her hand in his, bringing it to his lips for a kiss. Her smile was sweet and the adoration in his eyes made me sigh. They were obviously very much in love and I watched them leave the hotel, my imagination working overtime.

"Ready?"

I glanced up to see that Devon had returned. His smile and the softness in his eyes made my heart turn over.

Our room elicited more wonder from me. As luxurious as the lobby, the décor was unlike anything I'd ever seen in a hotel. The pattern was a beautiful blue, echoed in the upholstery and wallpaper. A king-size bed dominated the bedroom, while a sofa and dining table adorned the sitting room. The window caught my eye and I realized it wasn't a window, but the entry to a terrace.

Hurrying to it, I stepped outside. The wind was cold but I ignored it, my eyes transfixed on the view of the Eiffel Tower proudly extending beyond the rooftops, the glow of its lights blurring slightly in my vision.

"Do you like it?" Devon asked, his arms curving around my waist to pull me back against him. His lips nuzzled my neck and I tipped my head to the side.

"I-it's . . . amazing," I stammered. "I have no words for this." I had no idea how he was able to afford to stay in a place like this, but I was really, really glad he could.

We stood there like that for a few minutes, just taking in the view. Well, I took in the view. Devon was much more concerned with kissing my neck, not that I minded.

"Welcome to Paris."

⤳

The next day, it seemed Devon was determined to show me everything Paris had to offer, dragging me from bed early in the morning to have fresh chocolate croissants and coffee in a very French café. He sat close to me, lightly touching me while we talked, whether it was my hand or my shoulder, tucking a lock of hair behind my ear or pressing his knee against mine. It made me feel . . . special, for lack of a better word. His attention was solely on me, his focus absolute, and I wouldn't have traded it for anything.

By the time we'd finished with breakfast, the shops had opened. Devon hadn't been exaggerating when he'd said a "shopping spree." He bought me designer jeans and blouses, skirts and dresses, and enough lingerie to fill my drawers back home.

"Stop!" I finally said, decidedly uncomfortable at the amount of money he was spending on me. "I don't need any of this."

We were in the private dressing room area of one of the high-end stores and Devon had just handed the saleslady a pile of clothes. He rose from the chair where he'd been waiting, evaluating the outfits I'd paraded in front of him.

"I never said you did," Devon replied, resting his hands on my waist. "But I want to buy it for you, so let me. You like them, don't you?" He tugged me closer until our bodies touched.

"That's beside the point—"

"Not to me, it isn't," he interrupted. "You wear these clothes like you were born to it." He placed his lips by my ear. "I adore it. Adore watching you. Your face lights up and it's almost as though merely touching the fabric is enough to make you come."

My pulse shot up at that as his hands drifted down to cup my rear.

"Leave us," he suddenly said, his voice a firm command. I started, glancing over his shoulder to see the saleslady had returned, but was now walking quickly away. Somehow he'd heard her approach.

Devon backed me into the alcove where I'd been changing, closing the door behind him. When he turned back, he pulled me into his arms, his mouth landing hard on mine. The skirt I wore began sliding up my legs, his fingers tugging at the fabric. I pulled at his belt and had his pants unfastened by the time the skirt was at my waist. He shoved my panties down my legs and I kicked them off.

Lifting me, he set my back to the wall while I guided his cock to my entrance. A hard thrust and he was inside, filling and stretching me, forcing my body to accommodate his length. I was wet for him, my body so in tune with his demands that I was already primed and aroused, my clit pulsing with need.

His tongue was a soft slide against mine, a stark contrast to the fierceness with which he took me. I hooked my ankles behind his back and held on for the ride. His fingers dug into the soft flesh of my rear, the friction of his cock hard and fast. In moments, I was shattering around him, my cries swallowed by his mouth covering mine. I had to turn away, sucking in a breath. The pounding of my heart was loud in my ears as Devon's lips fastened to a spot on my neck. He hadn't slowed, despite my orgasm, and I could feel the pressure build again as he thrust into me.

He sucked hard on my neck, the slight pain sending a shiver through me. He was close, his cock growing even larger inside me. The slide of his flesh against mine was almost too much, too intense, but then I was coming again. His pelvis ground against mine as he climaxed, the pulse of his cock emptying inside me, prolonging my orgasm. I couldn't stop the cries falling from my lips, his groan echoing in my ears as my nails dug into the fabric stretched across his shoulders.

The world slowly righted itself as I panted for breath. His lips trailed a path from my neck to my mouth for a slow, deep kiss that made my toes curl. He pulled out of me and used his pocket square to wipe between my legs, his touch gentle against my overly sensitive skin. I righted my clothes as he tucked himself back into his pants.

"So, I'm thinking we probably just bought this skirt, too, right?" I asked.

Devon laughed outright, his eyes twinkling in a way that made me wish I could snap a mental photo.

"Worth every penny," he teased, leaning down to kiss me again.

He had our packages sent back to the hotel, taking me to lunch before hitting up more stores, this time in search of a ball gown.

"I thought we'd go see *The Nutcracker* tonight," Devon said, pulling me into a shop with windows full of floor-length gowns. "They perform it at the Opéra Bastille through December. Would you like that?"

I nodded. "I would love that." Which was an understatement. In a part of my mind, I couldn't believe this was happening. It seemed too good to be true. A romantic tale straight from a fantasy, yet the solid presence of Devon's hand clasped around mine proved it was very real.

The ball gown was Oscar de la Renta and it was the stuff fairy tales were made of. Strapless, the champagne-colored dress had a fitted bodice and waist, with soft tulle making the skirt poof out as it fell to a couple of inches off the floor. Gold paillettes sparkled in the skirt, increasing toward the top of the dress until the bodice was nearly covered in the glittering spangles.

Now I stood, staring into the mirror at a stranger. I'd pulled my hair up and added long earrings to complement the dress. The color of the dress, the champagne and gold, combined with my blonde hair to make me look as though I were a princess. I was almost afraid to go to dinner—I didn't want to get anything on the dress. But that wasn't really an option, and with a sigh, I left the bedroom and walked into the sitting room where Devon was waiting.

He turned, his brows lifting slightly when he saw me.

I did a slow pirouette, the skirt billowing out around my ankles. "How do I look?"

Devon set aside the glass he'd been holding. "You are the most beautiful woman I've ever seen." The roughness of his voice combined with the look in his eyes made my smile so wide, I thought my face would crack. I'd never felt so adored before, and I would have given anything to bottle up the feeling so I could use it again later.

Dinner was an elaborate event at a restaurant nearly as fancy as our hotel. Devon spoke fluidly in French to the waiter, and soon I held a flute of sparkling champagne.

"Let's have a toast, then," Devon said, raising his own glass. "To a Christmas spent with a stunning woman whose beauty is only matched by her strength and courage."

I stared wide-eyed at him, rendered speechless. Is that what he thought of me? Tears stung my eyes as he gently clinked his flute against mine.

"No one's ever said something like that to me before," I managed to say.

"They have now. Cheers." He took a drink, his eyes still on mine, as I copied him. The champagne was cold on my tongue, the bubbles tickling my nose.

I had no idea what we ate or what time it was as course after course appeared. If I saw something that made me hesitate, Devon would take a tiny bit of it on his fork and make me try it. More than once, it turned out to be something incredibly delicious.

I was feeling pleasantly full and a bit tipsy when we left. The opera was close enough to walk and I begged that we do so.

"Please? I'll fall asleep if I don't walk off some of this rich food," I said. "Plus, I want to see the lights."

Devon gave in and I clung to his arm, his hand covering mine as we walked. There was a huge Christmas tree in sight and I marveled at the elegant buildings stretched above us with their balconies etched in snow. I sighed, utterly happy and content.

"Have you enjoyed today?" Devon asked.

I looked up at him and smiled. "You have to ask?" I teased.

His smile was soft. "I know you like the clothes, that goes without saying. I was wondering, and hoping, actually, that you . . . enjoyed the company as well."

Devon's British circumspection made my heart ache. I stopped walking, pulling him to a halt, too.

"I don't care about the clothes," I said. Devon raised an eyebrow. "I mean, I do, but they don't matter. Not really. I'm just happy to be with you. Please don't doubt that."

Devon's face was serious now. "In spite of what I've brought down on you? The pain you've had to endure because of me?"

"You're worth it," I said with a shrug.

Devon studied me, his gaze intent, and I didn't look away. After a moment, he leaned down, his lips brushing against mine with the tenderness of an angel's wing.

And I couldn't have dreamt of a more perfect moment, place, or person as the lights of Paris twinkled in the night and Devon's arms wrapped around my waist to pull me closer.

Cheerful bright light streamed through the window when I woke on Christmas Eve morning. I stretched my arms over my head, then pulled the sheet up to cover me from where it had fallen to my waist.

"And here I was enjoying the view."

I turned to see Devon sitting by the window, reading the paper and drinking a cup of tea. He'd put on a robe, but I was still naked.

"Good morning," I said with a smile. "What time is it?"

"Late," he said, putting down the paper. "You've been lying about all morning, you lazy wench." Getting up, he sat beside me on the bed, tugging the sheet down to bare my breasts.

"It's your fault," I said. "You kept me up too late."

He was kissing my breasts now, his hands curved around my ribs. "Are you saying you didn't enjoy the entertainment?"

I buried my fingers in his hair, the slow rasp of his tongue against my nipple making me sigh in pleasure. "Are you talking about the opera or afterwards?" We'd made love twice last night, once when we'd returned to the hotel and Devon had peeled the princess dress from me, and again in the wee hours of the morning when I'd woken on the brink of an orgasm to find his head between my legs.

"Both."

"You have to ask?"

He laughed deep in his throat before moving from my breasts to my mouth. I quickly turned away. "Not until I brush my teeth," I insisted.

"As if I care," he said, but acquiesced, kissing the tender skin underneath my jaw instead.

I giggled and pushed him away, escaping from the bed and his clutches. Naked, I walked to the bathroom, glancing over my shoulder to see his eyes devouring me.

When I emerged from the shower, I was toweling my hair dry, but stopped short at what lay sitting out. Devon had unpacked, and the leather journal I'd stolen sat on the antique coffee table in the sitting room; the pendant Galler had given me was lying on top of it. It was the first time I'd seen him with both items since the day I'd given him the journal.

"Did you find someone to translate the coded pages?" I asked.

Devon glanced up from the newspaper he was reading. "I did."

"What did they say?"

He hesitated, then said, "It's the instructions for formulating the vaccine."

My heart stuttered. "Why did you bring it here if you're not on the case anymore?" I asked him, striving for nonchalance. I took a croissant and café au lait from the tray that room service had delivered. The croissant was pristine on a beautiful china plate that was so delicate it was slightly translucent.

Devon took another drink of his coffee, surveying me across the top of the cup. "I have to dead drop it," he explained. "They'll need it."

"They?"

"The people I work for," he said.

"The Shadow?" I asked around a bite of croissant, recalling what Heinrich had said.

Devon was suddenly right next to me, his hand closing none-too-gently on my arm. I let out a squeak of surprise.

"Don't ever say those words," he hissed.

My eyes were wide at the urgency in his voice, and if that hadn't convinced me, the deadly earnestness of his expression would have.

"If they find out you know that name, they'll kill you," he continued.

I swallowed the lump of croissant, the flaky pastry now tasting like dust in my mouth. I couldn't think what to say, so I just nodded. Devon gazed intently in my eyes, as though ascertaining that I understood the seriousness of what he'd said. At last, he gave a curt nod and let me go.

"I'm going to shower," he said easily, as though nothing had just happened. "Then we'll see what shops are open in Paris on Christmas Eve. I don't think we bought you nearly enough shoes yesterday to go with all those clothes."

I managed a weak smile and hugged him, wrapping my arms around his neck. "That sounds wonderful," I said. "But kiss me first."

Devon gave me a chaste kiss on the lips, but I pressed against him, curving my hand around the back of his neck and holding him close when he would have pulled away. I traced the curve of his lower lip with my tongue until he took the hint and gave me a real kiss that I felt all the way to my toes. I memorized the taste and texture of him, the feel of his body, the scent of his skin faintly tinged with his cologne. Finally, we parted.

"Any more of that and your shoes will be delayed," he gently teased me, rubbing his nose alongside mine.

"Sorry," I apologized. "Save it for later, right?"

"We'll make it the quickest shoe shopping in Paris history."

I forced a laugh at his joke, then watched as he disappeared into the bathroom, my smile fading once he closed the door.

Now I had to betray the man I loved.

CHAPTER
EIGHTEEN

I dressed in record time, throwing on skinny jeans, a long black sweater, and my black boots. I grabbed my purse, slipping the journal and pendant inside as I heard the shower start from behind the bathroom's closed door. Shrugging on my coat, I cast one last eye toward the bathroom, wishing desperately that things could be different. But wishing was for children, and I'd stopped being a child a long time ago.

While I walked down the hallway, I dialed the number I'd memorized. When it was picked up, I said, "I have it." The voice on the other end gave me instructions and I ended the call. A moment later, I was riding down the elevator.

Flipping to the back of the journal, I didn't hesitate before tearing out all the pages Devon had said were written in code. I had to do what I had to do, but I wasn't about to be responsible for helping unleash an incurable virus on an unsuspecting populace.

Going to the front desk, I took out the card Agent Lane had given me, handing it and the pages to the man behind the marble counter.

"I need these papers to get to this man, just as soon as possible. Can you do that for me?"

"*Oui, mademoiselle,*" the man said, taking the papers. "I will see that it is done."

I thanked him, then hurried outside. The air was crisp and cold, everything covered in a carpet of white from snow that had fallen overnight. I took a long look around, taking everything in while I waited at the curb a short way from the hotel.

It didn't take long, perhaps two minutes, before a shiny black sedan pulled up. The back door opened, but no one emerged. The car was for me.

Taking a deep breath, I headed for the car. I'd put one foot inside when I heard a commotion and turned back.

It was Devon. He'd emerged from the hotel and was frantically glancing left, then right. He spotted me, and the look on his face made fear spike hard in my veins. Pure rage shone from his eyes, his lips twisted in a growl. I froze in terror. Then the moment was over and he was running flat out toward me.

I dived inside the car and pulled the door shut behind me as the driver stepped on the gas. Devon made a grab for the handle, missing by inches. I twisted in the seat to stare out the rear window where he stood, watching the car drive away.

"Cutting it a bit close, aren't you, my dear?"

I turned to the man sitting beside me in the backseat.

"I'm here, aren't I?"

Heinrich just smiled. "Let's have it then," he ordered.

I swallowed and dug in my purse, unearthing the journal and the pendant. "Are you going to keep your side of the deal?" I asked, handing the items to him.

He didn't even glance at me, his fingers thumbing through the journal, pausing in several spots to study it. "You'd be unwise to question me," he said mildly.

"I did what you said," I reminded him, something close to panic rising to engulf the regret that threatened to drown me. "Despite the fact that you nearly killed me with the virus."

"Yes, you've been very useful," Heinrich said, closing the journal and fixing me with a calculated look. "Infecting you was an experiment. And since you're still alive, that means it worked."

"What are you talking about?" I asked. "We made a deal. You let him live, I deliver the journal and pendant."

"And that's been done," he said with a smile that sent a chill through me. "But you're living proof that Devon has the vaccine."

My face paled. I remembered the man who'd given me an injection and taken my blood when I'd been so sick. Was Heinrich right? At the time, Devon had said I hadn't died because I wasn't exposed long enough, but had that been a lie? Had Devon cured me, then lied to me about it?

I opened my mouth to ask more questions, but the driver interrupted.

"Sir, we're being followed."

Both Heinrich and I turned to look out the back window and my heart leapt to my throat.

Devon was chasing us on a motorcycle.

"Oh my God . . ." I breathed.

Heinrich laughed. "Mr. Clay is rather determined. Lose him."

The car put on a burst of speed, pushing me back against the seat. We weaved through traffic, breaking, I was sure, at least a hundred traffic laws. I held my breath, certain at any moment we were going to wreck.

I craned my neck to look for Devon, who was managing to keep up with us. I was terrified he was going to crash. He didn't even have a helmet on.

The car fishtailed around a corner, throwing me against the door, then we were going down into a tunnel and I lost sight of Devon.

We emerged going so fast that the car hit the top of the ramp and was briefly airborne. My teeth clacked hard together as I was tossed around again in the backseat.

"He's still behind us, sir," the driver said.

"I'll take care of this." Heinrich reached inside his jacket and pulled out a handgun. He rolled down the window on his side and leaned out.

I watched in horror as he took aim at Devon, now only three or four car lengths behind us, who showed no sign that he saw the impending threat. Or if he did, he was too angry to care. Instead, his speed increased.

I threw myself at Heinrich just as he pulled the trigger. The shot ricocheted off a nearby car, making the vehicle swerve into the path of his motorcycle. Devon jerked the bike to the side and I saw him go flying, then we were out of sight.

"You stupid bitch," Heinrich seethed at me. "I nearly had him. Don't interfere again."

He drew back his arm, then slammed the butt of the gun against the side of my head. A searing pain went through me, then everything went black.

⤮

"Please, I'll do whatever you want," I begged. "Please." But I had no idea what they wanted from me. They hadn't asked me a single question. All they wanted from me was my pain.

"Enough, gentlemen," a new voice said.

I heard another yell from Devon and it made me want to die. He was being hurt, I'm sure worse than me, tortured just steps away. And I could do nothing. My very presence had put him in this situation. It was a very real possibility that neither of us would survive the night.

The hand holding me up disappeared and I folded limply to the floor. Staring up, I saw a man I hadn't seen before. He was dressed expensively and was smoking a cigarette.

"Please," I managed to croak. "Please don't hurt him anymore." Just talking made pain ricochet through me and I swallowed on a dry throat.

"Devon Clay, you mean," he replied before taking a long drag.

I gave a fractional nod and forced my lips to move again. "I'll do whatever you want. Just please, don't kill him."

Another muffled yell from across the hall that I felt down to my bones.

"Will you?" the man asked, eyeing me. "Will you really?"

I tried to take a deep breath, but it sent a stabbing pain through my chest. "Anything."

The man sat down, casually crossing one knee over the other. He took another drag on his cigarette, then stubbed it out on the arm of the leather sofa.

"Mr. Clay has something I want," he said. "It seems we're getting nowhere in our efforts to . . . persuade him to give it to me. I imagine he won't walk away from tonight unscathed, if he walks away at all."

I made a noise of distress at this, the pain at the thought of Devon dying more acute than any of the physical trauma I'd suffered.

He fixed me with a calculating look. "However, I will agree to let both of you go, if you bring me what I want."

My heart leapt even as a sense of dread formed like a rock in my stomach. "What do you want?"

"Mr. Galler had a journal he kept that was his father's. I've seen it. There's an insignia on the front that matches a pendant he carried. Do you know either of these items?"

"He gave me the pendant," I rasped.

The man smiled. "Excellent. The pendant is key to unlocking part of a code in that journal. Do you have the journal?"

"No."

"Know where he kept it?"

"No."

He made a sympathetic noise. "That's too bad." Looking up at one of the men in the room, he said, "Tell them to break both his legs."

"No!" I yelled, trying to scramble off the floor despite my injuries. The guy nearest me shoved me back down with one booted foot, then stood on my arm to hold me in place. I grimaced at the pain, turning to the man who was obviously in charge. "I'll get it," I managed to gasp. "I'll get it and you can have them both. Just please, let him go."

He held up a hand, halting the guy who was leaving to do his bidding. I let out a breath in relief.

"You swear to me?" he asked.

"I swear. I'll get it."

Bracing his elbows on his knees, the man leaned down toward me.

"If you don't," he said, "I won't just kill him. I'll make him suffer an agonizing death. And you will watch him die. Have I made myself clear?"

I nodded. My arm was numb now, but I'd disassociated myself from the pain, as I'd done so many times before. It was like it was happening to someone else, as though I were a bystander.

The man studied me intently, as though ascertaining for himself that I understood he meant what he said, then he smiled. "Memorize this," he said, then recited a telephone number. I had to say it several times before he was satisfied. "When you have the items, call that number."

He got to his feet, adjusting his suit jacket and buttoning it. "Keep in mind," he said. "We'll be watching. Any hint that you've told Clay about this conversation or are attempting to double-cross me, and I'll know." He headed for the door.

"Wait," I said, and he stopped to glance back at me. "Who are you?"

"You may call me Heinrich," he said, then turned to the men still in the room. "Make it look good, gentlemen, but no permanent damage." The door closed behind him.

The men were good at their job and I barely remembered the hits I'd taken after that until I'd lost consciousness. But the number . . . the number I didn't forget.

❧

Pain. That was my first thought when consciousness came. My head was killing me.

I groaned and sat up, my hand going to my head, coming away sticky with blood that matted my hair and had dried on my cheek.

Looking around, I saw I was in a small room lying on a cot. An opaque window was on one wall, whereas the other walls were all solid with no decoration of any sort. There was no way for me to tell what hour of the day it was or how much time had passed.

I already knew before I checked the door that it would be locked, but I tried anyway before returning to sit on the cot. Even the short walk to the door had made me light-headed.

I had no idea what I was supposed to do now or what was going to happen to me.

I thought about the deal I'd made with Heinrich. At the time, I'd have done anything to save Devon's life, not realizing until later that doing so would mean betraying him in the end. But he was alive, and that fact alone kept the regret at bay. If I was faced with the choice again, I'd do the same thing.

I wondered where Devon was, if he'd escaped from the accident unscathed or if he was badly hurt somewhere. The look on his face as he'd emerged from the hotel would be burned into my mind for a long time to come. Always so circumspect, seeing his fury so plainly written made me shudder at how enraged he must have been . . . must still be. I hadn't wanted to see that, hadn't wanted to know the faith and trust Devon had lost in me. I imagined he'd remember me with loathing and disgust, which was a far cry from how I'd remember him. A man I loved enough to betray him.

My stomach rumbled, reminding me that it had been a long time since I'd eaten, but there was nothing I could do about it. Pulling my knees to my chest, I waited.

I didn't know how much time had passed when the door finally opened. I glanced up, afraid of what would happen next, and it was Heinrich who entered, accompanied by Hugo.

"My dear, we have a problem," he said. He was smoking another cigarette and he dropped it to the floor, then ground it out with his heel.

"What's that?" I asked, my mouth suddenly dry.

"The code. I'd hoped the journal held the formula for the vaccine. Alas, it doesn't."

"That's not my fault," I said quickly.

"There are several pages missing," Heinrich continued, "torn out, actually."

I swallowed, but didn't respond.

He towered over me. "You may not have outlived your usefulness after all."

"How so?"

"Clay has an antidote. He gave it to you to save your life. I want it. I have you. If he was willing to save your life once, let's hope he'll do so again. For your sake."

"He's here," Hugo interrupted, his fingers touching his earpiece as he listened.

"Excellent," Heinrich said. "Bring her and we shall await Mr. Clay."

Hugo's hand clamped around my arm and dragged me to my feet, pulling me out of the room and down a hallway after Heinrich.

We emerged into a spacious room that was much nicer than the room I'd sat in all day. Ivory rugs carpeted the floor over shining hardwood. Two curved sofas in matching chocolate leather faced a fireplace with a fire dancing merrily in the grate. Windows curved along the walls and I could see lights twinkling outside and snow falling. We appeared to be high up, but were outside the city proper.

"Get me my revolver, Hugo," Heinrich ordered. He glanced at me as he gestured to one of the sofas. "Sit."

I had little choice but to obey. I was so scared my knees seemed barely capable of holding me up. I didn't want to be beaten again, or shot.

"Devon's not going to give you what you want," I tried.

"That's where you'll be useful," Heinrich said, taking the revolver from Hugo, who'd quickly returned. "I'm betting he'll go to great lengths to protect you from harm, lengths that are decidedly unwise for a man in his position."

"And what position is that?"

I jerked around, my breath catching at the sight of Devon standing, his silhouette a shadow against the dark windows. He stepped forward, making the light fall on him, and I gasped.

His shirt was torn and dirty and I could see bloody scratches and scrapes on the exposed skin of his arms. Dried blood marred the corner of his mouth and his brow, and a bruise darkened his cheek, but his voice was utterly calm and the hand that held his weapon was steady.

"There you are!" Heinrich exclaimed. "We were expecting you."

Hugo had some kind of long machine-gun type thing pointed straight at Devon, who didn't seem to notice, or care.

"I wouldn't want to disappoint."

"Miss Mason and I were just discussing how foolishly sentimental it was of you to save her life."

"What are you talking about?"

"The antidote," Heinrich clarified. "You tipped your hand. She was infected with the virus, yet here she sits." He moved behind where I sat, his hand settling heavily on my shoulder. "I want that antidote, Mr. Clay, or the immediate future of Miss Mason is in decided . . . jeopardy."

Devon's gaze was ice-cold as it moved over me, pausing so briefly at the blood on my head that I might have imagined it. "I didn't give her an antidote," he denied. "I imagine you need more research on your virus. Obviously, it doesn't affect everyone the same way. She survived. Not that I care one way or another." He shrugged and a stab of pain twisted my stomach. "She's *your* spy, Heinrich."

"Come now, Mr. Clay, you didn't think I let you go that night out of the goodness of my heart? That you refused to give me the information I sought, so I threw up my hands in frustration and left to lick my wounds?" He laughed again. "Hardly. Ms. Mason saved your life. All I asked in exchange was for her to . . . acquire . . . the items I sought."

"She betrayed me," Devon said, his voice flat.

"She saved your life, you bumbling idiot." Heinrich's scathing condescension took me by surprise.

Devon didn't reply, but his hand tightened on his gun.

"So now, if you don't supply the antidote, her life will be forfeit. After all she's gone through for you, you'll let her die now? Come, Mr. Clay. There can be a happy ending for even star-crossed lovers like yourselves. I know it was in the journal, just as I know you took those pages from it. Now hand them over."

Devon's eyes flicked to mine, then back to Heinrich. "I told you," he bit out. "I don't have it."

Heinrich heaved a sigh. "I don't have time for this."

I felt the press of metal against my temple. It was the revolver Hugo had brought.

"This is a very special weapon, Mr. Clay," Heinrich said. "It's an Italian-made replica of an original antique Remington .44 caliber single-action six-shot revolver. I had it specially crafted. Do you like it? There's only one bullet in it, which means Miss Mason has a relatively good chance of surviving . . . if you cooperate."

"She's got nothing to do with this," Devon argued. "This is between you and me. You want that antidote, then let her go."

"Time is running out, Mr. Clay."

The revolver clicked, the hammer falling on an empty chamber with what seemed to me a deafening clang. I flinched, instinctively jerking away, but Heinrich fisted a handful of my hair and yanked me back.

"Do be still, Miss Mason," he said, his voice coldly cordial. "I trust you'd prefer death to permanent brain damage."

My breath was coming so fast, I was nearly hyperventilating, and my whole body shook with tremors. My eyes were glued to Devon's, though he was watching Heinrich—not me.

"What'll it be, Mr. Clay? A happy ending . . . or a tragic one? And she's so lovely, too. I can see why you'd want to keep her."

"Her life is nothing in the face of the millions you plan to infect," Devon retorted.

"Is that so? Well then we should just dispose of her, shall we?" Another click. I jumped, choking back a sob. I squeezed my eyes shut and prayed it would be quick and painless.

"Stop!"

Devon's shout made my eyes pop open in shock. His jaw was locked tight, his cool blue gaze now on me.

"Stop," he repeated more quietly. "If you kill her, you lose the antidote."

"I'm not playing this game—" Heinrich growled.

"I mean it!" Devon cut him off. "Galler injected her with the only formulated vaccine he'd created. That's why she didn't die. I didn't give her an antidote. I didn't need to. She'd already been vaccinated for the virus by Galler himself."

Those words echoed in the silence, sinking into me with the force of knives. The needle we'd found in Galler's desk, the one that had pricked me. Devon must have known—must have figured out somehow—what had been in that needle, but hadn't told me. What he'd said about the journal, how the vaccine formula had been in it, that had all been a lie.

"If she dies, you'll never be able to re-create it," Devon continued. "You need her blood, and last I checked, dead people don't make a lot of blood."

Heinrich seemed stunned at this revelation, then he burst out laughing.

"How incredibly marvelous! How clever! And you, Mr. Clay, keeping her as your lover all this while so you'd know exactly where the vaccine was at all times. You are a devious one, I have to hand you that."

I could literally feel the blood drain from my face. I stared at Devon, begging him with my eyes to contradict what Heinrich had said. But his focus was no longer on me.

A sound outside caught my attention, and Heinrich's. The whipping sound grew louder and I recognized the turn of a helicopter's rotors.

"What's this?" Heinrich asked, his hold on my hair loosening, though the barrel of the gun remained steady at my temple.

"It's backup," Devon bit out. "It's over, Heinrich. Even as we stand here, your computers are being erased, all files on the virus permanently deleted. What you've managed to manufacture is being confiscated. Let the girl go and I'll allow you to live." His words were like ice, bit out sharply as though he just managed to control his rage.

The helicopter was right outside the windows now, the bright lights shining inside. Guns were mounted to the helicopter and I was terrified of the damage they could do. I heard shouts from below and didn't doubt for an instant that everything Devon was saying was correct.

"Do you think that kind of weapon is just going to go away?" Heinrich asked, and this time there was no accompanying laughter. "If I don't sell it, someone else will. You won't be able to keep it under wraps forever. And Miss Mason here will be locked up in a lab, studied and dissected until they can re-create the vaccine or formulate an antidote, and then she'll die. Because you can't just have the vaccine up and walking about now, can you."

His foretelling of the dire future ahead of me made my empty stomach churn with nausea.

"Better I just end it now," Heinrich said. "It's really the merciful thing to do." The barrel pressed harder against my temple.

"No!" Devon shouted, just as all hell broke loose. Glass shattered and bullets flew. I saw Hugo go down, his rifle spewing bullets, and suddenly Heinrich no longer had a hold of me. I dropped to the floor as more glass shattered. People shouted and I covered my head with my arms.

Heinrich's people were putting up a fight and I was caught in the cross fire. I crawled toward the one door no one was guarding. Broken glass bit into my skin, but I made myself keep going, tears pouring down my face. When I got to the door, I glanced back.

Heinrich was flat on his back on the floor, a pool of blood spreading from underneath his body. Through the chaos, I saw Devon just as he saw me. Our eyes locked and I couldn't read anything on his face. Time seemed to stand still for a moment, then he turned away and disappeared from view into the smoke and wind whipping through the glassless windows.

I fell through the door into a stairwell. It was empty and I scrambled to my feet. I lost track of the floors I passed, my thoughts in panicked disarray with the sole focus of escape. I hit the bottom floor and pushed through a door marked Exit.

I was at the top of a hill, apparently having come out the back. The wind swirled snow and I started shivering. Without thought as to where I was going or what I should do, I ran. The urge to run, to get away as far as I could, was too pressing of a primal need to resist, no matter the bitter cold outside.

I slipped and slid down the hill, my clothes getting wetter with each step. I could hear the chaos behind me growing fainter the farther I got. I prayed no one would follow, sure that they'd kill me if they found me.

Nearing a village, I saw people and cars. Some had paused to stare up at the building with the helicopter circling, but I ran on, my feet on solid ground now. The cold seared my chest as I sucked in air and I could no longer feel my feet, they were so frozen inside my soaked shoes.

Finally, I had to stop. I couldn't run anymore. I stood on the sidewalk, chest heaving and my limbs trembling with cold.

"*Eh! Mademoiselle! Ça va?*"

I jerked around in dismay to see a man approaching me. Big, with a full beard and swathed in a huge coat, he looked like a lumberjack bearing down on me. Scared, I held up a hand to ward him off and began backing away.

"S-stay away from m-me," I stammered, my teeth chattering so hard it was tough to talk.

"*Arrêtez!*" he called out. "*Regardez! Derrière vous!*"

I couldn't understand, his alarm incomprehensible to me. When he began hurrying faster toward me, I panicked.

"No! Leave me alone!"

The sound of a horn blast and tires squealing made me spin around in time to see a car stopping inches from me. I stared in shock. Then I crumpled to the ground.

Chapter Nineteen

When I opened my eyes, I found I was in a dimly lit room, lying on a bed with a thin blanket covering me. Confused, I looked around. Where was I? What had happened to me?

"Bon. Vous êtes éveillé."

I turned around and saw a woman—a nurse?—standing next to me. She wore a kind smile, but I hadn't understood a word she said. By her uniform, I figured I was in a hospital . . . somewhere.

"Where am I?" I asked.

She switched to heavily accented English. "You are in the Hôpital Saint-Louis."

"How did I get here?"

"A man found you on the street. You were unconscious. People who saw say you were almost hit by a car, but you had other injuries. He brought you here for treatment."

It all came rushing back to me now. Heinrich. Devon. The attack and my escape. The man who'd tried to warn me about the car. Looked like there were still some good Samaritans out there after all.

She fiddled with my IV and took my blood pressure. I rested my head back on the pillow, the effort of holding it up too much for me, though I didn't know if that was due to my injuries or my heartbreak.

Devon had lied to me. Used me.

"You have no identification," the nurse said, dragging my attention back to her. "What is your name?"

I swallowed. My purse was gone and so was my passport, which had been in my wallet.

"Ivy," I replied. "Ivy Mason. I'm American."

She nodded. "The police will be glad you are awake. They want to question you." After adjusting the IV drip in my arm, she left the room.

The police.

I was in a foreign country with no ID and no money. I couldn't tell the police anything about Heinrich or Devon or the Shadow. In fact, considering that Heinrich had wanted to kill me and I was reasonably sure Devon wanted to as well—or possibly stick me in a lab—telling the nurse my real name had been a really dumb idea. For all I knew, the Shadow could have someone monitoring the Paris hospitals for a woman of my description.

You can't just have the vaccine up and walking about now, can you.

Which meant I didn't have much time.

Taking the IV needle out of my arm hurt more than it was probably supposed to, but I'd never done it before. My clothes and shoes were in a plastic bag on a chair in the room and I dressed as quickly as I could, wet clothes and all. My body ached and my head was pounding. There was a bandage on my forehead covering a knot that felt the size of a walnut—a memento of hitting the concrete when I'd passed out.

Easing open the door, I peeked into the hallway. It was late in the evening on Christmas Eve and the halls were nearly empty. Had it just been last night that I'd eaten a seven-course French dinner in a designer ball gown? It felt like a lifetime ago.

Spotting a sign that looked like stairs over a door at the end of the corridor, I took a chance and started briskly walking toward it. I had to cross another hallway that intersected this one and I paused, hearing voices.

"She said her name was Ivy Mason," a woman said.

"Yes, that's her. Thank you for finding her. What's the room number?"

I stopped breathing. Oh my God. It was Devon.

Unable to help myself, I glanced to my right just as he turned . . . and spotted me.

Time froze for a moment as our eyes met. I searched his face for any hint that I had nothing to fear from him as I teetered on the brink of indecision, wanting so badly to go to him, then Devon reached inside his jacket.

I ran, my shoes skidding on the linoleum floor as I hit the stairwell door. I could hear Devon's footsteps as he ran toward me, but the knob turned easily and I was through.

I flew down the stairs, hearing the door come crashing open above me, but I had a decent head start. I burst out the bottom floor onto the street, sending up a quick prayer of thanks that it was so crowded.

Melting into the flow of people, I had to remind myself not to run, which would stand out in this crowd and call attention. Resisting the urge to look behind me, I ducked into a café. The place was teeming with customers, the fluid sound of rapid-fire French swirling around me like the aroma of espresso.

At first, it seemed to be a bad idea, as moving through the tightly packed café was harder than I thought. But I kept going, heading toward the back and ignoring the irritated glares sent my way. At last I found the rear exit, then I was outside again. I crossed the street and repeated the process, this time impulsively grabbing and pocketing a cell phone I saw lying on a table while the owner was bent rummaging through their bags, which were resting on the floor. Now I was three streets from the hospital and a block down. Not safe, but not in immediate danger either. I hoped.

I walked down the narrow street, my arms around my middle as I tried to stay warm. My breath was a puff of fog in the chilled air as my feet crunched the ice and snow covering the sidewalk. Festive lights glittered and people laughed as they walked by, jostling packages. Occasionally, a door to a restaurant or café would open and the strains of conversation and music would fill the air.

I'd never felt so alone.

I lost track of time and location, walking aimlessly as I tried to think what to do. Tears leaked from my eyes to immediately freeze on my cheeks. My body was racked with chills.

The sound of a pipe organ caught my attention and I glanced up. I'd come upon a church, the stained-glass windows gleaming in the night. People were going inside. Of course! Midnight Mass. I could get warm for a while.

I hurried to the doors, my fingers so frozen I couldn't feel them curve around the door handle as I pulled it open. The rush of warm air made me release a long sigh. Walking inside, I saw the place was full, but there were some empty spots in the last few pews. Keeping to the very last one, I gratefully slid in and took a seat.

The service was already starting, and since it was in French, I couldn't follow what they were saying. But it was Christmas Eve, so I could guess well enough. The music was beautiful, haunting, and echoed in the old stone church well after the last line had been sung. I listened to the priest, the unfamiliar language soothing in a way. My gaze caught on the many candles dotting the altar and all around. The dancing flames mesmerized me.

I had no plans beyond the immediate one of getting warm. My stomach cramped with hunger pangs and my eyes were heavy with exhaustion. I found myself nodding off and jerking awake again.

A hand on my shoulder made me start, and I realized I'd fallen asleep completely. I'd slumped over in the pew and now sat up quickly, realizing as I did so that the church was nearly empty of people. Some still filed past me, but most had gone.

"*La masse est terminée, ma fille.*"

A priest stood by me, a look of kind concern on his face. I couldn't understand the words he'd said, but I got the gist well enough. Homeless weren't welcome to sleep the night here any more so than at a church back home.

"Um, yeah, yeah. I'm going." I got to my feet, grabbing on to the back of the pew when the room spun and my vision grew dark. I didn't want to pass out. But after waiting for a moment, the spell passed.

The clock outside chimed the hour as I stepped out of the building. One toll. One hour after midnight. Merry Christmas to me. It seemed unreal that just twenty-four hours ago, I'd been with Devon, leaving the opera house in a ball gown and happier than I could ever remember being.

I'd known it was too good to last. Nothing like that ever does.

The cell phone seemed to burn a hole in my pocket as I walked. I found a small alcove between two buildings and took as much shelter from the wind there as I could. Taking out the phone, I stared at it. Who in the world could I call? Who could possibly help me?

But I did remember a number, one I thought I'd never use, and I dialed it. I waited as the connection went through, wondering why in the world I was calling. No one could help.

To my surprise, it picked up, and hearing the voice on the other end say hello was such a relief, it rendered me momentarily speechless.

"Hello?" the man asked again. "Who is this?"

I forced my mouth to work. "Agent L-Lane, i-it's Ivy. Ivy Mason." The cold made my teeth chatter.

"Ivy, where are you?" Gone was the slight irritation and only concern laced his words now.

"I-I'm really far away," I said, "but I need help. I don't know what to do." My face crumpled and I started to cry.

"I'll help you, just tell me where you are."

But I was crying too hard to talk, the helplessness and heartbreak hitting me hard.

"Please," Lane begged. "Ivy, please, talk to me. Where are you?"

"P-Paris," I managed to stammer through my sobs. "H-he brought me here, b-but now I think h-he's going to k-kill me." That started a fresh round of crying.

"You're in Paris?" Lane asked.

I sniffed, wiping my streaming nose on my sleeve. "Yeah."

"Okay, listen to me, Ivy. You're going to do as I say, okay?"

I closed my eyes and leaned against the building, so tired I could barely stand. "Okay."

"I need you to find a hotel. Is there one near you?"

"Um, I don't know," I said. "I can't go to a hotel. I don't have any money or ID. I lost my passport."

"It's okay," Lane assured me. "Just find one. Stay on the phone with me and walk until you find one."

"All right." I pushed myself off the wall and started walking again. Luckily, I found a little place just a block down. "I found one," I said.

"Go inside, and give the person at the desk the phone. Don't talk, okay?"

"Okay." It sounded bizarre, but I had no other options. Obediently, I went inside. A woman who was maybe fifty and looked every year of it sat behind the small counter. She glanced up as the door swung shut behind me.

"*Bonsoir*," she said.

I didn't speak, just handed her the phone. She looked questioningly at it, but reached out and took it.

"*Allô?*"

I stood and watched as Lane spoke to her, but couldn't hear any of what he said. She listened, though, her gaze on me. The suspicious look on her face changed to one of sympathy, then she scrawled something on a notepad, nodding her head as she did so.

"*Oui, oui*," she said, then handed the phone back to me.

"Okay, now listen," Lane said. "I told her you're my wife and that I was supposed to be there, but my flight was delayed. I said you'd gotten mugged tonight and are traumatized. She has my credit card so she's going to put you into a room. I want you to sit tight until I get there."

I swallowed, the relief washing over me so intense I thought I'd start crying again.

"Ivy? Are you there?"

"Yes," I whispered.

"Get some rest," Lane said. "I'll be there as soon as I can."

"Okay." I ended the call, pushing the phone into my pocket.

"*Suivez-moi*," the woman said, motioning for me to follow her up the rickety staircase.

We walked up two creaking flights before she unlocked a door with the number thirteen on it. Going inside, she kept up a rapid chatter that I couldn't decipher as she flipped on a light and showed me the small bedroom and bath.

She left, returning quickly with a plate of bread and cheese and a glass of wine. I thanked her profusely, but she just blushed and said, "*Joyeux Noël.*"

I ate half the food, saving the rest for later, and drank the entire glass of wine. The shower was tiny, but the water was hot enough. I couldn't bear to put on the same dirty and torn clothes, so I crawled beneath the covers of the bed and fell instantly asleep.

I woke slowly, my body not wanting to give up the dreamless sleep I'd been enjoying. I stretched, then winced at the aches and pains that produced.

A blanket was tugged up to my shoulders and my eyes popped open with a start.

Agent Lane stood above me.

I gasped in surprise, grabbing the blanket and pulling it to my chin. "What—how—" I stammered.

"You've slept a long time," Lane said. "Must've been exhausted. It's"—he glanced at his watch—"almost noon."

I sat up, keeping my chest covered with the blanket. "How did you get here? How did you find me?"

He looked at me strangely. "Don't you remember calling me last night?"

I pushed a hand through my tousled hair, trying to remember. I'd been at the hospital, seen Devon, and ran. There'd been a church and somehow I'd gotten a cell phone. I remember looking at the numbers, thinking who could I call . . .

"I remember now," I said. I shook my head. "They must have given me painkillers in the hospital. I'm so sorry. It's Christmas, and you flew to Paris . . ." I was stunned that he'd done that and appalled that I'd asked it of him. "I'm sorry," I repeated.

"There's nothing to apologize for," Lane said. He glanced around and spied a wooden chair, which he dragged closer and sat on, with a small sigh. "You were hurt and said he was going to kill you. And I wasn't far."

At my questioning look, he explained. "Interpol flagged Clay when he left the country. Video showed you with him. I arrived yesterday."

I felt slightly better that I hadn't made him board a flight to France on Christmas Day, but still. "How long have you been *here*?" I asked, pointing down to indicate the room we were in.

He shrugged. "Since last night. You were pretty out of it when I got in, so I let you sleep."

Lane had been here all night and I hadn't even known? Maybe it should have creeped me out, but the kindness and compassion in his eyes eased my trepidation.

"So you want to tell me what happened?" he asked, nodding toward the bandage on my head. "Who's trying to kill you? Clay?"

I sighed, took a deep breath, and told him everything—well, almost everything. I didn't mention the Shadow, Devon's warning still echoing in my ears, and I had no wish to put Agent Lane in any further danger than I had already. But I did tell him about Mr. Galler and the pendant, Devon and the bank robbery, the journal, Heinrich, and the virus. I ended with confessing how I'd escaped and was on the run from both of them.

"I don't know if they'd go to the trouble to hunt me down now and kill me," I said. "But Devon might."

"I thought you and he were . . ." Lane let the sentence trail off, but I got his meaning. I appreciated his tact in not saying "sleeping together."

"He . . . used me," I said, going for vague. I had the gut feeling the fewer people who knew about the vaccine inside me, the better. Likewise, I didn't tell him about the pages I'd mailed. Without the key, he wouldn't be able to decrypt them anyway. "And I betrayed him. I think that puts us firmly in the past tense," I said, swallowing the growing lump in my throat.

I was still having a hard time wrapping my head around the fact that Devon had been playing me that whole time, buying me clothes, showing me Paris, telling me he wanted to be with me longer. All of it had been an act, an act to keep me close so Heinrich wouldn't find out the truth and the Shadow would have the vaccine.

"You weren't betraying him, you were saving his life," Lane said, the bitterness in his tone taking me aback.

"I don't think he sees it that way."

Lane's lips pressed into a thin line, but he didn't say anything.

"You knew Devon was in Paris, but why would you come?" I asked. "I thought you'd been told to stay away from him?"

"Galler was identified as a possible terrorist threat by FEMA," he replied, "due to his work as a bioengineer. His murder raised red flags, as did Clay's presence in the city. We knew something was going on, and I've been trying to put the pieces together. Now, thanks to you, I have."

A thought occurred to me and I chewed my lip, trying to figure out how to ask what was on my mind. Lane must have read my consternation because he frowned.

"What is it?" he asked. "Are you hurting?"

"No, not that," I said quickly. "It's just, um, it's Christmas and . . . well, surely you have a family? A wife? Someone that this," I waved my hand, "is keeping you from?"

Lane relaxed a little at my question, his lips curving into a smile. "My parents are accustomed to my work schedule being a little . . . unpredictable. My dad was a cop, too. He retired a while back. As for a wife, no, I'm not married."

I thought about asking if he had a girlfriend, but bit my tongue. It wasn't any of my business, though I was curious about this agent who'd taken such an interest in this case—enough to follow Devon to Paris.

"You realize that if Devon works for the British government, you won't be able to touch him," I said.

Lane shrugged, unconcerned. "If he comes after you, I'll take him out and there isn't anyone who can stop me, no matter what government he works for."

I forced a weak nod, though the thought of anyone "taking out" Devon made me sick to my stomach. But I wasn't crazy about the idea of him killing me, either.

"I got you some clothes," Lane said, getting to his feet. He grabbed a paper bag from the floor and handed it to me. "I saw you didn't have anything last night so I took a guess on your size."

"Thanks," I said. I swung my legs over the side of the bed, but stopped, my gaze lifting to Lane, who still stood next to me. His eyes were on my bare thighs.

"I'll just get dressed," I said pointedly.

"Oh! Yeah, right, sure." He quickly turned his back and I could have sworn his ears turned red.

I dropped the blanket and dumped out the bag, glad though slightly embarrassed to see he'd even bought me underwear. No bra, but I guess for a man that would really be pushing it. The jeans were a little big around the waist, but would do. The top was a thin, pale pink sweater, its cut simple with long sleeves and a V-neck.

It was obvious I was cold, but there was nothing I could do about that. Maybe in Paris, no one would notice my lack of appropriate underwear. The clothes were quite different from the designer brands I'd worn yesterday, but I didn't complain. It had been exceedingly thoughtful of Lane to get them for me.

"I don't have a brush or anything," I said, trying to finger-comb my hair.

"Oh, yeah, I got you a few toiletries," Lane said, digging in the pockets of his coat. He deposited a pile of things in my hands: a little toothbrush and travel tube of paste as well as deodorant and a purse-size brush. "Once you're ready, we'll get you something to eat. The embassy is closed on Christmas, so we won't be able to replace your passport until tomorrow. We'll have to stay another day here, is that okay?"

It seemed he'd thought of everything and, for a second, I was overwhelmed at the kindness of a near stranger. I looked up at him and the tears shining in my eyes seemed to alarm him.

"What's wrong?" he asked. "Did I forget something?"

I shook my head. "I'm fine," I managed. "It's just been a . . . really tough couple of weeks." Understatement of the century. My life had been turned upside down and inside out, my body taken more abuse than it had in years, and my heart . . . my heart was a dead ache inside my chest. Glancing up at Lane, the concern in his eyes was my undoing and a lone tear escaped to trickle down my cheek.

Lane stepped closer and wrapped his arms around me, cautiously pulling me toward him. I let him, leaning my head against his chest while he rested his chin on the top of my head. He was a big guy, his arms and chest solidly muscled, and it made me feel better to stay like that for a few minutes. I didn't feel quite so alone.

We didn't speak as we stood there, and finally I pulled back. "I'd better finish getting ready," I said, swiping a hand across my wet cheeks. I went into the bathroom, spending an inordinately long time brushing my teeth, washing my face, and generally just going through the motions. My hair was almost too much for the little brush, but I used it carefully, brushing my long hair until it gleamed, the white-blonde strands thick and straight as they fell over my shoulders and down my back.

When I emerged, Lane was sitting in the chair, his elbows braced on his knees and his hands loosely clasped as he studied the floor.

"Ready," I said.

He glanced up and went still, his eyes taking a quick journey from my head to my toes and back. Then he cleared his throat.

"Great. Let's get something to eat. You've gotta be starving."
He got to his feet and reached for his coat, swinging it over my
shoulders. "You need this more than me."

"It's okay, you don't have to—"

"Give me a little credit," he interrupted with a grin. "I have
some manners."

I smiled back, pushing my arms into the way-too-long sleeves.
The coat was big on me, ending mid-thigh, and smelled like Agent
Lane, a spicy kind of musk that was comforting.

The streets were nearly deserted and we walked a few blocks in
search of a restaurant that was open. When we came across one, I
hesitated. It seemed the only restaurants open in Paris on Christmas
Day were the kind Devon had taken me to the other night—the
expensive kind. I knew Lane was a kind of cop, and I knew cops
didn't make much money, plus I didn't have a dime on me. He
opened the door, but I stayed on the sidewalk.

"What's wrong?" he asked.

I shook my head. "Let's not eat here."

"You don't like this place? Um, okay. Well, we can keep looking."

That made it sound like I was being a pain in the ass, but I'd
rather he viewed me as that than say anything about money. Men
usually didn't take well to that sort of thing.

We were nearing the real hoity-toity part of Paris now and the
next two places we found open were the same—high class and high
dollar. After turning down the second, Lane confronted me.

"Okay, what's the problem?" he asked.

"Nothing," I said. "I thought we'd just try to find a, you know,
a place that's not quite as . . . fancy."

Lane frowned. "You're kidding, right?"

My face warmed in embarrassment and I blurted, "These places
are really expensive."

He looked at me strangely. "Yeah, I know."

I shrugged helplessly. "I don't have any money."

Lane finally seemed to get it, his frown melting into a smile. "Ivy, it's okay. Though the circumstances are a little . . . unusual, the fact is that I'm in Paris, on Christmas Day, with a stunning woman. Let me buy you dinner." He shrugged. "Call it a once in a lifetime event, but I'd rather enjoy the experience and not sweat the price tag."

His words eased my trepidation and I let out a breath in relief, giving him a shy smile. "Okay."

We were near Place de la Bastille and the restaurant was full, the smell wafting through the doorway when we entered, making my mouth water. Though they were busy, they found a corner table for two and soon we were seated. I was self-conscious given what I was wearing compared to the other patrons, but there was nothing I could do about it so I just held my head high and ignored the looks cast our way.

Lane leaned toward me. "We may be a little too American for this place," he said in an undertone, then gave me a wink.

I laughed lightly. He'd caught the disapproving glares, too. "Maybe," I agreed.

They had a prix fixe menu for Christmas so there wasn't much choosing to do, which was fine with me. It all looked good. Though when the cold oysters arrived, Lane eyed them skeptically.

"Have you ever had oysters?" I asked.

He shook his head. "My protein is usually the kind that roams the fruited plain."

I grinned. "Try it," I said. "Here, like this." I picked up a shell, turned it to the wide end, and slurped the fish and liquid into my mouth. I chewed a couple of times, then swallowed. "Yum." I smiled. "Your turn."

"Well I'm not about to let a girl show me up," Lane teased, then copied my movements. He grimaced a bit when he chewed, but swallowed the oyster.

"What'd you think?"

"I think I prefer hot wings as an appetizer," he deadpanned.

I laughed out loud at that. "More for me," I said, reaching for another oyster in the tray of ice.

Lane watched me finish off the tray, and as the waiter removed it, asked, "So where did you learn to eat oysters?"

I shrugged, taking a sip of the champagne paired with the course. "Fancy dinner dates. I like to try new things. And my grandma always said I had champagne taste on a beer budget."

"And where's Grandma?"

"Back in Dodge City."

"That's where you're from?"

I tipped up the champagne flute, letting the cool liquid slide over my tongue as I eyed Lane. Once I emptied the glass, I set it aside. "You're telling me you don't know that already."

He had the grace to look a bit sheepish. "Yes, I've looked at your records," he said, "but I wanted to hear it from you."

The waiter brought the next course then, thin slices of foie gras with toast paired with a sweet white wine. I took a bite, savoring the delicacy, before answering Lane.

"My parents died when I was little. I was raised by my grandparents. Have a useless degree that I still enjoyed getting, and a job that pays the bills but isn't exactly rocket science. End of story."

"And the stepbrother out on parole? The one who attacked you in the parking lot?"

I sat back in my chair, raising an eyebrow. "Really? You want to bring that up *now*?"

He hesitated. "Fair enough," he said. "So tell me what this stuff is."

I explained the awesomeness that was foie gras, and he liked it better than the oysters. By now I was feeling pretty good after drinking the wine and champagne. Maybe a little tipsy, but it would be tacky to get tipsy on Christmas, so I decided I was just really relaxed.

"So do you have a first name, Agent Lane?" I asked. "Or shall I keep calling you *Agent*?"

He grinned at my teasing, resting his arm across the back of my chair. "I do, actually. It's Scott. Scott Lane."

I held out my hand. "Nice to meet you, Scott Lane."

Scott took my hand and turned it palm down before brushing his lips across the back of my hand. "It's a pleasure to meet you, too, Ivy."

My eyebrows flew up in surprise.

He shrugged, his lips tipping up in a one-sided smile. "When in Paris . . ."

His chocolate eyes were warm and deep enough it seemed I could drown in them. My hand was gently cradled in his, his thumb softly sliding across my knuckles in a chaste caress.

Uh-oh.

Pulling my hand from his, I cleared my throat. "So Scott, do you have a girlfriend back home?" Usually the reminder made men draw back from flirting with me, but Scott just gave me a mischievous grin.

"Nope."

That was unexpected. "Why not?"

He laughed. "Not exactly a tactful question."

I blushed. "Sorry. That just kind of popped out."

"It's all right. Once a woman finds out what I do for a living, they usually lose interest pretty quick if they're the marrying kind. The one-night stands don't care, but I'm kind of over that."

"Why do they lose interest?" I didn't see the reasoning behind that. Scott was a really attractive guy, fabulous build, nice, funny, and had a steady job. What wasn't to like?

"Some don't like the fact that the profession is dangerous and I travel a lot. Others are a little more . . . avaricious."

Oh.

The returning waiter saved me from having to reply to that. I asked Scott about his job and where he grew up, resorting to my usual trick of getting a man to go on about himself so as to avoid talking about myself. There were few topics that interested a man more than his own accomplishments. But with Scott, it didn't last for long. We were finishing off the main course, lamb ("Finally some meat," he'd said), when he brushed off another of my questions.

"Enough about me," he said. "Tell me more about you."

"I already did," I insisted.

"Did not."

"Did too."

"Did not."

I narrowed my eyes at him, but he just grinned. "I've got four siblings," he said. "I can do this all night."

That got a reluctant laugh from me. "Fine, you win," I conceded. "What do you want to know?"

"So what's your favorite color?"

"Aqua."

"Favorite song?"

"Anything by Pink."

"Movie?"

I sighed dreamily. "*Titanic.*"

Scott snorted. "You're such a girl," he groused.

"So glad you noticed."

"Worst movie ever. There was room on that door for two people."

"There was not!" I argued. "They would have sunk and then they *both* would've died."

"Now *that* would have made it a good movie," he deadpanned. I hid a grin and rolled my eyes at him.

He kept quizzing me through the cheese course and I started turning the tables on him, asking him what his favorite things were.

"Gee, a cop whose favorite movie is *Die Hard*," I teased. "Could you be more of a cliché?"

"It's agent, not cop, and I'd hate to disappoint you."

What could have been an awkward evening turned out to be one of the more enjoyable Christmas dinners I'd ever had. By the time we'd finished the bûche de Noël dessert, I was so full my jeans were no longer big around the waist.

It was dark by the time we were back outside and I shivered, even wrapped in Scott's coat. He curved his arm over my shoulders and drew me close to his side as we walked back to the hotel.

"It's your last night in Paris," he said. "Anything else you want to see or do?"

I hesitated, sure he had to be freezing. "Um, no, that's okay."

"Tell me," he prompted.

"It's just so beautiful," I said. "But I know you're cold."

He stopped and looked down at me. "What do you want to see?" His smile was indulgent and his eyes kind. I relented.

"Notre Dame."

"You're in luck," he said. "I actually know where that is from here." He pulled me close to his side and we set off again. It was a bit of a hike, but not too far. The streets weren't teeming with pedestrians, which was really nice. We crossed the Seine onto the Île de la Cité, and once we were in sight of the cathedral, I gasped.

Ablaze with lights, it was a sight to behold. A huge Christmas tree stood in front and there was no line to get in.

"Is it still open, do you think?" I asked.

"Let's find out."

It turned out we were just in time to be the last visitors of the day. The inside was even more beautiful than the outside and I lingered a long time looking at the stained glass and the crèche. Finally, we had to leave.

"That was . . . amazing," I said to Scott as we began the walk back to the hotel. "A really bad day has turned out to be one of the best Christmases I've ever had." I looked up at him. "I don't know how to thank you." Despite the knot of lead in the pit of my stomach that had Devon and his lies written all over it, Scott had managed to give me a precious gift that I'd remember always.

"Thanks aren't required," he said. "I'm glad I was here. I'm even gladder that I was the one you called when you needed help."

We stopped by a crêpe stand near the hotel, which also happened to have hot wine. Scott teased me over my ability to still eat a Nutella crêpe even after the meal we'd had.

"There's always room for chocolate," I said around a mouthful.

He stopped by a car I assumed was one he'd rented and took a suitcase from the trunk before going into the hotel. It wasn't until we were back in the room that I realized this might be awkward since there was just one bed in the tiny space.

Scott seemed to read my mind because he said, "Don't worry. I'll sleep in the chair."

I eyed the wooden chair dubiously. "You can't be serious."

"What can I say? I'm a gentleman."

I laughed, his joking and easy manner calming my nerves. "I think I can handle staying on my side, so long as you agree to stay on yours."

He raised three fingers in a Boy Scout salute. "Scout's honor." Reaching into his suitcase, he pulled out a worn T-shirt and handed it to me. "Thought you might like something else to sleep in."

"Thanks." I disappeared into the bathroom and considered briefly before taking off my underwear and washing them in the sink. I hung them to dry and carefully folded the clothes Scott had bought for me. The T-shirt was as long as a nightshirt on me and I trusted that Scott wouldn't try anything.

He was checking his cell phone when I came out of the bathroom and he glanced up. His gaze took in the T-shirt and I saw his Adam's apple bob as he swallowed. But he said nothing, politely turning his back to give me some privacy. I was exhausted and slid gratefully into bed, pulling the covers to my chin.

"Are you coming to bed?" I asked.

He turned back around. "Shortly," he replied. "You go ahead and go to sleep."

I yawned. "Thanks again," I sighed.

"You're welcome," he said. "Merry Christmas, Ivy."

"Merry Christmas."

I was dozing, halfway between sleep and awake, when I felt the bed dip. I cracked my tired eyes and saw Scott had lain down next to me on his back.

"Aren't you going to get under the covers?" I mumbled.

"Nah," he said softly. "Better this way." He turned to look at me, a rueful smile on his lips. "I wasn't really a Boy Scout."

That made me smile, then I was out.

CHAPTER TWENTY

"Come on, Ives, please come out with us tonight."

I sighed in exasperation. "Logan, I told you, I really don't want to do the New Year's Eve party thing."

"But I'm going to feel bad, thinking of you sitting here in the apartment all by yourself while I'm out having a good time," he said, waiting patiently while I finished tying the bowtie on his tux.

"I sincerely doubt that," I retorted. "I'm guessing you'll have a blonde on each arm long before midnight rolls around."

It had been five days since I'd flown back to the States with Scott—Agent Lane—and I'd thrown myself back into my "normal" life. It was a life that had seemed so dull before, but which was now a welcome respite after what I'd been through. I'd told none of what had transpired to Logan—nothing about the virus, my sickness, or Paris—I'd only said that it hadn't worked out between Devon and me. He hadn't had much to say about that, but I could tell by the relief in his eyes that he wasn't unhappy about it.

Logan shot me a wicked grin. "A threesome you say? Why you naughty girl."

My cheeks grew hot and I slapped his arm, pushing him away. "Go on, get out of here. I'm sure Lee and Sam are waiting for you."

At the mention of his work buddies, Logan glanced at his watch. "Yep. Already late." He shrugged on his tuxedo coat and slid his cell into the inside pocket.

"Have fun," I said with a smile. I was sure Logan would have no trouble finding female companionship tonight. The tuxedo was tailored and fit perfectly, accentuating his wide shoulders and lean hips. The black fabric went well with his dark hair, making his blue eyes stand out. I felt decidedly underdressed in my T-shirt and leggings.

He glanced over at me, his gaze softening, then he was back and hugging me.

"All right, you don't have to come, but no moping, okay?"

I squeezed him back, glad that things were right between us again. When he loosened his grip, I stretched up on my toes and pressed a kiss to his cheek.

"That's the kiss I get for New Year's Eve?" he joked. "You can't do better?"

"I'm saving myself," I teased.

Something passed across Logan's face, but I couldn't read what it was. Disappointment, maybe?

"I'll see you later, Ives," Logan said. "Happy New Year."

"You, too."

After he left, I stood there staring at the door for a few minutes, trying to figure out if I had missed something between Logan and me, why he'd seemed subdued when he left. It was out of character for him, but there was no reason for it. Perhaps he was just feeling moody. The holidays did that to people.

Shoving my lingering unease aside, I made a pan of brownies and broke open the cheap bottle of champagne I'd bought and stored in the refrigerator. Curled up on the sofa, I was in the last hour of *Titanic* and halfway through my bottle of champagne when there was a knock at the door.

I jerked up from where I'd been lying, immediately thinking of Jace, and wished I still had my gun. But the last I'd had it, I'd nearly shot Devon. I hadn't seen it since dropping it on the floor of his closet.

Cell phone in one hand, I cautiously approached the door as the knock came again. Peering through the peephole, I let out a sigh of relief. I pulled open the door.

"Is the FBI making house calls now?" I teased.

Scott grinned, a hint of relief crossing his face. "Thought I'd drop by on my way home, see how you were doing."

"I'm good, thanks," I said, stepping back so he could come inside. "How are you?" I closed the door behind him.

"Well everyone's jealous that I got to go to Paris for a few days, so I'm taking a lot of shit about that," he said.

"I hope you didn't get into any trouble," I said.

"Nah. It's fine."

"You didn't . . . tell . . . anyone about the things I told you, did you?" I asked. I'd thought about that later, wondering at the wisdom of all that I'd confessed to Scott in that Paris hotel room.

But he shook his head. "No. And I didn't give anyone these either." Reaching inside his jacket, he removed a manila envelope. Taking it, I noticed it was postmarked from Paris. The journal sheets. "I assumed you sent these to me for safekeeping?"

I nodded, leafing through the pages. I wondered what it said. Devon had lied about it being the vaccine. What else could it be? I guess I'd never know.

"Thanks for bringing it by," I said, stuffing the papers back into the envelope. "So what are you doing about the case then?"

"Short of Devon Clay confessing and corroborating everything you told me, nothing," he said. "Nothing can be proven, and without another witness, it's all hearsay and speculation."

Hearing Devon's name spoken aloud was still a shock to my system, but I kept my expression carefully blank.

"But I also wanted to tell you that we found the guy you told us about," he continued. "The one who you said was there the night Mr. Galler was murdered."

My eyes flew open wide. "Really? You found him?" I knew I'd been right about that guy.

"Well, yeah, but he's dead," Scott clarified.

Of course he was. I sighed. I wasn't sure how to feel about Mr. Galler. He'd inherited a disturbing legacy, but his continued research into a vaccine had consequences that had hurt people. Whether he'd done it for nefarious or for philanthropic reasons, only God knew.

"We're marking the case as unsolved for now," he said.

I nodded, then caught him glancing at my clothes. I self-consciously ran my fingers through my hair. "Sorry," I said. "I wasn't exactly planning on company—"

"You look beautiful," Scott blurted.

A slow smile curved my lips. "Thanks. You don't look half bad yourself."

Gone was the cheap tie. Tonight he was wearing dark jeans and a charcoal Henley, a heavy leather jacket over that, and he looked nothing like an FBI agent. The scruff of a couple of days' growth of beard darkened his jaw and his dark hair fell over his forehead in a wave. He moved to smooth his hair and I saw the glint of his gun in its holster underneath his arm.

"Listen, I, um, I'm not trying to interrupt your evening," he said. "I just . . . wanted to tell you that and, um, well, I wanted to ask you if you'd like to go out sometime. Maybe grab a drink, or dinner, or something?"

He was nervous, which was so sweet. My smile widened and I nodded. "Yeah. I'd like that."

Scott beamed at me. "Perfect! That's great! Okay, well, I'll give you a call then."

"Okay."

"So, Happy New Year," he said, reaching to hug me. I automatically hugged him back. The scent I remembered from Paris drifted from his clothes and I inhaled deeply. The hug went on just a tad longer than it probably should have, but for once it was with a man that I didn't mind.

"Happy New Year," I echoed. When he let me go, I added, "I'm glad you came by."

"Me, too."

He hesitated for a moment, his gaze dropping to my lips, but he didn't kiss me. I was okay with that. A date was one thing. I wasn't sure if I was ready to be physical with another man so soon after Devon. But maybe Scott wouldn't mind taking things slow.

"Well, good night," he said, releasing me and heading for the door.

"Good night." I watched him walk down the hall and disappear into the stairwell. He glanced back once before going through the doorway and I gave a little wave. Then he was gone.

I smiled to myself as I closed and locked the door. Maybe something good had come out of all that. I liked Scott. I liked him a lot.

I'd missed Kate and Leo's last kiss, but sat and watched the rest of the movie anyway, forgetting to watch the clock to ring in the new year and by the time I remembered, it was already half past midnight.

"Oh well," I said. "There's always next year."

I finished off the bottle of champagne, feeling decidedly tipsy now, but I didn't care because I was just going to bed. The alcohol would also help me sleep. I'd had a couple of bad nightmares since

I'd been back, waking up in a cold sweat and tangled in the sheets, but I hoped they'd just go away with time.

I also hoped I'd be able to sleep without dwelling on Devon. I'd replayed every moment, every conversation between us since the first time I'd laid eyes on him in the bank. I had no one else to blame but myself for falling for his lies. If only it hadn't seemed so real. I remembered the way he'd helped me talk about Jace and my past. How could someone do that if they didn't care about me at all, but were just using me?

Questions like these had swirled inside my head since Paris, and I had no more answers tonight than I had at any other time.

Pushing the disturbing thoughts aside, I got ready for bed, pulling on an expensive champagne-colored silk nightgown that Logan had gotten me for Christmas. (*"Really, Logan?" "What? You love pajamas!"*) After plugging in the Christmas tree lights in my room so it wasn't dark, I climbed into bed, pulling the heavy covers up over me. The only way not to freeze in a tiny nighty in the middle of winter was with a ton of blankets.

I stared at the Christmas tree until I fell asleep, willing myself not to think about Devon or wonder where he was, what he was doing, or if he thought about me at all. . . .

⁓

A hand covered my mouth and I woke up with a start, a scream climbing from my throat and my hands flying up to pull at the arm holding me down.

"Shh. It's me."

I froze at the words, the voice, blinking and trying to focus on the figure looming over me. Slowly, the hand peeled away and he sank down to sit beside me on the bed.

"Devon?" Stunned, I just stared, then panic hit. With the covers over me, I couldn't squirm away. So I lashed out with my fists, trying to hit him, but he caught my wrists. I pulled as hard as I could, but couldn't get free. "Please," I gasped, terrified. "Please. Don't kill me."

"Kill you? What are you talking about? Stop fighting me."

Cautiously, I stilled.

"Is that why you ran? You thought I was going to kill you? Bloody hell, Ivy, you nearly gave me heart failure that night when I couldn't find you."

In one swift movement, he yanked back the blankets, exposing my skin to the chill night air.

"What're you doing?" I squeaked.

"I'm checking to make sure you're in one piece," he retorted, and sure enough, his hands were touching me everywhere, as though checking for broken limbs. I tried to bat him away, but he was too quick and, in another moment, he'd grabbed my arms and hauled me upright until we were face-to-face.

"Are you feeling all right? Heinrich didn't give you anything, did he?" He pushed the hair back from my face, turning my head so the dim light fell on me.

"N-no, he didn't," I stammered, utterly confused. I'd nearly given Devon "heart failure?" He wasn't going to kill me?

"Thank heaven for that," he muttered. Both his hands slid behind my neck to cradle my nape and then he was kissing me breathless, like he'd been gone for a year and thought we'd never see each other again.

He pulled me in, like he'd always been able to do, bending me to his will. But I was confused and upset and after several long moments of his tongue sliding against mine, my head trapped by his hands, I tried to turn away.

"No, stop!" I tugged at his arms and he finally eased up, his hands dropping to rest on my arms. "What the hell are you doing here?" I asked. I had many questions, but this one fell out first.

Devon sighed. "You're angry," he said.

"Really? Are you picking up on that?" I retorted. "You lied to me. Used me—"

"And you lied to me. Betrayed me," he interrupted.

"I did that to save your life! Heinrich told me he'd kill you if I didn't bring him the journal and pendant." I shook my head. "I wasn't about to let that happen—"

"Neither was I." Devon's voice was loud in the room, and it shut me up. For a moment.

"You knew I'd been given the vaccine," I accused, my voice more calm.

"I *suspected*," he said. "I didn't know for sure. Not until he exposed you to the virus."

"So that was an experiment?" I hissed, outraged. "To see if I'd survive?"

"No," he bit out. "I had no way of saving you. I didn't know if you'd live, or if you'd die in my arms that night. It made you ill, but the vaccine was enough to fight it off. That's when I knew."

"And you didn't think it was a good idea to tell me?"

"Why? To frighten you? Make you run from me? The safest place for you was at my side. Once Heinrich realized you were still alive, he was bound to come after you."

The truth, though I'd suspected all along, was a lot harder to hear coming from Devon's mouth. My eyes stung and my throat closed.

"So the whole thing," I managed in a choked whisper, "Paris, you and me, all the things you said, it was all a lie. Just a way to keep me with you."

Devon's hands slid up and down my chilled arms. I wanted to move away, make him stop, but part of me craved his touch.

"Is that what you think?" he asked.

"You lied to me. You said the vaccine was in the journal."

"It was."

I stared at him, confused. "But, you told Heinrich—"

"What I had to tell him to save your life," he interrupted. "If he thought the only vaccine available was inside you, I hoped he wouldn't kill you."

"So the coded pages," I said, trying to understand. "It's really the formula."

Devon nodded. "If you'd given them to Heinrich, it would have been very, very bad. But when he said the pages were gone, I realized I'd underestimated you." He said this with a little smile.

"But you saw me go," I reminded him. "You were so angry and then he was dead and I saw you. I saw you watching me . . . and you let me go. Alone." The terror of that evening came back to me and I swallowed hard.

"Ah, sweet Ivy," he murmured, tucking a lock of hair behind my ear. "If I hadn't let you go, the Shadow would have you now, and you'd be beyond even *my* reach."

I frowned in confusion. "What?"

"No one knows you carry the vaccine," he explained. "Heinrich is dead and I've told no one the secret. I destroyed all his records of you. The Shadow knows you only as an innocent civilian caught up briefly in this web."

"But you could've lied to them—"

"I had a very brief amount of time where I could have gone after you, or destroyed all evidence of you in Heinrich's labs and servers. I chose the latter."

I stared into the cool blue of his eyes, wondering if I could believe him. I wanted to. I wanted to so very much. But that left a lot of questions, and he still hadn't answered the very first one I asked.

"So what are you doing here?" I asked again. "Especially if they'll come for me if they find out what's inside me?" But he didn't answer my question. Instead, he replied with one of his own.

"Do you have the pages?"

My heart sank. So that's why he was here. I hid my disappointment, shaking my head as I lied. "Sorry, but you're too late. I destroyed them in Paris."

Devon searched my eyes and I held my breath. At last, he gave a little nod. "That's unfortunate," he said, "but it's not the sole reason I'm here."

"Then why?"

"Isn't it obvious?" His voice held a trace of bitterness. "You've gotten under my skin, little Ivy, something I'd vowed would never happen again. I wanted to stay away, and yet, here I am."

I looked down so he wouldn't see the tears filling my eyes. It was less than I'd been hoping for, but more than I thought he'd say. My hair fell in a curtain to conceal my face and Devon brushed it back with a gentle hand.

"You could have died," he said. "Heinrich nearly killed you. I almost lost you. Twice. Both times, right in front of my eyes and not a damn thing I could do about it. Why would you put yourself at risk?"

I shrugged, slightly embarrassed. "I had no choice," I said, lifting my gaze to his. I hesitated, but knew I had to say it. I had to tell him the truth.

"I love you."

Devon didn't speak. He didn't even move. I held my breath, afraid of what he'd say—or wouldn't say—next. When he did speak, his voice was a broken rasp.

"You shouldn't."

He dragged me onto his lap, his lips finding mine in the semi-darkness. My arms twined around his neck as we kissed, desperate and fevered. It took only a moment for me to undo his tie and slip it from underneath his collar, then I went to work on the buttons of his shirt while he shrugged off his jacket and holster, his gun thudding softly to the floor.

Devon pressed me back on the bed, kissing me hard before sitting up to strip off his pants and shoes. I bent my knees, spreading my thighs for him to lie between as I reached eagerly for him.

"This is pretty," he murmured against my lips, his fingers tugging at the silk nighty. His mouth trailed down my neck and I gasped.

"Thank you. It . . . was a gift," I managed to say. My hand reached between us, grasping the hard length of him.

"A gift from whom?" he asked, his head lifting slightly. The warning in his voice should have alerted me, but I was too busy squirming out of my panties.

"Logan gave it to me for Christmas."

The straps bit into my shoulders and the next moment, the fragile silk was being torn, shredded in two down the front of my body.

"Devon!" I squeaked. "What are you—"

"The only man who will be buying you lingerie is me," he growled.

I had no opportunity to argue, his mouth descending on mine with a force I couldn't deny. I wrapped my legs around his hips, urging him inside me, but he pulled back.

"Sorry, darling," he said, moving down my body. "Give me a moment. I've been craving the taste of you."

His head settled between my thighs, pushing them farther apart. His fingers spread the folds hiding my core and the warm slide of his tongue against me made my eyes slam shut.

"Oh God," I moaned, burying my fingers in his hair. Any lingering shyness I'd had over this particular act was long gone, his passion and skill overcoming all that.

And Devon was incredibly skilled at this, the touch of his lips and tongue slow and searing, gradually building my arousal until I was panting and my legs trembled. My clit throbbed with each teasing brush of his tongue. He slid a finger inside me and I moaned at the sensation.

"Oh God, yes, please, Devon . . ."

Coherent thought was beyond me now as he focused his considerable attention on my clit, flicking it with his tongue in hard, fast strokes. His finger pumped inside of me and a constant litany of moans and gasps fell from my lips. I was so close . . . and then I shattered completely, riding the wave of pleasure as he continued to lap at me.

I tugged at Devon's hair, needing to kiss him and feel the hard length of his cock inside me. Crawling up my body, his lips met mine in a searing kiss and I could taste myself on his tongue. I was so wet, the thrust of his cock penetrating me was easy.

I whimpered deep in my throat at the sensation of Devon filling me, possessing me. I'd tried not to think of how much I'd missed him, missed this, but now it all came rushing back.

"So good," he murmured against my lips. "So perfect with you."

He wrapped his arms around me and pulled me up to straddle his lap as he sat back on his knees. My legs were spread apart, pushing his cock deeper inside me. I still had the silk nightgown hanging from my shoulders and he slid the straps down my arms before tossing the fabric aside.

His mouth moved to my neck, sucking hard at the tender skin, while his hands settled on my hips. My head fell back and my eyes slid shut. I could feel the brush of my hair against my lower back.

Devon thrust into me, his hold on my hips moving me, too. The slide of his flesh against mine was addictive. I could feel my body straining for release again, but I fought it, not wanting this to end. My breasts were pressed against his chest, the faint scattering of hair teasing my overly sensitive nipples.

A harsh groan left Devon as he pulled me down to him and

the pulse of his cock as he came was more than I could stand. My orgasm rushed over me again, my body gripping his and tearing another groan from his throat.

His breath was hot against my neck as we both gulped in air. My body felt boneless in his arms, his fingers lazily tracing a pattern against the skin of my back. My head rested on his shoulder and when he lay down on his back, keeping me in place on top of him, I didn't resist. I could hear the beat of his heart as I lay there, and I memorized the sound.

Devon's fingers combed slowly through my hair and we didn't speak, which was fine. There was plenty to talk about, but I just wanted to enjoy this moment for a while longer.

"How did you know you'd find me here?" I asked.

"I spent two days searching Paris, then saw your name listed on a flight manifest back to the States," he said. "How did you get back here? You had no money and no passport."

"I, um, called that agent," I said. "The one I'd spoken to earlier."

Devon's hand stilled. "What did you tell him?"

"It turned out he was already in Paris," I said, avoiding the questions. "He followed us. Well, you, really. He was able to work with the embassy to get me a new passport and fly me back home."

"What did you tell him?" Devon repeated, this time tipping my head up so I was forced to meet his eyes.

I swallowed hard, then lied to him. "Nothing," I said. "I didn't tell him anything. Just that you and I'd had a bad fight."

Devon searched my eyes as though gauging the truthfulness of my words. I'd lied instinctively, afraid of what he'd do if he knew I'd told Scott so much. What would he do to me? What would he do to Scott?

"Scott came by earlier and told me they were closing the case as unsolved," I said, anxious to move on.

"Scott?"

"Agent Lane," I clarified.

Devon's hand resumed stroking my hair. "And you're on a first-name basis?" he asked.

I shrugged, settling my head back against his chest. "He was nice to me in Paris."

"How *nice* was he?"

Even I wasn't deaf enough not to hear the note of jealousy in Devon's voice. Resting my arm on his chest, I propped my chin on it so I could look at him.

"Are you jealous?" I teased.

"I don't get jealous," he said.

"Hmm. Are you sure? That sounded an awful lot like jealousy to me." I winked at him.

Devon didn't reply, he just brushed his knuckles down my cheek, his eyes serious. My grin faded and in my gut I knew something bad was coming.

"I have to leave in the morning," he said. "I won't be back."

My stomach dropped to my toes.

"What do you mean?"

"I've told you this can't last," he said, tucking a lock of hair behind my ear. "It's dangerous. *I'm* dangerous."

I couldn't argue with that, but still . . . "I don't care."

"You're young," he mused. "Too young to understand, I think."

My chest was tight as I could see I was getting nowhere in trying to persuade him. Tossing aside my pride, I flat out begged. "Please, Devon, please don't say it's over. No one has ever made me feel like you do." At the question in his eyes, I took a deep breath. "Before you, I could barely tolerate a man kissing me, holding me, without feeling trapped and afraid. You broke through all that, somehow, and I'm afraid that if you leave . . . I'll never have that, or *want* that, with anyone else ever again. So please, I'll take anything you'll give me. Just, please, don't say I won't see you again."

I didn't care how needy and pathetic I may have sounded. I was desperate not to lose him and if I thought something I might say had a chance of changing his mind, then I was going to say it, pride be damned. I held my breath, waiting.

"It's been . . . a very long time since I've cared for someone," he said at last, "and I told you the reason. I'd rather say goodbye to you on my terms, rather than at someone else's hand."

My eyes slipped closed in dismay, the tears I'd been holding back now spilling out. It was over then. He wouldn't change his mind.

Devon's thumb brushed my cheek, wiping the wetness away. "I can't offer you anything you'd want, any sort of proper relationship. I can't even say how often you'd see me."

A spark of hope flared inside me, and my eyes flew open to meet his, their clear blue steady and resigned.

He smiled, though it was a little sad. "What do you say to this—I won't put you in danger, but I promise that you *will* see me again. Is that better? Is that enough?"

My smile was tremulous. "Yes." It would have to be. The alternative was unthinkable. I couldn't begin to cope with never seeing Devon again.

Rolling us over, he put me on my back as he leaned over me, one leg insinuated between my thighs. He lowered his head and kissed me, as though to seal our pact.

"I have a request," he murmured, sliding his nose alongside mine and pressing his lips softly to my cheek, then the corner of my eye.

"Anything." His skin was warm beneath my fingers as my hands skated over the muscles in his back and shoulders.

"I want you to move out."

My eyes popped open and I frowned. "Move out? Why? Where would I go?"

"You can stay in my flat," he said.

"But you're leaving."

"Which means you'll have it to yourself until I return. No one knows about it but me. You'll be safe there."

I thought about it. Logan was going to be pissed, not so much that I was moving out, but at where I'd be moving to and with whom. But this was my life, and I wasn't stupid. I wasn't so blinded by my love for Devon that I didn't know the likelihood of how this was going to end . . . with my funeral.

It was a chance I was willing to take, though Logan would never understand. Having to deal with the stress of his disapproval combined with Devon and Logan butting heads every time they were in the same room had me agreeing to Devon's request.

"All right," I said. "I'll move out of here and into your apartment."

Devon flashed a satisfied smile. "Brilliant." He started kissing my jaw, his lips trailing a path down my neck.

"Though I do want my gun back, or another one, please," I said, tipping my head to give him better access.

"I can accommodate that," he replied.

"Especially with Jace still roaming around," I said, unable to stop the shudder that went through me.

"I told you, you don't have to worry about him anymore." Now his lips brushed my shoulder and his hand drifted down my stomach.

I frowned. "Why not?"

"I'll take care of it."

His mouth fastened over my nipple as his hand slipped between my legs. My flesh was still slick from our lovemaking and the slide of his finger made my questions drift away.

I trusted Devon. If he said he'd take care of it, then he would. He'd keep me safe . . . from Jace, from everyone. He cared about me, even if he hadn't said he loved me. I could, and would, wait for his return, and his love.

⌒

In the morning, he was gone. On my bedside table I found three things: a gun, a set of keys, and a note.

Happy New Year, sweet Ivy.
Until we meet again—
—D

# EPILOGUE

The man flipped through the channels on the decrepit television. There was nothing on.

"Piece of shit," he groused to no one, tossing aside the remote. The cheap motel had the most basic of cable packages. But what had he expected? He was practically in the middle of fucking nowhere to find a motel where they took cash and looked the other way.

He was out of cigarettes, too. Mumbling more curses, he grabbed his keys and headed outside to the stolen Cadillac that was so old, it probably predated him. A few minutes later, he was buying a pack of smokes and a six-pack. Glancing up at the television in the corner of the store while the clerk counted his change, he saw a blonde anchorwoman giving the news. Her hair was long and straight, but not as blonde as it should be.

Not as blonde as Ivy's.

The mere thought of Ivy gave him a hard-on. Angry now, and frustrated, he slammed the car into gear and tore out of the lot.

It was getting dark and his mood was no better when he returned and unlocked the motel, juggling his beer in one hand

and the key in the other. Tossing the key onto the cheap table in the corner, he twisted the cap off one of the beers and took a long swallow.

It wasn't until he turned around that he saw the shadow of a man sitting in the corner.

He choked on the beer, the bitter liquid making him cough as he spluttered and reached for the gun tucked into the back of his jeans underneath his flannel shirt.

"I wouldn't do that if I were you, Jace," the man said.

Jace froze, now seeing the outline of a gun in the man's hand.

"Very slowly, take that gun and set it on the table. One wrong move and you'll be dead."

Jace complied, his eyes glued to the man's gun, which remained steady in his grip.

"Now put the bottle down," he ordered. He had some kind of British accent, his voice all calm, like they were talking about the latest football scores.

Jace did as he was told. "Who are you? What do you want? I don't have any money."

"That's good because I'm not here for money. Take off your clothes."

A cold sweat broke out on Jace's forehead and he didn't move. "I'm gonna yell, man. Even if you shoot me, the manager will hear the shot."

"That manager's been paid very handsomely to be utterly deaf until morning," the man said.

Jace began to panic. He knew very well how easily someone could be persuaded to look the other way, especially in the type of company he kept.

A shot rang out and Jace jumped about a foot.

"That's your only warning. Now take off your clothes."

Realizing he had no choice, Jace hurried to comply, stripping off the flannel shirt and cheap blue jeans until he stood in his socks and underwear.

"All of it." The man's voice was like steel and sent a cold shiver of terror through Jace. His hands shook slightly as he removed the rest of his clothing.

"Now use these," the man tossed him a pair of handcuffs. "Lie on the bed and cuff your wrists to the headboard."

Jace eyed his discarded gun on the table.

"Try it and you'll be dickless."

He glanced over. The man had his weapon pointed directly at Jace's penis. Without any other choice, Jace climbed onto the bed, acutely aware of how naked and vulnerable he was. It took a couple of tries to get the handcuffs fastened, but they finally clicked into place.

"What do you want?" he tried again, embarrassed at how his voice shook.

"What do *I* want?" the man asked, putting his gun into the holster hidden under the suit jacket he wore. "I'm here for some long overdue justice, Jace."

"How do you know my name?" Jace's thoughts scrambled, trying to think of whom he'd wronged that they'd send an assassin after him, because it was obvious that's who this guy was. It had to be someone with some serious cash because this guy had to cost a bundle to hire.

"I've heard it spoken," the man said as he reached into his pocket. "Told to me quite calmly in a story that would leave most sane people horrified. And I've heard it spoken in terror, in a nightmare that I could only imagine paled when compared to reality."

He paused and pulled a switchblade from his pocket, hitting a button that flipped up a six-inch blade. "Tonight, you're going to feel that terror, Jace, and feel the utter despair of knowing that no one is coming to help you."

Fear washed over Jace in a cold rush and his arms jerked at the handcuffs, which held fast.

"Who the fuck are you?" Jace yelled.

"I'm a friend . . . a very close friend . . . of Ivy's. She sends her regards."

All the blood left Jace's head in a rush as he stared, horrified, at the man.

"So I have quite the evening planned for us, Jace," he said, walking to the corner and returning with a wooden broomstick, minus the broom. "First, I'm going to acquaint you with this, hit you about a bit, tenderize you, so to speak. Then I'm going to sodomize you with it. Will that be a new experience for you, Jace? I do know you were in prison. Perhaps you were someone's bitch? A pretty boy like you had to have had a boyfriend or two."

"You're fuckin' crazy," Jace choked out, but the man didn't look it. He was dressed in a goddamn suit, for chrissakes.

The man's face turned hard and cold, his eyes inhuman and terrifying. "I'm not the one who likes to rape little girls."

"She wanted it! She liked it!"

The slam of the wooden handle across his crotch made him scream as pain licked him like fire, curling up his belly and into his throat. Vomit spewed from his mouth, dribbling down his chin and coating his chest. He choked and coughed, drawing his knees up in a futile attempt to ease the pain.

"Don't be so dramatic, Jace," the man chided. "If you're having that much of a fit because of a little bruise, you'll no doubt cry like a baby when I cut it off." He slammed the knife down, point first, into the wood of the bedside table. The light glinted off its blade.

"Was there anything else you'd like to say?" the man asked,

again so calm. "Maybe you'd like to beg. I think I might like that. Yes, I'd like to hear you beg for mercy."

Jace began to cry. He knew with a dead certainty that this night would be his last, and that it was going to be filled with terror and pain like nothing he'd ever known. He also knew that the only thought the man would have as he stood over his dead and mutilated body was to make sure there was no blood to mar the pristine silk of his tie.

✺

Two days later

"So tell me again what this relationship *is* exactly?"

Marcia looked confused as we stood in the break room fixing our coffee. She'd hounded me that morning about whether or not I'd texted Devon or gone by his place, and I'd caved to the desire to tell someone about him. I'd glossed over the details—saying he worked for the government and traveled a lot, most of the time doing things that he couldn't tell me—but enough to where she got the gist. I'd finished by telling her that I was going to move into his apartment and that I'd see him again . . . sometime.

"It's the greatest sex you've ever had," she continued, "but you can't call him, don't know when he'll be back, and he never said he loved you or admitted to any kind of feelings at all?"

Well, when she put it like that . . .

"Um, yeah, I guess that's about right," I mumbled, dumping creamer into my coffee.

Marcia sensed my chagrin because she softened her words. "I'm sorry. I'm just trying to understand. It seems you're in this . . . relationship . . . that most men would kill for and most women would run from. He owes you nothing, isn't committed to you in any way—he's not secretly married, is he?—but can just stop by and have sex with you whenever he feels like it?"

"I love him," I said stubbornly, despite the way I knew my cheeks were burning.

The sympathy in Marcia's eyes bothered me, as if she knew this was destined to be an epic fail. "I know," she said. "I really do. There isn't a woman alive who hasn't been where you are—in love with a man who won't commit. I just want you to be aware of what you're doing. I'd sure hate to see you get hurt, Ivy."

"I do," I insisted. "I know what I'm doing." The chances of Devon and I ending up together—safe and happy—were minuscule. But I had to try.

"So long as you're going into it with your eyes wide open," she cautioned.

"I am."

We fell into a kind of awkward silence as I finished stirring my coffee. I did know what I was doing. Maybe. Probably.

"What's that? What happened?"

I glanced at the television behind me and it was flashing one of those news alerts. We both moved closer and Marcia turned up the volume. An on-site anchor was standing outside one of those strip motels that were cheap and ubiquitous, renting rooms by the hour. The banner across the bottom of the screen read "Escaped Parolee Found Murdered."

". . . Jace Croughton, a released felon wanted for not reporting for parole a few weeks ago in Kansas, was found murdered inside this motel. Though the owner says he didn't see or hear anything, the victim was found to have been brutally tortured for hours before bleeding to death . . ."

"Oh my God," I breathed, my eyes wide.

"Wow, that's like totally medieval," Marcia said. "Probably some kind of gang or drug thing." She shrugged and grabbed her cup of coffee before heading back to her booth.

I didn't answer, still reeling. Devon had killed Jace, there was no doubt in my mind. I wanted to tell Marcia, but couldn't. It surely spoke to some kind of feelings Devon had for me that he'd done this—committed murder to avenge me. But that wasn't exactly something you wanted to point to as a sign. *He killed my stepbrother who used to abuse me, so he must love me a little, right?* Yeah, somehow I didn't think she'd take it as proof of Devon's devotion. Mental instability? Yes. Love? No.

I felt . . . relieved that Jace was gone, but I shouldn't be glad at someone's death. That seemed wrong somehow, to not just be relieved but to have that spark of satisfaction, of joy even, that he was dead.

But no matter my confusion over my feelings, one thing was crystal clear. Devon had been right. I didn't have to worry about Jace any more.

Acknowledgments

This book would not have been possible if not for the loving encouragement of Kele Moon and Paige Weaver. Thank you both for your advice and your friendship. I treasure both.

Thank you and much love to my wonderful betas—Nicole, Leslie, and Tiffany—whose love and enthusiasm for my writing keeps me going on the tough days. I love you all and am blessed to call you friends.

Thank you to my wonderful editor, Maria Gomez. I treasure your steadfast cheerfulness and the way you persist in pushing me just a little bit more, which makes the manuscript so much better. You're going to be an awesome mom.

Thank you to Melody Guy for pointing out those plot holes to be filled.

Thank you to Marina Adair for making sure I was on the right track.

Thank you to Jennifer Armentrout for telling me the single best piece of advice upon finishing one series and starting another. I wrote it down and look at it every day before I begin writing. You're awesome and I love you.

To my agent, Kevan Lyon, you're a rock star and I thank you.

To my amazing husband, my best friend, Tim, for your support and belief in me. Thank you for being you, which makes me a better me.

And, as always, my thanks and appreciation to all those at Montlake Romance for their continued support in creating a wonderful platform and an amazing team to sell my books. You are all fantastic and it's a privilege to work with you.

CONTINUE READING FOR
AN EXCITING PREVIEW OF
SHADOW OF A DOUBT,
BOOK 2 IN THE
TANGLED IVY SERIES

Shadow
OF A DOUBT

A TANGLED IVY NOVEL

TIFFANY
SNOW

PROLOGUE

He came in the dead of night.

I was accustomed to his unannounced arrivals, so when I woke to the feel of a man sliding under the sheets with me, I wasn't afraid.

He was already naked and it only took a moment for him to slip my nightgown over my head and toss it aside. He kissed me and I wrapped my arms around his neck, pressing my body against his.

His skin was warm, his body hard. His taste and touch were addictions I craved more fiercely than the most avid heroin addict.

We didn't speak. I didn't welcome him home or ask about his day. He couldn't tell me about his job even if he wanted to, though I suspect that fact didn't bother him. It was the nature of spies to be secretive, though since I'd known only one, I supposed I wasn't an expert on the subject.

These thoughts were driven from my mind as his hands skated down my body. He shifted my legs apart, moving to lie between my spread thighs. I focused on him, memorizing the feel of him pressing against me, inside me.

The night passed in a blur of whispered sighs and moans, sweat and skin beneath tangled sheets, until the pleasure he'd wrung from me forced me into an exhausted and sated slumber.

When I woke to sunlight streaming through my window, he was gone.

CHAPTER
ONE

I was hard-pressed to keep a stupid grin off my face as I got ready for work.

Devon had come last night.

It had been weeks since I'd seen him, each night going to bed hopeful, each morning waking up disappointed. My cell phone hadn't rung with a call in the middle of the night, the number blocked. Its silence mocked me.

But I hadn't been disappointed last night.

My body still tingled when I thought about what had passed in the early hours of the morning, a shiver running down my spine.

I finished running a brush though my hair—long, straight, and pure white-blonde. My makeup was minimal. Blessed with beauty, I was glad for my looks for the first time in my life. Without it, I doubted I'd ever have caught Devon's eye.

Some men were attracted to lush figures, which I didn't have. Tall and on the too-skinny side of thin, I had the perfect shape to wear the designer clothes I couldn't afford that filled my closet. That shape was not one men usually drooled over.

Other men were all about the face. Devon was one of those men. He didn't seem to mind my angles and planes where there should be soft curves. He liked my face. He liked it a lot. And he'd once told me he liked the way I moved, the way I walked.

Maybe influenced by one too many runway shows, I tried to do justice to the clothes I wore. So I stood tall, shoulders back, chin up, and sashayed my ass down the street, usually in four-inch heels. It made me feel good about myself and gave me a confidence it had taken me years to acquire.

Glancing at my watch, I saw I was going to be late for work if I didn't hurry. Worcester Bank opened early and I had to be there even earlier for my job as teller. I'd been daydreaming of last night, putting me behind schedule.

Hurrying into the kitchen, I grabbed a mug and filled it with coffee. I needed a quick fix before I left. That's when I saw it.

A stack of money on the kitchen counter.

I stared in confusion for a moment, then set aside my mug and reached for the money. Next to it was a note.

For anything you might need, luv.
-D

Absently, I counted the stack. It was about a half-inch tall and only contained hundreds. When I was through counting, I just stood in amazement.

Ten thousand dollars. Devon had left ten thousand dollars just . . . sitting on the kitchen counter.

My happiness abruptly deflated like a popped balloon. Last night had seemed special—a wonderful reunion after too many weeks apart. But now it was sordid, tainted by money left figuratively on the bedside table, as though Devon were compensating me for having sex with him.

I didn't know what to do with the money. It wasn't like I felt like I could leave it sitting out. Going back into the bedroom, I hesitated, then put it in the top drawer of the nightstand. That was probably the most appropriate place for it anyway, I thought somewhat bitterly.

Now I was really late for work. I drove my own car although I had the keys for Devon's Porsche. He'd left them when he'd left the keys to his apartment and a directive to move out of my best friend Logan's place and into his. But driving such an expensive car made me nervous, so my old sedan was preferable.

Marcia, another teller at the bank and one of my few close friends, was pouring herself a cup of coffee in the break room by the time I hurriedly clocked in and tossed my lunch into the communal refrigerator.

"Oh, pour me a cup, too, please," I said, somewhat breathless from my dash into the building after I'd parked my car.

She obliged, pouring a second cup and eyeing me. "You look a little tired today," she said. "Everything okay?"

"Devon came last night," I said, taking the cup from her. We fell into step together as we walked to the front of the bank and our teller booths.

"That's, what, the sixth time he's been back since New Year's?" she asked. "That should make you happy." Her voice was carefully even. She didn't really "get" my relationship with Devon, but wanted to support my decisions, which was more than I could say for Logan.

"I was," I said, pausing outside my booth, "but then this morning, I saw he'd left money on the kitchen counter."

Marcia raised her eyebrows. "Money?" I nodded. She frowned. "How much?"

I glanced around before answering, then lowered my voice. "Ten thousand dollars."

Her eyes flew open wide. "Ten thousand—"

"Shh!" I shushed her, glancing around again, but no one had paid attention.

"Ten thousand dollars," she said again, this time much more quietly, but no less astounded. "Are you kidding me right now?"

I shook my head. "I counted it."

"Did he talk to you about it?"

"No. He just left a note."

"And it said?" she prompted.

Pulling the scrap of paper from my pocket, I handed it to her and she read it, then handed it back.

"What do you think it means?" I asked.

She shrugged. "I have no idea, but you know I don't understand how this relationship works anyway. Maybe it's just what he says. Some money in case you need it."

"But I'm already living in his apartment. He pays all the bills. Why would I need money?"

"Girl, if you think you're going to get sympathy from me because your boyfriend gave you ten grand to spend on whatever you want, you're looking in the wrong place." Her dry comment prodded a grin out of me.

We had to stop there because customers had entered the building. I was busy all day and when I did stop to eat lunch and chat with Marcia, we didn't talk about Devon or dissect the events of last night. Not that it stopped me from dwelling on it all day.

Was I making a big deal out of nothing? Ten thousand dollars was a lot of money. Maybe it was a goodbye gift? Maybe I wouldn't see him again?

The thought made my stomach clench as anxiety struck. Surely he'd tell me if he wasn't coming back? He wouldn't just leave and not say a word?

But I wasn't one hundred percent sure he wouldn't do just that.

I had no way of reaching him. When he called, his number was always blocked, and he didn't call that often anyway. There was no predictable pattern to it and he rarely stayed on the line for long.

Warm spring air greeted me when I stepped out of the building a little after six o'clock. I was tired. The lack of sleep last night and a long day at work had taken their toll and I couldn't wait to get home and relax.

Home.

Was that how I thought of Devon's apartment? Home?

It was the closest thing I'd had to a home since moving to St. Louis from Dodge City, Kansas last summer. I'd stayed with Logan for a while, but then Devon had swept into my life and one of his conditions for *remaining* in my life was that I move out of Logan's place and into his. Since he was hardly ever home, I had the place to myself. A perk I'd gladly give up if it meant I'd get to see him more often. Six times over the past four months wasn't enough, especially when the longest visit had been only ten hours.

I unlocked and climbed into my car, tossing my purse onto the passenger seat. I pulled my door shut with a slam just as the rear door opened and a man slid into the backseat.

Alarmed, I reached for my door handle. "Hey! What're you—" But I was cut off when he reached over the seat and took a fistful of my hair, yanking my head back. I gasped in pain, and with my next breath, I felt the cold slide of a blade against my throat.

"Hallo, luv. Been a while, eh?"

I caught sight of the man in my rearview mirror.

Clive.

He used to work with Devon, if I used the term *work* loosely. The details were sketchy. What I did know was that he'd once betrayed Devon and left him for dead, and that Clive's brand-new wife had been murdered by a poison that had also infected me. I, however, had survived.

I swallowed. "What do you want?" I asked, proud of my steady voice.

"I want Anna back, but that's never going to happen," he said, speaking of his dead wife. "So I'll settle for the next best thing."

He stopped and I thought he wanted me to ask. His fingers pulled harder at my hair and tears of pain burned at the corners of my eyes. My fingernails dug into my seat as I scrambled to think what to do.

"What's that?" I managed.

"Revenge."

About the Author

Photo by Karen Lynn, 2014

Tiffany Snow has been reading romance novels since she was too young to read romance novels. After many years of working in the information technology field, Tiffany now works her dream job of writing full-time.

Tiffany makes her home in the Midwest with her husband and two daughters. She can be reached at Tiffany@TiffanyASnow.com. Visit her on her website, www.Tiffany-Snow.com, to keep up with her latest projects.